DEEPWOOD MOUNTAIN

COMPLETE SERIES

LEXI HAYES

Published by No Regerts Press, LLC

NO REGERTS
PRESS, LLC

Cover Designed by Cormar Covers

ISBN 978-1-957933-15-3 (print)

Join my mailing list here:
www.lexihayes.com

CONTENTS

HIS BIG RIDE

HIS BIG AXE

HIS BIG HAMMER

HIS BIG RIDE

CHAPTER 1
WILLA

"Oh my god, it's *huge*."

Ash's eyes go wide on the other end of our video call.

"Willa," she drawls, a warning note in her voice. "Whatcha talking about?"

I throw the rental car in park and gape up at the massive estate before me.

"Sorry. It's just Dash's enormous...house."

I turn the phone around to show her.

She shakes her head. "Not cool, girl, baiting your best friend like that."

I laugh and gaze up again at the home that looms like a magnificent citadel on the mountainside.

Dash McCafferty's mansion is all aged wood, stone, and giant windows, surrounded by tall pine and spruce that is green and lush in the height of spring. It's older and more rustic than my dad's place on the other side of Deepwood Mountain, and has a certain wildness to it—a riot of different textures and shapes, mixed with natural, earthy components.

It dominates the landscape while still blending seamlessly with it. Larger than life, just like the man who owns it.

"Lucky for you that your dad's place is being remodeled yet again," Ash snarks good-naturedly.

Dad is forever changing his mind. That means more renovations to the place he wants to make his permanent home here in town. It's not remotely in a habitable state right now, but he's in Hong Kong on a consulting job, so he doesn't really care. I, however, need a place to stay while I get settled into my new job at the library. His best friend, Dash, offered to put me up at his house. His truly enormous house.

Growing up, I lived with Mom in L.A., and then went to college to get my Master of Library Science degree. Between school and visiting Dad while he was working abroad, I rarely came to Deepwood Mountain, this small town in western Montana where Dad and Dash were raised. When I did make it out, Dash was either off filming his former reality TV show or customizing a motorcycle for some celebrity somewhere.

I've known Dash since I was a baby, but the last time I saw him—besides on TV, of course—was when I was sixteen.

So why is my belly filled with butterflies?

"Earth to Willa. Earth to Willa. Come in, Willa."

I startle, having nearly forgotten she's there. "Sorry." I turn the phone back to face me and her dark eyes study mine.

She presses her lips together with that all too knowing look of hers. "You're thinking about him again."

"Am not," I mumble, slumping down in my seat.

"Are too. You're nervous."

I sputter. "Of *course* I'm nervous. I'm going to be staying with a TV star and starting a new job. It's all a little...overwhelming."

"Come on, babe. What have you got to worry about? Dash is a former *reality* TV dude. You know I love my reality TV, but he's not a movie star or anything. Like, Timothée Chalamet he ain't. Besides, you told me yourself he's completely down to earth." She peers at me. "Second, you're going to ace the new job. You're an actual librarian. I can't remember you ever wanting to be anything else. How many people can say they have their dream job?"

"I guess…" I sigh, glancing again out the window.

"Yeah. So let's talk about the real reason you're on edge."

I give her a skeptical look.

"You're worried that crush you had on Dash might still be lurking around."

Ugh. Why did she have to know me so well? *And* have such a flawless memory? Because, yes, years ago, I used to be obsessed with Dash. So sue me, I was a teenager with raging hormones, and he was famous, and charming…and smoking hot.

"Okay, fine! I don't want to make things weird or embarrass myself if…"

"Your panties get soaked when you see him?" she finishes with a wink.

"*Ash!*" I frantically thumb the volume on the phone lower. She laughs. "You're a menace," I grumble, and get out of the car, looking around to make sure no one heard her.

"Just chill, will ya? Even if you discover when you see him that you're still smitten with this guy, he'll probably just find it cute and move on. Don't make drama out of nothing."

I take a deep breath. She's right. I can handle some awkward moments. What's he going to do—throw me out? No way. My dad would kill him. Maybe I won't even feel anything when I see him anyway—and all this fretting will be for nothing. I'm a grown woman now with different priorities. Books over men, for a start.

"Yep, I can do this." I straighten my shoulders.

Ash smiles at me. "That's my girl." She glances at her watch. "Shit. I gotta run or I'll be late for yoga."

I nod sadly, remembering our regular yoga classes back in L.A.

"Enjoy cobra pose. Talk to you later." I wave into the phone. "Miss you already."

Ash blows me a kiss. "Me too, babe. Me too."

The screen blinks back to my wallpaper as she hangs up.

Lowering my phone, I admire the chunky cobblestone driveway and lanterns lining the edge of the drive.

Then I hear the purr of a motorcycle and turn to peer at the rider backlit by the afternoon sun. I can't tell who the big man in full gear and helmet is, but I'd recognize that bike anywhere: *Blue Steel.* A big metallic blue speed bike that Dash customized for himself. His pride and joy. I can't believe he still has it after all these years.

The garage door opens and he pulls in to a stop, then turns the bike to face toward the street. He quickly tears off his shiny slate helmet as he dismounts.

"Hey, stranger," he calls. His voice is deep and rough, like water rushing over river stones.

The world tilts on its axis as I gaze at him, and the air wrenches from my lungs in one big breath.

He's…*ravishing*…a word I never thought I'd use to describe a man, but in this moment it's the only one that does him justice.

A muscle works in his perfectly square jaw as he ruffles his short, jet black hair, with gray scattered at the temples and through the top. His ice-blue eyes, two arctic lasers, pin me to the spot. He could be Henry Cavill's long-lost twin. Superman, for heaven's sake! Yet more rugged, more sexy, more… everything.

My knees wobble.

I'm doomed.

"Hey," I finally reply, my voice barely above a whisper. My heart is lodged somewhere between my chest and mouth, and it's pounding like crazy.

He's staring, and I self-consciously push up the corner of my glasses.

"One sec. I'll help you with your luggage!"

It gets worse. He takes off his motorcycle jacket to reveal a pale blue Henley that clings to his toned body. Paired with worn jeans hugging him in *all* the right places, I'm instantly sweating.

Jesus.

He strides over to me, and before I can react, he's hauled me into his arms, lifting me clear off my feet in a tight bear hug.

I should be scrambling to get down. I don't. Instead, I close my eyes and melt into his strong, protective embrace. His scent surrounds me—motorcycle leather, pine, and warm sunshine —and I inhale against his neck like I'll never get the chance to breathe in again. Our clothes do nothing to mask his sculpted frame. It's almost obscene how clearly I can feel every cut of his chest and shoulders, every hard ridge of his abs, even the steely bulge of his—

"How long has it been, Willa?" he asks, stopping my train of thought. My name spoken by his ragged voice sends an unholy shiver down my spine.

In a daze, I reply, "It had to be back when I was in…high school?" On the words "high school," he sets me down almost comically fast, leaving me on unstable legs.

"Are these your only bags?" He quickly moves to grab the two bigger suitcases.

I nod, taking my small carry-on and purse. "The rest of my stuff was sent to Dad's place. Things I won't need right away."

7

"Makes sense."

I follow him up the driveway as he effortlessly carries my bags—you'd think they were empty.

"These are filled with books, right?" His grin is cheeky.

I stammer, "N-no! Why does everyone assume I lug tons of books around?!"

Just then, one suitcase bursts open and my books come tumbling out like so many little traitors. Fantastic. I scurry to pick them up while Dash lays the bag down and opens it flat for me.

"So I like having my books with me," I mumble.

Dash gives me a wry smirk. "I didn't say a word."

He squats down to help and reaches over to grab a book at random. "*His Burning Desire*," he reads. His eyebrows shoot up as he takes in the cover of a half-naked man embracing a busty woman. Then he flips through it, stopping at one page: "Kendrick pressed his aching—"

My cheeks ignite in flames, and I snatch the book from him before he can continue. "It's a romance!"

"I noticed. I mean, *Kendrick*?" Dash chuckles. "But hey, nothing wrong with enjoying…reading."

"Now you're making fun of me." I punch his rock-hard bicep. It nearly bruises my knuckles.

He winks before closing the bag. "Never."

I grin and we continue into the house. It's beautiful: impossibly high ceilings, warm wood beams, natural variegated floors covering the entire space. The sun floods into the living area, illuminating every nook and cranny with its golden light, almost dreamlike. Everything screams "Dash", from the charcoal and blue color scheme to the chrome accents. Swanky automotive-chic bachelor pad meets lumberjack's log cabin.

"This place is stunning." I run my hand appreciatively over the smooth wood of the staircase railing as we ascend.

"You like it?" He turns back, throwing me a proud smile and emphasizing that sweet dimple on his left cheek.

The sight still sends an electric current straight to my core. "It's very you."

"I'm glad you think so. We can explore more after we drop off your, ah, reading material."

I cringe momentarily as he leads me down a hallway and into a gorgeous bedroom overlooking the valley below. There's a big wall-mounted flatscreen TV, stone fireplace, gargantuan bed, and an ensuite bathroom.

"It's lovely." I put down my things and Dash drops my other bags neatly off to the side.

"Thanks. It's not as sleek or hi tech as your old man's setup, but I like it."

"Dad's place is way too modern for my taste." I eye the oversized, knotted wood headboard. "Almost sterile. This place has character."

He grins broadly. "You know, I forgot how much I liked you." He bumps his shoulder against mine, firing up every nerve in my body. He claps his hands together and adds, "Now —how about that tour?"

I bite my lip. "Do you mind if I take a quick shower first?" Honestly, I need a moment to get hold of myself if I'm going to be around Dash for any length of time.

"Oh, sure." He gestures to the ensuite. "Towels, toiletries and all that's in the bathroom closet. And if you need any help with the shower—I mean—you know what I mean—just let me know." A blush creeps over his stubbled cheeks and he rubs the back of his neck. "I'll be down in the kitchen. Hungry?"

I tuck a piece of hair behind my ear. "No, thanks. I ate on the plane."

"Well, if you change your mind and need a snack, you

know where to find me." Then he bolts for the door, waving once before closing it hastily behind him.

Holy shit. I can't believe *my* awkwardness has made even Dash uncomfortable around me.

I remove my glasses and face-plant into the sea of pillows on the bed. An alert sounds on my phone, and I roll over, fishing it out of my pocket.

Dad.

Guilt over these wicked thoughts about his best friend twinges in my gut. I really hope Dash doesn't tell him how much of a hot mess I am. Dad will know for sure something is up then.

> Did you make it?

> Yep, safe and sound at Dash's place.

> Great. How do you like it?

I glance around the room, checking out the hipster/goth vibe, between the iron wall sconces and slab wood nightstands.

> It's unique.

(Utterly perfect. Just like Dash.)

> Nicer than my place?

> No comment.

I stifle a chuckle.

Listen, I'm really sorry I can't be there right now, honey.

Soon, though.

It's fine. Dash is great.

(It's me that's the problem.)

He's the best, isn't he? There's no one I trust more with my little girl. Talk later. 🥹🤍

Night, Dad 🤍

I roll onto my back, and stare up at the ceiling.
Oh, Dad, if only you had any idea.

CHAPTER 2
DASH

This must be my punishment.

Payback for all the stupid things I've done in the past. That's the only explanation why I'm suddenly smitten by Willa Layne.

When did my best friend's daughter go from an awkward teen with braces and pigtails to this tantalizing creature in sexy, adorable glasses? All grown up with a body that begs to be worshipped. No plastic or fillers or inches-thick makeup like most of the women from my past.

The moment I first saw her standing in the street, it felt like time had stopped. Her amber gaze stripped me bare. And in my arms, she just felt so *right*—her body molded against mine, bringing to life every, and I mean *every*, dormant part of me.

As if. Gavin would bash my brains in if he knew what was running through my head about his daughter—his twenty-three-year-old daughter, if my math is correct.

I turn forty next year.

Christ! I'm officially a dirty old man.

At the kitchen sink, I splash ice-cold water on my face. I should be pouring it down my pants. Burning with...desire.

Just like that goddamned romance novel that fell from Willa's suitcase. I know exactly what ache Kendrick (Kendrick!!!) was talking about.

Willa strolls into the kitchen and I stifle a groan. Her honey-blonde hair is up in a messy bun, a few stray tendrils that couldn't be contained curling along the column of her slender neck. She's wearing neon yellow joggers and a tank top that's much too big for her small frame, but her clothes can't conceal the sexy curves underneath completely.

"You okay?" she asks, an uneasy crease on her brow.

Nope, not in the least. "Fine. Enjoy your shower?" I try to forget how I embarrassed myself earlier in her bedroom. It's almost like the more I try to keep my filthy thoughts from surfacing, the more my mouth decides to make a fool of me.

"It was great." She pulls at a few strands of hair near her shoulder. "Super luxurious."

Images of her body, naked and wet, soapsuds cascading down her slick skin as she lounges against the shower bench, accost my brain—

Shit. I open the fridge quickly and grab a cold beer bottle. "Do you want something? Wine maybe? Food? I'm having a beer." *Shut up, Dash. You're babbling.*

"I'm good, I promise." Her fingers drum absently on the island countertop.

"You're welcome to anything in the house, Willa, remember that." *Including me.*

She smiles. "Thank you. That's very kind of you."

I wave a hand dismissively and take a swig of beer. "Ready to see the rest of the joint?"

"Sure." She adjusts her glasses.

I loosen up a little as I take her around the house, the conversation easier now that I'm talking about my friends and how we built this place. I explain that around five years ago, me and my best buddies, who had all grown up in Deepwood Mountain and had created multi-million-dollar businesses out of our blue-collar roots, started work together on the McCafferty home.

Willa already knows our group of six well, since we're all super close and go back years. Nick's our contractor, Logan does the woodwork, Sully handles plumbing, Reece supplies labor (and food from his ranch), and Gavin's the electrician. Every one of them has a home here that we pitched in to build together. We've also made a point to give back to the community that made us the men we are today.

Willa and I take a tour around the ground floor, passing through the games room, mudroom, outdoor kitchen, and pool and spa area. She laughs at all my dumb jokes, and I find myself wondering if she'd laugh like that when I'm kissing her most ticklish places. I bite the inside of my cheek to stay calm as we go down another hallway.

"This place is enormous, Dash." She looks around, eyes wide. "And it's really only you?"

I knew she had probably seen my reality show, where the footage was edited together to make me look like some sort of womanizer always on the prowl. It wasn't true—sure, I had dated a fair bit in the past, but I was never really interested in anything serious, and I was always honest about that right out of the gate with the women I went out with.

Suddenly, I wish Gavin had told her how much I've changed over the past few years. I no longer fill my nights with meaningless dates, even for the cameras; instead, I've started focusing on becoming a better man.

"Just me," I finally murmur, leading her into the den.

"Do you ever get lonely?"

Her question catches me off guard. I want to answer honestly, but part of me is embarrassed by the truth. In the past, yes, those meaningless dates would have been what filled the emptiness. But now? "Sometimes." I shrug, avoiding her gaze. "But I have Gavin and the rest of the crew. And this town has some great people who are incredibly welcoming. I'm sure you'll find that out for yourself soon enough."

I flip on the lights and her eyes drift around the den.

She's smiling softly, yet there's something sad about her expression. "I hope so. I miss my mom and my friends back in L.A., and I'd rather not be lonely here."

I reach out and squeeze her shoulder, then pull back when she flinches. "Sorry, I didn't—"

She waves off my apology. "All good. It's just nerves." She wraps her arms around herself as if for comfort.

I can only imagine how alone and afraid she must feel now, so far away from home. "It's a big change," I agree, taking another sip of beer. "But you're smart and capable, Willa. You'll be fine."

Her face flushes. "Thanks, Dash."

I nod and gesture to the room. "This den is where I spend most of my time."

"It's definitely the coziest space I've seen so far."

"Wait until you see my bedroom." As soon as the words fly out of my mouth, I wish I could jam them back in. What is my problem? "I didn't mean…" I rub the back of my neck as heat rises to my cheeks, words failing me.

Instead of taking offense at my inappropriate comment, Willa simply grins and shakes her head, her own face reddening. "It's okay."

I take a deep breath and gesture for her to follow me up the stairs. We explore the second floor—the study, my home office, and various guest bedrooms. I hesitate only briefly before I usher her into my room. She immediately heads to the floor-to-ceiling windows. She stops and puts a hand over her heart. "That view is spectacular."

"Sure is…" I say. But I'm focused on the angel in front of me, not the massive trees or the sun setting over the sprawling mountain outside.

Against my better judgment, I drift toward her, unable to control the need to be near her. I shove my hands into my pockets to avoid doing anything reckless.

Eventually, I'm close enough that she can lean into me gently to rest her head against my shoulder. She used to do this as a kid, though she only came up to my ribs then. I'm hoping she feels just as safe with me now. She smells like vanilla and the fragrant spring vines planted in my yard—the ones with pale pink flowers as delicate as her lips. I want to wrap my arm around her and press her body against mine, but I resist.

"I'm really glad you're here, Willa," I say. "I need you to know that."

"Thanks. Me, too." Her voice is sleepy, with an underlying hint of uncertainty that makes me wish I could prove just how much having her here means to me. But I choose to leave that for another time.

We watch the sky transform from bright yellow and fiery orange to the deep violet and indigo of night, the stars twinkling into view.

She finally lifts her head and yawns widely.

"Am I boring you?" I ask.

"I swear, it's not you." She chuckles. "It's just been a long, exhausting day and I don't want to be struggling tomorrow at the library. I should probably get to bed."

"Understandable."

She turns toward me, and every cell in my body reacts

when she places her hand on my forearm, her touch searing right through my shirt.

"Good night, Dash. Thanks again."

"Of course." I'd give anything on the planet to pull her into my arms right now. "Night, Willa."

As she walks away, my eyes are drawn to her achingly sweet backside.

Jesus, I need a shower.

An ice-cold one.

Later, back in the den, I idly flip through channels on the TV to keep my mind off Willa. What's wrong with me? It's only been a few hours, but she's taken over my world. So many times I've had to rein in an impulse to "go check on her", knowing that if I did, I'd want nothing more than to crawl into bed next to her and make her mine.

Gavin texted earlier to say Willa let him know she arrived. What else did she tell him? That his best friend is a creepy weirdo? That he can't stop acting like a nervous teenager? Is she secretly laughing at the pathetic old man who's way too old for a young, beautiful sprite like her?

I hear footsteps coming down the stairs and look over to see Willa, hair disheveled and eyes hooded, like a damned wet dream.

"What's wrong? Everything okay?" I jump up quickly from the couch.

She shakes her head. "All good. I just couldn't sleep, so I made some chamomile tea." She lifts the mug in her hand, the one Nick got me for my last birthday: *Never Underestimate an Old Man with a Motorcycle.* He's such an asshole.

I slump back onto the couch with a wave of relief. "I'd sing you a lullaby, but that might do more harm than good."

She pushes up her glasses. "Um, yeah. I heard you sing on *McCafferty Customs*. You should seriously never do that again."

I laugh. "You actually watched the show?"

"My best friend Ash is obsessed with reality TV. It's not usually my thing, but I made an exception in this case." She avoids looking at me.

"It's not really my thing either." I think back to some of the ridiculous stuff we did on the show and how they wanted me to keep up that playboy persona with a different woman on my arm every week. "You do know that most of it is made up by the producers, right?" I glance up hopefully.

"That's what Ash tells me." She sips her tea quietly, and shame fills my gut at what is left unsaid. I can't take any of those shenanigans on the show back, no matter how much I'd like to.

She moves over to scan the photos on the wall.

"You customized a bike for *Ryan Reynolds*?" Her voice is filled with awe.

"Sure did." My chest swells with pride. "Gave him the sweetest ride. Super nice guy, too."

I watch her eyes light up when she sees another photo. "And Pink?!"

I grin. "Her ex-husband is a former motocross star. They were a blast."

She worries her lip as she continues to browse my memorabilia. "Wow. You've worked with some amazing people." She glances over, leaning on the arm of the couch. "So... What's next for you?"

I pause, rolling the question around in my head. "Probably going back to doing what I did before the show—helping people build their dream bikes. Not necessarily celebrities, but regular people. It makes me happy. And that's what matters, right?"

"Yup." She nods. "You won't miss the fame or the traveling, though?"

"Nah." I scratch my arm. "I'm not against taking jobs abroad every once in a while, but constant travel actually gets to you after a while." My eyes meet hers. "I'd much rather settle down and put down some roots."

"R-really?" she sputters, choking on the last of her tea.

"I'm thinking about it real hard."

She blinks, clearly taken aback.

Finally, she says, "Well, maybe you're right. I mean, Dad travels a lot, and meeting him in exotic places is fun, but... yeah. I can't imagine doing that all year around." Her eyes turn soft and a little sad. "I really miss him."

"Me too," I agree. "Hopefully after this renovation is complete, he'll stick around in Deepwood."

Willa smiles and I gesture toward the couch. "Have a seat. I don't bite." It rolls off my tongue without a thought and I wince.

Dammit. Any more stuff straight out of an after-school special you'd like to share with the class?

She just laughs softly, her cheeks slightly pink and, god, do I *ever* want to bite her gently...all over...as she moans my name...

Down, boy.

I swallow back my arousal and she takes a seat at the far end of the couch.

Smart girl.

We pick a show on the wildlife of the Serengeti, which is fine, but I hope the animals won't start humping. *Awk. Ward.*

"What about you?" I ask. "Your dad tells me you're here to revolutionize our ancient little library."

She snorts adorably. "He's such a big talker. But it's true, one of the reasons I was hired was to bring the Deepwood Mountain Library into the 21st century. It's a great opportunity."

Her intelligence and modesty only make her more attractive. "That's impressive."

"I think I still need to get Mrs. Holloway on board with some of my ideas. She's been head librarian here for over thirty years, can you believe it? I've been warned she's not fond of change or upsetting the status quo."

"Change is hard for us old fogies," I say with a healthy dose of self-deprecation.

She rolls her beautiful amber eyes at me playfully. "Please. Don't call yourself old. Your few gray hairs only make you look distinguished."

I raise my eyebrows skeptically. "You mean haggard."

She scrunches up her nose. "How about well-seasoned?"

"That makes me sound like a chicken pot pie." She giggles.

"Well-*worn*, then? Like a favorite pair of jeans?"

Hell, I'd love to be her favorite pair of jeans—close enough to feel every inch of her softness and curves against me. I clear my throat and say gruffly, "I think I can handle that."

She bites her lush lip and sighs. "I just want to make Mrs. Holloway's life easier, you know? While making books and library programming more accessible to the community. You'd think she'd be overjoyed."

"You're young, smart, energetic, and full of innovative ideas. That can feel threatening to someone in her position."

She ducks her chin. "Thank you, Dash. I honestly have no intention of taking her job; I want to learn from her and be her partner. I hope she realizes that. Mrs. Holloway *is* the Deepwood Mountain Library. She knows it like nobody else."

I sigh. "You have a good heart, too."

She blushes. "You're biased. That's my dad's fault."

Not exactly, but I'm not going to say anything. "Maybe."

Willa sets her mug on the coffee table and we settle into a comfortable silence, focusing on the program.

After a while, she snuggles into the sofa, resting her head on a cushion. Her eyelids droop. It's sweet and innocent and makes me want to wrap my arms around her. Protect her. Claim her, like some wild mountain man. The fierce possessiveness bubbling up out of nowhere catches me off guard and I scrub my face.

Christ, Dash. You need to back the fuck off. You're acting like a lunatic.

I watch Willa drift off, and it's not until her slow breathing fills the air that I dare get up and drape a blanket over her. She moans quietly when I brush her temple as I remove her glasses. Sensations roar through me so hot and deep as to set my groin on fire.

I hurry away after turning off the TV and lights, hard enough to split a tree.

CHAPTER 3
WILLA

I hear the clink of a mug on the table, and register the heavenly aroma of freshly made coffee before I even open my eyes.

"My god, I love you," I purr, sitting up and stretching awake like a cat. I turn to see Dash standing behind me, smiling in amusement.

"Oh." Heat blooms on my cheeks. "I forgot where—I—I thought you were Ash. She's my best friend—my former roommate." I fumble around, feeling for my glasses near the mug. Dash slides them quietly into my hand and I mumble my thanks. Can't I go one day without embarrassing myself in front of this gorgeous man?

He laughs softly. "No big deal. Now I know how to stay in your good books. Get it? Librarian? Books?"

I laugh, turning to look at him. "How did you know what kind of coffee I like?"

He grins. "I have...sources." He holds up his phone. I can see Dad sent him a screenshot of my usual Starbucks order.

"But... There's no Starbucks here."

He snorts. "It's just an Americano. I've got an espresso machine. It's not that hard."

I breathe in the aroma and take a sip. *Delicious*. "This is perfect, Dash. I'm impressed." Hmm. If he can make espresso this good—maybe I *do* love him.

Before he looks away, I swear I see a faint blush on his face as he stammers a hesitant thanks. I'm not entirely sure what to make of it. That's more *my* usual reaction to compliments. I wouldn't have thought it would have been his.

He clears his throat as I set the mug down. "I just thought you wouldn't want to be late on your first day."

Late?! I spring off the couch. "What time is it?" I step forward and yelp as I slam my toe into the table leg. "Shit!" I collapse back, cradling my foot. "Ow ow ow ow oww."

"Jesus, Willa." Instantly, Dash is at my side, kneeling and prying my hands away from my toe. "Let me see."

His rough hands feel really good against my skin, even though there's a bit of pain as he examines the appendage.

"There's no bleeding, but it'll probably bruise. I'll get you an ice pack." He rises to his feet. "It's only 6:30. The library doesn't open until 9, right? But I wanted you to have enough time to get your day started off right. Now relax and try to enjoy your coffee."

I breathe a sigh of relief, far too aware of his closeness. "Okay. Thank you. Again."

He grins down at me. "I'll be back with that ice pack and your breakfast."

My eyes widen. "Breakfast too? You don't have to do that."

His voice is thick with amusement. "Too late. I already did."

"I should walk with you, then." My toe throbs, and I can't help wincing from the stinging sensation that shoots through me when I try to flex it.

A trace of a smirk plays around Dash's lips. "No, you rest," he orders. Then he tilts his head. "Unless you want me to carry you, that is."

My my stomach flip-flops at the thought of being carried in Dash's arms like a damsel in distress, no matter how silly or embarrassing it would be in reality. And no *way* would I be able to control myself.

"No, I'll stay," I squeak out.

Dash chuckles deeply. "Good girl." *Oh my god*. Those two words set fire to my veins and spread through every inch of me like a low electric hum, waking me up better than any caffeine hit ever could.

I slowly push open the heavy library doors, my stomach still full of my delicious bacon and egg breakfast. It really was unnecessary, but Dash wouldn't take no for an answer. He insisted breakfast would "set me up for success"—especially when dealing with Mrs. Holloway—and I had to admit I was pretty sure I'd need all the help I could get there. He was adamant I take a packed lunch as well. When I told him he didn't need to do any of this, he said he kind of liked it. The comment made my insides go all jumpy and squiggly as I considered its implications.

Stepping into the small library feels like entering a moment frozen in time. Despite its age, the vintage furniture is well-maintained and cozy, the comfy overstuffed armchairs beckoning me to take a seat and lose myself in some fictional world. Bookshelves of old polished oak, packed with volumes of every size and color imaginable, line the perimeter. Berber carpets, worn in some places from years of use, are still soft underfoot. The scent of ink and paper hangs in the air, a tantalizing hint of all that lies within these brick walls.

It's exactly as I remember it from the few times Dad brought me here as a child. However, it lacks some much-needed updating. I can only see one ancient clunker of a computer at the circulation desk. One!

"Hello! How may I help you?" A small brunette with cherry-red lips and dark eyes smiles at me from behind the desk, which wobbles on two slightly uneven legs when she stands.

"I'm Willa Layne—"

"Oh! Our new librarian!" She hurries over to me, taking my hand in both of hers. "Miss Layne! Wonderful to meet you. I'm Ms. Alvarez." She leans closer and lowers her voice. "Please call me Eden when we're not at work. It's just that Mrs. Holloway prefers we address each other and the patrons formally here."

"Of course." Formality from Mrs. Holloway doesn't surprise me at all. "I'm thrilled to meet you too, Ms. Alvarez."

Eden's age is impossible to guess. She has a delicate face and bone structure and wears her makeup in a retro style. She could have stepped out of an old movie. Her colorful floral dress matches her cheerful personality, and the way she carries herself makes her seem friendly. I feel instantly at ease with her.

"Mrs. Holloway asked me to show you around when you arrived." She points to my lunch bag. "We'll start in the break room so you can leave your lunch in the fridge."

For the next half hour, Eden takes me through the maze of bookshelves, reading rooms, study areas, and multimedia racks. I ask a ton of questions to get a better feel for the place.

Noticeably missing are computers, places to plug in your own laptop, and other modern amenities. Directly in the center of the main space, flanked by tables and chairs, is a relic in dark wood, gleaming with brass plates and hardware.

"Yes, we still have our original card catalog," Eden says, running her fingers along the first plate where the edge meets the table. "Mrs. Holloway insists on keeping it as a backup."

I blink. "In case there's a library emergency because the digital system goes down?"

"Don't joke about such things, Miss Layne. It's a very serious concern," Eden says in a stern voice. Then immediately she breaks into giggles. "Sorry, I couldn't resist giving you my best Mrs. Holloway impression."

I laugh along with her, until we both clap our hands over our mouths, remembering we're in a library. But the few patrons milling about don't seem to mind.

"This would be the perfect space for new computer workstations," I say in a lowered voice, tapping the stained wood thoughtfully.

"I agree. However, you'll not only need to convince Mrs. Holloway to get rid of the card catalog, you'll have to find the money for the tech and the furniture. Plus someone on call for IT issues."

I nod. I knew going into this that it would be a challenge to implement any changes. I'll make sure my research is rock-solid before I meet with Mrs. Holloway to go over my proposals.

Eden leads me to the children's section, where the bookshelves are lower to give the little ones better access. Child-sized tables and chairs in colorful, sturdy plastic are nestled amongst cushions and bean bags; a cork board with playful drawings in crayon and marker runs the length of the back wall. It's adorable.

Eden reaches out, adjusting a piece of artwork featuring a giraffe stretching his neck up high to eat an apple. "Storytime's at ten-thirty. Anyone can volunteer to read to the kids." She fluffs up a cushion automatically as we pass. "Though it's mostly parents." She points to a sad little clipboard on the wall near the main entrance with a stubby pencil attached to it with string. "They just need to sign up."

I knit my brows. "They have to physically sign up in person? Can't you just have them fill out an online form?"

"Ha!" she barks. "Have you *seen* our website?"

"Oh. Good point." I have. With its clunky interface, garish colors, and outdated animated images circa 1995, the website is another project on my long to-do list. "I've never seen that much comic sans serif in one place."

Eden smirks. "Yeah, it's rough."

I sigh. "We definitely need an updated website with fillable forms. We'd get much higher engagement with all of our programs and events."

"Hey, you're preaching to the choir here." I follow her to a row of offices off the lobby. "This is you." The door squeaks loudly as she opens it. The room is small, but perfectly functional. I'm sure I can make it my own with a few personal touches—artwork, a photo here and there, a couple of knick-knacks. A new computer sits on the desk, the one I asked for in my contract. It looks sorely out of place.

Finally, Eden takes me to the office across the hall from mine. The door is ajar, and she knocks softly. "Mrs. Holloway?" she murmurs. "I have Miss Layne here."

"You may come in," a voice calls back, and Eden and I enter.

Seated behind a plain wooden desk is a woman with a withered and worn face, her hazel eyes magnified by thick horn rim glasses as she looks up from her newspaper. The paper rustles in her hand as she sets it down, her movements rather graceful. I can't help but wonder when I last saw someone reading an actual print newspaper.

Her gray hair is pulled back into a tight, sleek bun,

revealing a high-collared lavender blouse—clearly starched and pressed—and her face is etched with lines like intricate spiderwebs, a testament to years of experience and wisdom. She glances at me through lips that are pursed, whether due to the ravages of time or a sour mood I don't know. Maybe both? She looks exactly as I had expected, even though I'd only talked to her over the phone for my interview. No Zoom calls for Mrs. Holloway, no sir.

"Miss Layne." She stands, posture ramrod straight. Her charcoal-colored skirt is form-fitting on her thin frame. "I expect you to be on time."

I furrow my brow. "I believe I walked in at 9…?"

She clasps her bony hands in front of her. "You did not. It was 9:02."

Okay, then.

Her eyes drift to Eden. "I trust Ms. Alvarez has given you the tour." She frowns at me.

"She has, and I'm excited to get to work in this charming library." I hope a little flattery will help smooth things over. "It's obvious a lot of love goes into looking after it every day."

Mrs. Holloway's face softens for a moment, but it's gone so quickly I could have imagined it. At least she's not glaring at me anymore.

"Let's keep it that way, please."

Already starting off with an unspoken warning. Terrific. I give her my most winning smile. "Of course." I'm definitely not going to pick a fight on my first day.

I get settled into my office, already on a mission even as I feel Mrs. Holloway's eyes on me everywhere. I want to be ready to go with my prioritized list of projects to discuss with her when we have our first meeting tomorrow. Then...*bam!* I'll hit her with my proposals that'll knock her right out of her ancient pantyhose and into the 21st century.

I'm furiously typing away at my computer when Eden walks in.

"Already penning your resignation letter?" she jokes, and I'd playfully chuck something at her if I had anything besides a pen and pad of paper on my desk.

I shake my head. "No way! I'm just getting started here."

"I have a good feeling about you, Miss Layne," she says, standing at attention, doing another Mrs. Holloway impression.

"I'm glad someone does," I reply with a smile.

She grins. "Let me take you to lunch. I like to stretch my legs during my breaks, especially when it's so nice out."

I consider the lunch Dash so generously packed for me; it would keep until tomorrow, and a chance to see some of the town would be nice.

"Sure," I reply. "It's okay with Mrs. Holloway? Does she want to join us, since Janette is here?" Janette is the part timer who, I've been informed, comes in three days.

"I always ask her, but she continues to say she wants to stay and watch the children read."

"That's sweet."

Eden's brow raises skeptically. "Yeah, or creepy." She gives me a wicked grin and we laugh.

The sun is out and the air is warm, with a subtle hint of fresh soil and wildflowers, as we walk to Marge's Diner. Eden mentions that it's the only restaurant in town besides the pizza parlor. Well, and the Rustic Ridge Bar, but "it's a ways down off the main drag and doesn't open until four". Over the three blocks Eden gives me the rundown as we pass a bunch of Deepwood Mountain staples, pointing out a general store, beauty parlor, and post office. A dozen or so people are out and about, but it's mostly quiet, except for the occasional soft sound of tires rolling over asphalt and country music drifting out of cars, along with the cheerful conversations of those heading down the sidewalk.

The parking lot of the diner is full, mainly with pickup trucks and older sedans. The place is busier than I imagined, but I guess when you're the only restaurant in town you get a decent lunch crowd. The bell over the door jangles as we enter and Eden introduces me to the others gathered around the entrance. It's strange, being new in a town where everyone knows one another.

A faded red vinyl booth near the back opens up as an older couple leaves, and Eden pulls me toward it. As I slide in across from her, I can feel everyone's eyes on me. I attempt to hide behind my menu.

"Afternoon, Eden. Who might this be?" A large man with a long gray beard and wearing a stained apron stands before us with a notepad and pen. He rests his hand on the booth behind Eden, obviously tired of standing.

"T, this is Willa Layne. She's working at the library now."

"Oh right, the fancy-pants librarian from Los Angeles with a degree and everything. Gavin's daughter."

I blush. Have people here really been saying that about me?

"T" pats my shoulder with his meaty paw. "Mrs. Holloway mentioned it when I ran into her at the general store the other day."

Oh boy.

"You waiting tables today, T?" Eden asks.

"Angie needed some help. Only one server today."

Eden nods and her gaze drifts around the room. "The lunch crowd seems to be growing. You might need to hire someone else soon."

"I know, I know," he grumbles. I get the sense this is the hundredth time this has been mentioned to him. "Anyway, welcome, Willa. I haven't seen your pa around lately?"

"He's in Hong Kong on a job."

T whistles through his teeth. "Man sure gets around for an electrician. Well, I'm glad you're here. New blood will do this town some good." He winks. "Now, what can I get ya?"

We order—turkey on rye for both of us, as per Eden's recommendation—and T hustles off to another table.

I realize my expression must've given me away when Eden says, "Don't you worry about Mrs. Holloway, by the way. That's her way of bragging about you!"

"Yeah, right." I give her a glum side-eye.

She taps my arm. "Seriously. I know I joke about her being uptight and stubborn as a mule, but she's not a bad person. Honestly. I wouldn't stay at the library if she was. You'll see."

I sigh and give her a skeptical look. "Okay. I'll give her a chance. It's just this is all so new to me. New town, new people. Some are nicer than others."

"You'll fit in just fine." Her brows wiggle up and down. "Now, important stuff: tell me what it's like living with Dash McCafferty."

Even hearing his name makes my heart skip a beat. But, *wow*. Everyone really does know everyone else's business in this town.

"Oh. Um. I'm only staying with him until my dad's house is finished with renovations." Why am I mentioning this? She probably already knows everything about me, my dad, *and* Dash.

She rolls her teeth over her bottom lip. "I bet that house gets a lot of action. That man is fine with a capital F, and I've never seen him without a hot model, actress, or bombshell fawning all over him."

31

My heart plummets into my stomach with I swear an audible plop, and I'm hit with a whirlwind of emotions—anger, jealousy, disappointment. I'm not sure why. This isn't exactly news. The entire world knows Dash's playboy history. They were witness to it every week on tv! Sure, Dash said last night it was fake, but *all* of it? Regardless, what does it matter? Dash has no interest in me.

I shrug, trying to keep my facial expression neutral. "I haven't seen any of that since I've been here, but it's barely been a day."

Eden is peering at me a little too hard when a middle-aged waitress slides glasses of water in front of us. "Hello there, Miss Willa." Her graying hair is piled up on her head, held in place with a clip that looks like it's made from a western belt buckle. A pencil sits behind her ear. "I'm Angie, T's wife. Nice to meet you."

I shake her hand. "Thank you for the warm welcome."

She nods. "Say hi to your pa for me. And tell Dash I've got a piece of pecan pie with his name on it." She grins and scuttles away.

"There is no way in hell Dash eats pecan pie," I whisper. "You can see each ab of his six-pack through his shirt, for god's sake."

Eden drinks, then raises her eyebrows and licks her lips. "Can you see anything else through his clothes?"

I spit out my water.

"I'll take that as a yes," she says, handing me a napkin.

I shake my head, chuckling. "You're so bad." Then I let out a long sigh. "He *is* one of the sexiest men I've ever seen, though."

Eden laughs. "I knew you weren't dead."

I clear my throat. "Please. I think even Mrs. Holloway would find Dash attractive."

We both have a good cackle at that.

The rest of our lunch goes well—the food delicious and the conversation lively. By the end, I didn't even mind all the stares or whispers from the diners eager to know all about the "fancy-pants librarian from Los Angeles with a degree and everything".

I spend the remainder of my day getting ready for my meeting with Mrs. Holloway tomorrow. I have to be well-prepared if I want to get anything worthwhile out of it.

As I'm packing up, Mrs. Holloway begrudgingly hands me the keys to lock up and bids me good night with a curt nod before leaving. I walk out with Eden a couple of minutes later and we get into our respective cars before she drives off with a friendly wave.

I press the ignition button. Nothing happens.

I press it again. And again. No lights, no sounds. Nothing.

Perfect...

I sigh and look around for anyone who might still be here, but the parking lot is deserted.

CHAPTER 4
DASH

I stare at the bike in front of me on the lift—a blank canvas of steel, chrome, rubber, and paint, full of potential. It's already a beautiful beast, but its owner Jason Momoa wants more—more power, more style. I'm excited to take his bike to the next level and give him the ride of his dreams.

But honestly? Right now, my mind is far, far away.

It's been hard to focus today. All I can think about is Willa. I want to know how her first day at the library is going. Is she loving her new job? Is she getting along with Mrs. Holloway? Is... Is she thinking about me?

Ridiculous, I know. She's a bright young woman coming into her own with a new career. Why would she care about an old washed-up has-been like me? She's a hazard, that's for sure. This shy little pixie with glasses and a sweet smile is more dangerous than any woman I've been with—and I've been with women who had MMA fighters as exes.

"Dash!" a voice calls out impatiently.

I turn, startled, to see Kyle, another mechanic at the shop, glaring at me.

"What is up with you today? I've been calling you for five minutes." He wipes his hands on a rag.

"Sorry, man," I huff. "I'm just distracted."

He shakes his head. "Well, you have a call on the landline. Someone named Willa."

I jump up—Willa? What's wrong? Why didn't she call my cell? I slide it out of my pocket—ah, crap, it's dead. I must've forgotten to charge it. Another casualty of my lust-addled brain.

"She sounds pretty cute," he says, then smirks. "But way too young for your old ass."

"Watch it." I narrow my eyes and give him my meanest growl as we pass each other in the lobby. He gives me the finger and rushes off before I can punch him even playfully. I pick up the receiver from where he's set it down next to the phone.

"Willa? What's going on?" I sound much too concerned and frantic and not like myself at all. But hell, she's calling me here —it must be urgent. I mean, not that I would've minded if she called just to say hi.

"Sorry to bother you, Dash, but your phone went straight to voicemail, and I need some help."

"What is it? Anything you need, I'm on it."

"I'm so sorry, but can I get a ride? The rental car won't start and the agency said they can't get someone out here to fix it until tomorrow morning."

"Sure, give me ten minutes." I fish my keys from my pocket. "You think the car just needs a jump?"

"I don't know. Dad always said that typically some lights come on in the car if it still has some juice. But I'm getting nothing at all."

"At least you listened when your dad tried to teach you

something about cars," I mutter. "He never wanted to listen to me—and I'm the mechanic!"

She laughs. My god, I could live off that sound forever. "Hang tight; I'll be there soon, okay?"

"Thanks, Dash."

"No problem, hon."

I hang up and yell to Kyle I'm taking off. He appears in the lobby just as I'm throwing on my jacket.

"Hot date with Willa?" he asks with a grin.

"Watch it, jerk, or I'll tell Aquaman you botched his exhaust pipe."

His face pales and he holds his hands up. "Okay, okay... Shit, no need to get nasty."

I chuckle. "Do me a favor. Call Sam's and get a tow truck over to the library."

"You got it, boss. Have fun with Willa." He winks and I roll my eyes on my way out.

When I pull up on my bike, Willa's amber eyes go wide.

I roll to a stop next to her where she's leaning on the fender of the car and push up my visor.

"Are you serious?" she asks, her jaw dropping. "I get to ride Blue Steel?!"

I swing my leg over and grin. "Only if you promise not to tell your dad." Again, I worry that's made me sound like a dirty old man, but without a pause she hands me her purse and I put it in the storage box at the back.

"I promise." She pretends to zip her lips and lock them with an imaginary key that she tosses away. It's beyond adorable how excited she is. I remember her begging Gavin to let her ride with me when she was a kid, but he wouldn't allow her anywhere near a motorcycle. Probably for the best back then, but, she's all grown up now. *Gorgeously* grown up. So she can make her own choices—even questionable ones, like getting behind me on a bike. Still, I tremble thinking of what Gavin would do if he found out.

I hand her a helmet, jacket, and gloves. Technically she should be wearing shin guards too, but we're not going far and I'll be more careful than I've ever been, knowing she's behind me. Thankfully, she's wearing slacks and boots today.

"Your toe doing okay?" I ask, eying her foot.

"It's still a little sore, but there's barely any bruising," she replies, before sliding her helmet on. "Strap me into this thing so we can get going!"

Her enthusiasm is contagious, and I'm grinning like a fool as I help her with the equipment. I pull at the chin strap to make sure her helmet is secure. "You keep your feet on those foot pegs, and your arms tight around me. Got it?"

"Yep!" As soon as I hit the seat, she's clambering up behind me. Her arms wrap tightly around my ribs. Her hands send a searing heat through me as they clutch at my chest. It feels spectacular in a way I can't explain. It also scares the hell out of me. I've had women on the back of my bike before, but it never felt like this.

I swallow the confusing feelings down. "Ready?" I ask, pulling my visor into place.

Her muffled "ready" comes from behind. She squeezes me tight and we're off, tearing down the road that is bathed in golden late afternoon light.

The journey up the mountain is like a dream I've never had but still seems oddly familiar. Every detail and sensation is perfectly vivid—from the roar of the engine to the crush of Willa's luscious body behind me. Even through the thick, protective fabric of our gear, I can feel her breasts pressed against my back and the rapid beating of her heart. I'm suddenly utterly content. Whole. Thrumming with excitement, and at the same time at peace with it all.

Fuck, what is happening to me?

We reach the house much too soon. I come to a stop in front of the garage and turn off the bike. She continues to hold onto me. I don't want to tell her to let go.

"How was it?" I ask, finally pulling off my helmet.

She shakes her head, as if waking from a dream. Surely not the same one I had? Pfft. Not a chance.

"Amazing," she says with a contented sigh. She moves her hands to my shoulders and dismounts, then I follow.

She pulls off her helmet and shakes out her hair. Her cheeks are flushed, and she looks at me with huge eyes that catch the dappled light, the flecks of gold sparkling back at me. She smiles brightly at me. "That was so much fun! I really don't understand why Dad wanted to keep me away from this."

The breeze blows across us, messing up her curls. "No, I get it." My heart beats faster as I stroke an errant tendril near her ear. "He wanted to keep you safe."

She looks down when my finger brushes her cheek, then back up at me. Her breath catches and I quickly pull back my hand. *Don't scare the poor girl, Dash.*

But she only smiles. "Stop defending him," she laughs, then removes her gloves. I help her with the jacket. "Can we go again tomorrow?"

I chuckle. "Spoken like a true biker. I think I've created a monster."

"That's on you, mister." She playfully swats at me and her fingers linger for an excruciating moment. I swallow and fish out her purse from the storage box.

As we walk into the mudroom, I say, "I'm ordering dinner for us tonight."

She rolls her eyes at me. "You do know I'm perfectly capable of making my own meals, right? So far you've made me breakfast and lunch, now you want to get me dinner too?"

"I'm sure you're capable." I put the rest of the riding gear away. "I just feel like treating you today."

She smiles softly. "Thank you, Dash. At least let me pay for it?"

"Not happening, hon."

"*Fine*." She huffs. "Where are we ordering from?"

I stamp down the urge to let my hungry gaze roam over her body. "Marge's Diner?"

"Awesome. I was there for lunch. The turkey on rye was delicious! The bread was buttered and it crunched just right when I bit into it..." She trails her hand down the doorframe, a grin playing at the corner of her mouth. "Eden, the library tech, invited me to go with her. I was curious to take a walk and see some of the town. I like her... She's fun."

"So I guess you didn't eat the lunch I packed for you?" I pout extravagantly. She bites her sweet bottom lip and I nearly groan.

"I'm just giving you a hard time, Willa. You don't have to answer to me...even if I *did* slave away at that almond butter and apricot sandwich, and goat cheese on water crackers to go with." I fake sniffle, then chuckle when she giggles and follows me back into the kitchen.

"I can't wait to have that for lunch tomorrow, then."

I duck my chin in appreciation and laugh. "I forgot Eden works at the library."

"You know her?"

I do. Eden is only a few years younger than me. She's grown up around here like me and the crew. Our paths have only occasionally crossed, though. "I know most people in this town."

"Of course." Willa sets down her purse on one of the bar stools. "Because it's so small."

I open the refrigerator and grab a beer. "That must be strange for you coming from L.A." I offer the bottle to her, silently asking if she'd like one.

"Very." She nods at the bottle, and I remove the top and hand it to her, getting another for myself. "Like, everything you do is everybody's business."

I scratch my arm. "Yeah, you'll get used to it eventually. I have my own share of rumors flying around out there, too. No one is perfect."

She nods and twists the little silver ring on her right hand. "What kinds of things do they say about you?"

I take a drink, then clear my throat. "It's not important. Those rumors are in the past. The thing is, no matter what people think or say about you, they don't really know who you are, and you shouldn't waste time worrying about their opinion. Right?"

"Right. I'm sorry, it was rude of me to ask," she murmurs, glancing down at the floor. "I didn't mean to pry."

I shake my head, attempting to reassure her. "It's not a big deal. I'd just rather keep some dignity, you know?" I lean back against the counter, the cool quartz pressing against my skin.

She nods slowly, still looking uncertain, and lets out a small sigh. She picks at the beer bottle's label.

"Don't worry about those wagging tongues, is what I'm saying. You also have a lot of people looking out for you." My voice is low and reassuring as my gaze travels over her face—studying the way her glasses sit slightly forward on her sloped nose, the rosiness of her plump cheeks, and the gentle curve of her lips that quirks upward when she's amused.

She fiddles with a button on her shirt, drawing my eyes to

her to chest, and heat floods my lower half. "I guess," she whispers. "It's going to take some time for me to get used to."

"But you've got time, right? You're not going anywhere for a while." I flash a crooked smile in her direction. "At least I hope not."

Willa grins back at me—still a little hesitant, but brighter than before.

"How about pizza, then, if you got lunch at Marge's?" I ask quickly, before she can say anything.

She nods. "Sounds great. I'm good with whatever toppings you want."

"Even pineapple? You're a dream." I grab the phone on the counter to place the order, and she scurries away to change. I know I'm walking a dangerous line, but the words come tumbling out too easily, without a filter.

She returns shortly in those mind-melting yellow joggers and a white tank, and I push down my filthy thoughts.

I grab plates from the kitchen and get everything set up on the coffee table. I carefully set aside the ceramic octopus in the middle that Julia Roberts gave me when I was in San Francisco last year working on her son Phinnaeus's bike, a gift for his eighteenth birthday.

"You don't use the dining table?" she asks, settling on the sofa and pulling her bare feet underneath her.

"Why, so I can sit alone and ask myself how my day was?"

She chuckles, giving me a saucy look. "No casual girlfriends?"

She leans back against the cushions. Is the little minx fishing?

"I date sometimes, but nothing serious. That whole scene has gotten stale for me."

"Well, I'm guessing there are very few models here in

Deepwood Mountain, Montana. But I'm sure Ryan Reynolds could hook you up with one of his single female friends."

"You think?"

She rolls her eyes. A few seconds pass and I can tell she has more she wants to ask about my past, but she keeps her mouth shut.

She leans forward to grab her beer from the table but suddenly flinches, grabbing at her neck. "Oof."

"What is it?"

She rubs at the junction between her neck and right shoulder. "I haven't been able to do my regular yoga practice and I can feel it. My neck is beyond tight."

"New job. New town. New everything. You're bound to be tied up in knots." I scoot closer to her on the couch. "Let me work them out. It's amazing how strong your hands get over the years working with metal, steel, and fiberglass." I hold them up, showing off my mechanic hands. "I'll use lotion and everything so they won't be rough," I add.

The fuck, Dash? I shouldn't be offering such a thing, knowing how much touching her will tempt me to want to do more. Then I can't keep my mouth from spewing even more words. "Money back guarantee if I don't live up to the hype."

She bites her lip in indecision. "I don't want to put you out."

"It's not about me." I grin. *And anyway, I would love to put out for you*. Stop it. Stop it. Stop it.

"Well, as long as you're sure you don't mind." She adjusts the puffy bun on top of her head, a tint of pink on her skin.

I get up to grab the lotion from the kitchen. "You can tell me all about how your first day went at work. How was Mrs. Holloway?"

She turns, exposing that sexy swath of bare skin on her neck and shoulders, as I sit close to her on the couch.

The moment I touch her I realize this is a horrible idea. Goose-flesh erupts all over her silky skin, and it's a fight to keep my breathing even and my lips from her ear. Her delicate, flower-and-vanilla scent tempts me even closer. What have I done?

"You didn't run screaming from the library this afternoon, so I can take that as a good sign." I hope words will distract me from Willa's tiny, cock-teasing gasps as I rub circles with my thumbs along her neck into her hairline.

She chuckles. "After being chastised for arriving two minutes late and then warned to basically stay in my lane, she left me to my own devices to get settled. I'm sure getting her to accept my proposals will be an uphill battle."

Mrs. Holloway was always stern with us boys growing up if we got rowdy, but never cruel. "Hmm... Possibly, but you might be surprised." Willa's muscles gradually loosen under my touch. "How's the pressure?" I manage to ask, voice rough. I struggle against the compulsion to bite the decadent flesh in front of me.

Her head drops forward and she groans. "Perfect…"

My cock is straining against the seam of my jeans.

"Eden said the same thing about Mrs. Holloway," she says. "So maybe you're right. I guess I'll reserve judgment until after our meeting tomorrow."

I move down her spine, eliciting more sounds of pleasure. When I move up again and fan out, rubbing down her neck and over her shoulders, kneading and rolling her muscles, something deep catches in her throat. "Dash," she moans, her body squirming. My throat goes dry.

I imagine slipping one of the straps of her tank top down, dragging my tongue and lips over her flushed skin. Picture my hands coming around to cup and tease her breasts until she's begging me for more.

The doorbell rings with our pizza delivery, and Willa and I both jump. *Holy shit.*

" That was…really nice. You had me in a trance. Thank you." She puts a hand to her chest, looking suddenly flushed, like she's just come in from a sprint down the street.

"You're very welcome," I reply, my ragged voice almost unrecognizable. I get up, taking a throw pillow with me to cover my erection, or else the delivery guy's going to think I get hard for pineapple on my pizza.

Fuck.

CHAPTER 5
WILLA

I t takes several moments for me to gather my wits after that massage. My heart is pounding and my skin prickling, as if I've been sitting too close to a fire. It's not fair that in addition to looking like a rugged superhero, Dash also has wickedly talented hands. My panties are drenched and I'm breathless from the effort of not acting like a sex-starved nymphomaniac in front of him.

I hear Dash at the front door, his voice raised and another voice booming. I turn to face the foyer just as Dad barges into the house past Dash. "What's going on here, Willa?"

"Dad!" I self-consciously wrap my arms around my body. "You're back from your trip?"

"Yes! And this is what I come back to! My best friend"—he glares at Dash—"*former* best friend feeling up my daughter?"

Dash places a steadying hand on Dad's shoulder. "Gavin, it was just a massage."

Dad angrily shrugs him off and throws his arms skyward in exasperation. "*Just a massage*? Bullshit. Look at you two!" He points to Dash holding a pillow in front of his crotch, and as for me—my face feels so hot it must resemble an overripe tomato, with sweat beading on my forehead.

Suddenly Mrs. Holloway is standing next to my dad, clicking her tongue in disappointment. OMG, where did *she* come from? "And you want to be the next Deepwood Mountain library director?" she huffs. "Fat chance."

"Willa, wake up."

I hear Dash saying the words, and his voice seems to come from all around me, but his mouth isn't moving. *"Sweetheart, you're dreaming."*

The crystal blue of his eyes has become the sea, and I am drowning in them—yet I am filled with a warmth that flows right through my veins to the farthest corners of my body.

My eyes fly open. It's pitch black. I can feel the heat of someone near me. "Dash? Is that you?"

"I'm right here, hon." His hand finds mine above the covers and squeezes. A lamp flicks on.

I squint as my eyes adjust to the light. Dash pushes my hair out of my face, and I fight not to lean into his soft touch. "I heard you calling for your dad all the way down the hall."

"Oh." Immediately I feel beyond foolish when I see the concern on his face. "Sorry. I was having a nightmare."

"I figured as much." He studies my face and I wish I could hide. "You want to tell me about it?"

I shake my head. "No. Nothing made much sense anyway." I definitely don't want to try to explain the feelings for him that are threatening to overwhelm me.

Gradually, as my mind clears, I realize he's shirtless and I'm transfixed by the sight before me; my god, he's a work of art. His chest rises and falls with each breath, broad and firm, as if chiseled from marble. His arms are thick and corded with muscle, and those abs—holy hell, I could wash my laundry on them. All this without my glasses! I feel light-headed just thinking about what he'd look like if I put them on.

I inhale deeply, taking in the warm musk of his body, and wonder if his skin tastes as delicious as it smells. He's close enough I can feel his hot breath on my skin, causing a shiver to run down the length of my spine.

Before my rational side can jump up and down, frantically screaming at me to stop, I reach out and touch his stubbled cheek, where that one dimple forms—it's rough under my fingertips.

"Willa..." he growls. The sound goes straight to my core, making my pussy throb.

I don't want to stop exploring. I trail my fingers over his jaw and down his throat, his Adam's apple bobbing under my touch.

Dash's breath goes ragged, and I can feel his heart racing under my palm as I slide it lower. I've never touched any man like this, but with Dash, I want to touch *everything*. My hand skates over his chest and grazes his nipple—he shudders. "Willa," he whispers again in a husky voice, "I... I..."

I move closer and brush my lips gently against his.

An impossibly deep groan erupts from his throat, and he launches himself from my bed as if burned by invisible fire. "I'm sorry." In a rush, he's out the door...and I'm alone again in the dark.

"It was a stupid error in judgment and I regret the entire thing," I say, then lean back in my office chair, the squeak of the hinges doing nothing to help my frayed nerves.

"Don't say that," Ash says calmly, buffing a camera lens.

"Why not? It's true. I feel like the biggest idiot in the world."

"Take it down a notch, Miss Dramatic." She puts down the cloth and picks up her phone to stare directly at me. "You took a chance. Sometimes it works out. Other times it doesn't. I'm proud of you, Willie."

I make a face.

"I *mean* it," she says, undeterred. "Look at the net positive here. You have closure with Dash now. You can get over him and move on."

Ugh. I really hate it when she's right.

"Why does that sound easier than it is?"

"Derr, because it's your heart, silly. I didn't say it would be easy."

Not easy? No shit. Whenever I close my eyes, I see Dash tripping over himself to get out of my room last night, fleeing from me as if I had some horrible contagious disease. Who knew a kiss from me was so terrifying? If it wasn't for the humiliation, I'd probably find the whole thing hilarious.

And so I avoided him this morning, staying in my room until it was absolutely necessary to leave. I mean, he *was* still my ride to work.

"About last night..." he said, the air thickly charged as we rode in his pickup truck.

I swallowed the lump in my throat. "I don't want to talk about it, Dash."

"I think we should—"

"Just leave it. Please?"

His jaw clenched and his grip tightened on the steering wheel— his face a mixture of anger, annoyance, and frustration. But he didn't say another word for the rest of the drive. I got out of his truck quickly before he had a chance to step out and around and open my door for me.

"I'll pick you up later, if your rental is still toast?" he called after me.

"Eden said she'd give me a ride home," I threw back. I hadn't even asked her, but I hoped she would, because I had no desire to face him and these feelings again so soon.

"But—"

I waved and hustled into the library—not looking back until I heard him drive off.

Ash tells me to stay strong and I end the call, my eyes wandering to the chip in my wooden office door frame. "Get over him and move on." "Stay strong." What does that even *mean*, Ash? How do I forget a man who lives in my head rent free? Thinking about it all makes my stomach churn, leaving me confused.

I swear Mrs. Holloway can smell my weakened state. She calls me into her office after reviewing the proposals I submitted earlier this morning, before my call with Ash that squashed my hopes when she was firmly on Team Get Over Him.

I sit down across from Mrs. Holloway and she laces her fingers on the desk. Her nails are longer than I expected, painted pale lavender. It makes her look like an evil grandmother.

"Are you sure you're all right, Miss Layne?" The chain on her glasses sways with her slight movements. "I can't help but notice that you seem a little...off...today."

My first reaction is to deny it. But I do feel off. Am I really that transparent? Finally I let out a deep sigh.

"I suppose I'm just finding it more difficult to settle in than

I expected." I quickly add, "But it has nothing to do with the library. I feel more at home here than anywhere else."

She takes a breath. "I see. Well, I know you didn't ask for my advice, but I'll offer it anyway, in the hopes it does you some good." She leans in and lowers her voice to a whisper. "People in small towns like to talk. Gossip gives them something to do instead of worrying about their own dull little lives. Take anything they say with a grain of salt and form your own opinions. It'll save you a lot of heartache."

I nod politely, but I'm not sure how these pearls of wisdom pertain to me. I always make up my own mind about things. What am I missing?

"Oh, and don't let anyone ruin your day." She gives me a small smile. "Especially a man."

That, at least, I can relate to. "Thank you, Mrs. Holloway. I appreciate it."

"Now, let's talk about your proposals." Her usually sharp gaze softens, and I'm struck by the pretty shape of her eyes. I suddenly realize with a pang that she's much more human than I initially thought. "I'm very impressed with your ideas and your research, but I have some concerns…"

We spend the rest of the morning discussing the details of all my proposals one by one. It turns out she's actually very *much* for improving the library and bringing it into the twenty-first century and beyond, but is afraid that a library so accessible online might mean patrons no longer visit the library's physical space. Who would've thought Mrs. Sourpuss didn't want to lose the patrons, especially the children, and was concerned this place would become a ghost town, all empty and lonely? Maybe she isn't so bad after all.

I was so worried, but in the end my proposals do their job of showing her how important the physical space is, and reinforce the idea that more technology and resources would bring people in, not drive them away. Hurray!

I'm still riding the high of excitement at lunchtime. Eden and I meet around a picnic table on the back lawn. There's a thick tree trunk at one end and she props her feet up on it while crunching on a carrot stick. I crack open the lid of my box and see the almond butter and apricot jam sandwich Dash made for me. I remember our conversation from yesterday, just before he gave me that massage, and I squeeze my thighs together. Why did he have to be so damn perfect?

While Eden is busy texting with some mystery man, I google Dash. I honestly hadn't yet, probably because I knew what I would find. My worst fears are confirmed. Models, celebs, beautiful socialites—Dash had been with them all at some point. Promotional photos for the show have him flashing that enticing dimple at any number of women. Paparazzi shots feature candid snaps while he's on holiday out in the tropics with women in tiny micro-bikinis or strutting in designer dresses on their way into a club or fundraising gala. The women are gorgeous, with bodies like fine sculptures, and hair and makeup straight out of the priciest salons.

It's painfully obvious why Dash wouldn't want me—little miss mousy four-eyes reading silly romance novels in her sweatpants. There's no glitz or glamour in my life. The women he's used to are worldly and experienced with grace and maturity. I have none of those qualities. I swipe my phone closed and sulkily set it face down on the table.

I won't dwell on it. Like Mrs. Holloway said, no man should ruin my day...even if it is unintentional on his part. One thing is certain. Ash is right. I need to get over Dash McCafferty, and fast.

"Whatcha doing after work today?" I ask Eden. As she

LEXI HAYES

looks up from her phone, twittering bird calls float in from the nearby trees.

She squints, a ray of sun in her line of vision. "There's a yoga class at the gym I'd like to try. Want to come?"

"They have yoga here?" I'm actually surprised Deepwood Mountain even has a *gym*.

She snorts and gives me a sideways look before tucking her dark hair behind her ear. "Not everything in town is as outdated as the library. But besides going to the Rustic Ridge Bar, there's not much else to do in the evening."

The last thing I feel like doing is subjecting myself to the bar scene. I rub at the knot near the base of my neck that has returned three-fold since Dash's talented hands made it disappear. Yoga would have to ease my tension, now. "I have nothing to wear, though."

"I've got an extra set of workout clothes with me."

I sit up straighter on the bench. "Yeah? Thanks! Let's do it."

CHAPTER 6
DASH

I t's gone dark outside, and the library closed hours ago. She should've been back by now.

I text Willa, my fingers flying over my phone screen.

> Where are you?

Her reply comes three agonizing minutes later.

> At the gym.

> The gym? Why?

> I'm finishing up a yoga class. Excuse me, I have to get back into downward dog.

Really? *That's* how it's going to be? All attitude?

I jump up and stride toward the garage. I try not to slam the door of my truck too hard as I get in and start heading to the gym. I'm not upset...fine, I *am* upset...but only because she didn't tell me she'd be late. If anything happened to her, I'd go out of my mind—not to mention Gavin would kill me.

I'm seething as I walk into the gym, fists clenched. The place is hot and smells like sweat, heavy and metallic. I can hear water splashing in an adjacent room. Heads turn my way, and a couple of people wave at me from their machines, but I don't have time for idle chit chat. I'm on a mission to find Willa.

At last I spot her near the door of the classroom in a baggy concert tee and purple leggings, her purse slung over her shoulder. Her hair is up in that messy bun, same as it was last night when I massaged her shoulders, except now the stray hairs are covered in sweat and sticking to her flushed throat and cheeks. Why this turns me on so much, I don't know. But if we were anywhere else right now, I'd devour her.

She's talking to some guy almost twice her size. He's built like a goddamned tree. She's smiling up at him like he hung the moon, and it makes me want to take down that tree with my bare hands.

When the guy turns, I curse. It's Rex "Raging Boner" Fletcher, my buddy Nick's younger brother. He's notorious for spreading his seed all over town. He's one of those assholes who gets away with bad behavior because he got really close to being a pro football player. It's revolting: even though his dreams never panned out, now he just goes from woman to woman and party to party to forget how pathetic his life's turned out to be and *nobody calls him on it*. He doesn't deserve Willa's attention, and here he is with his hand against the wall inches above her shoulder. My protective instincts claw at my insides. If he boxes her in any further, I'll have to rip his arm clean off.

Eden comes over to join her. Willa types something into her phone, then moves away, waving at Rex.

"I can't wait for this weekend," Rex calls out to her as the girls walk toward the entrance, and I gnash my teeth. The girls are still chatting and giggling when they get to the door, then Willa looks up to see me standing there.

"Dash?" Her brow furrows.

I glance at Eden. "No need to give her a ride, thanks, I've got her."

Eden grabs Willa's wrist. "It's no trouble, Dash," she says.

"It's okay," Willa replies, patting Eden's arm. "I'll wash your clothes and return them tomorrow. Thanks again."

Eden nods once and looks up to me for a second before her eyes flick back to Willa. A silent exchange passes between them; I'm sure I look half-crazed right now. Eden should know I'd never hurt Willa. My hand drifts to Willa's lower back as I guide her to the truck and open the door for her.

As I climb into the truck, Willa sits back and folds her arms across her chest.

"Rude," she grumbles as we pull out onto the road.

My blood boils. "*Rude*?" My smile is tight and forced; it feels like the skin stretching over my face might split open. "You mean like not telling me you'd be late tonight was rude? I was worried!"

"I didn't know I was required to check in with you like a teenager with a curfew. I'm an adult now, if you haven't noticed."

Hell, have I ever. "An *adult* would have the decency to let the person waiting for them know where they are." My voice comes out sharper than I'd like.

"Okay, Dad, whatever," she mutters under her breath.

Did she just—

"I am *NOT* your father," I spit out, my knuckles turning white as I grip the steering wheel. "And if you call me that again—"

She glares out the window, the streetlamps reflecting their light off her glasses. "You'll what? Ground me?" she hurls back.

A flush of heat rises up my neck, and I take a deep breath. She's right. What *would* I do? Lock her in her room? Spank her bare bottom? I shake my head, quickly pushing the second image out of my mind.

"Why were you talking to that walking hard-on Rex Fletcher?" I ask.

She clears her throat. "He's a personal trainer. He offered his services."

"Oh, I bet he did."

She smacks her forehead in exasperation. "Dash, I'm sorry for not letting you know where I was. I just wanted to go out with a friend and blow off some steam in a yoga class. I didn't think it would be such a big deal."

My jaw is as tense as a steel trap as I wait for her to continue.

"And as for Rex, it's really none of your business."

"He only wants to get in your pants, Willa. I know him. That's his MO."

"Well, maybe that's all I'm looking for right now." She huffs. "Again, not that my love life is any of your business."

I want to pound the steering wheel into oblivion. "You want to be used, like a piece of meat?"

She lets out a frustrated sigh. "Don't be so patronizing, Dash. Who's to say I'm not the one using him? If you must know...I'm a virgin. Is it so wrong for me to take control of my own pleasure and go after someone experienced enough to show me what I need?"

My jaw drops open. Willa is a *virgin?* And she's ready to sacrifice her beautiful body to that douchebag? There's no way he knows how to worship a woman the way she deserves.

She lifts her chin defiantly. "Just because I may not meet the standards of beauty, sophistication, and maturity that *you* require, doesn't mean there aren't other men out there who'll find me attractive."

I hit the brakes so hard they squeal in protest, and we fly forward against the seatbelts. I hastily steer over to the side of the road and stop the car. My heart is racing in my chest. "What are you talking about?"

She's still gripping the armrest, nearly out of breath. "Not *all* men need to have models and the most beautiful women in Hollywood to be satisfied, you know. Some men—"

"Stop right there." I reach over and slide my hands under her chin, gripping her sweet face, soft and delicate, in my big palms. "You think I'm not attracted to you?"

She shakes her head as best she can in my grip. "Why would you be? I'm not a famous actress, or a beautiful model. I'm not even pretty."

Instantly, I'm livid. Livid that she would believe this about herself and that I played any part in her thinking it. I want to pull her into my lap and whisper in her ear how sexy she is and do every dirty, filthy thing I that fills my mind. But there's this goddamned center console between us.

In a matter of moments I've gone around to her side and yanked open the door, lifting her down to the ground. My body is flush with hers and I thrust my hands into her hair, tugging it free from her bun. She sinks against me, her eyes wide, glowing in the silver light of the moon.

"Now you listen to me. I've *never* been more attracted to any woman in my entire thirty-nine years on this planet, Willa. From the moment I first saw you in my driveway, all I can think about is you and what I want to do to your gorgeous body."

She opens her mouth, probably to protest, but I press my fingers to her mouth. God, her lips are like velvet.

"I'm not done, sweetheart. Models and celebrities have

nothing on you, because you're real. Your beauty is natural. From your scrubbed face to your sensible shoes, I'm addicted to the whole package—inside and out. I'm attracted to *you*." My hand drags down from her mouth to her chest, and I stroke the spot where I can feel her heart beating as fast as mine.

"Then why..." She furrows her brow. "Last night... You ran away after I kissed you." Her voice is breathy and my swollen cock fights against the zipper of my jeans.

"That has nothing to do with how much I want you." I exhale slowly. "And everything to do with your dad. The last thing I want to do is anger him or damage our friendship."

She slides her hands up my stomach and then around my back. My entire body trembles under her touch.

"I used to have the biggest crush on you." Her fingers twist the fabric of my shirt. "But it's grown into something much more intense. I want you, Dash, more than anyone I've ever wanted before. If my dad can't accept that..." She trails off, her hungry gaze drifting to my mouth. Her tongue darts out to wet her lips.

And all my willpower goes right out the window.

I need her to be *mine. Now.*

Consequences be damned.

My lips crash down on hers like a mountain storm, rough and forceful. As my name spills from her mouth, I moan into it, the taste of her sweeter than I imagined. Our tongues dance and play together, and I pull at her bottom lip with my teeth. Her nails scratch my back, and she gasps and whimpers, the sounds etching themselves forever into my brain and making my cock throb, feeling as if it could explode without a single touch.

I gather her to me, one hand in her hair. I grasp her firm ass with the other to fit her against my aching cock. When she throws her head back and cries out, I come close to losing it. I rush to trail wet, open-mouthed kisses down her neck and into the hollow of her throat, tasting her salty skin. She grinds against me desperately until I'm on the verge of coming undone. I'm wild with need for her, my self-control shattered by the intensity of her passion.

I shift her aside and scramble to open the cab door, my hands shaking. "Lie down," I rasp, my voice deep and savage. She stumbles backward into the cab with my help, her body pressed up against mine, her breasts crushed against my chest. I crawl into the seat on top of her, pushing her down. Her sharp intake of breath makes me ravenous.

"I need to taste your fucking pussy."

The words come out harsher than I intend, a dirty growl instead of a seductive whisper. I worry I'm scaring her. She's new to all of this and here I'm barking orders at her.

"Yes." She moans loudly, digging her nails into my biceps. Shit, that only spurs me on more.

I move back and remove her shoes, then grab her leggings and yank them down as she lifts her hips. In a rush of desire, I grab both sides and they rip apart at the seams.

She gasps. "Oh! Those were Eden's."

"I'll buy her ten new pairs," I growl, capturing Willa's mouth in another savage kiss and once more pressing her back onto the seat.

I kiss down her throat, knead her breasts under her t-shirt, then push it up to tongue her soft, trembling belly. I skirt the edge of her thin cotton panties. Cotton. Not lace. Not silk. Not a thong. Just good, wholesome, cotton. "I love these panties."

"I'm going to go with...thank you?" she chuckles and grinds against me with a shudder.

"No... Thank *you*." I shove my face against her drenched

center and drag my teeth over her through the glorious things. "Christ, you smell delicious."

She gasps and her hands find my head, tightening on the back of it.

Goosebumps erupt over my skin, and I snarl. I could so easily tear off these panties just like I did the leggings, but I should take my time with her. Please her like she deserves. Not like some feral beast without a shred of self-control.

I slip my hands into the panties at her hips and pull, moving back to slide them down and off. I toss them away.

In case someone passes by, I hit the switch to turn off the cab light. Because at this point I couldn't stop for anything.

Willa is *mine*.

This pussy is *mine*.

I kiss up her leg from her ankle to the inside of her knee, then higher, into the hollow of her creamy white thigh. She squirms and groans as my tongue teases her there.

Her pussy lips are so wet, so plump, and so pink, and her blond pubic hairs tickle my face. I haven't seen pubic hair in a while, either. I love it. I feather my fingers through it. Beyond sexy. So natural. So feminine.

"Dash, please," Willa pleads.

"You're going to tell me if anything doesn't feel good. You won't hurt my feelings, got that?"

"I'll tell you."

My fingertips stroke along her slick folds and her body quivers beneath my caress.

"Tell me this pussy right here is mine, Willa."

She nods, trying to catch her breath.

"Say it out loud, sweetheart."

"Yes, yours," she cries.

"Good girl."

She moans softly as I lick her from the bottom up, slowly

snaking upward and then back down. Her breaths are quick and shallow, and I can see her pleasure in the way she writhes beneath me, lifting up to meet my tongue, straining toward my mouth like a flower reaching for the sun.

"You okay, hon?" I ask, as I feast on her.

She opens her eyes and smiles. "Yes. *God*, yes. Don't stop."

I slow down and tease at her sweet flesh, my cock throbbing with each beat of my heart, demanding release.

"I'm not stopping until you come all over my face." I slide my hands under her ass and pull her closer to my mouth, cupping the perfect curves I haven't been able to stop dreaming about ever since I saw her again. I devour her with kisses and licks, exploring every last inch of her wet folds with my tongue and lips.

She squirms and her breathing is getting even wilder as I trace circles around her sweet spot. Her fingers spear through my hair. "Oh, Dash..."

"Yes, love…" I murmur, lost in the depths of her pleasure.

I tease her clit, and she lets out a low whine. I hear the slide of her fingers as they leave my head and clutch at the armrest behind her. "Mmmm, yeah," she purrs. "Just like that. *There*!"

My breath is hot on her sensitive center. "Is that the right spot, Willa?" I carefully lick over her silken flesh, wanting to tease the orgasm out of her. My hands anchor around her thighs as I wreak tender havoc on her most intimate spot.

She sputters in response, her body trembling like crazy.

"Are you going to be a good girl and come for me?" I rasp.

"Yes..." she replies. Her moans grow more desperate as I continue my sweet torture. "That's…yes…I'm coming!" She keens and her hips start to quiver and buck, but I hold her firmly and bury my face in her flesh, absorbing all of her climax.

"Dash! Oh…oh, god…" I will never tire of hearing my

name as she comes all over my tongue. I leisurely lick at her until the tremors subside and only her heavy breaths remain in the air.

She gets up onto her elbows and I kiss the insides of her thighs. It's dark, but I can see the reflection of the moon in her glasses.

"That was—" she starts to say.

A siren chirps a single staccato note behind us.

And then I look up to see flashing red and blue lights cutting through the night sky.

CHAPTER 7
WILLA

The Police? Are you freaking kidding me?! "What do we do?" I ask, as Dash wipes his face on the front of his shirt.

"Uh… Don't panic?" He gives me a cheeky smile.

"Dash, I don't have any pants on…or panties!" I sit up and try to pull my t-shirt down over my lower half. I probably look a complete mess, still reeling as I am from the most amazing orgasm of my life.

Dash runs a hand through his hair. "Yeah…about that… uh…" He briefly looks around the cab. "Sorry. They're gone."

I bite my lip, shaking my head in disbelief.

The police officer steps out of his Ford SUV. He's a mountain of a man. Maybe as tall as Dash, and extra thick, with a dark brown beard and a cowboy hat. He strolls over to us.

"Evening, Sheriff Quinn," Dash says, standing in front of the cab. I try not to squeak in alarm. Not just a cop, but a sheriff? *Shitshitshitshitshit.*

"Dash." He tips his hat and looks toward the truck. "Everything okay?"

Dash nods. "Everything's fine, Sheriff. We only stopped for a moment. We'll be getting back up the mountain now."

The Sheriff doesn't budge. "Move aside, Dash." He stops and flicks his flashlight into the cab and onto me. "Hello there? Miss? Can you come out here, please?"

I squint, shielding my eyes from the light. "Um…" I start. "I—"

"She's not…fully clothed, Sheriff. Can I get her a blanket or something?"

Quinn rolls his tongue around his mouth and nods. "Sure, and then I'll need to see her ID."

I groan as he keeps his light on me—thankfully, just the upper half.

Dash grabs a blanket from the back and flaps it open. I wrap it around me like the world's fuzziest sarong, and he helps me down as I give him an icy death stare.

"It'll be okay," he whispers, trying to comfort me. Then he gives me a quick peck on the cheek. His breath smells like me and I blush despite my discomfort.

Dash hands me my bag and I slowly reach in to get my wallet with my ID.

The sheriff takes it from me. "Willa Layne," he reads, then looks up at me. "Oh! Gavin's daughter? The new librarian?"

I give him a weak smile, not sure if I feel embarrassed or relieved I'm recognized. "Yes, sir," I mumble.

He glances at Dash and shakes his head in a curious, amused way. "Miss Layne, why are you out here on a public road half-naked?" He puts up his hand. "Before you answer, let me say I can guess why. But I need to hear it from you. If you need my help, just say the word."

Dash starts. "Sheriff—"

"I asked Miss Layne," he interjects sharply.

"I'm fine, sir. We just got a little"...I swallow..."*amorous* and pulled over to be safe."

This time it's the sheriff's turn to crack a smile. "Well, while I appreciate your concern for road safety, it's illegal to get this"—his brow arches up as he draws the light down my legs —"*amorous* out in public, and it comes with pretty serious consequences here in Montana."

For some reason that doesn't surprise me. Dash circles my waist with his strong arms to hold me steady.

"But knowing your pa, I think what you're going to get from him when he finds out what you two were up to will be punishment enough." He winks. "You're free to go."

Dash corrals me into the passenger seat just as the sheriff leans down and picks something up off the ground with his pen.

When I see what it is, my face bursts into flames. *No. Please, no.*

"These belong to you?" he asks, holding my panties out in front of him, dangling from the tip of his pen.

Dash snatches them, mumbling something.

"Welcome to Deepwood Mountain, Miss Layne," the sheriff says, then he grins and tips his hat.

"Thank you," I croak, from behind hands that are now covering my face.

"Sheriff Quinn," Dash says, and I peek between my fingers to watch him walk over to the Sheriff's SUV.

"What're you thinking?" the officer says in hushed tones, but I can still hear him. "Gavin's going to murder you."

"I know..." Dash trails off, running his hand distractedly over the back of his neck. "It was a terrible mistake. I should've known better."

My heart drops into my stomach. Is that what Dash thinks of us? Of me? A terrible mistake? I feel sick.

"Just be careful," the sheriff warns him.

They wave goodbye to each other, and the sheriff drives off.

Dash gets back in the truck and puts the car in gear, pulling out onto the road. I can feel his eyes on me, but I keep mine straight ahead.

"Well *that* was an adventure," he says with a laugh, reaching for my hand. I hesitate, torn between my desire to feel his touch and my sadness at the idea that I'm just another mistake. I want to be more to him than a momentary distraction.

"Willa?"

My heart warms at the sound of my name on his lips, but still I pull away. "I need a few moments, okay?"

He presses his lips together and nods slowly. "Sure." Disappointment is clear in his gaze as he turns his full attention back to the road.

The rest of the ride home is quiet; I do my best not to sneak glances at him, with mixed results.

When we arrive at the house, he helps me out of the truck. I'm lifted into his arms before I can protest and the next thing I know he's carrying me over the threshold like a bride.

"What are you doing?" I hold on to his neck, partly to keep myself from falling, but also because being this close to him is truly intoxicating.

"You're not wearing shoes," he says, then he gestures to where the blanket is still wrapped around me. "Or much else."

My cheeks flush with heat as a grin spreads across his handsome face. Despite how badly I want to return it, his charm will not win me over this time.

He sets me down in the living room, and I pull the blanket tighter around me. "I feel so dirty," I mutter, my voice barely above a whisper.

"Let me run a bath for us, then."

I shake my head. "No, I'm tired. I'll just take a quick shower and go to bed."

"Alone?" he asks, confused.

I hesitantly nod, avoiding his eyes.

"So...what?" He crosses his arms over his chest. "We're just going to pretend this never happened?"

I meet his eyes. "Isn't that what you want? You said it yourself: I'm a terrible mistake. A dumb reminder of your lack of judgment and self-control."

"*What*?"

"That's what you said to the sheriff. It makes complete sense. You just got a little too wrapped up in the moment. I'm much too young, plain, inexperienced, and *risky* for you. I get it."

His jaw grinds. "Willa, *you* weren't the mistake. Stopping at the side of the road to eat your delectable pussy was. And I'd do it again and again, even if they locked me up for it. Because yes, you *do* make me lose all control. You also make me feel invincible and like I'm the luckiest guy in the world. All I can think about is how many different ways I can make you scream my name."

I open my mouth to speak, but for some reason the words get stuck in my throat. Dash has said it before: he wants me. He's kissed me and tasted me until I couldn't hold back anymore. Why am I having such a hard time believing him?

He moves closer and sweeps me into his arms. "You need more convincing, sweetheart?" He presses his lips to mine once, then again with more intensity. "I'll gladly do whatever it takes, for as long as it takes, until you see just how crazy I am about you."

I'm in a daze, still reeling from the weight of his words,

when he tugs away the blanket and I'm instantly tossed over his shoulder like a sack of potatoes.

"How about we continue this in the bedroom?" he asks, my stomach quivering in anticipation. "Unless you still want that shower."

"N-no, the shower can wait for now," I stammer, draped on his shoulder.

He smacks my bare ass once and then squeezes. "This ass...mmmf."

The stairs are a blur, and when we get to Dash's room, he lets me slide deliciously down the front of him and onto the massive bed. His ice-blue eyes flash with desire, locked on mine, and a wicked smile tugs at his lips. My pussy throbs once again, still aching in the best way from my last orgasm, and I'm already soaked. I want his cock inside me. Filling me. Stretching me. Claiming me.

Dash turns on a soft light near the bed. "I need to see you." He studies me intently, and there's a tremor in his voice when he says, "The last thing you are is plain, Willa. You're a genuine beauty: it honestly hurts me to hear you say otherwise."

He squeezes the massive bulge in his jeans, and I gasp at the size of it. "This is what you do to me, just being near me."

He begins to take off his shirt, but I sit back on my knees and grip his arms. "Wait," I say. "Let me."

He stops, one elbow over his head, the other arm hanging at his side. "This night is all about you, sweetheart," he says. "You're in charge."

"I am?" I ask, sitting up straighter.

He nods and puts his shirt back on with a wry grin. "On one condition."

"And what would that be?" I ask, watching him carefully.

His smile broadens and his eyes dart toward the t-shirt I'm wearing.

"That ridiculous shirt needs to come off."

I laugh and look down at my chest, the soft material clinging to my curves. "*Frankie Says Relax*, Dash? This is vintage 80s!"

"How would you know that? Frankie was way before your time."

I shrug. "I like antiques," I say, and arch a brow at him.

"Oh, you are so going to pay for that." He reaches under my shirt and grabs at my sides, tickling me mercilessly.

"No!" I wriggle and laugh under his fingers. "Classic!" I shriek. "I meant classic!"

"Right…" He smirks, stopping his assault.

I'm left breathless when he rips off my shirt, leaving me completely bare. He groans. "Christ, Willa." My nipples get impossibly hard under his hungry stare. He leans forward and nuzzles my chest, kissing and licking my breasts.

Softly moaning, I thread my hands through his hair, pulling him closer to me. His tongue swirls around a tight peak before he sucks it into his mouth and grazes it with his teeth. A molten puddle of heat pools between my legs and I drop my head back in pleasure. He repeats the process on my other breast, giving it the same undivided attention. When his hands knead my ass cheeks he groans, his breath turning ragged and shallow like mine.

I nudge him away from me. "You distracted me from getting this shirt off you. I want to see you, too." My voice is deep and breathy, unrecognizable to me.

He moves back and I push his shirt up until he lifts it off the rest of the way, tossing it across the room. "Now I understand how my panties went astray," I whisper, and he smiles, his dimple driving me into a frenzy.

My fingertips explore the contours of his powerful chest and shoulders even as his intoxicating musk lingers in the air. I press my lips to his neck, gently nipping and kissing, moving downward. A deep groan runs through him when I circle his nipples with my tongue.

"Naughty girl," he murmurs, and gives me a spank on my ass.

I drag my nails over the ridges of his chiseled abs, feeling the muscles ripple beneath my touch. When I reach his jeans, I can't help but run my hand over the hard length of him. It feels like it's ready to tear right through the denim.

"Fuck..." he curses, and his cock jumps.

I undo the button of his jeans and slide his zipper down with a hiss. I feel his fingers skim through the slickness between my legs. Electric pleasure courses through me and a gasp escapes my lips.

"Goddamn." He groans and his thick finger slips inside me, stretching my tight entrance. "You're so wet, sexy."

I can barely think as my trembling hands struggle to remove the rest of his clothing. I moan when he strokes against my g spot, teasing me.

My legs buckle, threatening to give out.

He holds me up around the waist, his grasp firm. "Feel good, baby?"

"So good. Too good," I croak, shivering.

His throaty chuckle vibrates through me but he doesn't stop. Somehow, I manage to pull down his jeans and boxers while he brings me dangerously close to the edge.

"Dash, if you keep doing that, I'll—"

"Come?" he finishes, brushing my lips lightly with his fingers. "God, that would be so hot...but right now, I'm only trying to get you ready for my cock. It's aching to get inside your sweet pussy, baby."

His gaze falls on the formidable length between us—so hard and *so big*.

Will that even fit inside me? He stretched me with just his finger.

Dash must sense my apprehension, because he lifts my face to look into his eyes.

"We don't have to do this if you're not ready. I know I'm your first. If you want to wait, I would never force you to do anything."

I melt. Truly, Dash is a decent, caring man with a heart of gold. Kind and tender, just like the heroes from my romance novels. He's perfect. "Dash, I really do want you inside me, but I'm nervous." I take a deep breath. "In case you haven't noticed, you're huge."

The corner of his mouth quirks up in a half-smile, and that dimple sends more heat straight to my core. "We'll go slow, sweetheart. If it gets too much, we can take a break and work back up to it. I'm not going anywhere." He caresses my cheek and my entire being screams how much I love this man.

Yes, there it is. *I love him.*

I reach out and grasp his thick cock in my hand, my small fingers barely able to wrap around it. It feels like velvet over steel, hot and smooth, pulsing with life. I lick my lips in nervous anticipation.

He squints as if pained. "I hope I can last more than a few blazing hot seconds with you, my sexy girl." He turns and fishes out a packet from the drawer of the nightstand. Then he tears it open with his teeth and rolls on the condom.

"Umm… What do I do?" I ask, unsure where to start.

He climbs onto the bed and lies down on his back. The soft light falls over him, and my eyes zero in on his cock standing at attention. He strokes it languidly a few times and looks up at me with a seductive grin. "You're going to ride me."

I blink back at him, and his heated gaze lights sparks inside me.

"That way you get all the control. You decide how much and how fast." His hand engulfs mine as he brings it to his lips. "Now bring that pretty pussy over here and get on like I'm your personal Blue Steel."

I obey without hesitation, swinging my leg over him, my pussy poised over his cock. He lets out a low groan as I press my tender flesh against his tip.

Closing my eyes, I slowly sink down onto him, inch by inch, breathing through the slight pain.

"Hell, baby," Dash whispers. "You feel so good."

He brushes his fingers up my thighs, his touch soothing me.

"Look at me, Willa," he growls, his voice filled with need.

I open my eyes and meet his gaze, reveling in the sensation of his cock buried completely inside me. The stretch is intense, but my feelings for him are even more so.

"You're gorgeous and you feel incredible," he says, roughly.

My heart races as he rolls his hips, and I can only whimper in response.

"Easy, hon. Let your body lead."

I lean in and move with a slow, purposeful rhythm. Resting my hands on either side of his shoulders, I grind against him.

"I'm seeing stars," he grits out. "You're so hot, tight, and wet...I can barely stand it."

The pain gets less and less with each thrust, replaced with an overwhelming pleasure that blooms through my core like wildfire. "Ohhh, god..." I remove my glasses, placing them on the nightstand, and arch my back, driving against him faster.

"Fucking hell, Willa," Dash roars, kneading my breasts. "You're a goddamned vision."

"More, Dash...more!" I plead, helpless in the face of this craving.

"Take it all from me, baby." He pulls me down to him, flattening a hand over my lower back as he pumps his hips, meeting each of my desperate thrusts. "I'll give you everything I have." His lips find mine and his kiss is hungry and deep. We're moaning loudly, the tension building hot and fast in my belly.

"I'm going to come," I break from the kiss to pant.

"Yes." Dash presses me closer to him, his firm, slick shaft sliding over my inner walls, his body rocking against my clit.

My orgasm crashes over me in sudden waves, pleasure zooming into every corner of my body. I shatter and cling to him for support.

"Willa!" Dash cries out hoarsely, bucking beneath me. His breathing is wild, and he babbles incoherent phrases as he comes, peppered with expletives and words of admiration.

My heart pounds and a sheen of sweat slicks my skin. I lay my head on Dash's chest, hearing his heart beating just as fast as mine.

He kisses the top of my head. "You are amazing."

We stay in each other's arm, immersed in warmth and bliss. I attempt to move, but he pulls me closer. "Please stay, sweetheart." How could I refuse such an irresistible request?

I would lie here forever with this man if he asked.

CHAPTER 8
DASH

I quietly set the breakfast tray on the nightstand and perch next to my sleeping beauty. She stirs and groans, still half asleep, rolling over. Her eyes flutter open.

My cock swells, even though I've lost track of how many times we woke up throughout the night to make love.

"Mmmm...again?" she asks groggily.

I shake my head. "This time, it's just for breakfast."

"What time is it?" She stretches sleepily and turns toward me.

"Almost time for work."

"Oh!" She bolts upright and grabs her glasses, shoving them on. Her blond hair is disheveled and sexy as hell, and her breasts are bare. My sweet little librarian isn't so shy with me this morning, and I love that.

"You won't be late, hon."

She pauses for a moment, then sighs. "Sorry. Old habits."

Her eyes roam over me from head to toe. "You showered," she purrs. "And you're wearing gray sweatpants."

"So?" I raise an eyebrow.

"So you look like you just stepped out of one of my steamiest romances."

A sly smile plays at the corners of my lips. "Do I, now."

She nods slowly, her gaze smoldering. "*And* my filthiest fantasies."

My cock is back to full-blown steel. Her eyes light up hungrily and she runs a finger along my waistband.

"So naughty," I chuckle.

She pulls down my sweats to find I'm going commando and bites her lip seductively. She strokes me with her soft hands, and I'm already moaning.

"Baby, what do you think you're going to do with that?"

My heart races as she lowers herself down, locking her amber eyes on me. Her soft lips touch my weeping tip and a shiver snakes down my spine as I let out a hiss.

"I'm going to suck you until you come in my mouth," she murmurs, her hot breath trailing over me.

My legs nearly give out and I thrust a hand into her hair. "You can't say things like that, Willa. I won't be able to control myself."

She simply gazes back at me with eyes of fire. Licking a slow path along the length of me, she starts off easy, then gently increasing the pressure as my breathing grows more labored. I arch into her, begging and moaning for more as her mouth works its magic.

She takes me deep enough that she begins to gag, and I'm trembling with pleasure, grasping her shoulders for stability.

"You're my good girl, you know that?" I growl. "And *all mine*."

She responds with a low moan around my cock. I'm so close to exploding.

Her fingers slip down and massage my balls until I don't know how much more I can take. Then she draws soft circles just behind them, stroking and exploring the sensitive skin there. I'm a goner.

"Willa, I'm—"

Before I can finish the sentence, I'm coming down her throat. My hand tightens in her hair, my body taut and trembling—and the world melts into blissful oblivion around me.

I expect her to slip off me, but instead, she clamps down with her plush lips as I praise her like the goddess she is. I feel her swallow with deep, contented pulls until I'm spent, lost in a euphoric haze.

"Where did you learn how to do that?" I gasp, when I finally catch my breath.

She daintily wipes her mouth with the back of her hand. "Librarians read a lot."

"You never have to buy yourself a book again. I'm officially bankrolling all your book purchases from now on."

She clears her throat and laughs. "You'll regret that, I'm sure."

"Never." I lift her face to look at me and admire the flushed pink in her cheeks, like the color of fresh roses.

This woman is everything.

I pull on my sweats and point to the tray near her. "I made you Eggs Benedict for breakfast. The eggs are a little runny this morning, though. Sorry."

She looks at them and grimaces. Then her face goes green. "Oh, god—" She covers her mouth and runs to the bathroom. A second later I hear her heave in the toilet.

I cringe. Poor thing. She might need to go easy on swallowing my come before she's had any breakfast.

~

Later, I take Willa to the library on the back of Blue Steel. What can I say? She can't get enough of my big ride. And I'm more than happy to have her on my bike with me. I honestly wonder if I can ever ride solo again.

I grin at that thought as we walk in and chat with Eden and Mrs. Holloway—at, I might add, two minutes *before* nine. Then I follow Willa into her office.

The office is plain and generic, and I make a note to help her add some personal touches.

"How about we go into Missoula tonight for a nice dinner?" I ask, watching her drape her cardigan over the chair. "It's not too far."

She grins. "I'd love that."

I reach out and pull her into my arms, holding her tight against me. I study her beautiful face—the fiery amber eyes, the delicately sloping nose, the lush lips. It's truly a marvel she's mine. I lean down and claim her sweet mouth.

"Surprise, honey! Congrats on your new—" Gavin stands in the doorway with a big bouquet of flowers. Willa and I turn to stare at him in shock, arms still locked around each other.

"Dad," Willa whispers.

I'd actually clean forgotten about the Gavin issue in the exhilaration of our last hours.

I feel like I'm watching a movie in super slow motion as Gavin's face contorts, realization dawning on him. He hurls the flowers onto the desk and pulls at his tie, loosening it as he rushes toward me.

I let go of Willa and hold up my hands. "Gav, please, hear me out—"

"*You bastard!*" he roars. His midnight blue eyes are black with rage as he hauls back and decks me.

Pain slices through my jaw, and I fall flat on my ass. He

77

leans down, grabbing at the collar of my shirt, winding up to punch me again.

"No, Dad!" Willa cries out. She pushes Gavin back from where he was hovering over me. "Stop it!"

Mrs. Holloway and Eden appear in the doorway, their eyes wide.

"What in heaven's name is going on here?!?!" Mrs. Holloway booms in a voice that can probably be heard all the way down the street. "Gavin Jacob Layne and Dashiell Adam McCafferty—if you don't take this outside and away from the library this instant, I'll be forced to call Sheriff Quinn!"

I pull up short when I hear Mrs. Holloway's fury. You know she means business when the full names come out. All I need is another visit from the sheriff… I wince.

Gavin looks down at the floor. He pauses, takes a deep breath, holds it for a moment, then releases it with a loud sigh. That's one of his anger management techniques that I'm eminently grateful for…though I would've preferred it if he'd used it *before* he punched me.

"Yes, ma'am," he finally says, hoarsely. "Sorry for the trouble," He glares at me. "Dammit, why do you have a jaw made of stone, asshole?"

"Language!" Mrs. Holloway snaps, and Gavin storms out in a huff.

"You okay?" Willa leans down and offers me her hand. I pull myself up and she strokes my face with the backs of her fingers, her brows knit together. "You're going to need some ice."

I kiss her hand and grimace at the twinge of pain. "Nothing I haven't dealt with before. Gav and I are old pros when it comes to busted jaws." I smile and look into her eyes. "Let me go talk to him."

She nods and I squeeze her hand before apologizing profusely to Mrs. Holloway on my way out.

Gavin's angrily kicking at the dirt out back with his hands on his hips when I walk over to him. It still surprises me to see him in a designer suit and fancy tie. We grew up poor together as grungy country kids who turned into grungy blue-collar workers. Only recently has each one of our crew become a millionaire. And Gavin's been my best friend through it all, the guy who had my back from the beginning.

"What the fuck are you doing, Dash?" There's hurt in his eyes when he looks up at me. "I trusted you. Willa's everything to me, you know that."

I rub my sore jaw. Time to lay it on the line. "I love her, Gav."

He reels back, stunned, like I'd punched him. "What did you say?"

"I'm in love with Willa."

He shakes his head. "Is this some kind of sick joke? Because it's a terrible one."

"No joke. I'm dead serious."

He laughs dryly. "Please. You've never been in love. You're always saying a woman's never made you feel anything. It's always just been sex..." He scowls and closes his eyes, fists clenching. "You'd better move now, or I'm going to hit you again."

"Gav, listen." I back up from him just to be safe. "I'm being completely honest. You're right, I've never been in love. I didn't know what it was or what it felt like. Willa changed that in an instant."

"It's been three days!" he yells. "How can you possibly fall in love that fast?"

"I don't know." I shrug. "But the moment I saw her, something just...clicked. Like a light switch being flipped on. She's completely different from the women I've been with before. She's smart, kind, funny…a pleasure to talk to…and naturally beautiful, without all the fake stuff."

Gavin shakes his head. "I'm still not sure I believe you. Not about Willa—she's a delight. I mean about your feelings."

"Have I ever lied to you before? You think I wanted this to happen?" I clear my throat. "I tried to ignore my feelings—so hard—shoving them down inside, hoping they'd go away because I didn't want to hurt you. But they just found a way to escape, and rip my heart out to lay at her feet." I move closer to him cautiously. "All I think about is Willa, and what I can do to make her happy. She fills me with genuine love and satisfaction. It's something I've never felt before. And it's the most humbling thing in the world."

"I love Dash, too, Dad."

Gavin and I turn to see Willa standing at the picnic table. How long has she been there?

Her golden hair glints in the sun as she walks toward us, her lovely eyes sparkling with something I can only assume is for me. "He's sweet and generous and always looking out for me." Her voice catches for a moment, but she continues. "And he gives me confidence, because he believes in me. I enjoy just being with him."

She loves me. Willa loves me. My heart is going to burst. I can't help it; I rush over to her and lift her into my arms. She laughs and I hold her as tight as I can as she kisses my good cheek.

"Ugh!" Gavin gags. "This is going to take some getting used to."

"But you'll try?" Willa says hopefully as I set her on the ground.

"You know I'd do anything for you, pumpkin." He sighs.

"Even if it involves this filthy bastard." He grins my way, and she launches herself at her father, giving him a huge hug.

"I love you, Dad." She beams at him.

He kisses the top of her head. "Love you too."

I go over and clap him on the back. "So...back from Hong Kong already?"

"Only for the weekend. Thought I'd surprise Willa. Little did I know *I'd* get the surprise." He smirks.

"Need a place to stay?" I ask.

He eyes the two of us dubiously. "Only if you promise to keep it strictly PG while I'm there."

"I think we can manage that." Willa smiles.

"Hold up." I narrow my eyes suspiciously. "How long will you be staying, again?" Gavin punches my arm. "Kidding, kidding!"

Gavin straightens his tie and adjusts his suit jacket. His expression turns serious. "Now, tell me why there are *two* helmets on Blue Steel out there in the parking lot."

Willa and I look at each another.

We're so dead.

EPILOGUE - WILLA

I'm outside leaning against the garage door, too excited to wait for him inside. I almost start bouncing when I hear Blue Steel's familiar rumble coming up the drive. It's not unusual for me to be ready and waiting for my husband on my short days at the library, since they're also typically our date nights. We've been together for about a year now, married after only three months. If it had been up to Dash, we would've gotten married within a week, but I wanted time to plan, and make sure all our most important loved ones could be there with us on our special day.

The wedding was beautiful, held in Dash's yard among the tall pines and wildflowers—one of my favorite places in the entire world. It felt as if the entire town came out to wish us all the best for our marriage.

Dad has come to accept our relationship, despite the rocky start. Mostly, I believe he enjoys having his best friend around. He just doesn't want to hear *any* intimate details. Thank god!

The library is quickly becoming a hub of new and innovative activity. We finally got rid of the card catalog, and Dash's friend Logan is making it over into something that Mrs.

Holloway can cherish for years to come. Even better, the space left behind is earmarked for brand-new computers graciously donated by a group of anonymous Deepwood Mountain donors. Many of our programs have gone hybrid, bringing even more foot traffic to the library and generating more interest in our services. And Story Time has grown into a highly sought-after event amongst the preschool set! We've had to turn away volunteer readers because we have too many. Our website is modern and functional, and now we're branching out into social media. Mrs. Holloway has even threatened to retire in a year or two, confident I could take over when she left.

Needless to say, I'm ecstatic with how my life is going.

So, when I got this joyful news today, it was like the icing on the cake.

"There's my gorgeous girl," Dash says, removing his gear, still as hot as the day we met right out front of this house.

He pulls me into his arms, kissing me until I nearly forget my name.

"Mmm, I can't wait to take you out tonight." He plays with a strand of hair fallen from my bun.

I smile up at him, thinking about how lucky I am to have such an adoring husband.

"I have good news, hon," he says.

"Oh! Let's hear it."

"I may have a social media manager for you. Logan's daughter's best friend. Logan said she's moving to Deepwood even as we speak."

"Wow. Sounds great! Tell him to have her send me her resume. I'm excited to meet her."

"You bet." He pauses. "It's the strangest thing. As you know, Logan's not one to say more than two words at a time, but he sure went on and on about this woman."

I gave him a look. "Maybe...?"

We both think for a moment. "Nah," we say together, and then laugh.

"Actually, I have a project for Logan." I say. "There's a piece I'd like him to build."

"Yeah, what's that?" Dash asks absently, already headed to the mudroom door.

"A crib."

"Nice. Someone having a baby?"

I exhale. "Yeah."

He waits for me to continue. "Who is it?"

I bite my lip and smile at him mischievously.

His eyes go wide. "Are you serious?" His mouth drops open and he grabs me, searching my eyes for any hint of deception—even though he knows I'd never joke about something like this.

His ice-blue eyes tear up. "Really?" he chokes out.

I nod as my eyes fill with happy tears of my own. "You're going to be a daddy."

"This is amazing." He hugs me tighter than I ever thought possible and peppers my face with kisses. "I love you so much, Willa." He puts a hand on my belly.

"I love you, too," I reply, nuzzling him.

He takes my hand, and we walk inside. "Wait—have you told your dad yet?"

"No. Only Mom and Ash know."

He takes a deep breath. "I can handle Gavin." He sounds like he's trying to convince himself. "He wouldn't hurt the father of his grandchild, would he?"

"I...doubt it." We look at one another and grin.

We're ready for anything that comes our way. I mean, it's all about the ride, right?

And we're on it together.

HIS BIG AXE

CHAPTER 1
MADDIE

There's nothing quite like the Montana mountains in the summertime.

The familiar scent of fresh pine and sweet wildflowers is floating in on the breeze and as I ease out of my car I soak up the comforting aromas, along with the warm afternoon sunshine.

I'm from the East Coast, where summers can be muggy and downright miserable, so I consider myself lucky to have escaped to Montana for college. UM is where I met Blair Everett—my dorm roommate and instant bestie. Four years ago, she brought me here to her dad's Deepwood Mountain cabin, and the place is etched into my soul.

Real talk: calling the Everett place atop the mountain a "cabin" is like calling Buckingham Palace a "cute townhouse". Blair's dad is the former owner of Everett Logging, the largest logging company in Montana. I say "former" because he sold the company a while back for millions. With its three stories, soaring gables, floor-to-ceiling picture windows, and wood and stone everywhere, yeah, the house may have some rustic elements, but referring to it as a cabin is just silly.

Making my way over to the railing of the multi-level wrap-around deck, I break into a wicked smile. The really scenic view has nothing to do with the majestic Montana landscape.

Bare-chested and glistening with sweat, Logan Everett works in a methodical rhythm as he splits logs down in the side yard. His sun-bleached hair is tousled, falling into his eyes, his attention squarely focused on the wood beneath his big axe.

If anyone thinks that because Logan used to own the company, he never worked a day in his life felling trees, sawing wood, or operating any of the heavy machinery, they'd be dead wrong. He's been working with wood since he was a kid—his father hiring him on as a lumberjack as soon as he graduated from high school. Since then, he did every labor-intensive job at the company just the same as his employees until the day he sold it.

And he has the thick muscles to prove it.

I'm mesmerized by each swing of his axe, heat pooling between my legs at the sheer masculinity of it all. I can't help it. Since Blair invited me to spend our freshman year Spring Break with her and her dad, I've had a secret crush on Logan. It's honestly impossible for me not to drool over him. He's tall, strong as an ox, ruggedly handsome, and the most down to earth, gentle man I've ever met. And now, watching him in his element, his body thrumming with primal energy, my heart starts pounding harder in my chest.

Logan's axe lands on the block with a final thud, splitting the log before him neatly in two. He straightens, wiping his brow with his forearm, and turns to look up at the house. His gaze lands on me, and a pleased smile tugs at the corners of his mouth.

"Maddie!" he calls, resting his axe against the woodpile. "You're early."

There's a familiar flutter in my belly when I hear him say my name. "Logan," I reply, my voice a bit too breathy. "Traffic was lighter than I expected."

He nods. "Blair still enroute?"

"Guess so," I say with a shrug. "She had a later start but should be here soon."

He rolls his eyes. "She takes after her mother there."

I smile. Logan and I both like to give Blair a hard time about her tendency to be late. It's become kind of an inside joke between us, and his comment just now felt intimate in a way it probably shouldn't have.

There's a loud, deep bark from somewhere nearby, and a flurry of black, white, and rust-colored fur hurtles toward me. "Hank!" I exclaim, as Logan's massive Bernese Mountain Dog knocks me down onto the deck. I'm instantly covered in aggressive licks and wet nose rubs. He dances on excited paws, tail wagging furiously, his entire body shaking with joy as I hug and pet him. "Hello, boy. I missed you!"

I glance down at the yard, but Logan is gone. In a moment, I hear the sliding glass door open behind me. "You okay?" Logan asks, suddenly next to me, pulling Hank off me. "Don't be so damn rough, Hank."

I laugh as Hank nudges his enormous head under my palm, demanding pets. "I'm fine."

Logan offers me a hand and I take it, electric sparks zooming through my arm at his touch. He pulls me up with more force than I expect, and I bump into his rock-hard body. "Oh," I gasp, moving away until my back hits the deck railing.

His gaze locks on mine. I haven't let go of him, and I'm physically unable to look away from those deep green eyes. I'm still too close, helplessly intoxicated by his heady musk and hot breath. His built chest heaves, and I want nothing more than to taste his slick skin.

"Yoohoo! Hey! Anybody home'?" Blair calls out, and Logan and I split apart so fast that poor Hank flinches. I swear I didn't even hear Blair drive up. Go figure, she's actually on time.

"*Ew*! Dad! What did I tell you about walking around without a shirt? No one wants to see all that." She gestures to him and grimaces. "You're sweating all over my BFF."

"It's fine," I protest in a small voice. Logan just mumbles an apology, then heads toward his daughter with his relaxed mountain-man gait.

Blair clambers out of her red convertible, her long wavy hair so much darker than her father's as it peeks out from underneath an absurdly large sunhat. She yanks an over-stuffed suitcase from the trunk.

The woman is a boisterous and clumsy ball of energy, insanely driven, a genuine whirlwind of excitement wherever she goes. You'd never think upon meeting her she's wanted to be a therapist since she was a little girl. But once you get to know her you realize she's the most kind and empathetic person you'll ever meet, only ever wanting to help people—not to mention the best listener in the world. I'm lucky to have her as my best friend, despite her flair for the dramatic.

I smile as she gives her dad a quick peck, holding onto her hat, careful to steer clear of his sweat.

"Good to see you, kiddo." A pang of something undefined hits me as I watch Logan with Blair. He's such a great dad. Shaking it off, I remind myself that I need to get my emotions in check. I'm pining for a man who's completely off limits.

"Hank toppled her. Again," Logan explains.

Blair shakes her head. "Seriously? I think that dog likes Maddie more than he likes you, Dad."

He winks in my direction. "He's a smart dog. I'm sure he does."

My cheeks heat and I hurry over to throw my arms around Blair, giving her a hug. "Hello, my beautiful riot. On time for once?"

She grins. "Amazing, right?"

Logan takes my small bag from where it sits outside my car, then looks down at Blair's suitcases. He glances at her. "Did you pack for *two* summers?"

"Oh, hush!" Blair takes off her hat and swats him with it.

We all laugh, and Blair and I follow Logan into the house. I try not to notice how his broad shoulders and back flex as he moves, or how his jeans cling to his chiseled backside. It's a struggle.

Logan starts up the stairs but stops at the first landing to turn to us. "I'm firing up the grill for dinner."

Blair immediately brightens, then says, "Maddie's a–"

"Vegetarian," Logan finishes. "Yes, I remember. I've got a bunch of vegetables ready to go. Even a new recipe for grilled eggplant and peppers."

Warmth spreads through me at his thoughtfulness. "Sounds perfect, Logan. Thanks."

He nods his head toward me, his gaze lingering for a moment, before turning to go up the stairs. A strange look flashes in Blair's eyes as she glances at me, and I can feel a flush creeping up my neck, my heart in my throat.

Does she know what I'm thinking? That I would happily climb her dad like a towering Montana pine?

Blair shrugs, her mossy green eyes sparkling with something I can't identify. "You look like you're about to overheat," she says, with a half-smile, and I freeze. "Let's kick off this vacay with some drinks, shall we?"

I let out a long breath.

How am I ever going to survive the summer?

CHAPTER 2
LOGAN

I shouldn't be thinking about her like this.

It's not right.

But as I flip the eggplant slices on the grill, the aromatic smoke filling the air, only one thing consumes my thoughts.

Maddie.

I glance over at her and Blair lounging by the pool, their laughter drifting over to me on the warm early evening breeze.

I'm known for not saying much, but I could recite lengthy sonnets about Maddie.

Easily.

Those wild copper curls framing her face, the mischievous glint in her deep brown eyes, her contagious laughter and the genuine warmth of her smile—it's enough to drive a man crazy with desire.

My gaze travels over her as she reclines in the deck chair, Hank nestled contentedly at her feet. She's absently stroking the wood of the hand rest, her profile turned to me, lips curving up in a smile as Blair recounts yet another outrageous story. She's radiant in the fading sunlight, and my heart squeezes.

She's different from all the other women I've ever known: independent and smart, with an energy that's infectious. The memory of her eyes on me earlier while I was chopping wood seeps back into my mind. I'd sensed her gaze, noticed a subtle shift in the air, felt a prickle on the back of my neck. There was an appreciation in her eyes, a hint of approval that caused a strange jolt in my gut...and lower. I'd liked it. Way too much.

If Blair hadn't shown up when she did... God help me. The woman makes me think and want to do things I never have before. Dirty things. Romantic things. Wildly inappropriate things.

She's not just my daughter's best friend—Maddie's a woman who's ignited a fire in me, a fire I'm not sure I can or want to control.

But I have to. I'm nearly twice her age! Besides, I don't want to force her into something she's not ready for, like I did with my ex-wife, back when we were too young to know any damned better. I'm determined to steer clear of anything that could harm the close-knit relationship Maddie, Blair, and I have formed over the years. Maddie deserves to live her life and follow her dreams, without me screwing it up.

As if she'd ever want anything to do with an aging lumberjack that ogles her like a hormonal teenaged boy, anyway.

My attention returns to the grill as the vegetables start to blister and char.

"Are these chairs new?" Maddie calls to me, leaning over to peer at her deck chair more closely.

I'd secretly hoped she'd notice. "Yeah, they're pine." I slide a few charred pepper slices onto a serving plate. "Figured I'd do something different."

She smiles. "They're so comfortable." She follows the grain with her fingers. "Beautiful work."

"Yeah, pretty darn sweet, Dad," Blair adds.

I feel my cheeks heat and mumble a thanks to the grill, while scratching the back of my neck.

The girls return to their conversation and I plate the food, setting it all on the outdoor dining table. "Come and get it."

They wander over with the fruity drinks Blair made as I lay out the condiments and sauces for their meals.

"Everything smells delicious," Maddie says.

Blair grabs a burger and piles it high with fixings. "Don't look," she says to Maddie, as she takes a big bite. "Sorry, cow."

Maddie waves her off. "I don't care if you eat meat. It's your life."

"Well, and the cow's," I add, eliciting a mid-chomp glare from my daughter.

Maddie swallows and shakes her head playfully. "Thank you for the reminder."

"I'm just giving you a hard time," I say, fixing my burger, adding some grilled vegetables on the side.

Maddie gives me a warm smile and makes a burger with a slice of eggplant substituting for the meat patty. I'm always impressed by how appetizing she can make a meatless burger look. Her Instagram feed…yeah, I check it…is filled with recipes and photos of veggie dishes, mostly her own creations. I'm rarely on social media—but I do like to see what Maddie's up to.

Five minutes into our dinner, Blair's phone buzzes on the table. She looks at the screen and groans with exasperation. "It's Trent," she says. "I *told* him not to call me until later tonight."

"It's fine. Take the call," I murmur, trying to keep my voice even. She knows my strict rule about no calls during meal-times, but I also know how much she likes Trent, even if I'm not entirely sold on the guy yet myself.

Blair shoots me a grateful smile before answering. "Hey,

babe. I told you I'm out at my dad's..." Her brow furrows as she listens to Trent's reply. "Okay, okay. Hold on." She gets up from her seat, phone pressed to her ear. "I'll be right back," she mouths to us apologetically, and disappears into the house.

I glance at Maddie, who's just dipped a spear of grilled zucchini into the tahini sauce.

She licks the sauce off the tip of the spear, and the whole world spins. I rest my forearm on the table for stability.

She catches my eye and quickly wipes her mouth with a napkin. "Sorry. I'm probably making a complete mess."

Of me, yeah...I clear my throat, unable to reply right away. Thank god I'm sitting down with my lower half covered. I take a sip of beer to wet my suddenly dry mouth. "What do you think about Trent?" I finally ask, trying to distract myself.

She finishes chewing and swallows. "I guess he's okay. I haven't had a lot of time to get to know him, but he seems to make Blair happy, so..."

I nod, crunching on a pepper dipped in ranch dressing.

"Do *you* like him?" she asks.

I shrug. "I don't know. I can't get a good read on the guy, for some reason."

"Interesting," she says. "Maybe you should spend some time with him."

The skeptical look I give her makes her giggle, and she rolls her teeth over her bottom lip. "Okay, maybe not."

"I mean, I'm not against it."

"You might end up liking him."

As much as you can like any guy who's doing your daughter. "I'll think about it."

"That works." She finishes another bite of food. "Everything I've had so far has been really tasty. For a steak and ribs guy, you sure know your way around vegetables."

"Thanks," I reply. "This old dog might have taken a look at someone's Insta to pick up some new tricks."

Her face lights up. "You read my content?"

"I...browsed."

She laughs and as we continue to eat under the dusky Montana sky, a warmth blossoms inside me. *This* is what I want. Lazy summer dinners by the pool. Easy conversation. Someone companionable with whom to share my evenings... and my bed.

The patio door slides open and Blair emerges from the house, her face pale, phone still clutched in her hand. "Sorry about that," she says, a worried frown creasing her brow.

"What's up, kiddo?" I wipe my hands on my napkin and guide her into the seat next to me, tucking her under my arm.

"Trent's grandmother just passed away," Blair blurts, her voice shaky. "He was really close to her. I think I need to go back and be with him."

Maddie's face softens with sympathy. "Oh, Blair, I'm so sorry."

"Yeah, sorry, hon," I add, rubbing her shoulder.

"I really should go," Blair says, wringing her hands anxiously. "But Maddie...our hike to Emerald Falls... It's the last week before it goes dry for the summer."

Maddie dismisses Blair's concerns with a wave of her hand. "Don't worry about it, girl. I can do the hike alone."

My head snaps up. "Absolutely not," I announce firmly. "It's a two-day hike, Maddie. You're not going alone."

Maddie's eyebrows rise defiantly, her back straightening. "I'm an experienced hiker, Logan. I'm perfectly capable of taking care of myself."

I shake my head. "If you're that experienced a hiker you would know it's not safe to do that hike alone."

Blair nods vigorously. "Dad's right. I'm sorry, Maddie. Anything could happen on that trail."

"I'm. Going," Maddie insists, folding her arms on the table.

My gaze meets Maddie's stubborn one, and I sigh, knowing I'm fighting a losing battle. "Then I'm going with you."

Maddie's mouth falls open, but before she can protest, I raise a hand to stop her. "No arguments, Maddie. If you're going, I'm going with you. That's final."

With that, I push myself up from the table and start clearing away my dishes, effectively ending the discussion.

I'm going on a hike with Maddie, alone.

I'm terrified.

This summer is already turning out to be far more challenging than I'd anticipated.

CHAPTER 3
MADDIE

I follow Blair into her childhood bedroom, the walls still lined with posters from high school and the shelves filled with mementos. It's cozy and familiar, yet this evening it doesn't calm my nerves.

"I'm so sorry about this, Maddie," Blair says for what feels like the hundredth time, taking a blouse from her big suitcase and placing it in a smaller bag. "I really wanted to do this hike with you."

I force a smile, scanning over the mementos of Blair's childhood—a pink jewelry box, an old stuffed panda bear, a picture of her with Justin Bieber. "It's okay. Trent needs you. I get it."

"But you'll be alone with my dad," Blair hisses. "I'm sure that's not what you had in mind when you pictured a *fun* hike." She puts the word fun in air quotes.

I nod, painfully aware of the implications.

I'll be alone with Logan.

The thought is unsettling. What if I can't control myself around him? What if I spit out something I can't take back? "He's just being protective, Blair." I clear my throat. "He'd be like this with any of your friends. It'll be fine."

"Yes, but you're special to him," she says, and my heart stops. My face must betray my thoughts, because Blair narrows her hazel eyes at me. "You okay, Maddie? You're acting kinda weird."

"Special to him? Why?" I ask, ignoring her question for a moment.

She frowns incredulously. "Because you're my best friend. Like, duh."

Right. I take a deep breath. "I'm just...nervous, maybe," I admit, flopping down on her bed. "It's awkward."

Blair shrugs, continuing her packing. "Nah. You know how easy he is to get along with. As much as I hate to admit it, he's actually pretty good company."

I can't help but smile at her casual dismissal of her dad's *significant* appeal. "Yeah, I guess."

Just then, a loud thump echoes from outside, followed by Logan's exasperated voice. "Hank! Settle *down*!" We glance out the window to see him pulling out the old camping gear from storage, with Hank bouncing around him excitedly. It's such a heartwarming and wholesome sight that I sigh inwardly.

A hike with Logan.

Only the two of us.

I'm toast.

Blair's voice pulls me back to reality. "Don't worry, Maddie. Everything will work out." She zips up her bag with finality. "Who knows? Maybe you'll finally figure out what you want to do with your life on this hike."

I let out a laugh. "True. A little clarity in the Montana wilderness wouldn't be such a bad thing."

"Clarity...that's it..." Blair echoes, shooting me an odd smile.

～

The next morning is crisp and clear, aka the opposite of my foggy brain. Blair leaves in a wild flurry of hugs and reassurances, setting off toward Missoula. I watch the dust settle in the wake of Blair's car peeling away, a twinge of sadness in my heart for Trent. I hope he knows what an amazing woman he's found in her.

"Ready to pack up and go?" Logan rasps from the doorway, his voice still husky from the early hour. My stomach does a little backflip.

I turn to him, taking in his towering, solid form. He's wearing a weathered flannel shirt over a white tank, his muscled chest peeking out from where he's left the top buttons open. I groan internally as the fabric stretches to accommodate his thick shoulders and biceps. My mouth is a little dry, but I manage to croak out, "Yes, let's."

We work together to load up our backpacks, tent, sleeping bags, food, and other necessities. The physical weight of my gear matches the one in my heart. Dreams of Logan had permeated my sleep, and now watching him bend over, filling out those dark khaki tactical pants so perfectly, I can barely swallow.

"It can get cold up there at night sometimes," Logan says as we secure our packs. "But I checked the weather. We should be fine." The lines of his face soften as he smiles at me and the subtle change makes me ache, from my chest right down to my core. It would be so easy to fall into his kindness, his protective nature. I steel myself, having a stern word with my heart not to make a fool out of me.

We load our gear—and Hank, of course—into the truck; the vehicle rumbles to life with a familiar, comforting sound. The trailhead isn't far, and as we drive, I catch glimpses of the wilderness, vast and unending. It's beautiful and intimidating at the same time—much like the man driving.

As we pull up at the trailhead, nervous energy is buzzing through me, but I fight to keep my face neutral. I've been looking forward to this hike and I'm going to enjoy it, my feelings for Logan be damned.

We set off in silence after strapping on our packs. Hank runs in circles around us, his excitement contagious—nipping at the long grass on the trail, chasing butterflies, hopping over rocks and tree stumps. Logan and I say very little as we walk, but it isn't really uncomfortable. I'm still acutely aware of him trudging along behind me, where he insists on staying. I hear the cadence of his breath, the slide of his clothing as he walks, the sound of his body moving through the brush, and the crunch of his big boots over pebbles and roots. I find I enjoy having him back there, watching, keeping me safe.

Logan checks in every so often, asking if I'm okay. Am I hungry? Thirsty? Do I need a bathroom break? I know he's used to taking care of Blair, who's pretty high maintenance on a hike compared to me, so I give him a pass there.

After a couple of hours, I can hear the rush of the river ahead, wild and rough.

"Sounds like the river's full," Logan says behind me. "Must've been all our May rain."

"That'll be good news for Emerald Falls," I reply happily, as we make our way to the crossing.

He nods decisively. "I'll go first." Without waiting for my answer, he follows the precarious path of wet, slick stones. They look like they're wobbling and teetering in the swift current, but he navigates everything with an ease born of experience.

I grin. *Such a showoff.*

His call cuts through the rushing noise of the water. "Your turn," he says, waving from the other side.

"Go on, boy," I say to Hank, but he just sits there, waiting for me. "Fine, you silly dog."

The water isn't deep, but it's fast enough and the thought of falling into it wearing my pack makes me nervous. With a deep breath, I place my foot on the first stone. Once I'm secure, I go to the next one, and continue on like that, my focus sharp.

Halfway across, my heart is thundering with a mix of pride and adrenaline.

I'm doing it!

But when my foot touches the next stone, it tips to the side. A gasp tears from my throat, the world tilting sideways as I windmill my arms for balance. Hank barks from behind me and something splashes into the water. Suddenly, Logan is there, gripping me under my arms, strong and unyielding.

"I got you. Just hold on to me," he orders, and I obey as he hauls me the rest of the way across.

My heart continues to pound when we arrive on the other side, for two reasons now. I keep clenching onto his biceps, and his hands remain on my back and waist to steady me. His heat radiates through my clothes, sending fresh tingles up my spine. I look up at him, meeting his intense gaze. There's something there, something that makes my stomach twist and my breath hitch. *Does he feel it, too?*

No way.

"All good?" he asks as he releases me, his attention shifting back to the trail ahead.

Hank darts past us, shaking himself dry.

I nod heartily. "Yup. Thanks for the help." I realize with a thud that as much as I normally don't need anyone, he sure came in handy just now.

And I'm left standing there, wondering what that could mean.

CHAPTER 4
LOGAN

W e stop and have lunch on a flat, rocky outcrop that overlooks a sweeping valley.

I have to admit, hiking with Maddie is fantastic. I worry too much when I'm with Blair, because she's always getting herself hurt or lost from not paying attention to her surroundings. Maddie's more than capable of looking after herself, and that independence is damn sexy. Saving her from falling into the river was more for my peace of mind than anything…and, well, so she wouldn't have to walk the rest of the day in soggy shoes.

Our fingers brush together briefly when I hand Maddie a cheese sandwich. The fleeting touch stirs something in me yet again, that desire I'm so desperate to keep at bay. I hastily turn my attention back to my own food.

"Thanks for making lunch," she says, stretching out on the rocks, showing off her long, firm legs. They're clad in gray hiking pants, but I can picture the creamy, freckled skin underneath. "I would've helped you, but Blair had a fashion emergency. Apparently, it's incredibly important to wear the right thing when consoling your grieving boyfriend."

My smirk wins out.

"Sorry, that was insensitive and bitchy of me," she huffs. "I've just been in a mood lately."

"What about?" I ask, as she contemplates her carrot sticks.

"Oh, lots of things." She snaps a carrot stick in half. "Mainly, it's that I have no idea what I want to do with my life."

I snort. "You just graduated from college, Maddie. You don't have to know right now."

Her head whips to me dramatically. "Yeah? Tell that to my parents. For people who had very little interest in me during my formative years, they sure won't leave me alone now. And their expectations are so unrealistic! They can't understand why I don't have a plan and why I haven't figured out my entire future yet."

I cross my arms. "They're not impressed that you finished a degree in communications and marketing?"

"They think that was a bad choice of program." Her words tumble out with a raw, unfiltered honesty. "My degree doesn't come with a 'viable set of skills'. Their words. If I don't make something of myself, they've made it clear they'll think it was a waste of time, effort, and money."

Shit. Blair has mentioned that Maddie's parents were sometimes critical of her, but I never realized they were this unsupportive. There's a vulnerability to her right now, a stark contrast to the vibrant, confident woman I've grown accustomed to, that stirs up a protective instinct inside me—a desire to take away her worries, to provide some kind of solace.

"You're already something, Maddie. Honestly? You were perfect before you got that degree. That piece of paper is just the icing on the cake." Maybe I've said too much, but hell, someone needs to tell her they believe in her. Every damn day.

She grins, her cheeks turning pink.

"Please don't tell Blair, but it's extra hard when your best friend has known her life's path for years. She has her dream job lined up already and everything!" She takes a swig of water. "I'm not used to being jealous."

My heart twinges. I knew all about that kind of certainty. I'd been sure of my path once too, so sure I'd forced it on someone else. And as it turned out, I was wrong.

She looks up to meet my gaze, her dark brown eyes clouded with ambivalence. "There's so many things I could do. It's almost overwhelming, you know? I'm not sure what I want."

I wish I could relate, but I can't. By the end of high school, I was already a dad, the weight of the world on my shoulders. Meanwhile, my own dad was grooming me to take over the family business. I didn't have much chance to try my hand at anything else, was just shuffled straight into the logging industry. But I knew that's what I wanted to do at the time. In a way, I'm glad that track was solid.

I also had the support of the five best friends anyone could ask for. Gavin and I in particular leaned on one another quite a lot, because he also had a daughter about the same time I did. But I'm proud that to this day Blair calls every one of them Uncle.

"It's okay to be unsure, Maddie," I finally reply. "You've got time. You don't need to prove anything to anyone…least of all your parents."

I lucked out with my dad. He never pressured me into anything, but once I showed interest in his work, he took me under his wing and showed me the ropes. And I surrendered to the fact that wood is just in my blood.

She presses her lips together and nods, gazing off into the middle distance. I'm struck by what a natural beauty she is.

"Just remember, it's *your* life," I advise. "Who cares what anyone else thinks?"

Her smile is oddly shy, and it hits me square in the chest. "Thanks, Logan. I really needed to hear that."

After lunch, we get back out onto the trail and settle into the same rhythm we established this morning. I keep her ahead of me, admiring her copper curls tied up in a ponytail, some wavy strands trailing down. As she expertly navigates the tricky terrain, I can't help but watch her slender arms assist her balance, the curve of her mouthwatering ass as she steps over rocks, and the way her breasts jiggle as she jumps down grassy embankments, causing me to hold back a groan.

It's sweet torture keeping my cock in check. All I want to do is lay her down in the grass and ravish her.

I'm a sick, sick man.

As we move along the trail, dark clouds begin to gather in the sky, casting an ominous shadow over the rugged terrain.

"Rain's coming." I'd hoped the weather would hold until we reached the campsite, but no such luck.

Maddie stops and looks around. She gestures to a nearby outcrop of rocks along a hill. "Should we try to take cover over there?"

I nod and we hurry over, the clouds closing in and the sound of thunder in the distance.

Maddie removes her pack and squeezes under the rock ledge. There's not much remaining space. If I got in there too, I'd be dangerously close to her.

She must notice my hesitation. "Get in already. The thunder is getting louder and I can feel the moisture in the air."

I steel myself with a deep breath and remove my pack. Pressing my big shoulders in close, I try to avoid Hank with my lower half, who's sitting dutifully against her shins. *Big lug.*

Though the raindrops are cold and the temperature has dropped, I'm burning up. From my face down to my groin, it's hot as hell in here. My side is nestled against hers as we huddle together, the scent of her—an intoxicating mix of sweat and her tropical sunscreen—doing strange things to my self-control. I do my best to push the thoughts aside.

Suddenly, the rain and thunder explode, loud and hard on the rock face.

Maddie gasps and grips my thigh. I tense involuntarily, trying to keep the other reaction in my pants from scaring her off.

Hank barks in alarm.

"Sorry." Her voice is soft as she takes her hand away. I'm relieved, yet instantly miss her touch like crazy.

God, I'm insane.

"S'okay," I reply, but I'm not sure she can hear me over the thunder and the pelting rain, not to mention my pounding heart. My eyes land on her shadowed lips as she licks them, and my gut clenches.

I force myself to meet her gaze—or what I imagine is her gaze in the darkness under the rock. All I can feel is our hot breath mingling together, my mouth alarmingly close to hers.

With my thoughts running wild, we remain in that position for what feels like an eternity.

Eventually, we realize the rain is letting up, and a rustling in the nearby undergrowth catches our attention. We both turn to look and spy a fawn, its spotted coat slick from the rain. Hank chirps a bark, but Maddie whispers, "Hank, shh…" and *the dang dog obeys her*, nuzzling into her legs.

The fawn's mother comes up behind her little one. Maddie's gasp is soft in the now-quiet space between us, and it makes my insides churn. She's smiling as we watch the creatures, sharing whispered observations, sending shivers through me with every word—both because I want her so badly, and because her love for nature, her awe and appreciation for the great outdoors, is clearly as deep as my own. It thrills me, this shared love for the wild. I find myself lost in her, and the raw potential of what we could be together.

Maddie's face turns up to me, the soft glow from the breaking clouds illuminating her features. I can see the freckles scattered across her nose, the light smattering of raindrops still on her eyelashes. Again, my gaze drops to her lips as they slightly part.

A thought, unbidden yet unmistakable, hits me.

I want to kiss her.

My heart hammers against my ribs, breath hitching in my throat. This isn't mere physical attraction. It's something deep, something real. Something that's been brewing for a long time.

I wrench my eyes away, holding myself back, the stark reality of the situation crashing back into me.

Maddie's my daughter's best friend. I couldn't possibly cross that line.

Or could I?

The question haunts me as I feel her heat next to me, my body aching to close the miniscule gap between us. The moment feels suspended in time, an anticipation building that I don't know how to navigate.

The doe and fawn scamper away, and the spell breaks.

For now.

I still can't shake the feeling, the intense desire consuming me. A desire not just for her body, but for her spirit, her zest for life. It terrifies and excites me all at once, making me feel a whirlwind of unexpected emotions.

Maddie emerges from the space and holds her arms out

while looking up at the sky. "Still some clouds, but it's not raining anymore."

I clear my throat. "We should get going." It comes out harsher than I intend, but there's no taking it back now. "Let's go, Hank," I say, but he's already in front of Maddie.

We shoulder on our packs and I try to remember why I insisted on going on this hike with a woman who makes my entire body ache with need.

CHAPTER 5
MADDIE

I t's the screams of laughter in the distance that tell me we've made it to Emerald Falls. I can't help but smile at the sounds of pure enjoyment.

They're a good distraction after the last hour with Logan. Something changed in him after we were taking shelter under the rocks. He'd looked at me like maybe he wanted to kiss me... No, I'm sure I'm just projecting there. Because being that close to him, inhaling his musk and pine scent, I would've eagerly kissed him back... *and then some.*

Since then, though, he's been on edge to the point that I almost asked him if he was mad at me. Did it piss him off when I grabbed his thigh? I had been startled by the thunder-clap. Maybe he's just sick of me. We've been together for almost a day now, with no reprieve. Maybe I should give him some space.

We head into a heavy thicket of trees and emerge to see Emerald Falls dead ahead, magnificent in its height and power.

"It's breathtaking," I whisper, awestruck, Hank running up

ahead and then looping back, his enormous tongue flopping out of his mouth. *Goofball*.

The water cascades down in a thunderous, steady stream, crashing onto the rocks below and creating a white, glowing mist illuminated by the soft, dying light of the day. This place has always intrigued me. The water carries a unique mineral that gives the falls a stunning, emerald hue. The basin below is also green-tinted, and local legend says that bathing here brings vitality and youth. A small crowd of people is scattered around, taking photos and swimming, enjoying the perfect summer day.

I turn to Logan and catch him staring at me. He quickly looks back toward the falls, rubbing a hand absently over the back of his neck. "We should set up camp for the night."

Yep, he's definitely irritated with me. But I ignore that for now to focus on our tasks. We find a quiet area out of the way from the other campers and pitch the tent. I create a makeshift fire pit and ready the stove for dinner.

"I'm going swimming," I announce shortly after, as I grab a swimsuit and towel from my pack and put them in a small duffel. I'll give him some time alone.

"Sounds good," he replies, setting out two folding chairs. "I'll join you."

"You don't have to if you don't want to," I say.

"Why wouldn't I want to?" he asks, his brow furrowing.

I huff. "Okay." *Men*. And they say women are the difficult ones to understand!

We head to the public restrooms to change. When I come out, Logan's already in the water, doing somersaults. He pops his head up and waves at me. Then he swims to a shallower area and surfaces.

Oh my.

Water slides off his toned muscles, his skin shimmering in

114

the last bit of sunlight. He looks like a Greek god, tanned, sculpted, the epitome of chiseled perfection...and fine enough to eat.

I shiver.

He slicks his hair back from his face and calls out. "Water's great, Maddie!"

Every woman within hearing distance turns to look at him, their eyes wide, lips parted, as if this merman has hypnotized them. A strange knot of jealousy tightens in my stomach, and I shake my head. *As if he's mine.* I'm just a regular girl in a sensible swimsuit, surrounded by women far more beautiful showing a lot more skin.

As I walk into the emerald water from the embankment, Logan comes over and offers me his hand for stability. Normally, I wouldn't take the help. I could manage on my own. But something makes me want to hold on to him. Claim him in front of these women. *Back off, bitches.*

Good lord, I'm hopeless.

Despite all the attention from the other women that he *has* to have noticed, Logan's gaze doesn't leave me, and a special thrill runs down my spine.

I smile at him and dive into the water, darting away from him. Hank and Logan chase me, and before they can catch me, I rear up splashing, my laughter echoing off the surrounding mountains. We swim around and explore different parts of the basin, delighting in the falls' beauty.

Every so often, I catch his eyes on me again, shining, a soft smile playing on his lips. How can one look hold so much promise, so much possibility? It's such a change from earlier when I thought he might've been upset. *This* is the Logan that makes me feel truly seen, filling me with a sense of exhilaration that I can't ignore.

But what could you do about it, girl?

Hank gets up on some rocks and shakes out his fur emphatically.

"How about a race?" Logan asks, one hand on a rock as he treads water.

"You sure you're up for it, old man?" I tease, getting ready to duck under into a handstand next to him.

"I forgot about your trash talk," he says. He grabs my ankle when I'm upside down.

I manage to twist out of his grip and come up for air, laughing. "How could you forget it? Especially when I beat you at the Everett Challenge nearly every year?"

He narrows his eyes. "You mean whenever you cheat?"

"I do *not* cheat!"

"You're just a natural at axe-throwing even though I'm the lumberjack?"

I pop up out of the water and shrug. "Guess so."

He grins, and I swear it's dazzling to see. "Ok, Miss Confident. First one to that big rock with the forget-me-nots growing on top of it wins."

I spot the rock with the blue flowers across the pool and nod. "You're on."

He steadies himself against the bank. "On your marks. Get set." He side-eyes me. "*Go!*"

We take off and I immediately lean into a freestyle stroke, ploughing through the water as fast as I can. Logan appears in the corner of my eye, but I keep my focus on the rock ahead. The splashing of the water next to me lets me know he's keeping up with me. I'm not able to come up with some super burst of speed, but I keep pushing on. I'm close! The rock is right ahead! My palm smacks onto it and I yell, "Finish!" like we always do.

He finally glides in. "You win," he says gallantly, and I hoot and holler.

My heart is pounding, both from the exertion of the race and from the excitement of victory. I can't help but feel a rush of joy, even if I deeply suspect Logan *may* have gone easy on me.

"Yesssss!" Without thinking, I jump into Logan's arms, delighted giggles bubbling up from my chest. His arms wrap around me, holding me close, and then we're spinning. Water swirls around us as he turns, my laughter ringing out over the falls.

When he finally stops, we're chest to chest, my arms still around his neck, his around my waist. For a moment, we just float there, treading water together. I swallow, acutely aware of his heart beating against mine, the heat of his warm skin, the firm hold of his big hands on my hips. A soft smile plays on his lips as he gazes at me; the silence is filled with unspoken words and...could it really be feelings?

There's a sense of intimacy in the way he holds me, a familiarity that goes beyond—

SPLASH! Hank jumps into the water next to us and I squeal.

"Dammit, Hank!" Logan exclaims as we move apart, laughing.

Later, after a delicious dinner of hearty minestrone soup and soft pumpernickel bread, Logan and I sit by the fire at our campsite. The sounds of nature serenade us as we gaze quietly up at the stars in the night sky. For the first time in a long while, I feel content with my direction...or rather, my lack of it. I'm fine just being here, enjoying the moment. I'm sure that has a lot to do with Logan and his advice. The possibilities are endless and exciting now, rather than overwhelming.

"Why did you decide to sell Everett Logging?" I ask. Blair had mentioned her dad had wanted to work on his creative side, and I'm curious to hear more about that.

"Wanted to pursue something that brought me more peace, more happiness," he says, staring into the fire. He glances at his big, calloused hands, and flexes them thoughtfully. "I like working with my hands. Making furniture." His face softens, the firelight dancing in his eyes. "There's something magical about transforming a raw piece of wood into something not only functional, but beautiful, too."

I nod. I can understand that, considering I enjoy creating beautiful content online via social media outlets. Sharing beauty with the world in my own small way.

My phone buzzes. It's a text from Blair.

> How's it going? Any poison ivy or broken ankles yet?

I glance over at Logan and, smirking, show him my phone screen.

He grins. "Tell her nope, since she's not here."

I shake my head, laughing.

> Your dad is making me say no, because you're not here with us.

> RUDE!

I chuckle.

> Srsly, all good. We just finished dinner at the campsite. Emerald Falls is stunning. I'm sorry you had to miss it.

> Me too.

How's Trent doing?

> Grieving, but he's a trooper. He's stepped up to help his family and I'm really proud of him.

That's sweet.

> It'll be another day or two before I get back home, sorry.

No prob. Your dad has been great.

> He always is, Maddie.

You told me so.

> See you soon!

"Everything okay?" Logan asks, poking at the fire with a stick.

"Think so. Trent is doing well, helping his family, and Blair is getting him through it."

"I'm glad." He rests his elbows on his knees. "Blair's good at that."

"What's her mom like?" It just pops out, then I realize that maybe I don't want to know. Would it make me jealous thinking about her with Logan if I had more of an image of her? And is it too personal a question? "Sorry." I shake my head. "Forget I asked." But he waves me off, his attention still on the fire.

The corners of his mouth turn up a bit. "Think Blair but without the selflessness and drive." He shrugs. "Sorry. That sounds harsh. Jo has some good qualities, but she and I never had much in common. We were young and naive. She got pregnant, and I did what I thought was the right thing. Looking back, I think she only went along with it because I

119

was so hell bent on doing it my way. I didn't exactly give her much choice in the matter..." His voice trails off, a mixture of regret and quiet acceptance on his heavy brow.

Seeing him like this, open and vulnerable, makes my heart hurt. "Have you dated at all?" *Again? Why do I insist on asking these private questions about Logan's love life? Am I some sort of masochist?*

But he answers without much hesitation. "I tried a few times, but no one ever made me feel"...he pauses and turns to me..."like I want to stick around." Suddenly, everything else disappears. All that exists in the universe is Logan, and the firelight, and some weird tension in my belly.

In the soft glow of the fire, my heart pounds with a mix of anticipation and pure vulnerability. Eventually I have to confess: "When I first met you, I thought Blair was pranking me."

His brow furrows. "Pranking you? How?"

"I mean... There was no way that the hot guy she introduced me to was her father. I thought she hired you or something to pretend to be her dad. I crushed on you so hard...still do, a bit." A shaky breath escapes my lips.

Logan looks at me, surprise and something else flickering in his eyes, quickly replaced by amusement. "You think I'm hot?"

I bite my lip and nod. *Good lord, what have I done? Remember what we talked about, Maddie? About not spitting out something you can't take back?* I cover my face with my hands in embarrassment. Telling him just makes me sound like a silly, foolish girl. Even if it is true.

"Don't be embarrassed, Maddie," I hear him say near me. He sighs. "I might have a bit of a crush on you, too."

My heart leaps into my throat and I move my hands away

from my face to see him giving me a small smile. "Y-you're just saying that to be nice," I stammer.

He chuckles, shaking his head. "Come on. You're beautiful, independent, modest to a damn fault, and fiercely stubborn. And those freckles drive me out of my mind." He gives me an incredulous look. "I mean, how could I not have a crush on you?"

I'm silent, but my insides are screaming and I think I'm going to faint. Logan has a crush on me?!

What do we do now?

Logan's sad expression threatens to pierce my heart. He averts his gaze and looks down at his hands, rubbing them anxiously on his pants. "I… We can't do anything to threaten our friendship and relationship with Blair. And with me being so much older… It's just not right, Maddie."

The words hit me like a cold bucket of water. A lump forms in my throat, and I nod, not trusting myself to speak.

Why? Why am I feeling this way? Of *course* Logan and I could never be together. Sure, he said all those sweet things about me, about having the same feelings I have for him, but he's probably trying to save me all kinds of embarrassment. He is that kind of man. Decent. And a decent man does what he feels is right, especially when it involves his daughter…and his daughter's best friend.

Despite all that, I had something akin to hope before. Now, it's like those hopes have been dashed.

Gone forever.

I get up from my chair, heart ripped in two, and nod solemnly. Then I retreat to the tent without another word, leaving Logan alone with the dying embers of the fire.

CHAPTER 6
LOGAN

I jolt awake, my body rigid and alert. Hank's whines cut through the silence, the sound instantly setting off alarm bells in my head.

Something's wrong.

Shifting my gaze in the dark, I spot Hank nestled next to Maddie, just a few feet away. He's restless. He keeps creeping closer to her, snorting and snuffling.

"Maddie?" I say, my voice hoarse. There's no response, but I hear what sounds like teeth chattering and she stirs. Barely.

Instantly, I'm wide awake, throwing the top of my sleeping bag back, turning on the light on my phone, and crawling over to her.

"Maddie, talk to me." I touch her neck and almost hiss at how cold she is. She's like an ice sculpture. She moans faintly and her teeth chatter again. I curse under my breath; the temperature must have dropped due to a sudden cold front, and I never checked before we left to make sure she had a proper sleeping bag, not this thin little thing. I need to warm her up quickly before hypothermia sets in.

"We need to get you warm, Maddie." My voice is surprisingly steady despite the panic rising in my chest. "Skin-to-skin is the best way. I promise not to look at your underwear."

I peel off my flannel shirt and pajama pants, then help Maddie out of her tank and little shorts. What was she thinking sleeping in only this? By the blue glow of my phone, I do my best to ignore the fact that we are both almost naked. My focus is entirely on getting her body temperature up.

(*Honest.*)

I bundle her into my sleeping bag. She's weak, her movements uncoordinated and sluggish, and all I can get from her are sounds, not actual words. Jesus, I need to be quick.

My arms and legs wrap around her and I feel better about my chances of warming her up, even though she trembles against me, her skin cold and clammy. I get to work, rubbing her arms and back with my thick arms, trying to stimulate her blood flow. I run my legs up and down hers and breathe hot air onto her neck and shoulders, desperate to give her my heat. Her nipples against my chest are as hard as glass, and a brief thought of taking them into my mouth to warm them pops into my head—

Nope. Can't do that.

Or using my mouth on her earlobes, neck, fingers, toes...

Focus, dammit.

I cup her hands in mine and blow hot air over them.

My cock rages below. Regardless of the dire circumstances, I finally have Maddie in my arms. I give up on telling him to sit down and be quiet. I don't have any time to waste. Saving Maddie is my priority.

Time seems to stretch on as I continue my task. After what feels like hours, but is surely not, her movements gradually increase. Her sounds get louder. Words fall from her lips, even if they are only "cold" or "more." Her trembling slowly subsides, and her breathing and heartbeat mirror my own.

Soon, I notice her drifting in and out of sleep. She's curled up against me tight, and I slide my hand into her hair, thankful she's okay.

"Don't stop," she whispers into my neck, her lips grazing me. I shudder.

"Still cold?" I whisper in her ear.

"No."

The air is thick and hot and tense. She's warm now. *And she doesn't want me to stop touching her.*

My cock throbs in my boxers at the idea.

"You sure you're feeling okay, Maddie?" My hand tangles at the base of her hairline.

"I feel great," she says. "You saved me. You're really good at this saving stuff, you know that?"

I chuckle. "But are you sure you want *this*?" I ask, tightening my grip in her hair.

"Logan," she moans, and it goes straight to my rigid cock. "You're the only thing I'm sure of in my life right now."

I groan and stare up at the ceiling of the tent.

I hear her swallow thickly. "But if you don't want me...that way...I'll understand."

"Don't want you? Woman, can't you feel my rock-hard cock against your hip?"

She huffs. "I thought they had a mind of their own and if a guy was in this situation with any near-naked woman, they would do that."

I chuckle. "Well, Maddie, with me, it's you. Only you." Then I draw her earlobe into my mouth with my teeth.

Her gasp turns into a moan, and I feel a shiver run through her body.

Goddamn, I want her.

She works her arm out from the sleeping bag and moves

back an inch to caress my stubbled cheek. "Thank you for saving me. I owe you one."

"You don't owe me any—"

She presses a finger to my lips. "I don't want to ruin anything with Blair, but how I feel about you is so special. It's unlike anything I've ever felt before. I can't help but think that it must be worth the effort."

I adjust the sleeping bag around us and roll on top of her. "How did you become smarter than this grizzled old lumberjack?"

"*Grizzled?*" she sputters, laughing. "I've seen you throwing around that big axe of yours *and* wading through Emerald Falls—both while half-naked. *Grizzled* is not a word that ever came to mind. Now, *sexy, buff, chiseled, cut, built, panty-melting—*"

"Ooh, 'panty-melting'," I repeat, nodding. "I like that."

She smiles, her dark eyes reflecting the blue glow of the light in the tent.

My thumb strokes over her cheek. "Maddie, I've never cared what people think, but I worry about what *you* might think further down the line. I don't want to force you into something when you have so many possibilities available to you. I did that with Blair's mom. And I'd never forgive myself if you ended up looking back on your life only to realize you made a mistake by hitching your wagon to an old man who promised you the moon and couldn't deliver."

"Logan..." She runs her hand down my back and squeezes my ass cheek. "Has anyone ever told you that you worry too much?"

I inhale with a start and smile, shaking my head no.

"I want you. I want you to be my partner, to support me, and...love me. You'll never have to worry about not being enough or holding me back from my dreams. I'm in perfect control of my dreams. I just want someone to be there with me as I head toward them. Mine and yours."

Can a mountain man swoon? Well, this one just did. "You keep talking like that and I'm going to rip off those polka-dotted panties, missy."

Her eyes fly wide. "You said you didn't look at my underwear!"

"You heard that?"

She nods, her lips curling into a shy smile.

"Sorry, I peeked," I admit, closing in on her sexy mouth.

"Such a bad boy…" she whispers before I kiss her soft lips.

We both groan as we sink into each other, tasting and teasing and exploring. I'm so lost in her already.

I kiss down her jaw, her throat, and sexy collarbone, already addicted to the taste of her skin. She's so responsive to my touch. It only makes me want more of her sweet body.

I unzip the sleeping bag further so I can move down to capture her breasts—one in my hand, as my fingers play with her pebbled nipple, the other deep in my mouth.

She arches up into me as I lick, suck, and tease the peak, listening to her breathing becoming erratic. My tongue rolls around her velvety skin, my teeth grazing the hard tip.

"Fuck, Logan," she moans frantically, making me growl.

I move my mouth to her other rosy breast, savoring it with the same vigor as the first. Maddie grips my head close to her, her nails pricking at my scalp and sending shivers throughout my whole body.

I don't think I've ever been this hard in my life, and I worry that just one touch will have me coming all over her innocent polka-dotted panties. The image isn't helping me hold back.

My hands reach down to pull those pretty panties down, and I push the sleeping bag all the way open. I'm moaning as I kiss down her belly, the hot, sweet scent of her pussy consuming me in the best way.

"Take off my panties," she breathes. "I want to spread my legs wide for you."

The request has me near climax. "Maddie, please. I'm trying not to blow too soon here…"

She giggles, as if I'm not serious. Then I tear those panties off like they're on fire.

She spreads her long legs and I get lightheaded just from her luscious scent. I grab her underneath her ass and haul her up close to my face, inhaling her aroma. "You smell like my dreams," I whisper before rolling my tongue over her pussy.

"Oh fuck…" she moans, her hips lifting to my mouth.

She's decadent. Like a luxurious, creamy dessert, her tender flesh soft and wet, trembling under my tongue. She tries to writhe, but I hold her ass cheeks tight, my thumbs around her hips as I lap at her delicious center. Her copper curls tickle my nose and lips, and I'm moaning along with her. She's shaking like a crazy thing, biting her lip, and grasping at the flannel of the sleeping bag.

"God, Logan. That's so good."

"I want you coming all over my mouth, Maddie," I demand.

"Yes. *Shit*," she gasps as I lick at her clit.

I slide my tongue and lips back down, circling lower, then back up again, loving her little gasps and groans. I relish teasing her pussy, working it into a frenzy, for as long as I can hold out.

As I circle her clit again, she's still arching and grinding into my mouth. "Please, Logan," she begs. I can't deny her any longer. I focus on her tender center, circling and sucking—the sounds coming from deep within her throat driving me close to the edge.

Maddie's thighs shake and her head tosses from side to side. "I'm going to come, Logan. God!"

I nuzzle my face into her pussy as she detonates, hips snapping, body convulsing. I just keep licking her, tasting her sweet nectar, wringing out every last drop of pleasure from her core.

She's moaning and panting like she's just run a sprint, and I lower her back down to the floor, and nestle between her legs, drawing tender licks up her seam as she comes down from her orgasm.

Her legs slide down and out, my tongue causing little aftershocks that make my cock jerk.

"Okay?" I ask, in between kisses and licks.

"*Okay*?" she breathes. "You have a very skewed view of reality, sir. That was…" She lets out a long, contented breath. "Masterful."

I feel like pounding my chest with pride as she lies there, utterly spent.

"You ready to sleep?" I ask, crawling up next to her.

She turns to me and runs her hands up my chest, shaking her head.

"No?" My eyes drift shut at her touch…then fly open again when she drags her nails down my stomach and into the waistband of my boxers. When her hand curls around my cock, a low hiss rises from deep within me. "Maddie…"

"I want to suck you, Logan," she says, placing soft kisses on my mouth, cheek, and jaw.

"Damn, Maddie, you'll be the death of me."

She chuckles. "You'd really rather we go to sleep?"

I roll onto my side and begin pulling off my boxers. "Let's not be too hasty."

She laughs, until my cock is free. Her eyes fixate on it, widening.

"We don't have to—"

"Shush," she says. "It's just…big. Bigger than I've ever seen… And for the record, there's nothing *grizzled* about it."

That's it. I'm going to marry this woman.

"You realize you'll just kiss the tip and I'll be done for." I position myself directly in front of her on my knees, then lean back to sit on my heels.

She rolls onto her stomach, scooting toward me. Just seeing her there in front of me, licking her lips, already has my cock leaking precum.

She reaches out to wrap her fingers around the base, and my eyes drift closed. "Hell…"

She strokes up the shaft and over the tip, and I shiver.

"I dreamed about touching you like this last night," she whispers, her soft hand pumping me torturously slowly.

I groan. "Maddie, you're in my dreams every goddamn night."

"Really?" She scoots closer and gently licks a line from the base of my cock to the tip.

I gasp at the heat and wetness of her sweet, soft tongue. "Really."

Then she moves my swollen head around her lips, and I almost die. "Holy…hell," I grunt, my voice rough and unrecognizable. My stomach clenches with need.

When she slides me into her hot mouth, I make a sound only meant for beasts. Primal. Savage.

Hank snorts from the other side of the tent.

I lean back on one elbow and place my other palm on her head. I thread my fingers in the back of her hair as she sucks and licks, my muscles tightening and shaking, trying to hold back. "God help me," I whisper in between moans and grunts and curses. It's too good…

I could come at any second. She moans on my dick, her hand squeezing the base, and I cry out.

She slides her mouth off me for a moment, smiling brightly as her eyes flick up to mine. "You're delicious, you know that?"

Then she slides back down, taking me as deep as she can.

I'm done for. "Maddie! God, please, I'm…" I tremble. "I'm going to come. You'd better move."

But the woman clamps down on my thick, hard tip, rolling her wet tongue over me while hollowing out her cheeks.

"*Fuuuuucck…*" My cock erupts hard and fast into her hot mouth, and still she doesn't pull off. She grabs at my hips as they shake and jerk, all of my muscles straining at once. I fall back and she continues to lick, softer now, milking the last of my seed from me, her throat working to swallow every single drop.

"You are so hot," I say, trying to catch my breath. I jump as she licks my slit. "Careful, I won't be responsible for what my cock does if you do that."

She grins. "I could play with you all day."

"Yeah, he won't calm down if you keep talking like that."

"I also love how loud you are during sex—considering you're the strong, silent type."

My face heats, and I'm glad she can't see it in the dark.

"I know you're blushing, Logan."

Dammit.

I slide my boxers back on and pull her into the sleeping bag with me. The feel of her naked skin on mine is a heady mix of sensuality and comfort.

She burrows into my neck, and I kiss the top of her head.

Hank snores from across the tent, asleep on top of Maddie's sleeping bag.

"I hope we didn't offend that poor dog," Maddie whispers, and we chuckle, drifting off to sleep, our bodies twined together in the crisp mountain night.

CHAPTER 7
MADDIE

My eyes crack open as a sliver of sunlight breaks through the tent. Warmth radiates from Logan, his breath steady against my neck. The heat that had once been for survival is now a reminder of what we did last night.

I lie there quietly for a few moments, taking in the feel of him. The way his body fits so perfectly to mine.

I move my hands tentatively, tracing the lines of his muscles. When my fingers start exploring the contours of his cock, hard against my hip, he stirs.

"Mmmm..." he murmurs. "I'm so glad you aren't a dream." He grasps my face and pulls me into a searing kiss that sends even more heat coursing through my veins and pooling in my core.

I continue to stroke his thick rod.

"Now, what do you want with that, Maddie?" he growls against my lips.

"I want it inside me."

He growls. "My god, woman..." He rolls on top of me. "You're perfect in every way." He rocks against me and hisses. "Fuck, you're already so wet."

"That's because I woke up thinking about you," I purr, meeting his hips. The way his cocks slides through my folds, I swear I could come just like this, the tension in my pussy already building.

He shakes his head, his green eyes gazing at me as if he doesn't believe I'm real. "Are you"...he clears his throat..."on the pill, or...?"

I nod and bite my lip, wanting to get the embarrassing admission over with quickly. "Yes, but... It'll be my first time."

He searches my eyes. "You're a virgin?" He blinks rapidly. "But all of that last night—"

"Oh, I've done *that* stuff before, just not...ya know...full meal deal."

He lifts off me and hunts frantically for his boxers. "Then let's get going. We need to get back. Your first time will not be in a grungy ol' tent on a hard dirt floor next to..." He looks up as Hank raises his head, tongue lolling. "Hank. No offence, Hank."

I chuckle. "I don't care where it happens, as long as it's with you."

He leans down to take my face between his hands and kisses me briefly. "You are the sweetest thing ever, but no. I want to take my time and do this right—also, then we can be as loud and go on as long as we like." He starts gathering up our clothes and gear. "We need to pack up and get back to the house, pronto. You said Blair will be back in a day or two?"

"Yes, sir," I reply, smiling until he mentions Blair's name.

What are we going to tell her?

We get everything together faster than I would ever have thought possible, then hustle back through the trail, only stopping for a quick sandwich and a make-out session (or two) against a thick pine tree.

When we finally get back to the house, we trip over one another as we stumble upstairs and straight into the shower, kissing and stripping off one another's clothes, feverishly tossing them aside. Under the water, we soap our bodies thoroughly but quickly, washing away all the grub and grime from the last two days on the hike.

Once toweled off, Logan lifts me up and I wrap my legs around him as he carries me to his big hand-carved bed that he made himself.

"How many nights I'd pass your bedroom door, fantasizing about what you might be doing in this bed," I moan, as he lays me out on his soft sheets. I wish I could roll around in them to get his intoxicating scent all over me permanently.

He crawls over me, pinning my wrists over my head. "If you were here in this house, then you know exactly what I was doing."

"That's so hot." The thought of him jerking himself off to me sends fresh heat between my legs, and I rock upward, desperate for the weight of his powerful body on me.

"Easy, kitten," he murmurs, before kissing me deeply, making me dizzy.

His mouth wanders down my throat and my chest, his hands dragging down my arms and holding them down as he takes the peak of my breast into his mouth, swirling his tongue around it.

My head drops back, and I moan. "Logan, that feels amazing."

"Good." He bites my nipple gently with his teeth, and I gasp.

He continues his kisses down my belly, and then sits up, massaging my breasts. His green eyes are dark and intense in the fading light from the massive windows. He's the most magnificent man I've ever seen, and he's looking at me as if I'm an angel sent from Heaven. I could soar into the clouds with how wonderful that makes me feel.

My legs splay apart for him as his palm strokes over my pussy.

"Yes," I whisper.

"I love how wet you get for me," he growls, slicking his fingers through my folds. "But I want you to come before we do this, so you're relaxed and properly prepared."

I just nod as he slides his finger into me, the stretching feeling already noticeable. "I know you'll make it good for me."

"That's all I ever want," he says, sitting back on the bed. "To make it good for you."

I smile and let him work his talented finger inside of me, moving in and out, the sensations making me clench around him. He curses. "You're so tight. How does it feel?"

"Incredible," I say on a breath, my hips rising to meet him.

He adds another finger, and even though it stretches me even more, it still feels spectacular. I'm already so close. "Logan…" I plead.

His fingers do something inside me…curl?…and I nearly hit the roof. "Oh, god! Yes…"

"That's it, baby," he murmurs, as he continues to work at my pussy, and I moan louder.

My legs begin to shake, my pelvis gyrating, the tension a rubber band pulled so tight it's about to snap. "Don't stop, I'm—"

"Never…"

My climax shoots through me as I grab at the sheets, arching and convulsing under his expert touch.

"Fuck, you're so beautiful when you come," he rasps.

I'm trembling, my heart pumping like mad.

Logan slows his hand movements and eventually slides out of me.

I lie there, sweating and satiated, as he crawls over me.

"So, intercourse is like that?" I ask breathlessly.

His brow jumps up, and he grins. "Better."

"Oh my god…" I groan, and he palms his cock once in between us before nudging my opening with the tip.

"It might hurt at first," he says, as he inches into me. "But if it's too much, you just say the word and we'll stop."

I swallow and nod. It does hurt a little, giving me a burning and stretching feeling, but I inhale and exhale slowly, reveling in the fact that Logan Everett, the man of my dreams, is making love to me.

"You still okay?" he asks. I can't believe still there's more of him.

I close my eyes. "Yes," I croak.

He pauses. "That wasn't very convincing."

I open my eyes to see him with a pained expression, eyes screwed shut and mouth pressed into a thin line.

I stroke his back. "What's wrong, Logan?"

He manages a smile. "You just feel so goddamn good. I'm trying not to come right here and now."

I chuckle.

"No!" he huffs. "No laughing. Shit…"

I bite my lip. "Okay. No laughing."

"That's it. I'm all the way inside you, baby. I'm so close…"

His body is flush against mine and I'm riding my edge as well, just knowing I'm giving my body to Logan completely.

We start to move together, and yes, it's rough at first, but gradually, he stirs up and releases something deep and primal within me. His cock reaches secret places that now have been discovered are aching to be pleasured.

I shift my hips, and he chokes back a curse when he feels the new angle. "God, Maddie…"

"More, Logan! More…" my voice cracks. "It feels amazing."

He snarls at that and anchors me with his weight, thrusting into me in heavy, deep strokes.

"Fuck, Maddie…your body is like sweet fire, burning me up to the core."

My gruff lumberjack, such a poet in the throes of passion.

"I can't…" he grunts. "I'm so close."

"Me too," I whine, his thrusts verging on erratic.

He grabs my face and kisses me possessively, then forces me to look into his intense green eyes.

"You're mine, you hear me, Maddie?" he whispers. "*Mine.*"

"Yes, yours," I echo breathlessly, his words setting me off, my climax tearing through my body. "Logan!"

"Fuck, yes!" he roars over me.

The world around me disappears into nothingness as I lose myself in my orgasm. The only thing I'm only able to focus on is my body, and Logan pumping hard and deep into me as he comes undone.

I wrap my legs around his hips as he fills me with his wet, hot seed, and hold onto him as we shiver and jerk together.

After a few moments, he presses a kiss to my forehead, sliding out and rolling off me onto the bed. We lie there for a few minutes in silence, catching our breath.

"Maddie," he begins, his hand finding mine. He turns and I love how completely wrecked he looks—his hair a mess, his skin sweaty, his eyes hooded. I'm sure I look just as disheveled.

"I know it might be a little strange, considering I'm Blair's dad. But what I feel for you…" he trails off with a helpless sigh. "It's love. I love you, Maddie."

The words hang in the air between us, raw and powerful, filling me with unending warmth and a whirlwind of emotions.

"I thought I might've been in love with Blair's mom years ago, but what I feel for you is completely different. It's so much...*more*." His gaze intensifies. "It's all-encompassing, like a wildfire I can't control. It makes me feel invincible."

Logan pauses, shaking his head. "I don't care what anybody else in town thinks. I don't care about society, or their norms, or expectations. All I care about is you and making you happy. If Blair can't understand that, well... we'll just have to make her."

He strokes my cheek. "Because you're the most amazing woman I've ever met, Maddie. And I want you to be mine, end of story."

Again, for a man who doesn't say much, when he does speak, it's utter beauty and he renders me speechless with every word.

When I don't respond right away, his expression takes on one of worry, but then I give his hand a reassuring squeeze. "Logan, I've been in love with you since I met you that first Spring Break."

A look of pleased disbelief spreads over his face.

"I've tried to date, really, I have. Ask Blair," I chuckle.

He averts his eyes. "I *have* asked."

I giggle. "You did not. Oh my god."

He shrugs and gives me a shy smile. "I made it seem like casual conversation."

I shake my head. *This man.* "No one could compare to you, Logan. No one makes me feel the way you do, just by being there for me." My voice wavers, but I keep going. "My feelings for you...they've only grown deeper as time has gone on. I was afraid of them at first. But not anymore."

I start to tear up. "I love you, Logan. I want to be yours."

He grins and hauls me into his arms, holding me tightly against his chest. He kisses my head, his voice raw and full of emotion. "I've hoped to hear those words for so long, but never dared to believe I would."

And in that moment I know exactly where Blair got her big, caring heart from…

Her hopelessly romantic dad.

The next morning, the enticing smell of breakfast wafting from the kitchen gets me up and out of bed faster than usual. Though I love the warmth of Logan's bed, it's not the same without him in it. My skin still tingles from where his hands touched me the night before, when we made love until we both were utterly exhausted.

I slip into one of his flannel shirts—which hangs more like a dress on me—and blunder sleepily toward the aroma with Hank at my heels. My heart flutters when I see Logan in the kitchen, flipping pancakes and tending to some sizzling bacon.

"Morning," he rasps in the rough voice that makes me wet instantly. He looks drop-dead sexy in a t-shirt and sweats. I sidle up to him, and he pulls me into a warm hug. "Sleep well?"

"Like a baby," I reply, unable to stop the smile from spreading across my face. He grins back at me as I pour myself a cup of coffee and sit at the table. We don't say much. I'm still processing everything we said and did last night. As we eat in comfortable silence, a contented happiness settles over us like a blanket, our goofy smiles and long gazes giving it away.

The sudden sound of the front door opening jolts me out of my reverie. "Hiiiiyeee," Blair calls, and Logan and I look at one another in surprise. I thought we had one more day! We didn't even plan what we were going to say, or how we were going to tell her.

I start to get up in a panic, but Logan puts his big hand on mine. "No. Stay."

And that's how we are when Blair enters the kitchen.

Her eyebrows raise as her gaze lands on us at the table, my hand in Logan's. Her eyes then drop to the flannel shirt I'm wearing.

"Um… Is that Dad's shirt?" she asks.

My face heats, and I desperately want to bolt from the room. But Logan doesn't let go. I look at him, flustered, then turn to Blair.

"I-I'm sorry. I didn't want you to find out like this," I confess.

"She's right," Logan adds, his eyes anxious. "We didn't mean for you to—"

"Just stop, okay?" Blair says, holding up a hand. "Both of you." A small smile tugs at the corners of her mouth. "I'm not mad. I've known for a long time how much you like each other. I mean, I'm a trained therapist. My business is observing and understanding people. Not to mention, *helping them*."

She pauses and puts a hand on her hip, her smile widening. "I knew something would happen between you two while I was gone. You've been dancing around each other for way too long. Someone was bound to make a move eventually."

With relief and maybe a little embarrassment, I squeeze Logan's hand and let out a long breath.

"So—who *did* make the first move?" Blair asks, looking between us.

Logan and I glance at one another. Emerald Falls…dropping temperatures…one sleeping bag…

"It's, uh, sort of a long story," Logan offers. "You probably don't want to hear it."

Blair grimaces. "Enough said."

Logan chuckles, his relief palpable. "You've got no idea how glad I am that you're okay with this, kiddo."

She huffs, crossing her arms. "Honestly, I'm more upset that there isn't any breakfast left."

Logan quickly moves to remedy that, pouring more pancake batter onto the griddle, while I get Blair some coffee and we chat about her trip, and Trent.

"One other thing," Blair says, as I sneak Hank a piece of bacon. "Being with Trent got me thinking about family, and how short life is, yada, yada, yada, and I think I'd like to spend the rest of the summer visiting mom in Oregon."

"And did you talk to her about this?" Logan asks.

Blair nods. "She called me while I was at Trent's and we talked about it. I think it would be good for both of us."

"When would you go?" I ask.

"Maybe in two weeks? We'll still be able to go on a few hikes and spend time together, Maddie." She shrugs and smiles slyly. "And you'll get plenty of alone time with my dad—I mean, your new boyfriend."

My eyes go wide. "Logan and I haven't really talked about any of that—"

"No, please, stay with me, Maddie," Logan interrupts. "I'd like nothing more." A soft smile appears on his face. "It could also give you a chance to figure out what you want to do. Or not. It's your summer. And I know Hank would be over the moon about it." He pats the dog's head.

The idea of spending a dreamy, lazy summer with Logan exploring our feelings for each other is more than appealing. It feels right. It feels like home. "I'd love that, Logan," I finally answer, giving Blair a hug, my heart as huge as all the Montana mountains surrounding us.

EPILOGUE - LOGAN

I'm marinating steak for me and portobello mushrooms for her in the kitchen when Maddie bursts into the front door.

She dashes into the kitchen, her eyes dancing with excitement.

"I got it!" she yells, nearly knocking me over as she vaults into my arms.

Hank jumps up next to us, barking and spinning in excitement.

I laugh, holding her close. "The social media job at the Deepwood Mountain Library?"

She nods, rattling off details about Willa and Eden, our local librarians, and their plans for the town library. I've never seen her so excited. I smile, listening to her gush about her new job. "I'm so proud of you, Maddie," I say, my voice choked with emotion.

She grins and kisses me with such passion this old lumberjack gets weak in the knees as my hand tangles in her hair and my tongue dances with hers. We've been inseparable all summer, and it just keeps getting better. I'm addicted to everything about her.

Finally, I set her down and pull away. "Come with me," I murmur, taking her hand and leading her out to the deck.

Her breath hitches as she takes in the scene before her— dozens of candles in hurricane lanterns flickering in the breeze, twinkling fairy lights strung up along the rails of the deck and suspended from above, a table set for two with a small arrangement of wildflowers in the middle. "What's all this?" she asks, her voice barely above a whisper.

I tear off my apron and take her hands in mine. Looking deeply into her eyes, I drop to one knee.

"This has been the best summer of my life, Maddie. You've shown me what true love really is and what it feels like to be loved for who I am."

I take a deep breath, reaching into my pocket to pull out a small velvet box. She gasps and covers her mouth.

"I love you, Maddie, more than I can ever say. I'm terrified of losing the one person who makes me feel like everything in my world is finally right." I open the box to reveal the emerald engagement ring I bought from the antique store in town in only the second week of her stay. I chose it because it reminds me of Emerald Falls and our time there. I gaze into her soulful brown eyes. "Will you please marry me and make me the happiest man in the world?"

Her eyes fill with tears as she nods, whispering a soft, "Yes."

Hank, sensing the joy in the air, lets out a long howl at the beautiful moon above. Honestly, the way I feel right now, I could howl along with him.

But instead, I rise and slide the ring onto my future wife's finger before pulling her into the most passionate kiss this ridiculously happy mountain man can give her.

EPILOGUE - MADDIE

SIX MONTHS LATER

A s the last few wedding guests trickle out of the house, I sink deeper into Logan's lap on the couch, joy and excitement finally giving way to exhaustion. The day has been a wild and wonderful ride, but finally, it's just the two of us—except for Blair, asleep on the couch next to us, and for Nick, one of Logan's groomsmen, who's outside on the deck talking on his cell.

Nick's voice, gruff and tired, carries through the open window. He's arguing, his tone polite enough but firm. "I just don't understand why we can't work with one of the guys we've used before. All these new designers are completely unrealistic and demanding—like, they're certifiable divas." He's obviously exasperated, poor guy.

Logan shifts underneath me, his hand tracing gentle circles on my back. "Sounds like Nick's going to regret coming out of retirement for that project," he says, sympathetic amusement in his voice.

I nod, stifling a yawn. "Sure does."

From the corner of my eye, I see Nick pacing on the deck,

his free hand running through his dark hair. He lets out a huff of resignation.

"Well, if your wife insists, of course, Mr. Donovan," he mutters tightly before hanging up, his face etched with annoyance. He stands still for a moment, phone in hand, as if he's contemplating throwing it into the vast forest beyond the deck. After a moment, he shakes his head and sighs, leaning against the railing.

Logan's chuckle brings me back to our own little world. "I think it's time I take my wife upstairs," he murmurs into my ear, his hot breath sending a shiver down my spine. "Nick can show himself out."

I manage a sleepy smile. "That sounds like a wonderful idea," I reply, allowing him to lift me into his arms and carry me upstairs to our bedroom, ready to begin our new life together as husband and wife...with Hank close behind, still in the bow tie that he wore as our ring bearer.

HIS BIG HAMMER

CHAPTER 1
VIOLET

This must be it. Yes!

I turn onto the gravel road, barely visible in the cluster of tall pines. The uneven terrain jostles my little car, and I'm bounced all over the seat.

"You did it, Minnie! I'm so proud of you!" I cheer, patting the dash of my Mini Cooper affectionately. The poor girl is more accustomed to the pavement and city streets of Los Angeles, not the uneven roads and steep inclines of Deepwood Mountain, Montana.

The struggle getting here was worth it. As I pull up to the construction site, I can't imagine a more beautiful spot for the Donovan family lodge...even if right now it's only a pile of concrete, wood, and metal on a sprawling mountainside lot.

This project is the opportunity I've been waiting for. The canvas where I'll paint my dreams and kick-start my career as a successful designer.

For bonus points, I'll be working under Nick Fletcher, the legendary contractor who specializes in luxury mountain residences. It's like he has a magic touch, with everything he works on turning to gold. And all his awards and accolades certainly back up the hype.

I've admired his work since design school, following his career until he went into semi-retirement a while back. I've been out of school for a couple of years now, trying to build my portfolio with any work that comes my way. When Mrs. Donovan contacted me about this job, and I found out I'd be working with Nick, I knew this could be my big break.

I've only talked to Nick via email so far, going back and forth over design plans. His messages are brief and to the point without a speck of personality. But that's email…right?

I get out of my car, the cardboard tube with my renderings clutched to my chest. I smooth down my pencil skirt and walk toward the site, silently cursing as my heels sink into the soil. Probably not the best choice in footwear, but too late now. I take a deep breath, drinking in the cadence of construction around me, my jangling nerves soothed by the familiar clatter of tools and buzz of conversation.

Before I can take another step, a loud, sharp whistle stops me. Glancing around, I spot a tall, muscled figure in a hard hat striding closer through a swirling cloud of dust—like some action hero in a movie.

Oh my god, it's Nick Fletcher.

I instantly recognize him from the photos I've seen, though they clearly don't do him justice. He's even more imposing and attractive in person. At the moment, though, his incredibly handsome face is drawn tight with annoyance. My eyes follow his gaze to where a group of workers is struggling with a hefty wooden beam, perilously close to damaging a half-built wall.

"Careful with that!" Nick's voice booms. He swiftly redirects the beam to its proper place, his movements fluid, confident, and oh so strong.

I fight back the urge to sigh like a swooning fangirl as I take a step toward him. Then my high heel catches, and I flail. Everything switches to horrific super slow motion as I go sprawling onto the ground with a yelp.

Great first impression, Vi.

I lift myself up onto my forearms, a large pair of beige work boots in my line of sight. Before I can react, I'm hauled up by two massive hands and set back on my feet.

Tall, hulking, Nick tilts his head slightly to the side, his piercing green-blue gaze finding mine. "You must be the new designer."

I nod, trying to still my racing heart, doing my best to brush off the dirt and humiliation.

It's not working.

"Yes. Violet Bridges," I say, extending my hand after I wipe it on my now-dusty skirt. "Thank you for the help." A nervous smile tugs at my lips.

His handshake is warm and firm and all-encompassing, and it sends an electric jolt through me. "Nick Fletcher," he replies, with the smallest hint of a smirk. "You okay?"

"I'll be fine."

"Good. I don't have time for princesses who throw tantrums because they've ruined their fancy clothes."

Excuse me... where did *that* come from? I did no such thing!

I square my shoulders, refusing to let the sudden rude outburst faze me. "I can assure you, Mr. Fletcher, I'm not about to throw a fit over a silly fall." I shake my head ruefully. "No matter how badly I've sprained my dignity."

I thought that might get at least a little smile out of him, but he only presses his lips together like he's exasperated with me. *With me!*

Jerk.

The tension between us is almost tangible, crackling in the air like static. His gaze drifts down, taking in my outfit. He arches an eyebrow, his eyes lingering on my heels before traveling up my legs.

Heat coils around my insides, despite my irritation.

"You can't waltz around a site dressed like that, Ms. Bridges. Now you know why," he says smugly.

"I *wanted* to make a professional first impression for my new boss," I retort defensively.

He scoffs, crossing his brawny arms. "If you really want to impress me, show me you can navigate a construction site. Those heels are a safety hazard."

I feel a surge of indignation. "I can handle myself just fine," I snap back.

"Yes, as you've so expertly demonstrated." His eyes narrow on me. "Go home. Change into something more appropriate. Then come back."

I stare disbelievingly. "You want me to go home? Right now? You can't be serious."

"If you don't go yourself, I'll have to escort you back to your car. You're a liability on the site dressed like that."

"Why do I get the feeling that by "escort" you mean haul me off, caveman style?"

Nick shrugs his thick shoulders.

Wow. This man is a lunatic. But boss or not, I won't let him intimidate me.

"You wouldn't dare," I retort. To my surprise, my tone is a mix of anger...and maybe a wee bit of curiosity to see if he actually *would*.

Yes, he would.

Before I can fully register what's happening, Nick's scooping me up and slinging me over his shoulder. My eyes widen in shock and my heart races. Not from fear. It's a potent mix of outrage and something else that I feel down in a secret place I really, really shouldn't. It's a dangerous feeling to have for your certifiably insane boss who's just crossed a super inappropriate line.

"Put me down, Mr. Fletcher!" I demand, my voice sharp.

He starts walking, each step purposeful. "I warned you, Ms. Bridges."

Of all the crazy, arrogant, overbearing... More choice words run through my mind.

Reaching my car, Nick finally sets me down, leaning me back against the door. I huff, adjusting my clothes. Our eyes lock, and I swear there's a fleck of amusement dancing there.

"You think this is funny?" I ask, my voice low and intense.

He leans in, his voice a hot whisper against my ear. "Kinda, yeah." He smells like fresh linen and wood shavings. Not anything that typically turns me on, but here I am, fighting the urge to grab hold of his firm shoulders and pull him closer to me.

What? No! Vi!

He finally straightens up and adds in that husky rasp, "Don't provoke me again, Ms. Bridges."

I want to reply with "What if I do?" just to see what would happen, because I have clearly suddenly gone crazy, too. But I don't. That's a great way to get fired on my first day.

With one last glare at him I climb into my car, slamming the door. As I drive off, I can't help but look at him in the rearview mirror. Nick stands there, a giant mountain man in a hard hat and flannel shirt, hands in his jean pockets, watching me leave with an unreadable expression on his face.

My heart is still pounding, my mind in a whirl. I can't believe he just sent me home to get changed. I feel like a schoolgirl being scolded for wearing a skirt an inch too short. Ridiculous.

One thing is clear: Nick Fletcher is a force to be reckoned with. A storm on my horizon. And whether I like it or not, I think I'm about to be swept up in it.

CHAPTER 2
NICK

Fuck. My. Life.

My new city slicker designer speeds off in that tiny Barbie excuse for a car, and I'm left staring after her, wondering what the actual hell just happened.

When she's finally out of sight, I blow out a breath. I rip off my hard hat and run a hand through my sweat-dampened hair.

How did this woman get under my skin so quickly?

I'm not one to get riled up easily. I pride myself on keeping my emotions in check. But damn, if she didn't reach in and pull everything out of me like it was the easiest thing in the world.

She should've known better than to come to a construction site dressed like that. She could have gotten hurt. I would've overlooked it today, if she hadn't been so goddamned sexy with those toned legs and tight ass, and then opened that smart mouth of hers...

I see a lot of overblown egos and entitlement with new designers. There's no room for that BS on my team. I expect everyone to work hard, get along, and follow *my* rules.

No one talks back to me. Ever.

Yet this woman with enough fire in her deep brown eyes to burn down this entire mountain didn't give it a second thought. I've got no time for lust, romance, and all that fantasy shit, especially not on a job site. But one look at her sleek black ponytail had me daydreaming about wrapping it around my palm and pulling until her pretty lips opened just for me.

Hoo boy, Nick, let's not go there.

I'm already having a difficult time keeping my cock in check.

Not only is she *my employee*, she's way too young for this old grump.

Not that I need to worry about that. Judging from the daggers she shot at me as she drove away, I'm sure I've just made the top of her least favorite boss list.

Two hours later, while looking over Violet's renderings, the sound of heavy, purposeful footsteps abruptly draws my attention. Glancing up, I find myself momentarily stunned, lost for words.

Violet's back.

Oh man, is she ever.

Gone are the pencil skirt and heels. Instead, she's wearing black form-fitting pants and steel-toed boots that look ready to kick me right where it would hurt most. And the hard hat perched on her head? Hot pink.

If I found her irresistible before in that ridiculous corporate getup, now she's a goddamned wet dream.

Fuck.

"Well, well," I say, nodding at her new footwear. "Someone's ready for battle."

She smirks, taking a few more steps toward me. "These old things? I thought they'd come in handy in case you tried to manhandle me like that again."

I nod, the tension from our earlier encounter simmering just below the surface. I really had taken it too far. "Won't happen again, Ms. Bridges."

She exhales, and her shoulders drop slightly. I'm glad. I never meant to put her on edge.

"Please, just call me Violet," she says.

"Only if you call me Nick."

"Deal, Nick," she says, the hint of a smile on those pretty lips.

More footsteps approach us.

"Can this be...Ms. Violet Bridges?" Hector Rivera, the architect on the project, walks up with our forewoman, Tasha Williams.

"It sure can," Violet says, smiling Hector's way.

He clasps her hand, sandwiching it between his. "Ah, *Dios!* Beautiful *and* talented. A great pleasure to meet you." He's a few years older than me, with more gray on his temples, and he's got that suavely confident Latino thing going on that's suddenly supremely annoying to me as his eyes rove over Violet.

"Such a flirt," Tasha sighs, shaking her head slightly. "Hi, Violet. I'm Tasha." She offers her hand and Violet shakes it. "Love the hat. I wish I could get a different color, but the big boss here likes white for the supervisors." Tasha grins my way, and I cross my arms, glaring.

"Oh. Is this against your dress code, too?" Violet asks, casually pointing to her hat. There's a spark in her eyes that instantly makes my cock stiff again.

"Ms. Bridges," I warn, "as long as you're wearing a hard hat, that's good enough for me. I just want you safe."

Hector and Tasha stay quiet.

"Anyway, I'm glad you're all here," I say, moving on, "because I have some concerns."

"What kind of concerns?" Violet asks, as I swipe her renderings off the makeshift worktable and lead us all into what will be the main living space. Currently, it's just concrete underflooring and some wood framing, but it's easy to see how open and spacious it will be. I point to the area before me.

"Concerns over your vision for the sweeping staircase'," I begin, unable to stop the sarcasm seeping into my tone. "Things like this may look magnificent on paper. But they're an accident waiting to happen, especially in a family home."

She huffs. "It's about creating a statement, giving the home a unique touch. The engineering can be worked out to ensure safety."

Holding back an eye roll…just barely…I counter, "But it's not just about the aesthetics. It needs to be functional and solid, too."

Violet's nostrils flare, and she chews on the inside of her cheek. The fire is back in her eyes, growing in intensity. As much as it irks me to admit it, that fire is doing something to me, drawing me in, making me crave its burn.

She steps closer, challenging me. "Every choice I make is based on a combination of aesthetics and functionality. The staircase is the centerpiece of this home. It's meant to leave an impression."

"An impression is fine, but not when it compromises safety," I fire back, frustrated with her unwillingness to see reason.

She tilts her head, her lips pressed into a thin line. "The engineering team has assured me it's more than just possible— it's innovative."

I growl, feeling a vein in my temple throb. "You're not hearing me. It's not about whether it *can* be done. It's about whether it *should* be done. There are ways to make a statement without introducing, frankly, a potential hazard."

Her cheeks flush, a slight uncertainty coming into her eyes before she squares her shoulders. "I might be new to a project of this scale, but I've done my research and consulted with experts. They believe in this design."

"Can you back me up here, Hector?" I ask, turning to him. Honestly, I'd damn near forgotten he and Tasha were still here. Violet has taken all my focus and sent the blood rushing to my groin.

"Hold on a sec, please, Hector," Violet says, flaring her fingers in Hector's direction as he opens his mouth to speak. Her eyes lock on mine with a fierce determination. "I've poured my heart into this design. It's innovative, fresh, and yes, it might challenge norms. But isn't that what progress is all about? Pushing boundaries?"

I let out a scoff. "Pushing boundaries is one thing. Risking the integrity of the entire structure is another entirely. Real-world experience trumps fresh-out-of-college ideals every time."

She takes a deep breath, clearly working very hard to keep her temper in check. "My designs might be unique; that doesn't make them impractical. You just don't want to try something that goes against your old-school methods."

"Is that meant to be a jab at my age?" I chuckle, feeling the heat of irritation rise. "There's a reason certain methods are tried and true. They work. And it's my responsibility to ensure the final structure is safe."

"And it's *my* responsibility to ensure it's memorable," she retorts. "The Donovans hired me for my *vision*," she says, mimicking my mocking tone from earlier, "and I intend to see it through."

"Okay, okay, both of you. Let's just step back for a

moment," Hector interjects, as the rubber band of tension between me and Violet stretches to its limit. "I see the merit in both of your arguments. Maybe we can come to a compromise, yes? How about if we adjust the staircase to hug the wall around the outside, loosening the spiral and leveling it out more? That way it still maintains the integrity of the sweeping, luxurious design, but also satisfies the family's safety needs."

"I really think Nick is being overly cautious," Violet says, crossing her arms.

"And *I* really think Violet is being a stubborn—"

"Oh my god, you two, just *stop*," Tasha snaps before I finish my thought. She turns to Violet. "Violet, Nick is being extra cautious because he goes way back with the Donovans. They're family friends. He needs to be sure the house he builds for them is safe. And, well…perfect."

Violet glances at me, surprise on her face.

Then Tasha turns to me. "And Nick, you need to let my girl Violet here do what she does best: design. You know Mrs. Donovan will have your hide if she hears that you're shutting down her best ideas."

I narrow my eyes at Tasha. *Traitor.*

"Don't glare at me like that, Nick. I can make this project a living hell for you if you don't play nice." She whips her braids around and gives me a wink.

I reluctantly give in, because I know she's right. She's the best forewoman I've ever had, and she only took on this job as a favor to me.

"We should listen to Tasha and Hector, Violet."

Violet nods. "I'm fine with that."

I don't know what it is about Violet, but I just can't help but be provoked by the woman. Maybe it's that in all my years in this industry, no one has ever challenged me this directly before. Regardless, her stubbornness is poking at my ego, igniting a competitive streak I didn't know I had.

"How about we make a little game of it," I propose, stroking my chin. "Prove to Hector, Tasha, and me that your designs can stand up to the practical challenges on this job, and I'll personally handle any extra work they entail."

She tilts her head, clearly intrigued despite herself. "Okay," she retorts, arching her brow. "But you also need to come up with suggestions that don't strip the soul out of my ideas."

Hector and Tasha chuckle. "*Buena suerte*," Hector mumbles.

A smirk spreads across my face. The gauntlet has been thrown down. I can see the resolve in her eyes mirroring the steely determination in mine. And damn, that only turns me on even more.

"Deal," I say, extending a hand.

She hesitates.

"Oh—right. And no manhandling," I add, remembering what she'd said earlier.

She purses her lips and takes my hand, her grip firm, her skin soft. A rush of electricity zooms up my arm.

Tasha and Hector take Violet to show her around the site and introduce her to the rest of the crew while I get to work on my other tasks for the day. I'm struck by how this job has suddenly taken on a whole new dimension and become a battleground of sorts.

Word of our little competition spreads like wildfire, and I overhear snippets of conversation from the crew, some of them placing bets on who'll win.

I can't ignore the excitement bubbling up inside me. This job isn't just about erecting walls and putting up beams anymore; it's about proving a point, pitting my years of experience against youthful vigor.

As the day rolls on, amidst the clatter of hammers and the

hum of machinery, I catch a glimpse of Violet. She's deep in conversation with one of the workers, pointing out something on the blueprint. They both laugh at something, her laughter ringing out clear and bright. And in that moment, I know it isn't just the competition that's causing the strange sensation in my chest...and lower.

Violet Bridges has wormed her way even deeper inside me, and I'm starting to suspect that our rivalry is just the tip of the iceberg.

CHAPTER 3
VIOLET

F inally—home!

I tiredly push open the door to my rented cabin, the weight of the day settling over my entire body. The wooden floor panels creak under my boots as I step inside, tossing my bag onto the nearest chair. The room is dim, the setting sun casting a soft glow through the sheer curtains. This quiet solitude should feel comforting after a long, hard day, but all I can think about is the site, the crew...and, most of all, Nick.

Exhausted, I sit to unlace these heavy-as-fuck boots, my feet singing in relief as I kick them off. I'd driven straight to the mall in nearby Missoula after Nick chased me off the site and bought the most badass boots I could find, together with some seriously tight leggings. The pink hard hat was the perfect icing on the cake. I think the outfit achieved its purpose and let Nick know that how he had treated me was unacceptable.

And yet...I keep thinking about how easily he threw me over his shoulder, his big, rough hands on my bare thighs holding me in place.

God, that was hot.

Shit, why am I feeling like this?

I groan and reach for a bottle of wine from the counter, pouring myself a generous glass.

As I sink into the plush couch, my thoughts spiral back to the day's events. From our very first interaction, Nick had managed to push every single one of my buttons—incredibly bad and incredibly hot buttons, leaving me swimming in a sea of contradictory emotions.

Why did he have to question everything I did? Why couldn't he just go with my design, trusting that I saw the rationale behind every line and curve? Way to drive me crazy.

And underneath the frustration and the heated disagreements, there's an undeniable charge, a tension that refuses to be ignored. It goes beyond professional rivalry; it's personal, raw, and completely unexpected.

I take a long sip of my wine, trying to drown out these aching, overwhelming feelings. It doesn't work. Every time I close my eyes, I see him—those piercing eyes, that rough voice lecturing me on his vast years of experience. The way he challenges me, making me defend my decisions. It's maddening.

It's also exhilarating.

I roll my eyes at my own thoughts. *What are you doing, Vi?* He's my boss, for god's sake! And I'm already clearly testing the edge of his patience after today. I'm not here for that. I'm here to make a mark, to prove to everyone, especially to Nick, that I belong in this world.

I know he's trying to rattle me. Hell, he probably gets his jollies from crushing new designers.

Well, I won't let him crush me.

I run a bath after eating a quick dinner of instant noodles and make a note to go grocery shopping soon for proper food. Sliding down into the steamy water, I let the lavender bubbles soothe my body and mind. It only works for so long, though.

Leaning my head back, I close my eyes and almost drift off, picturing Nick swinging his big hammer over his head to demolish the fireplace I'd designed with such care for the home. I'm livid and striding over to him, but when I reach him, he grabs me and pins me against the wall, his thick palm at my throat. Flecks of amber, emerald, and sapphire flash in his eyes. I tremble, but not from fear.

"Don't tempt me, Vi," he growls in my ear, and I shiver.

My hand slides into the water and over my wet skin to my pussy, already aching and swollen.

Nick fits his hardness against me. "Is this what you want?"

I gasp, both in the fantasy and in real life, because as I rub my clit, I swear I can feel the friction from his cock.

"Yes," I whisper, as he uses his other hand to undo his belt and jeans and pull out his massive length.

"Louder. I want to hear you really say it." He yanks down my pants and my panties and spins me around, bending me over so I can grab onto what's left of the mantle on the crumbled fireplace. Why do I feel like I'm being punished? This is exactly what I want.

"Take me, Nick!" I moan, backing my ass into him.

"Fuck, Vi," he groans, his cock slowly pushing into my entrance. "You're soaking wet. And so tight."

"God," I moan, as he stretches me to the limit, fills me. I'm already so close.

He thrusts harder and faster. So deep. So good. So…

Holy—my climax tears through my body, and I'm soaring and trembling in the water.

I let the tremors subside, and catch my breath.

Wow.

I down the last of my wine and get out of the tub.

Time to rest and recharge, so I can weather the storm that is my boss the best I can.

Weeks pass, and the lodge is coming along nicely. We've completed the structural framing and are now working on the roof, main windows, and doors.

Our entire crew has fallen into a simple, generally predictable rhythm. Of course, every day with Nick is a test of wills, but somehow we manage to keep moving forward on the project and make it work, despite my inner turmoil and, frankly, my constant sexual frustration.

Tasha has become a good friend, but I don't dare tell her how I feel about Nick. I can't risk the humiliation.

The sun is barely peeking over the horizon as I arrive at the construction site today and there's a satisfying quietness everywhere, the stillness of a world not yet woken up. I glance around, checking that I'm indeed the first one here. Sure enough, the site is deserted, and I park around the side of a large pile of excavated dirt, making sure to keep my car well out of sight.

Because one way Nick and I keep from strangling one another…is with pranks.

What? It allows us to blow off steam harmlessly when things get too intense and too ugly in our arguments.

A mischievous grin stretches across my face as I pull the toy rubber snake from my bag. Last night, after a particularly exhausting day fueled by yet another argument with Nick over an archway in the foyer, I stopped at the general store and happened to find this gem. It's beyond silly, but the idea of seeing the stoic mountain of a man, Nick Fletcher himself, jump even a little bit was too tempting to resist.

I approach Nick's usual spot—the workbench laden with blueprints and papers (and hidden candy wrappers that he thinks nobody sees)—and carefully position the toy snake, ensuring it looks as real as possible. Standing back to admire my handiwork, I stifle a chuckle. I can already picture the scene.

Then I place a fresh cup of coffee on the edge of the desk as a peace offering later with a small sticky note attached: *Gotcha – Vi*

Satisfied, my heart thuds in excitement. The feeling grows as I hear the familiar rumble of Nick's truck approaching. I hide behind a pillar and watch as he steps out, looking as rugged as ever in his jeans and flannel, a couple of buttons undone, showing off his built chest. He approaches the desk and reaches for his pile of papers.

The moment he lifts the corner, he jumps back. "What the actual fuck?" he exclaims, his face briefly a picture of surprise before he relaxes. For a second, I worry he might actually be mad, but then I see the tiniest twitch of a smile. He goes for the coffee and reads the note as he picks it up.

Shaking my head, I emerge from my hiding place, trying to feign innocence but failing miserably. "Morning, Nick. Thought you might need a coffee after your wild reptile encounter."

His gaze travels over me, making me flush. He arches an eyebrow, the corners of his lips pulling up. "Trying to give me a heart attack so you can get a new boss?"

"Just ensuring you're wide awake and alert," I shoot back with a smirk, taking a sip from my own cup.

He lifts the coffee and gives me a wink. "Yep, I'm awake now." He takes a swig and groans, the sound making my lower belly tighten. "Caramel. You remembered."

I smile behind my cup. Of course I remembered! Any chance I can get to hear him make that husky groan of pleasure, I'm going to take it. Because I know that we'll be back at each other's throats soon enough.

We're enjoying a comfortable silence when I hear the crunch of tires over gravel. We turn and look out into the wide expanse of the driveway. Weird. The crew should be trickling in shortly, but I don't remember any of them having a Mercedes SUV.

"Good thing we're caffeinated," Nick remarks. "The Donovans just arrived."

CHAPTER 4
NICK

Violet immediately puts down her coffee to smooth her hands over clothes, adjust her hard hat, and fish out some lip gloss from her pocket. She runs the tube over her pretty mouth, and I'm instantly ridiculously jealous of that applicator.

"How do I look?" she asks, rolling her shoulders.

"Perfect," I say, without my trademark sarcasm for once, and she furrows her brow.

Oh, shit—

"You have whipped cream on your lip," she replies, ignoring my compliment.

I wipe my mouth with the back of my hand. "Better?"

She looks up and shakes her head, then reaches out and strokes her finger over my top lip to wipe the last of the cream away. I fight back a groan and blink rapidly as she stares at my mouth for what seems like forever. She's so close—her sweet lilac scent accosting my senses. My jeans get tight. Crap.

It finally seems to register in her eyes what she's doing to me. "Oh, god. I'm so sorry. I didn't mean—"

"It's okay. You did get all the whipped cream off, right?" I say, willing my erection to go down before we meet up with the Donovans. Talk about awkward.

She nods, and I lead us out to Mr. Donovan, the picture of debonair affluence with his styled hair and suit. He opens the car door for his wife: she's a tiny wisp of a lady, but she's also the epitome of elegance and poise. The atmosphere, up till now thick with the tension between Violet and me, takes on a different vibe with their arrival—warmth, yes, but also subtle apprehension.

Mr. Donovan isn't just any client. He's practically family, an old college buddy of my dad's. Over the years, our families have celebrated many occasions together, so there's a level of comfort with him around, but also a weight of expectation. I've grown up listening to stories of their youthful adventures, their practical jokes, their future dreams. And now, here I am, building one of those dreams.

He approaches with his familiar broad smile.

"Nick!" he says, wrapping me in a hug and patting my back. "So good to see you."

"Great to see you, too, Mr. Donovan," I reply. "Mrs. Donovan." I kiss her cheek. "May I introduce you both to Violet Bridges?"

"Well, of course," Mr. Donovan takes her hand and shakes it. "Good to meet you, Violet. My wife's a big fan of your work."

"Your wife is very kind," Violet says, throwing her a smile.

"How are you liking it here in Deepwood Mountain, dear?" Mrs. Donovan asks.

"It's beautiful. Truly stunning. Such a pleasant change from L.A."

"I'll say!" Mr. Donovan chimes in. "Less traffic, cleaner air, beautiful seasons. What more could you ask for?"

We all chuckle and nod in agreement.

"Violet's really taken to the project and gets along incredibly well with the crew," I add, and glance over at her. Her cheeks go as pink as her hard hat and it's goddamned adorable.

"Really?" Mr. Donovan peers at us suspiciously. "I've heard there's quite a bit of verbal sparring on the site. Even some wagers?"

"It's all in good fun, Mr. Donovan, I can assure you," Violet says, but I can see her paling.

"Violet and I like to keep each other on our toes. And I think the wagers increase morale. We want everyone involved invested in this very special project."

Mr. Donovan chuckles. "Well, you've convinced me. Now, how about a tour?"

As we take them around the space, Violet explains her plans for each area.

They both nod along with her. "You always come up with the most intriguing ideas, Violet," he praises her. But then with a deep sigh, Mr. Donovan turns to me, probably seeking the pragmatic perspective he's come to expect from me. "How do these ideas translate into reality?"

I hesitate for a moment, wanting to choose my words carefully. "Challenging," I admit, hyper aware of Violet's eyes on me. "Especially given the timeline and materials. The designs are captivating, but safety and stability are of course crucial."

Mrs. Donovan, till now quietly observing, steps in, her eyes sparkling with excitement. "But it's all so beautiful! It's why I wanted Violet and nobody else to design the house! Can't you see our grandkids here, running up and down the stairs, and enjoying the holidays here with all the family?"

I want to point out the risks but bite my tongue. This is their dream, after all.

Mr. Donovan places an arm around his wife. "We've

always admired your work, Nick. And we're thrilled with Violet's vision. But both of you"…he motions between us, emphasizing his point…"need to collaborate. This house is our legacy. I want it to be as beautiful as it is safe."

Violet, ever the professional, nods. "Of course, Mr. Donovan. Dazzling and durable. We'll make it happen."

There's a pause. The weight of Mr. Donovan's words, layered over the history we share, adds gravity to the situation. As the couple drifts away, discussing other aspects of the project, Violet and I square off. Her look is defiant, mine equally determined.

Neither of us is backing down.

Oh, boy. This should be fun.

The atmosphere at the construction site has shifted once again since the Donovans' visit two weeks ago. The stakes were already high, but now the rivalry between Violet and me is reaching a new crescendo. Everyone is focused on impressing the Donovans. Every design decision, every piece of material used, every nail hammered into place…it's all tinged with the spirit of competition.

Seeing Violet engrossed in her sketches, adding creative flourishes to the practical suggestions I'd given, I shake my head in amusement.

"Always trying to one up me," I mumble, sticking a pencil behind my ear.

She looks up. "It's really not that hard," she says mildly.

The crew laughs.

"Zing! It's about time someone other than me stood up to you," Tasha says, slinging her tool belt over her shoulder.

Violet laughs, still huddling over the blueprints. Her ass

looks like a perfect peach I could take a bite out of right now. My groin tightens.

The day's energy crackles with mischievous intent. The playful back and forth between Violet and me has escalated into strategic acts of sabotage. It's not about getting ahead now, but about pushing each other's buttons, and in a weird way, connecting through these minor battles.

Her most recent design is a big talking point—a gargantuan fireplace with a luxurious, ultramodern flair that is uniquely Violet. The crew gathers around, murmuring words of admiration. I feel a twinge of jealousy at her instant success.

Never one to be left behind, I undertake a covert operation of my own, slightly moving construction materials here and strategically placing a few boards there, until her prized mock-up is hidden behind a makeshift wall. It's subtle, and it's devious. It also works.

"Nick Fletcher!" she calls out from across the site in mock annoyance.

I look up innocently. "You're using my full name now?"

She places her hands on her hips, trying her best to look stern. "Where is it?"

"Where is what?"

"My fireplace mock-up!"

I shrug. "Must've gotten lost in the shuffle," I reply, suppressing a smirk.

She huffs and narrows her eyes at me before stomping off to find it.

At lunch, I grab my sandwich and boombox. It's so old that it has a cassette player as well as a radio, but it still works. I keep it for sentimental reasons; I bought it for my first job in construction years ago. All the stations are programmed to my favorite music, but when I turn it on, the sound of piano, violins, and cellos fill the air. Huh? This should be classic rock.

I flip to the next preset, which should be metal. More classical. And the next, instead of old country, is classical again.

Everything is goddamned Beethoven!

I glance up, catching Violet's eyes dancing with triumph.

"Thought you might like to hear the music of your youth," she quips, sauntering by.

"Funny. You'll be staying late to reprogram it all back," I retort, though the chuckle in my voice gives away my amusement.

As she breezes past me, her delicious feminine scent fills my nostrils. It's flowery and soft, such a contrast to the dust and grime of a construction site. The fragrance lingers, taking its own sweet time to dissipate, just like my thoughts about her.

And as the weeks stretch into months, I'm left wondering how I'm ever going to live without this woman once the project is complete.

CHAPTER 5
VIOLET

The end of summer has brought with it a noticeable change in the weather. The temperature has dropped and the air feels crisper, fresher. A golden hue bathes the construction site as Nick and I find ourselves embroiled in our last clash for the day: the kitchen countertops.

Around us, the crew—be it out of genuine interest or just for the thrill of the show—has gathered around, tools down, to watch the spectacle unfold.

"Quartz will last longer, and it's much easier to maintain," Nick argues vehemently, pointing at my draft, which calls for marble. "We want this kitchen to stand the test of time without being a headache for the Donovans."

I raise an eyebrow, leveling a withering gaze at him. "You can still find marble structures in Italy from ancient Rome. I'd say that's standing the test of time." I shake my head. "It not only provides classic, timeless design but also durability. Plus, its unique natural patterns will add character."

"You and your 'character'," he quips, a bit sarcastically. But I swear his eyes are twinkling.

"You say that like it's a bad thing," I say with a smirk.

We square off, neither willing to give ground. The crew chuckles, whispers, and place side bets on the outcome. I shudder to think how much money has been won and lost over these last few months because of Nick and me.

"Okay, okay, that's quitting time," Tasha calls out, bursting through the crowd of workers. "These two can continue hashing it out in the morning."

The crew grumbles in response but starts packing up, throwing in a few playful jibes our way. "Better decide or we'll just have to build two kitchens!" one of them shouts, eliciting a few laughs.

The bustling site quiets down, and before I know it, it's just me, Tasha, and Nick surrounded by a house that's taking shape before our eyes. It's exciting to think of what it'll look like when it's finally complete, and that I had a major part in it. I'll never tire of this feeling.

When Tasha returns from turning off all the lights and securing the site, I fall into step next to her. "You up for the Rustic Ridge tonight?" I ask. "I'm out of wine at home, and I could use a drink." I massage my shoulder, the tension of the day getting to me.

"Sorry, hon, I'm on Aunt Duty tonight," she says, gathering up her things. "My sister and her husband are celebrating their anniversary with a nice dinner in Missoula and I told them I'd babysit."

I nudge her shoulder. "Aww, you're such a sweet sister."

"I try," she says, grinning. "But hey, I'm sure Nick will go get that drink with you," she continues, much too innocently, and my stomach drops.

What is she doing?

Nick looks my way from where he's packing up. "Hell, if we can't decide on marble or quartz here, maybe we can at the bar." He takes off his tool belt and drapes it over his shoulder, then gives me a lopsided smile.

Oh god... I swallow. "Is that your way of saying you need some liquid courage to deal with my ideas?"

He snorts. "As if. But who knows? A drink or two might help us see eye to eye."

"*Or* it might help you realize I'm right." Good god, this can't in any way be a good idea. But I can't seem to resist his stupidly handsome face, or the possibility that I might actually change his mind on the freaking kitchen counters. "All right, let's go. But, fair warning: I can hold my liquor."

He smirks, falling into step beside me as we head to our respective vehicles. "We'll see about that. Last one to get tipsy wins?"

"You're on," I reply with a laugh. Yet another bet on the books. I really should start writing these down.

"Goodnight, guys!" Tasha calls to us, waving, as she drives away.

I remind myself to keep my wits about me tonight on the drive over. This is unfamiliar territory for Nick and me. Over the course of the project, I've been out with Tasha and Hector and their friends, but never with Nick. And certainly never alone.

I've worked very hard to keep Nick firmly in the professional realm, and out of the personal one. My mind and my body might constantly protest that. Hey, I'm only human. And the man is smoking hot.

But Nick and I together? At the bar? Drinking?

I didn't lie when I said I can hold my liquor. But there's still a tendency to...let my guard down...after a few.

You got this, Vi.

The homey ambiance of Rustic Ridge immediately

surrounds us as we step inside. Dim lights, wooden interiors, and the subtle scent of hops all set a cozy tone. I've come to like this bar, with its simple, down-home vibe that's a million miles from LA. I mean, yeah, I have some ideas if they ever want to add some additional style elements. But it's pleasing enough.

Nick leads the way to a booth in the back, waving to a couple of other patrons in cowboy hats that I don't recognize. The older bartender says hello to me and I mouth one back.

Before we can get settled in, a voice is interrupting us. "Where have you been hiding this one, Nick?"

I turn to find a tall, built man, strikingly similar to Nick but with a more roguish charm. His eyes sparkle with mischief as they size me up.

"Violet, meet Rex, my younger and clearly more annoying brother," Nick grunts, his tone less than warm. "I'm actually surprised he hasn't sniffed you out yet."

Rex winks and slaps his brother on the back, harder than necessary, before extending a hand. "Pleasure to meet ya, Violet. Did my big bro rope you into one of his boring construction projects?"

"Oh, I came willingly. Your brother's a legend in his field and I feel lucky to be involved in the project," I reply, honestly.

Rex leans in closer, but glances at Nick. "Whoa. You sure have her trained well."

"*Excuse me*?" I'm not afraid to use these boots.

"Never mind," he mumbles, then clears his throat, seeing that both me and Nick are glaring at him. "Well, if you ever tire of him, you know where to find a more entertaining Fletcher brother."

Nick's face tightens. "That's enough, Rex. Scurry along back to your little friends," he says, his voice tinged with frustration.

Rex laughs. "Always so protective. Fine, fine. Nice meeting

you." He throws another wink in my direction before ambling off.

Nick exhales deeply. "Sorry about him. He's...relentless."

I chuckle. "It's okay. I've survived much, much worse."

"I'm sure you have. You *are* amazing," he says. We sit, and I try not to blush. "You have brothers, then?"

I shake my head. "Nope, no sisters either. It's just me. But I have a lot of male cousins. They constantly tormented me growing up with wrestling matches and noogies," I laugh.

He nods, and we order some drinks, wine for me and beer for him. The conversation quickly shifts back to the kitchen design. We debate the counters, but it's less intense than before, mellowed out by the casual environment and the drinks in our glasses. We slowly reach a middle ground, and I feel a real sense of accomplishment there.

After that, the conversation veers away from the current job. Nick talks about a restoration project from a few years back. I watch as his gruff exterior softens. His hands move animatedly, and his eyes dance with a fervor I've rarely seen at work. The way he speaks about restoring and preserving the soul of a building makes me smile. There's so much passion and depth there. *This* is the Nick Fletcher I idolized from my studies in design school.

Feeling bold, I dramatically recount my first big interior design job right out of college, exaggerating my panic, the adrenaline rush, and the thrill of it all. I imitate the client's nasally voice, and he lets out a hearty laugh.

"You should've seen me, Nick. My god. I was such a mess, but it was all worth it when they ended up loving what I had done."

"I can imagine," he says with a smile, as the bartender brings us another round.

The more we talk, the more the walls between us begin to

crumble. Our laughter becomes part of the soundtrack to the evening, blending seamlessly with the hum of conversation, the twang of the background music, and the clinking of glasses around us.

In this space, our rivalry is forgotten. The blanket of competition, which can sometimes be suffocating, is temporarily lifted, affording me a brief, beautiful glimpse into a world of what could be.

The conversation falls into a comfortable lull. Taking a sip from my glass, I gesture around the bar, and then toward the window, which reveals a bit of the picturesque scenery. "This place...Deepwood Mountain... You seem very rooted here. Why do you love it so much?"

Nick leans back, his green-blue eyes growing thoughtful but warm. "It's home. Always has been. I've been all over the world on various contracting jobs, and I love exploring new places. But there's a connection to the land here, the trees, the people. Everything's genuine."

"And your house? You built it here, right?"

He nods, a proud smile playing over his lips. "Yeah—with the help of my five best friends. Each of them brought their own talent to the project. I'm telling you, my house is more than just a structure. It's memories, sweat, and believe it or not, a lot of laughter. Every beam, every nail has a story."

I smile, picturing Nick and his buddies building a home together. It's a beautiful image, and it makes me respect him even more.

"You seem content to be retired. Why take on this project?" I'd read that Nick and his best friends are all millionaires now, some of the most successful men to come out of Deepwood Mountain. None of them needs to work anymore, if they don't want to.

Nick looks into his drink for a moment. "I *don't* usually

take on anything new. But for the Donovans, I made an exception. My dad passed away about five years ago and my mom moved out west, fed up with the harsh winters. I go out to see her every so often, but the Donovans are my Deepwood family now."

"That's so sweet," I say, fiddling with the coaster underneath my glass, nervous again, because all this talk is not doing anything to snuff out my feelings for the man. "And then I come along and wreak havoc on what should've been a passion project for you. Up to and including the kitchen counters."

"Oh, I wouldn't go that far," he says, ducking his head slightly. "But truthfully? I was against hiring a designer that was new to me. I thought you'd be a high maintenance drama queen, coming here with an ego the size of that mountain out there."

I raise an eyebrow, not sure if I should be more amused or offended. "It all makes sense now. The initial judgment, the rage…"

He laughs awkwardly, looking into his beer. "Yeah, I'll admit, that wasn't my finest moment. But Mrs. Donovan insisted after she saw your portfolio. She fell in love with your style, and wanted to take a chance on you…and I'm glad she did." He glances at me, his eyes sincere. "You've certainly proved me wrong in many ways." He squints at me. "*Mostly*."

Blushing, I reply, "Well, I *do* have an ego, but it's probably just the size of a small hill."

He laughs, a deep, genuine sound.

Nick signals the bartender for the bill and pays despite my protests. "Come on," he says, "I'll drive you back to your cabin."

I start to object. "Nick, I can manage. It's just a couple of—"

But even as I stand up, the world tilts, and I realize perhaps

I am a little drunker than I thought. We were so busy chatting we didn't eat anything.

"You okay there?" Nick asks, his hand steadying my arm. His palm is so warm, and I desperately want to lean into him.

"You win," I huff. "I'm officially tipsy."

His eyebrows jump. "Sweet victory," he whispers to the ceiling. "But now I'm definitely driving you home."

I nod. As we make our way to the exit, I stumble over an uneven wooden step and pitch forward, but before I know it, powerful arms are encircling me, stopping my descent.

"Gotcha," Nick murmurs, holding me against him. I shamelessly enjoy the way his big, brawny body fits with mine. *Oh lord…*

When I try to take a step, pain shoots up my ankle. "Ow. I think I twisted my ankle," I yelp, clinging to his thick bicep.

"In that case, I have to manhandle you again. Sorry," Nick says, before gently placing one hand under my knee and another behind my back, lifting me with ease.

I just nod, because honestly, I don't mind one bit.

"We'll get you home and that ankle iced," he says with a determined look.

As we head toward his truck, me cradled in his arms, the line between rivalry and something else blurs even more. I inhale his woodsy musk and sigh.

Screw it. I'm going to let myself enjoy this, if only for a minute or two.

After the short drive, the warmth of my cabin welcomes us as Nick pushes the door open. The dim ambient lighting casts a soft glow over the living area. With the utmost care, he carries me past the rustic furniture and toward the bedroom.

He sets me on the bed and removes my boots. "Yeah, it's a little swollen," he says, after stripping my socks and tenderly feeling around the injured ankle. His touch is causing all sorts of chaos, but no pain. "I'll get you a bag of ice in a minute, but first I'll grab you some pajamas."

"Top drawer. No snooping," I say, with a grin.

He chuckles. "Promise." He quickly retrieves a nightshirt and some shorts for me. As he hands them over, his fingers brush against mine, sending a shivering tingle up my arm.

Watch it, Vi.

"I'll give you some privacy." He nods toward the bathroom.

"Thanks," I murmur, grateful for a moment to compose myself as I hobble on my good foot. Despite the slight ache in my ankle, there's an electric buzz in the air, a sense of anticipation. And I need to quash that. Pronto.

When I re-emerge, Nick is adjusting the pillows on the bed. Our eyes lock, and there's a flicker of something—recognition? Understanding? Blinding sexual heat? I let out a shaky breath.

He helps me settle in, propping my foot up on a soft cushion and placing the ice around my ankle. The sudden burst of cold helps momentarily quell the fire blazing in my core.

"You should see a doctor tomorrow," he advises, genuine concern in his eyes.

"I will," I promise. "Just to make sure it's nothing serious."

"I can take you," he suggests immediately.

I shake my head. "You need to be onsite. We can't get behind schedule."

Nick runs a hand through his hair, looking conflicted. "Are you sure?"

"Yes. We've both got jobs to do."

There's a pause, a moment that stretches out seemingly forever, filled with unsaid words and emotions. At least on my end. He's so close and so hot and he makes me so dizzy with want to touch him. Everywhere. I'm about to reach for his hand when he stands up.

"I'll have one of the crew drive your car back first thing in the morning. I'd do it, but I don't think I'd fit in that thing."

I laugh despite my sudden disappointment at him leaving, imagining Nick trying to stuff his massive body into little Minnie. "Yeah, probably not. Thank you."

He's about to leave when it just tumbles out. "You know, Nick, when we first met, I thought you were an arrogant, pig-headed asshole."

He looks taken aback, but amused. "To be fair, you were probably right."

I bite my lip. "Actually…I think I might've been slightly off in my initial assessment."

He grins, leaning against the door frame, looking more relaxed than I've ever seen him before. "Oh?"

"Maybe. The jury is still out. Maybe 80% jerk, 20% decent human being," I tease.

He chuckles, "I'll take that as progress. By the time we finish the project, maybe I can get those numbers reversed."

"It's always good to dream big," I wink.

As he turns, I stop him again. "Wait."

He looks back at me expectantly.

"Let's go with quartz. As long as you choose one that will mimic the marble in my design."

His grin is blinding. "You got it, Vi," he says, throwing a playful salute my way. It's the first time he's called me Vi, and it makes my heart flutter. "Rest up and take care."

I smile, settling deeper into the pillows. "Goodnight, Nick."

CHAPTER 6
NICK

"Cannonball!" I hear someone yell, before a loud exuberant splash follows, along with laughter and cheers. I step through the ornate wrought-iron gate and into the lush outdoor entertaining space belonging to Brock Donovan, the Donovans' eldest son.

The house itself is a masterpiece, but the yard is truly spectacular. The enormous pool dazzles in the afternoon sun, sending flashes of light bouncing around the trees and colorful patio furniture. Guests are everywhere—swimming, lounging in the sun, chatting together at various tables. There's even a small group playing cornhole on the lawn. Food, fun, and tropical drinks garnished with chunks of fruit—definitely my kind of relaxation, the kind you need after months and months of hard work.

The weather is still unseasonably warm, which is why we're able to have a pool party just days before Halloween. I'm already feeling the heat, so find an empty lounge chair and pull off my T-shirt. I scan the crowd eagerly for the only person who's ever on my mind these days.

Vi.

It's been a few weeks since I took her back to her cabin when she hurt her ankle. I'd wanted to stay so badly that night. Wanted to kiss her, and tell her how crazy she made me, how I couldn't stand thinking about not having her next to me day in and day out.

But I chickened out. I told myself she'd been drinking, and it wasn't right to take advantage, but mostly I worried she'd be afraid of the intensity of my feelings—the ones I never used to have before she came into my life, and that I'm now having a bitch of time hiding.

"Hey, boss man," Tasha says from behind me, startling me out of my thoughts. "Looking pretty jacked there."

I turn, and she pulls down her sunglasses and whistles at me.

I wave my hand dismissively, but inside I'm glad I did the quick set of push-ups just before I left to come here.

Hector walks up in neon swim trunks and a Hawaiian shirt. "You ready to relax, Nick? I know I am. Can't believe we're only about a month away from completion."

Shaking my head, I grab a tall glass of something frothy from a woman walking by with a tray, thanking her.

"Me neither," I answer, turning back to him. "Very cool of Mr. Donovan to throw this party to celebrate."

They both nod, Tasha swaying to the soft rock music filtering through the yard.

I take a sip of my drink. Pineapple and rum. "Wow. Delicious. I could probably drink ten of these."

Tasha counts on her fingers. "I think I've already had… three. Which means I'm gonna need some food. You guys want to come with?"

"I will," Hector says. "I saw *elote!*"

"I'm going to lounge for a minute and let this drink sink

in," I say, then ask as innocently as I can, "Has Violet shown up yet?"

Hector and Tasha exchange a look.

"Oh, she's here," Tasha grins. "Just follow the trail of drooling men."

What?

Hector and Tasha just laugh as they walk away.

What the hell did they mean by that? I scan the crowd, slower this time.

Finally, I notice a throng of men, young and old, their attention all focused on something. A couple of them move aside to let Violet through.

A rumbling growl catches in my throat.

Her sexy tanned skin is on mouth-watering display in the tiniest of black string bikinis. A sheer hot pink sarong is knotted around her waist, emphasizing her curvaceous, heart-shaped ass. Black stilettos showcase her toned legs. And her dark hair is pulled up into that sleek ponytail that haunts my dreams every night.

Lawd have mercy…

My heart pounds like I've just run a marathon, and I'm suddenly sweating all over.

To say she's the center of attention is an understatement. Whispers, stares, and raised sunglasses follow her everywhere. Admirers, both from our crew and Mr. Donovan's family and friends, flock around her.

A simmering anger bubbles up within me as the men gawk at her. I completely understand the ogling. Shit, I'm having a hard time keeping my eyes off her, too. But something's poking me in the chest.

I'm definitely jealous, seeing other men flirt with her so openly. But it's more than just that. It's…I blink…possessiveness.

I want her. And I don't want anyone else to have her. Because she's mine.

The thoughts tumble out from my subconscious quickly and fiercely. I'd say they were shocking, but they're not. They've been inside me, bottled up, since the day she walked onto my construction site.

And it's time I finally do something about them.

I set down my drink and cut through the crowd, making a beeline for Vi, and gently but firmly taking her arm. "Can I talk to you for a second?"

She looks up at me. "Well, hello to you too, Nick," she says, a hint of annoyed amusement in her dark eyes. Then she nods, letting me lead her away from the party, toward a secluded corner near the pool house.

"What the hell, Violet?" I mutter.

She raises an eyebrow. "What's *your* problem?"

I shake my head, irked that I'm coming off like an asshole. Again.

"*This*," I say, unable to stop from trailing a finger from her throat to the swell of her breasts.

Her breath catches, and I can feel her trembling under my touch.

"Sorry." I pull my hand back. I'm probably scaring the poor woman. "You just… You're so beautiful, and all this exposed skin. Those men…" I can barely speak, my words tight and low.

She leans in, murmuring softly. "Are you *jealous*, Nick?"

I take a deep breath, trying to calm the whirlwind of emotions this woman stirs up inside me. "I can't stand those guys hovering around you like that, touching you, eye-fucking you like it's okay."

Her eyes soften. "I can take care of myself, Nick. You know that."

I growl. "I know you can. But I want to be the one to take care of you. I want you to be mine." It pops out before I can stop myself.

She blinks back at me, eyes wide, stunned perfectly silent. "Did you just—"

"Come with me." I take her hand and try the door to the pool house. By some miracle it opens, and I pull her inside before locking it. There's a butcher block table in the empty kitchen, and I lift her sweet ass onto it.

I push my hips between her legs. "I want you, Violet Bridges." I take her chin in my hand and stare into her deep brown eyes. "I've wanted you ever since the first moment I saw you." I swallow. "Not just in my bed... and on this table, and against that wall..." I grin. "But in my life, every damn day, as mine and *only* mine."

Her breath becomes ragged, and her lips part. "I..." She can't finish her sentence, just leans forward in a rush, searing her sexy lips to mine.

I groan from a place deep inside me as her hands spear through my hair, pulling me close. "I want you, too," she breathes against my lips.

She wants *me*. She wants *this*...!

I'm delirious as I focus on Vi's delicious mouth. I slide my tongue against her lips and she whimpers, opening up to me. *Fuck me.* My cock is raging in my swim trunks, eager and aching for her.

When our tongues meet, I shudder, and she holds me tighter, clawing at my shoulders and neck. I wrap my big arms around her body, relishing the heat of her bare skin on mine. All I can think about is more. *More...*

I kiss across her cheek, licking and nipping down the graceful column of her throat, sucking on the luscious flesh at the curve of her shoulder.

"Nick," she whispers, her head thrown back. "Yes…"

My fingers slide along the inside edge of the triangle top, which is doing a poor job of covering her generous breast. I gently push the scrap of fabric aside, baring her soft skin and dusky nipple. It's already pebbled, the skin taut and needy, just like the bulge in my shorts.

I slide my hand under the globe of tender flesh, hefting the weight of it in my palm, before caressing her nipple. I can feel the tremors take hold of her as my fingers move in circles, carefully exploring and teasing, finding her most sensitive spots. Her tiny gasps and moans point me in the right direction and drive me wild.

Finally, I graze the tight peak and she cries out. "God…"

"I love how sensitive you are, Vi," I whisper, rolling the nub between my fingertips as her body arches and jerks. "You like my touch, baby?"

"Fuck yes…" she replies, her nails playing over my neck.

I dip down and take a stiff peak into my mouth, and she groans. My tongue rolls all over her flesh, her taste delicious.

"Oh, Nick… Nick…" she's saying, as I suck and lick, moaning. My other hand slides into the fabric over her left breast, teasing and caressing, her body still just as responsive.

I move to take that one in my mouth, too, lavishing the same attention on it. Her hands are fisting in my hair as she gasps.

"Lie back, sweet stuff," I mutter, coaxing her down onto the table. "And spread those legs like a butterfly for me. I need to taste that pussy."

Vi moans, untying her sarong, then doing exactly as I say without a moment's hesitation. "I'm not used to you being so obedient," I tease.

She scoffs. "Maybe if you'd led with wanting to eat my pussy, I would've been."

I hum with a smirk. "Duly noted."

She giggles and I lean forward to kiss down her stomach, feeling it flutter under my touch.

I run my tongue along her bikini line and up to the tie at her hip. I yank the string and it comes undone. I peel the fabric away, baring her pretty pussy to me.

"Fuck, Vi. Your pussy is breathtaking," I say, my voice husky. Her decadent pink skin and dark landing strip are too much to resist. I lightly run my fingers from her hip bone down the crease of her groin and into the soft hollow where it joins with her thigh. She shivers, biting her lip, watching my path with her eyes.

"Ticklish there much?" I ask, tracing the same path with my lips and tongue.

She giggles and gasps. "Maybe, but don't stop."

"Not a chance," I whisper, her heady scent speeding up my heart rate.

I'd love to tease her more, but I can't hold back any longer. I lick her from back to front, my tongue flat and thick against her already wet flesh.

"Oh my god, Nick," she wails, and I wonder if the entire party might hear. I don't care. I'm tongue-deep in Violet Bridges, and there's nowhere else I'd rather be.

I lick and kiss and taste her sensitive folds with my lips and tongue, holding onto her flanks as she writhes and wriggles under me, unable to stay still.

She shakes with every slide of my tongue, every soft press of my lips and light suction on her skin bringing her fresh sweet torment. Her back arches, and her nails scrape on the table. I love how wildly responsive she is. It's almost as goddamned addictive as her slick honeyed center.

"Nick...you're driving me...out of my mind," she moans,

her breasts jiggling as she thrusts them out, her head thrown back.

I reach up and palm one of them as I zero in closer to her clit, swiping just next to it with my tongue.

"I'm going to come. Fuck, I'm so close." Her words tumble out, and my cock threatens to explode at that alone. "Don't stop, please don't stop..."

"You'll never have to beg me for that, Vi," I say, before finally landing on her clit, feasting on her pussy like a man starved.

"Oh, oh..." she cries, and I let my tongue graze her secret spot, tease it, worry it, until she's a wet, blubbering mess. She reaches down and with trembling hands takes hold of my head, keeping my tongue on her clit.

"I'm coming! Nick! Yes! God, *yes*..." she screams, before her body detonates in a series of tremors and convulsions, her back bowed. I hold her down as best I can, finishing her, drinking her sweet nectar. She's pulling my hair, but I can't get enough, and I growl like an animal protecting its meal.

Violet just came undone right before me, because I made her body sing. I'm a happy, happy man.

"How you doing, sweet stuff?" I whisper after a few moments. Her tremors slow and I dance kisses across her thighs and stomach. Unable to resist, I lick inside her navel.

She laughs and gets up onto her elbows. "Help me off this table."

I lift her, setting her back down on her feet. The bikini bottoms fall the rest of the way off, and she's a delectable sight in just her heels and a bikini top that's pushed up, her breasts bare and luscious. I groan, my cock rabid by now, leaking at the tip.

As if understanding my pain, Vi grabs the waistband of my swim trunks and spins me so my back is against the table. She unties the drawstring and slips her hands into my shorts at my hips, pushing them down. My cock gives her trouble at first, the fabric getting caught on it. But soon she has them off my ankles and I kick them aside.

"Jesus Christ, Nick," she breathes, her eyes on my dick. "Where?....How? That's huge!"

I chuckle, not sure what to say. But when she grasps my length in both hands and starts to stroke, I choke on my own spit. "Vi…"

"Get up on the table," she orders. "Your turn."

I grin, suddenly all too happy to obey her as well. I jump up and sit on the edge, leaning back onto my forearms to watch.

She eyes my cock, standing at attention, precum at my slit.

"You gonna be able to handle that?" I ask, smirking.

"Probably. If not, guess I'll just have to practice until I can," she says, winking at me, running her fingertip over my cock head, massaging the slick around.

I exhale a shaky breath, then moan. "I'm so here for that."

"You'd better be," she says, then leans forward and licks my tip. We lock eyes and that fire is back, making my belly tighten. She must notice, because she rakes her nails down my stomach, watching it tremble under her touch, and smiles. "I can legit count your abs. That's hot, Nick."

There's not much time to revel in her praise, because the next thing I know she's steadying my dick with one hand and taking me into her hot mouth.

I let out a long groan. I could come from her sucking my tip alone. Hell, I'm already so turned on she could probably get me off with one hot *breath*. But now it's my turn to writhe under her lips and tongue. My skin tingles and burns in the best possible way, my balls tightening with each movement of her mouth. She slides down further each time, slow and deliberate. Just how I like it.

"God, you're good at this, baby," I manage, my voice hoarse and thick.

She moans on my cock, the vibrations adding to the pleasure. *Fuck, yes.*

I'm not going to last much longer. Watching her suck my cock feels like a dream. Sure, it's a fantasy I've had all these months, but the reality is better than anything I could have imagined. Eating out the hottest woman I've ever known and then getting my cock sucked by her talented mouth? I'm in heaven.

My balls pull up tight, and her fingers stroke the taut skin.

"Holy hell, that feels nice," I groan, my hips rolling with her mouth. "I can't hold out any longer, baby. I'm going to come."

Vi takes me as deep as she can, using her hands as an extension of her mouth. Jacking me slowly, steadily. It's dizzying.

"Yes, *fuck* yes… Here I come, Vi," I say, rambling off more incoherent words as my climax slams over me. "Fuck! Oh… oh…Jeezuuuuus." My body bucks and I come straight down her throat.

She doesn't stop, just keeps stroking and sucking until she's taken every drop of my come. "Baby…" I say, in complete awe of this woman.

I shake and jerk for a few moments until she slides off, and I let out the sigh of all sighs, falling back onto the table.

"That was incredible, Vi," I say to the ceiling. "What the hell am I going to do with you?"

"Anything you want," she laughs, and I lift back up onto my forearms. She's putting her bikini back in place and retying her sarong. "Seriously, you're going to take me back to your place and put some salve on the table burn from this butcher block." She turns and shows me her back, which is covered in red splotches.

I groan. "I'm so sorry. I'll kiss it all better." I hop down and put on my shorts.

"And you need to get us out of here without being seen."

"Your wish is my command." I pause, pressing Violet flush against me. "Wait. Aren't *I* the boss?"

"You are indeed, Nick," she winks. "And that's why you're going to tell me exactly how to take that cock when we get home."

I blink rapidly, stunned. "Shit Vi, then let's go. Now!"

CHAPTER 7
VIOLET

We're still laughing like lunatics when we get to Nick's house.

We'd left the party via the back of the pool house and had just started walking toward our cars when someone called out to us. Nick yelled "go go go!" and we bolted like naughty teenagers, laughing and whispering. Then I'd followed Nick up the mountain in my car to his house.

I didn't even have time to admire it properly since he whisked me right up the stairs to his bedroom and proceeded to kiss me hungrily like we hadn't just had some of the most mind-blowing sex ever.

Now, though, he's tending to my table rash, achingly gentle as he rubs the salve all over my skin. I'm giddy, still riding the high from hearing this man say he wants me—despite all our bickering, and the rivalry, and the constant challenges. Nick Fletcher wants me.

And I want him.

"How's that?" he asks, once he's covered all my red splotches.

"Wonderful," I say, turning back to face him. We're naked,

having ditched our clothes the moment we got inside. I'm entranced by Nick's body. His thick, cut muscles, massive chest, washboard abs, sculpted legs, and that cock…oh, that cock…no words.

He's staring at my body as well, and I love the hungry, possessive look in his eyes.

I reach for his cock, but he backs up. "Not just yet." His brows jump. "As your boss, I think you need to be reprimanded for that smart mouth I've had to put up with over these past few months. I'm afraid I don't allow anyone to talk to me that way."

He's got a twinkle in his eye that tells me he wants to play, and I'm instantly wet.

"Reprimanded?" I gulp. "What on Earth will you do, Mr. Fletcher?"

His cock twitches and he's hiding a smile as he sits down on the edge of the bed. He pats his lap authoritatively. "You need to be spanked for all your backtalk."

Heat blooms low in my belly. I lean over his thighs, his cock against my hip. I arch my back slightly to make my ass stick up. "Is this acceptable?" I ask, up on my forearms, turning my head to look up at him.

"Very," he croaks, and I smile with nervous anticipation.

He lays his palm over my tailbone and slides it down over the curve of my cheek. "You have such a gorgeous ass, Violet."

"Thank you…sir." It slips out, and he growls.

"Remember, Violet, this is for your own good," he says sternly, then pauses. "But if it gets to be too much, you have my permission to tell me to stop."

"Yes, Mr. Fletcher."

Suddenly he smacks me once, on the fleshiest part of my ass. I gasp at the sweet sting as he caresses the spot immediately afterward.

Then another smack, and another caress. Then again, and again. He doesn't hit *too* hard, for which I'm thankful, just firmly enough to make a nice slapping sound, give me a quick rush of heat, and I'm sure, make my rump jiggle.

I moan and gasp with each slap, and I can hear Nick's ragged breath.

"Are you okay?" he asks, his voice rough.

"Yes, sir," I reply, and I feel him shiver under me.

"You keep calling me *sir* like that, I'll have to fuck you right here and now."

I shiver at his needy words. "Understood..." I bite my lip. "*Sir.*"

He snarls and I feel him wrapping his big hand around my ponytail. "Don't say I didn't warn you," he says, and tugs at my hair until I'm up, kneeling beside him. His green-blue irises are mere rings next to his dilated pupils. His mouth crashes down on mine and I'm completely devoured—mind, body, and soul.

He lies back and grabs my ass, pulling me over his hard, thick body.

"I need you now," he grits out, searching my eyes.

"And I need you. I want you inside me," I reply, the ache in my core growing by the second.

"I don't think I have any condoms." Lines of worry crease his forehead. "I was not exactly expecting this."

I grin. "I'm on the pill. Tell me you've been tested recently."

"Not recently. But no reason to. It's been a long, long time."

"Ditto. The pill's just to keep my cycles regular."

He chuckles and flips me so I'm underneath him. "Then let's do this, sweet stuff."

And he kisses me again, deep and slow, and I wrap my legs around him, desperate for the friction.

He pulls away and slides his fingers into my wet folds. His touch is electric, and I cry out.

Nick hisses. "You're already so wet, Vi."

"I guess I really enjoyed playing together," I smile, as he positions his cock at my entrance.

"Yeah? You like getting spanked?" His chest heaves.

"Only if Mr. Fletcher is doing it."

He groans. "Good girl," he praises me, biting his lip. "You are perfect."

As he says *perfect*, he begins to push inside me, and little by little I'm stretched out like I've never been before.

"Oh…" I try to breathe through it, grabbing a handful of the bed sheets.

"You okay?" he grits out.

I nod. "Just trying to get used to how big you are. You?"

He smiles as if in pain. "Amazing. But you're so tight and wet, Vi. I'm not sure I can…" he trails off, and I will myself to relax and take more of him.

"Ahhh, that's it, baby, you're doing it," Nick says, and it feels like he's almost all the way inside.

Then he pulls back out slowly, and despite the earlier discomfort, my body suddenly feels empty. But when he pushes back in a second time, slick and easy, the pain subsides, replaced with a gnawing, tickling need.

"More, Nick," I hear myself say, and he growls, leaning forward and pumping slightly faster.

Oh my…this. This is good.

No, scratch that.

This is spectacular.

And then I'm moaning, wrapping my legs around Nick's flanks again, pulling him deeper, encouraging him to move.

"Fuck, you're killing me, baby. So sweet. Gripping my cock like a silky glove."

I can feel my orgasm building, climbing up some invisible ladder, and the harder he thrusts, the higher I go. When he leans over and whispers, "Come for me, sweet stuff," that's it. One moan, and I'm imploding, shaking, my fingers clawing at Nick's back.

"Yes, Nick!" I yell, holding onto him. Then his muscles tremble.

"Fuck, yes, Vi...I'm coming too!" He falls over me, his body wracked with tremors, and I feel him shooting his seed into me in hot, wet bursts.

We hold on to each other, letting our climaxes subside.

I'm a hot mess under him, but I don't care. I relish the beating of our hearts and the intensity of our passion.

Nick eventually slides out and flops over to lie beside me. "Hey gorgeous," he whispers in my ear, nibbling it.

"Don't get me going again," I mumble, drifting in and out of consciousness.

"No, let's sleep."

"But first—bathroom?"

He points behind us. "Right there."

I use the facilities, still drowsy, and back in the bedroom, Nick pulls the covers back for me. I climb into bed and curl up next to him.

"What do you want for breakfast tomorrow?" he asks, his lips against my shoulder.

"You," I reply, and I feel him smile.

"There's something to look forward to." He pauses, then adds, "Also. You'll stay here with me in Deepwood Mountain, right?"

"You want me to?"

"Yes. So badly."

"Then I will."

"Good. 'Night, my love."

And my heart takes flight.

The warmth of the sun's rays peeking through the curtains rouses me from sleep. A smile spreads over my face as all the memories come rushing back. It had been a night of laughter, passion, and vulnerability with Nick. Finally, it felt like the walls we'd built around ourselves had crumbled down. I snuggle closer to him, basking in the comfortable silence of the morning.

Nick's phone rings shrilly, shattering my moment of bliss. I feel him tense beside me, and I pretend to still be asleep, not wanting to interrupt him.

"Yes, Mr. Donovan?" I hear Nick answer, and my heartbeat picks up. Mr. Donovan rarely calls early unless there is a problem.

As their conversation continues, I can hear Mr. Donovan's booming voice on the other end of the line. It's clear he isn't happy with the stone accent wall in the great room, a design element I had spearheaded. My heart sinks, but what irks me the most is Nick's response. Instead of saying he needs to discuss it with me or defending our joint decisions (because that's what it was!!!), he's quick to pacify the man.

"I understand. We'll get it fixed. Don't worry," Nick says.

Anger brews in my gut and my heart. I wait until Nick quietly exits the bedroom to finish the call, assuming I'm still deep in slumber, before I sit up, shaking with a mixture of humiliation and fury. I trusted him. I thought we were a team. Especially after last night! But now, it seems like when push comes to shove, he still chooses the side against me. I thought we'd moved beyond the rivalry, but I guess not.

My eyes well up, but I refuse to cry over this right now.

I quickly pull on my clothes and scrawl a note on a pad sitting on the nightstand.

Nick,

I heard your conversation with Mr. Donovan. It's clear now where you stand on my capabilities as a designer. I thought you, of all people, would have my back. I thought we were partners. Regardless, I'll be at the site getting to work on removing that horrific accent wall. I won't let a hiccup like this ruin the project.

Violet

Bitter? Yes. Snarky? Also yes. Before I can second-guess my actions, I leave the note prominently displayed, grab my purse, and storm out the back door.

CHAPTER 8
NICK

Violet's note burns in my pocket as I speed toward the job site. My fingers tighten on the steering wheel as my mind races, piecing together the events of the morning. My guilt pangs deepen with every passing mile marker.

I hadn't wanted to wake her with the early call. I just wanted her to have a few more moments of sleep. But in my attempt to shield her, I've inadvertently caused her pain.

And after one of the best nights of my life, too!

Goddammit.

My phone pings with a flurry of incoming texts, most likely from Violet, but I don't dare stop to look. Instead, I focus on the road, and the conversation I'd had with Mr. Donovan. She only heard that first fraction of it. She didn't hear the rest, me defending her work, her vision, or my insistence that the Donovans see the wall in question in person before passing judgement. It's a brilliant design that deserves at least that much.

Pulling into the site, I spot Violet talking with the crew. I rush out, my boots kicking up dust. She spots me and turns to storm inside the lodge.

"Violet, wait!" I shout, catching her attention.

She turns back, and her eyes meet mine, ablaze with determination. "I'm fixing it, Nick. Just like you told Mr. Donovan you would."

I grab her arm gently, pulling her away from the rest of the crew. "You didn't hear everything," I start, taking a deep breath. "I defended your design. Told Mr. Donovan to come down and see it for himself. I said it was a perfect blend of style and practicality. 'I believe my exact words were 'a real show-stopper'. They're on their way."

Violet's fiery demeanor softens. "You...what?"

"I believe in you as a designer, and I believe in *you*," I continue, sliding my palm down her arm to take her hand. "I'm sorry for earlier, and I'm sorry that I made you feel that way. You've shown nothing but dedication, talent, and ingenuity on this project. You've proven yourself ten times over every step of the way."

The words spill out, a tumble of regret and admiration. Her brown eyes glisten with happy tears.

"And I know we're supposed to include the others to decide the winner of our initial competition. But in my books, you've already won. You worked your sexy ass off, creating a beautiful, luxurious family home, and you did it even as I fought with you the entire way. You deserve a medal for that, love."

She laughs through her tears.

"That's not all," I add. "I might've reached out to a friend who knows the editor of *Architectural Digest*. They're interested in doing an interview with you once this project wraps up." I'd called them the moment I read her note. She needs to know how gifted she really is.

She looks stunned as she processes it all. "Nick...I...I don't know what to say."

"You don't need to say anything," I say, pulling her into a tight embrace. She clings to me fiercely, and my shoulders sag with relief. "But you *could* tell me you loved me. Because I'm head over heels in love with you."

"I do love you, Nick. So, so much," she murmurs into my neck.

"Thank god," I groan.

"And for the record," she continues, "no matter what the Donovans decide, I stand by our work."

"That's my girl," I whisper.

One month later

As the applause from the toast dies down, I feel a rush of adrenaline as I stare out at the faces in the familiar crowd at the wrap-up party at the Donovans' new home. The lodge turned out even better than I think any of us ever hoped. And as I glance over at the stunning stone accent wall, I can't help but get misty-eyed. It was the first design element Violet and I defended as a team. We still enjoy a good debate, but these days it's more for fun. Though one could argue that it's *always* been just for fun with Vi.

I grab the microphone again with nervousness and determination. "Ladies and gentlemen," I start, my voice a little softer this time, "please bear with me for just one more moment."

I beckon Violet closer. She looks slightly confused, her brow furrowing in that adorable way I will never get enough of. "Violet," I call out, and as she walks toward me, in that sexy, sleek gown, the atmosphere in the room grows quiet and expectant.

"From the first day I met Violet, our journey has been… well, to put it mildly, a roller-coaster," I begin, addressing the audience with a smile. "We started off as a boss and an employee that butted heads on almost every design element, every idea. Every single day was a battle of wits and wills."

There are soft chuckles from the audience. Most of them have at least heard the stories, even if they haven't witnessed our head-to-heads firsthand.

"But as the days turned into weeks and then months, I came to realize something," I continue, my gaze fixed on her. "Behind those fierce debates, silly pranks and sharp retorts was a brilliant mind, a passionate heart, and an indomitable spirit. Violet, you've shown me a side of myself I never knew was there. You've taught me patience, humility, and the joy of collaboration. And most importantly, you've made me realize what's been missing in my life."

The room is pin-drop silent now, every pair of eyes locked on the scene unfolding before them.

I take a deep breath. "I love you, Violet. Like nothing else in this entire world." My words hang in the air. I reach into my pocket, pulling out a small velvet box containing the ring I had Tasha help me pick out. As I sink to one knee, there are gasps and murmurs around the room.

"Violet…my love, my sweet stuff…" My voice is low, but strong. "Will you marry me?"

For an agonizingly long heartbeat, time seems to stop. The anticipation is palpable. Then her soft voice, choked with emotion, breaks through. "Yes, Nick. Yes!"

I slide the ring onto her finger, and the room explodes in cheers, whoops, and applause. Rising to my feet, I pull her into

my embrace, our lips meeting in a searing kiss that consumes
me entirely.

EPILOGUE - VIOLET

ONE YEAR LATER

The gentle rhythm of Deepwood Mountain welcomes me back, and as I step out of the cab the essence of the familiar, comforting town fills my soul. Paris was terrific, don't get me wrong, but there's no place like my new home here with my doting husband.

Before I even make it to the front door, it swings open. My rugged mountain man that I adore so much, even more today, is all smiles.

"Missed me?" I ask, though his grin already confirms it.

"Like crazy," he says, leaning down to give me a tender, lingering kiss. He pulls back and takes my luggage, but not before I spot the playful twinkle in his eye. I'm sure he has special plans for us tonight, but I'll let him surprise me there.

"How was boys' night?" I ask, genuinely curious. With our circle of friends' lives constantly evolving, these moments the six of them carve out for themselves have become increasingly rare.

Nick chuckles. "Dash is drowning in diapers, Logan can't stop gushing about the wedding, Reece's ranch stories are as wild as ever, Gavin...well, who knows where in the world he is right now, but he joined for a while over Zoom. Sully just wanted to play board games all night."

I laugh, imagining the group together. "How's Reece doing? The last time he visited, he sounded a little down."

"When he's not raising hell, I think he's thinking about his life." He drops my luggage near the stairs. "If you ask me, he's lonely. I told him he should find himself a nice wife."

I grin. "Like it's that easy."

"Hey, mine walked right onto my job site. How hard can it be?" he shrugs, and I punch him playfully in the shoulder.

As we make our way inside, the delightful scent of dinner hits me, making my stomach rumble appreciatively.

"I hope you're hungry," he says, handing me a glass of wine.

I set the wine down on the coffee table, a nervous flutter in my stomach. "Actually, I think I'll pass on the wine for now."

Nick raises an eyebrow but doesn't press the issue. We settle onto the couch, and he looks at me, concern in his loving gaze. "You look exhausted, Vi. Maybe you should consider scaling back on at least your overseas projects for a while."

Wow. It's extremely rare for him to suggest I slow down, especially since he knows I thrive on the hustle and bustle of my work. Looking into his earnest eyes, I nod. "You might be right."

He looks even more surprised now. "Really? With no debate, even?"

Taking a deep breath, I meet his gaze, my heart fluttering. "Yes, really. I think... I think it's time for a bit of a break."

"Why the sudden change of heart?" he asks, a teasing lilt in his voice, but I can see the genuine curiosity behind it.

Grinning, I reach out and take both his hands in mine, licking my lips. "Because, Nick, in not even nine months... You're going to be a daddy."

It takes a moment for the realization to sink in. When it does, his eyes light up with a blend of shock and elation. "Are you serious, sweet stuff?"

I nod, laughing. "Dead serious."

In an instant, he's pulled me into his arms, holding me tight. "Vi," he murmurs, his voice thick with emotion, "this is the best news ever."

And we stay like that for a while, holding each other, my excitement growing at the knowledge that Nick and I are heading toward this new, wonderful chapter in our lives.

Together.

HIS BIG ROPE

CHAPTER 1
PAIGE

Marge's Diner has *the best* vegetarian club sandwiches.
They're not on the menu, but the owners, Angie and T, always make them special for me, swapping out the meat for cucumber, avocado, and a pile of golden onion rings.

I legit had fantasies about these beauties while I was away at college.

Taking a bite, I close my eyes and groan in ecstasy at the explosion of flavor and texture on my tongue.

"Been a while, huh?" Willa asks, handing me a napkin with a wink.

My sister Eden and I are sharing a booth with our friends, Maddie and Willa, who both work with her at the Deepwood Mountain library.

The diner is bustling as always these days, filled with the comforting aroma of coffee and lunchtime favorites from the grill.

"Too long," I finally mumble around my sandwich, before swallowing and dabbing at my face.

Initially, I did my undergrad degree at the University of

Montana in Missoula. Then I went to veterinary school for four more years in Bozeman. While I was at school I only came back occasionally at the holidays, preferring to keep my nose to the grindstone. But I missed my mama and sister, my friends, and this amazing little town.

So now that I've graduated, I'm back for good. Hurray!

"We need to go out, Paige," Eden says, tapping my arm with her short, manicured nails. "I met two firemen at Rustic Ridge last weekend and convinced them to sign up to read to the kids for Story Time at the library." She glances over at Maddie, who's in charge of the library's social media. "These firemen were *smoking* hot. Pun one hundred percent intended. You should feature them on our Insta, Maddie."

Yep, that's my older sister. Boy crazy since she turned thirteen, and always on the hunt for a man. She's got a bit of a reputation, but… It's a small town. People talk. And of course, I don't blame her one bit. I blame our rat of a dad, who left us when we were just kids. It affected us in opposite ways. I ended up not trusting men. Meanwhile Eden's desperate to find one. *Any*where.

"And since these two are taken"…Eden gestures to the girls…"it's just you and me, sis."

Willa is married to Dash, who builds custom motorcycles at a shop in town. Maddie's also hitched, to Logan, a local lumberjack-turned-woodworker. Both of them are wildly happy, which I'm sure only makes my sister even more eager to find Mr. Right.

Me? I have better things to do.

"How's the hunt for a space for the sanctuary going?" Maddie asks, popping a fry into her mouth. She's vegetarian too but prefers the diner's portobello mushroom burgers. Those *are* on the menu.

"I'm having a hard time finding something that works with my budget," I admit, then take a sip of my soda. "Everything is either too expensive, or needs way too much work before I can make it usable." I've toured a dozen places in the month that I've been back, but nothing yet has fit the bill. Who would have thought that finding the right property for a farmed animal sanctuary would be so difficult? It's discouraging, but I'm not giving up on my dreams.

Maddie smacks the table. "Oh! I totally forgot! Logan mentioned some big changes going down at Callahan Ranch. Reece sold off the bulk of his cattle and had to lay off most of his ranch hands."

"Right! Sounds like he's downsizing," Willa adds, poking at her chicken salad with her fork.

Maddie nods. "He might be looking to lease out part of the ranch. That could be the perfect place for you."

Eden shifts in her seat next to me. "Excuse me? You can't be serious." Her voice is sharp. "Paige should stay as far away from Reece Callahan as humanly possible. That man is *no good*. Trust me on that."

The table goes quiet. Willa and Maddie exchange a look. All that's left is the background hum of the other diners and the clink of silverware and dishes.

This is…tricky. About four years ago, Eden and Reece dated. It didn't last long. He ended it rather badly, and it broke her heart. She's made it abundantly clear how much she despises him ever since.

Meanwhile, Willa and Maddie are friends with Reece, since their husbands are super close with him. I know they want to be loyal and support Eden, but…yeah. Like I said: tricky.

"Oh! Hey! I have new baby pictures!" Willa announces, breaking the tension. She pulls out her phone and suddenly we're all oohing and ahhing over her sweet little daughter's big blue eyes and chubby cheeks.

Except even as I look at them and make the appropriate noises, I'm thinking about Reece, and there's a knot twisting in my stomach. His name alone stirs up a whirlwind of...stuff.

Remember when I said I have better things to do than search for a guy? Well, it's true. But a huge part of the reason I don't want to go looking is that there's no point. My heart already belongs to a man.

And that man is...drum roll...Reece Callahan.

I know. It's ridiculous. For god's sake, I've only talked to him once!

It happened a couple of days before Reece broke up with Eden, all those years ago.

It was a bright summer day and I'd just dropped something off at the post office. I was about to get back in my truck when I saw Reece atop his palomino, Ollie. He steered Ollie over to me, tipped his hat, smiled, and called me ma'am.

Ma'am.

One word had never done such arousing things to my body.

His green-eyed gaze held me captive for what seemed like an eternity but was in reality I'm sure only a minute. We may have made small talk, but honestly, I can't remember. I was too busy swooning over his broad shoulders, the tan chest peeking out from the collar of his shirt, and that slow, devastatingly sexy smile. And I've never been able to forget the feeling he left inside me, the sinful spark I've tried like crazy to ignore.

It felt like...love. I think. Or, at least, what love *should* feel like. Not that I have any experience with that.

"Just look at her. Spaghetti everywhere!" Willa exclaims, startling me out of my thoughts. Her eyes are so full of joy and love as she stares at the adorable photo of her daughter, and Eden seems to have forgotten all about the mention of Reece, asking Willa the next time she can babysit.

Me, I'm left feeling like a horrible person for wanting Reece like this when he kicked my sister to the curb so ruthlessly.

Yet, as I stare out the window at the sun dancing on Main Street, I know what I have to do.

~

After lunch, Eden, Maddie, and Willa all go back to work at the library.

And I drive to Callahan Ranch.

I'm chalking this up to pure desperation. Forget any feelings I have for him. This animal sanctuary is my dream, and I'm willing to do anything to make it happen.

Even if it means hurting my sister.

I'm still not completely convinced this is the best idea, as witnessed by the fact that I've hidden my truck from view of the main drive in a cluster of trees on the perimeter of the property. I want to take a peek at the place alone. And I *don't* want anyone to know I'm here, especially Reece. He's *way* too much of a distraction.

During my internships in private veterinary practices, I quickly found that working with livestock and other farmed animals was what I loved best. Ranching and the farm industry can mean a rough life for animals and I saw how much suffering truly went on in places that didn't care for their animals properly. It tore me up and led to my dream of a place where I could help neglected, injured, and abused animals heal and live out the rest of their lives in peace.

Also, I saw the potential to give back to Deepwood, the

town that had supported my mom when she found herself suddenly single and taking care of two children by herself back then. I figure the sanctuary can be a place to learn and grow, providing educational programs and other field opportunities for schools and the community at large.

So, long story short, sneaking around like a thief on the Callahan property is for a good cause.

Looking out over the land, I'm struck by its beauty, with rolling hills and lush pastures that seem to go on forever. It's a little slice of paradise tucked away in the mountains.

As I walk, I keep my eyes peeled for any of the ranch hands. They'd probably think I'm some sort of stalker.

I'm not sure why I even care. It was one moment in time. *Four years ago.* Reece was already like twice my age back then. Now he must be ancient, with skin like cracked leather from spending too much time out in the sun and premature wrinkles from partying it up at night, smelling of wet hay, booze, and stale sweat.

I hold back a dry heave.

Not to mention, if Reece is anything like most of the other crotchety old ranchers I've met, the last thing he'll want to do is get involved with helping the animals he's made a living off selling. It's a complete change of mindset and values. Not everyone is ready for that kind of mental flip-flop, particularly not those whose families have been ranching for generations.

Like the Callahans.

Nearing the animal pens, I hear voices, so I veer away, hiding in the shadows. A few chickens peck at the dirt around me. I duck inside the stables, horses peering out of their stalls to say hello. I pet the muzzle of a pinto with beautiful light blue eyes affectionately. Horses are one of my favorite animals, and the thought of working with them again fills my heart with pure happiness.

I make my way down the line of them, their low whickers soothing. I keep my movements slow so as not to spook them, then turn the corner.

In an instant, I'm grabbed roughly by a thick pair of arms, my scream choked off as I'm thrown to the ground and pinned under the weight of my attacker.

CHAPTER 2
REECE

I 'm walking toward the stable when I hear footsteps.

Instantly my body goes rigid, my senses on high alert.

Carter and Maverick are out fixing a busted fence, and I've just left my other men at the pens.

Nobody should be over here.

Dammit. Intruders on the ranch are a rare thing, but we've had a few horses stolen in the past.

I press my back against the wall as the footsteps come closer, waiting for the trespasser to turn the corner.

When he does, I'm on him.

The momentum carries us both to the ground, landing hard, and he exhales sharply as the wind is knocked out of him.

He fights back, limbs pushing and shoving and pounding me, though not as hard as I'd expect. And his sounds as we wrestle for dominance are...strange.

I get my forearm jammed against his throat, pinning him to the hay-covered floor as he struggles to speak.

Suddenly, I smell something sweet and flowery. I notice the body underneath me is compact, light—filled with adrenaline, but also somehow soft. I'm much larger, and for a moment, I feel like a beast looming over its prey.

Then I see small, slender hands pulling at my arms, and feel the swell of full tits at my chest. Strands of silky dark hair tickle my face.

Fuck me. I'm fighting a woman.

I relax my hold on her neck.

"Let go of me!" she shrieks, her voice cracked and raw.

I shift my weight, and finally get a look at her face.

My god. I'd recognize those eyes anywhere.

"Paige?" I grind out, confused. What the hell?

She blinks up at me. "Reece?"

"Shit, darlin', are you okay? Did I hurt you?" My hands roam over her, quickly checking for damage. If I've harmed her, I'll never forgive myself.

"Reece..." she breathes, as I continue my search for injuries. I can't stop touching her, feeling her soft, pliant flesh under my hands. "I'll—I'll be okay," she stammers. Her cheeks are flushed, her hair mussed. "Just a few bruises. You're a"... she winces..."big guy."

Christ. I'm furious with myself for being so rough. I slide my hand to the side of her face, her skin like the petals of a flower.

Paige Alvarez, the woman I never thought I'd see again, is underneath me, her pulse as rapid as mine, and I'm staring at her beautiful face, enchanting eyes, those parted lips—

Reece, enough!

She wriggles, which doesn't help curb my desire. Somehow I make myself get up before she thinks I'm a touchy-feely prick.

I climb to my feet and offer her a hand, but she ignores it, standing on her own and dusting off her clothes.

She's just as stunning as I remember. Even more so. Her

dark brown hair is back in one thick braid, her slim hips and thighs are clad in blue jeans, her magnificent round and tight ass is reminding me of a ripe peach in the summer, and the two glorious tits under a long-sleeved white t-shirt have me wishing it was raining.

"Fuck, Paige." I reach down to grab my hat from the ground and adjust myself, particularly my jeans which have, go figure, tightened. "What if I'd had my gun?" I shudder to think what could've happened.

She looks down at her feet for a moment. "I didn't mean..." She trails off and swallows, massaging her neck.

I'm at her side in a millisecond, pulling her hand away. There's an angry red mark on her throat where I pinned her to the floor. "Shit, I'm sorry, hon. So sorry..." And I can't help it. I'm running my calloused fingers over the mark and down the column of her neck, watching the goosebumps appear over her delicate skin.

"It's okay," she says, hoarsely. "It'll fade." To my surprise, she doesn't move away.

I'm still touching her when Carter canters around the corner of the stable on his horse and comes to a halt.

I step back from her as he takes in the two of us. We must look a mess, and I can only imagine what he's thinking. But he just tips his hat at Paige. "Ma'am."

"What is it, Carter?" I ask, my voice gruff.

"Sorry, Boss," he starts, "we've got a situation. Calf's caught in the north pasture fence. He's pretty cut and Doc Mahoney is out on an emergency call."

Paige stiffens and looks at me, then Carter. "I'm a vet," she says, her voice still a little gravelly.

Carter's eyebrows shoot up. "Yeah? You reckon you can help?"

Paige nods. "I'll do my best."

I knew Paige had gone to veterinary school, but had forgotten in the chaos. "I'll take her out there on Ollie."

"See you there," Carter says, spinning his horse around and spurring it into a hard gallop.

Paige and I exchange a look, but there's no time for me to dwell on the fact that Paige...*my Paige*...is right here in front of me. In the flesh.

"You okay to ride double?" I ask as I lead her over to Ollie, tied up out front of the stable.

"Of course," she says indignantly behind me. "I grew up here in Deepwood, Reece, you know that. Been riding since I was a kid. Me and my sis used to double all the time."

I cringe at the mention of Eden, then climb up into the saddle. She's already up on the fence waiting to get on.

"No, I meant because I just slammed you down to the ground. I'm concerned about you being hurt, that's all," I explain, nudging Ollie over to the fence.

"I'm fine," she replies, then swings up behind me. A jolt of surprise hits me, making me catch my breath, when her jean-clad thighs brush against my own and her slender arms wind around my waist.

"I'm tougher than I look, cowboy," she says near my ear, and I stifle a shudder. Yep, there go my jeans, getting tight again.

Dammit. Focus, Reece.

"Whatever you say, darlin'." I lean forward, urging Ollie into a gallop. Paige's arms tighten around me.

The ride out to the pasture is short, but I'm hyper aware of Paige pressed against me the whole way, and the way her hands grab at my stomach and chest as we ride. It's a special kind of torture.

But there's no time to dwell on it. When we arrive, the poor calf is wriggling about at the fence, his mother lowing in distress nearby. My other ranch hand, Maverick, has come to help as well.

Paige dismounts from Ollie, and I follow.

I watch as she assesses the situation. "You have wire cutters?" she asks Mav and Carter.

Maverick holds them up. "Sure do, ma'am. We tried to get him out already, but he keeps thrashin' something fierce."

Paige nods, then turns to me. "Reece, help me hold him still. I'll try to calm him, and when I say the word"—she looks at Carter—"you snip the wire as close as possible to his leg."

Carter nods, getting into position.

Paige pets the calf gently on his head and neck. "It's okay, buddy." He jerks at first, crying. "Your mama's right here, sweetie. She's just waiting for you to get free and all fixed up. Yeah?" With more pats and soothing murmured words, she nods my way and I hold on tighter, my arms around the calf in a hug. Eventually, I feel him relax.

"Now, Carter," she instructs. The calf backs up at the sound of the wire being snipped, but I hold him as he struggles, trying to calm him with my voice.

"It's okay, little one," Paige says, as she unravels the wire around his leg to reveal a nasty cut between the hoof and the fetlock. "We'll get this cleaned up and bandaged in no time."

Maverick offers Paige the first aid pack, and she works quickly and efficiently, her hands steady and confident as she tends to the wound. The calf has relaxed a lot more now that he's free from the fence.

Paige is clearly a natural, gentle and skilled, with a soothing voice. It's admirable. "Wow, you're great at this, Paige," I praise.

She glances up at me, her eyes sparkling. "Thanks," she whispers, her cheeks turning slightly pink.

I lean back, the mountain air suddenly thinning. It's the

only explanation for this lightheaded, giddy feeling that's come over me. Or maybe it's that this woman, who's haunted my dreams for years, is on my ranch, helping me.

Paige straightens up after patting the calf's flank, urging him back to his mother. He only has a minor limp. She wipes her hands on her jeans and pushes a few stray hairs out of her face. "That should do it," she says. "Watch him closely for the next few days, but I'm sure he'll be fine."

The men and I thank her, then Carter and Mav get to fixing the fence. I tell them to bring the calf and mother to one of the stalls for observation when they're done.

I take Ollie's reins, ready to lead him, and smile over at Paige. "Now... How about you tell me why you were sneaking around my property?"

I remember that summer day four years ago. Ollie and I had gone into town.

For the life of me, I can't remember why. All I know is that when I came to the post office, the most stunning woman I'd ever seen jogged out the front door and down the steps before opening the door of her Ford pickup. She turned briefly, and I nudged Ollie into her line of sight. She stopped and smiled at me, and it was as if goddamned Cupid's arrow had hit me straight in the chest with a twang.

It was just like in those stupid cartoons: my heart ricocheted out of my chest, my tongue flopped out of my mouth, and mini hearts sprang from my eyes.

No joke.

And I remember feeling like I could spend the rest of my life with this woman, even after I found out she was the little sister of Eden, the woman I'd just started to date. It didn't change that feeling deep in my bones.

It also scared the hell out of me.

I'd never thought of marriage. Why would I? I had a great life as a single guy. Endless casual flings. Partying with the ranch hands anytime I felt like it. And the unconditional support of the five best friends a guy could ask for.

The sudden, instantaneous longing for more—for *Paige*— came with an irrational fear that prevented me from doing anything about it after we went our separate ways that day.

And now Paige has come to my ranch, for reasons as yet unknown.

Maybe fate's trying to tell me something.

As we walk, with Ollie behind us, I can tell Paige is nervous. Her eyes dart about, hands fidgeting with her sleeves. And I hate that she feels anything but completely comfortable around me.

"You gonna spit it out?" I finally ask, when the silence has stretched on for longer than it should have.

She chews on her lower lip, gazing straight out in front of her rather than at me. "I want to open a farmed animal sanctuary here in Deepwood Mountain." She recites it like she's been practicing the sentence in her head.

"Oh?" It takes me by surprise, considering I didn't even know she was back in town, never mind to stay. "I've never heard of anything like that around here."

"Exactly. There isn't, for livestock," she says, shoving her hands in her pockets. "There's a few smaller operations, specialty rescues, and wildlife sanctuaries of course. But *my* passion is for farmed animals."

I smile at the determination in her voice.

"Ever since I finished my veterinary studies, a sanctuary has been on my mind. I want a place where farmed animals can come to live out the rest of their lives peacefully in a safe space where they are well cared for."

She glances up at me, and I can see the compassion in her eyes. She's brave to bring it up, I'll give her that. Generational ranchers like me can be a touchy bunch when it comes to farmed animals and animal welfare.

"That's a noble cause," I say. It is: I've done some research. "But what does it have to do with me?"

A sweet smile spreads over her face, making my heartbeat escalate and…dammit. Jeans even *tighter* now.

"I need land with proper facilities. Maddie said she heard there's been some changes on the ranch and that you might be open to leasing some of it."

Oh boy. The thing about small towns is that word travels fast. Not that what's happening here at my ranch is a secret, but telling one person is like sending out a news bulletin. I *am* making changes. I lightened my herd and relocated most of my hands to some of the best ranches in Montana.

"Yeah… Ranching made me and my pa our money, but I think it's time to go in a different direction. Sales are down, but the work is just as hard. So something has to give, you know? I'm looking at ways to make the ranch more modern and sustainable."

I can tell she wasn't expecting to hear that. "Really? Wow."

"I know," I chuckle. "I'm not sure how Pa would've felt about it, but I know he'd want me to blaze my own path. I like to think I'm different from the typical rancher. It's time to make some changes."

Her eyes light up. "Change can be very scary, but also incredibly exciting. Not to mention rewarding."

"You ain't kiddin'." I tip my head as I gaze at her. "But I'd prefer my excitement not to include attacking pretty prowlers."

She swallows loudly and looks away. "I'm sorry for all the cloak and dagger stuff."

"You could've just asked me, you know? No need to sneak around."

She rubs her arms and bites down on her lower lip, making it difficult to look anywhere else but her sexy mouth.

"It's not that simple," she finally mumbles.

"Why not?"

She huffs out a sigh of disbelief and rolls her eyes. "Because my sister would kill me if she found out I was here."

Yeah. Paige had turned everything I thought I knew on its head that day. I couldn't continue seeing her sister, knowing how I felt. It wasn't right. So a few days later, I broke it off with Eden.

Not that I did anything to go after Paige after that. There were too many reasons not to. One, I didn't want to get in the way of her getting her degree. Two, I didn't want to piss off Eden and her mama. And three, I *really* didn't want to look like the world's biggest creep, chasing after a woman half my age that I'd just met, claiming she was my soul mate.

Even now, it sounds ridiculous.

Instead, I had simply hoped I'd never run into her again.

But now that she's here, I'm terrified to let her go a second time.

"In any event, no matter what my feelings are about you and my sister," she continues, "I want to do everything I can to make this sanctuary happen."

I remember back to telling Eden we were through. I thought I'd been honest. Kind, even. But I guess she took it harder than I thought. She and her mama never talked to me again.

Somewhere in the distance a cow lows. I run a hand over

my face distractedly. "This land's not cheap. You sure you'll be able to afford it?"

Paige sticks out her chin. "I have some savings. And I'm not opposed to doing whatever it takes to secure more funding."

Determination flashes in her eyes. She's a fighter, that's for sure. I find this side of her enchanting.

"Listen," she says, reaching out and grabbing my sleeve. I come to a stop with Ollie nipping inquisitively my shoulder. "I know it won't be easy. But I'm not afraid of a little hard work. Heck, I got my undergrad degree in three years before attending veterinary school."

My heart aches at her innocence. "Oh, I don't want your money, darlin'."

Her brow furrows. "You don't?" She huffs again, and it's goddamn adorable. "So you're saying this is a no-go, then."

"Hang on, I'm not saying no," I say, lowering my voice.

"I don't understand. What do you want?"

Her gaze meets mine, and I want to tell her exactly what I want.

You. I want you.

In my bed. Under my tongue. Taking my cock. At my side for the rest of my life.

But that fear rears its ugly head once again.

"I want to be your partner."

"Partner?"

Just tell her already.

"Your business partner."

...Such a coward.

CHAPTER 3
PAIGE

"Really?"

My voice comes out as a squeak, betraying my excitement. Reece Callahan wants to be my business partner?

He nods. "We can use the money you have saved for start-up costs. I'm not charging you for the land, or the space, or anything."

I blink. "Ever?"

"Ever."

He moves in closer to me as we go back to walking, and a shiver runs up my spine.

For the record, Reece is *not* ancient. He's just as tall, broad, and rugged as I remember him—even more so now, with that sexy gray in his stubble. And he smells like freshly oiled leather and sandalwood soap. No wet straw, BO, or stale booze in a million-mile radius.

I could barely stand it when he was on top of me, touching me, his searing hot breath all over my face and neck. I'd wanted to wrap my arms around him and just hold him like that forever. My insides did backflips when I saw the concern in his eyes over the mark on my throat and the gravel in my voice. If he'd kept touching me with those gentle strokes and Carter hadn't ridden up when he did, I don't know what I would've done. Honestly, I was ready to offer him everything. This cowboy had me lassoed in his big rope like a helpless calf.

He grins, and I have an overwhelming impulse to lick the subtle dimple in his cheek.

Sheesh, Paige. Control yourself.

"Don't think I'll be taking over and making all the decisions, either," he adds. "I'm leaving that to you. This is *your* baby. I'll only be there when you want me to be."

Oh, I want you…there. And there. There, too, would be really nice.

I shake the haze from my head. His generosity is overwhelming. I'm hugely grateful for it, but Eden's voice is in my brain, telling me to watch out. It does seem too good to be true.

"Why?" I ask. "Why would you do this?"

"Because." He glances at me before gazing out at the surrounding land. "It's the perfect chance to take the ranch in a new direction, one that I can feel good about. Giving back to the animals I made my money from. Making amends." He shrugs. "And doing something positive for Deepwood and its people. Call it a way to create a new legacy for Callahan Ranch."

Good answer.

My insides squirm. "But why would you do this for *me*, Reece? You don't even know me."

A few raindrops start to fall, dotting the ground around us. When did those clouds move in?

"I know enough, darlin'. And by the fire I see in you, I'm sure you have a business plan and all the important details sorted out." He stops and his eyes are soft as they meet mine.

"Look, I'm in a position to help, and I want to. I want to be a part of this."

For a man who treated my sister with such disdain and has a reputation for loving 'em and leaving 'em, he's turning out to be nothing like I expected. Kind, thoughtful, and genuinely interested in helping his community? He's challenging every-thing I thought I knew about him.

And he's still hotter than a five-alarm fire.

Damn him.

The rain is coming down harder as we reach the stables.

He hands Ollie off to a ranch hand and grabs a raincoat from one of the racks.

"Ready to make a run for it?" he asks, moving in close to me and holding the coat over our heads.

I nod and we're off, dashing across the wet gravel and dirt toward the main house.

I wrap my fingers around his wrist to try to keep pace with him, but we inevitably jostle each other as we run, with his gait so much longer than mine. Being under his arm, in a cozy cocoon of Reece, is both exhilarating and comforting all at once.

We're laughing as we enter from the back deck of the main house, which is set up for entertaining with a lounge area and an outdoor kitchen. Inside, Reece directs us to the mud room where we leave our wet boots and socks.

He strips off his wet shirt as well, leaving him just in jeans and a white undershirt. I'm stupidly jealous of the fabric that gets to cling to his chest and washboard abs. The man is sculpted like a work of art. I mean, I already know firsthand, because when I rode behind him on Ollie, I couldn't help where my hands wandered.

What? I had to hold on.

His eyes fall to my chest, and he clears his throat. "I'll get you a dry shirt."

Crap. I instinctively cross my arms over my chest. I *had* to wear a white T-shirt today.

My cheeks heat when Reece returns with a completely dry, completely dark shirt. "There's a powder room just there."

"Thanks." I go in and quickly change, freshening up in the small bathroom, but not before pressing the shirt to my face and inhaling the fresh leather and soap smell deeply.

Don't judge.

When I wander back out, I'm impressed by the sheer size of the place. Eden told me that after Buck passed, Reece added a wing just for the ranch hands and updated and remodeled the rest of the house to make it more functional. His best friends Dash, Nick, Sully, Logan, and Gavin all helped, as they had with each of their homes. Eden and I affectionately nicknamed the group the Blue-Collar Millionaires Club, since they all started off in blue-collar trades, then built successful businesses around those trades that made them millionaires. Basically, good, down-to-earth men, who love Deepwood and its thriving community.

The living area, with its high ceilings and thick natural wood beams, is instantly welcoming. A massive fireplace and comfortable-looking seating area below appears lived in and cozy, but well-kept and tidy. And tons of light fills the space, thanks to the walls of windows.

"Are you dry enough? I can find you some more clothes, if you want," Reece offers, now wearing a button-down shirt.

Such a shame.

Even though the thought of wearing Reece's clothes makes

my core throb, I politely decline. "I'm good. I probably shouldn't get too comfortable. I need to get home."

Just then, a big crackling flash lights up the windows, followed by a thundering boom. The sky opens up and rain pelts down on the roof hard and fast.

Reece's brow shoots up. "Looks like you're staying for dinner, sorry."

"It's not that bad," I say, though the rain nearly drowns out my words.

"No way. I can't let you go home in this weather. What would your mother say?"

Funny thing, that. My mother would tell me that rain-slicked roads are way safer than Reece Callahan.

"Besides, what better way for us to get to know one another...partner?" He flashes me a lopsided grin and I fight off the blush I can feel spreading across my cheeks.

Business partner, Paige. *Business* partner.

As if on cue, there's another flash of lightning and thunder-clap, followed by more rain. *Ugh...*

"Okay, I'll stay," I say, rubbing my arms.

His smile widens. "Great. Come with me." He gestures for me to follow and leads us into the kitchen.

I run my hand over the enormous quartz-topped island and take in the six-burner gas range with a magnificent copper hood and a matching copper farmhouse sink. "This kitchen is amazing, Reece."

"Thanks. The ranch hands and I make a lot of meals together in here."

"You cook?"

"Yeah, but Maverick's the chef of the bunch. It's a real treat when it's his turn."

"Whose turn is it tonight?"

"Mine," he says, then chuckles. "The guys went over to Sully's for poker night."

"Oh, aren't you going?"

"*I* have company," he winks, and my stomach does another backflip.

Alone with Reece. This could be dangerous.

"What should I make?" he asks.

"I'm a vegetarian," I say. "But I'm not picky."

"I should've guessed the vegetarian part," he grins before opening the fridge. "You eat dairy? Eggs?"

"Yes and yes."

"Good, because I just milked our dairy cow Greta this morning, so we have fresh cream."

Don't picture him milking a cow right now, Paige. Just. Don't.

No matter: when he pulls an apron out of the pantry and ties it on, it's one of the sexiest things I've ever seen a man do. And it's downright erotic watching Reece's hands and arms, thick and corded from roping cattle, preparing a meal.

"How about pasta alla vodka? We can make a green salad and garlic bread to go with."

"Sounds delicious," I reply, trying not to drool. Over him *and* the meal.

"I want to help," I insist. "I usually make a vegetarian version of whatever my mama is making."

"How about you do the salad," he says, as he gathers vegetables from the refrigerator and then places them on the island with a cutting board for me. "What does your mama usually make?"

"For family dinners? Paella." I grab a knife from the block and get to work chopping as he starts the sauce in a big pot on the stove. "It's tradition."

"Sounds great. I'd love to try it sometime," he says,

sautéing some fresh garlic in the pot. The smell of it fills the kitchen, making my mouth water.

I just nod. My mama will *not* be inviting him over for supper, or any other meal. It makes me sad.

We pass bottles of spices and bunches of fresh herbs back and forth, the brush of our hands sending tingles up my arms.

I'm whisking together a simple vinaigrette dressing when Reece turns to me. "Come here and taste this."

I stop and wipe my hands on a dishtowel as I go over to him. He takes a spoon from the drawer and dips it into the sauce, holding it out to me. I take it from him, all set to put it in my mouth, when he grabs my wrist.

"Careful, it's hot." He blows on the sauce in the spoon, and I'm distracted by his mouth, so close to mine. "Okay, now," he whispers, and my cheeks heat when I realize I'm staring.

I take a taste, his warm, calloused hand still lingering on my wrist. The sauce is rich and bright. "This is fantastic, Reece. I could eat buckets of this."

A smile plays over his lips and his hand slowly pulls away. "Glad you like it."

I set two places at the long oak farmers' table off the kitchen while Reece finishes the bread and plates our meals.

"I have the perfect wine for this," he says, reaching into the wine fridge under the counter. "Gavin brought me back a Chianti from Italy when he was there last year on a job. I've been waiting for the right occasion to open it."

I laugh. "Cowboys are into wine?"

He grins. "Guess I broke the mold again, darlin'." He opens the bottle and pours us two glasses. He removes his apron, tossing it on a chair, then dims the lights before we sit. "To getting to know one another," he says, raising his glass.

The soft light makes his eyes glow as they lock on mine.

"To getting to know one another," I repeat, and clink his glass.

The wine truly is perfect for the meal, which is also spectacular. I'm impressed. And our conversation flows effortlessly. Reece asks me about college and veterinary school, and about my experiences as a vet out in the world since graduating.

He's flirty and charming, yet there's an authenticity to him that's disarming. I'm laughing and telling him things I rarely do to mere acquaintances, let alone male ones.

As we talk, I'm captivated by the way Reece's eyes crinkle when he smiles, and the gentle timbre of his voice, and, to be honest, by this entire side of Reece. And I'm having a really hard time imagining this man hurting my sister as badly as he did.

My phone buzzes on the island where I left it.

"You should get that," Reece says, getting up to clear our plates. "I'm sure it's someone checking on you, especially in this weather."

"You're probably right," I reply and get up to look.

It's a text from Eden.

> Hey, where are you? I went to Mama's but she said you hadn't gotten home yet. I thought we could watch a movie tonight?

My heart sinks a little, a twinge of guilt deflating the cozy bubble Reece and I had created.

> I'm at the mall in Missoula. Pick a movie. I'll be home soon.

Ugh, I hate lying to her, but I'm not ready to face all this right now.

"Everything okay?" Reece asks, seeing me staring at my phone.

"All good." I muster a smile. "But I should get going. The rain has let up."

From the way he eyes me, I almost imagine he can tell I'm not okay. But maybe I'm just paranoid.

"Oh, where are my manners?" I start gathering dishes. "I should help you tidy up first. You cooked. The least I can do is clean."

He places a hand over mine to stop me. "I can handle a couple of dishes. You're right. You should go before it gets too late."

His touch is very distracting. "Are you sure? It's no prob—"

"Paige," he says firmly, sending a coil of heat straight into my core. "I mean it."

I nod, mentally fanning myself, and grab my things.

Reece walks me out to my truck. The rain has stopped, replaced by a fresh, crisp night air that carries the lingering scent of wet earth. The sky is clear, revealing a blanket of stars above us. I inhale deeply as a different kind of storm brews within me. I unlock my door and Reece opens it for me.

I turn to thank him, and suddenly he's right in front of me. We aren't touching, but his sexy, wine-stained lips are dangerously close to mine, and his breath is hot against my face.

"Thanks for dinner," I say, my voice barely above a whisper.

"Pleasure's all mine, darlin'," he replies. "I had a great time."

Reece gently brushes some lingering chaff from my hair, his fingers lightly grazing my skin, and I struggle not to whimper. Our faces are inches apart, and the intensity in his gaze is overwhelming. I'm lost in the depths of his eyes, unable to move.

"You're coming over tomorrow, right?" he asks.

Wait, what? I'm suddenly as confused as I am flustered.

My expression must give that away. "For the sanctuary," he says gently. "I'll have my lawyers draw up the papers."

My sanctuary! Or I guess, our sanctuary. Mine and Reece's... I'd completely forgotten the reason I was here.

Business. That's all.

"Of course," I whisper, climbing into the driver's seat.

"Can't wait. Good night, Paige." Then he closes the door, leaving me to drive off into the night, my heart beating out of my chest. And my panties beyond *soaked*.

CHAPTER 4
REECE

averick and I watch as Buddy hops around the stall, nipping playfully at his mama. I reach down and pat the little calf on the head. "I think your mama's ready for you to join her back out in the pasture."

"Yep, he's healing up nicely," Mav comments. "Paige did a great job. She has a way with 'em."

"Sure does," I reply, my jeans getting a little uncomfortable just at the mention of Paige's name. I haven't heard from her yet today, but it's still early. Last night was...great. Having her there with me in the kitchen, and then talking over dinner—it was easy and exciting and damn frustrating all at once.

Seeing her in my T-shirt had my cock raging to the point of pain. I nearly excused myself to take care of things. But I knew it would probably only make things worse. Hell, the rest of the night was a testament to my Herculean self-control. There were so many times I wanted to pin her against the island and kiss her senseless. Or toss her onto the farm table and fuck her sweet, soft body until she screamed my name.

And yet, what really ate me up inside was how much I wanted to tell her how I feel. I couldn't bring myself to do it.

When I said goodbye, I could've kissed her. She had me convinced she wanted me to. But once again, I was a coward.

Mav leans against the pen and I feel his eyes on me. "You missed a doozy of a poker night, boss. Carter won big."

I raise my eyebrows and chuckle. "Damn, chose the wrong night not to be there." I can only imagine Carter's face when he won. He's one hell of a ranch hand, but the cards never seem to be with him, poor guy.

"You want to tell me what's going on with Paige?"

The question catches me off guard, but it's not all that surprising. I've worked with Maverick since he came to the ranch at eighteen. There's a level of camaraderie between us that has grown deeper over the years. He may be a lot younger than me, but he's earned my respect with his insight.

"I'm going to talk to you and the men about it tonight," I begin, "but I'm partnering with Paige to open a farmed animal sanctuary on the ranch." I've talked to Mav many times about the changes I've wanted to make concerning the future of the ranch. He's been on board from the get-go.

He smiles at me. "That sounds fantastic, Reece. I'm excited."

I grin. "Me too."

He gestures toward me with his chin. "There's more to it, though, isn't there?" His voice is low and soft, as if he's coaxing a skittish horse.

I rub my hand over my stubbled jaw. "N-no, not really."

My attempt to brush him off fails. "Reece." His tone is still gentle, but now there's a hint of steel. "Do I need to remind you about all the times I pulled your nuts out of the fire? I think I've earned the right to know when something's eating you."

I blow out a breath. He's right. I trust him.

"I love her, Mav," I blurt out.

His dark brows shoot up. "*Love* her? Hold up, didn't you just meet yesterday?"

I nod. "Yes, well, not really. I met her four years ago, only for a minute. That was when I fell for her."

He shakes his head, as if trying to understand. "And yesterday was the first time you'd seen her since?"

"Yeah."

His eyes go wide. "Oh shit! Did you hook up with her yesterday?"

"No! Of course not. Not that I didn't want to. But it wouldn't have been a hookup. I want her...forever." Now that I've said it, I feel like my innermost guts have been exposed and there's nothing I can do to protect them. I almost feel sick.

Mav's eyes go wide. "Who are you and what have you done with Reece Callahan?"

"Very funny." I swallow down the nausea.

"Sorry, boss," he chuckles. "So, tell me about that day back then," he says.

I relay the story. "And uh, I haven't slept with anyone since."

"*What*? Get out!" he exclaims, punching me lightly on the shoulder. "I've seen you with women."

"Swear to god." I hold up my hand. "I flirt, but never let it go too far."

Mav whistles low. "Four years. How have I not noticed?"

"I've kept busy?"

Seriously—it's been a long, lonely four years.

"Okay, Reece, let me ask you this," he says, chewing on a piece of straw. "What did you expect to happen? What was the plan right after you first saw her?"

"I never thought I'd see her again. Especially with me and Eden's history." I kick the dirt at my feet. "And I thought these

242

feelings would fizzle out, and I'd be back in the saddle again... so to speak."

Mav chuckles.

I take a deep breath. "I know I gotta tell her, but I'm scared shitless, Mav. What if I scare her off?"

"Then it's not meant to be."

My shoulders droop. "I'm not sure I could handle not having her in my life again." I run a hand through my hair. "And what do I do about her *sister*? I mean—Christ!"

Maverick turns and spits off into the distance. "You'd find a way to work that part out. Don't let the fear of what might happen stop you from taking a chance. You deserve to find your happiness."

I stare at Maverick, his young jaw set with conviction.

I nod. "I'll tell Paige today when she comes over."

He puts out his fist, and I bump it. "Good. You got this."

Do I?

I'm saddling up our pinto Mabel for Paige, but I'm a bundle of nerves.

I've already taken her through the stables and the pens and all the facilities near the main house, showing her what she's got to work with. But I want to ride out to the south pasture to talk. To tell her how I feel. How I've felt since the moment I saw her.

I've never been so nervous in my life.

As we head out, riding side by side, I look over at her. She's stunning; her dark hair back in that loose braid, showing off her slender neck, and her graceful hands on the reins directing Mabel. She wears a thin flannel shirt tucked into her form-fitting jeans, and well-worn leather boots. She rides with practiced ease, her hips rolling in time with Mabel's slow gait. It's goddamn mesmerizing. Oh, to be her saddle.

Fucking simmer down, Reece.

She's taking in everything around her, and the expression of her sweet face tells me she's full of ideas and excitement.

"Whatcha thinkin'?" I ask, steering Ollie closer to her.

She turns to me and rests her hands on the saddle horn. "Lots of things. I'm trying not to get overwhelmed by everything I want to do." She exhales slowly. "Are you absolutely sure you want to do this?"

She's already asked me more times than I can count. "I'm even surer every time you ask, darlin'."

Her lips curl up in a small smile.

"Have you thought of what you'd like to call this place?"

She shakes her head. "This is your *family ranch*, Reece. And Buck gave you his name. I can't ask you to change something like that."

Most of the town knows my story. How I ran away from an abusive home in eastern Montana at fifteen. Buck Callahan, who'd lost his wife at a young age and never had any children, took me in and showed me not only how to run a ranch and be a cowboy, but also what a real father and son relationship should be. He made it official by adopting me when I turned eighteen.

I smile as I get an idea.

"How about the Callahan & Alvarez Animal Sanctuary?"

"Reece, come on—"

"First one to the edge of the pasture near that row of spruce trees gets naming rights," I interrupt. "*And* you have to get off and touch the fence to win."

"But—"

"*Heeyah!*" I spur Ollie on, galloping off before she can protest.

"Hey! No fair!" she yells, and then I hear Mabel taking off behind me, as Paige whistles at her loudly.

She's gaining on me and Ollie, but I holler, "Come on, boy!" and give him more slack in the reins.

The pounding of hooves continues, until finally I near the finish line. I come to a stop, jumping off in the process and hurling myself at the fence.

"Callahan & Alvarez Animal Sanctuary it is!" I holler, as she jumps down behind me, laughing, and reaches out for the fence too late.

"Fine, you win," she says, almost tripping over a rock. I grab her before she falls, pulling her up against me, my back against the fence.

I open my mouth to speak, but now that she's right here in my arms, where I've dreamed about her being for years, I forget what to say.

She's gone quiet, those gorgeous eyes gazing into mine. I don't want to let her go. I want to kiss her, her mouth so tempting, her breath like a soft breeze stirring the hairs on my neck.

But I'm afraid of crossing that line and ruining everything.

She reaches up and runs her fingers over my lips. I hold back a moan at the tentative way she touches me, the way her soft skin brushes against mine, as if testing how far she can go. "You're playing with fire, darlin'," I growl, and her eyes flare. I kiss her fingertips, unable to stop my tongue from darting out to taste them.

She makes the sweetest sound in response, deep in the back of her throat. Which is, coincidentally, where I wish my cock was right now.

Have I crossed that line yet? Because god help me, I need more of Paige Alvarez.

Much, much more.

Her hands slide down my chest, her fists curling in my shirt.

"You should back away right now, hon."

"I should?" she says on a breath.

"I'm this close to taking you right here, right now in this pasture."

Line? What line?

I brace myself, waiting to realize I've gone too far. But her eyes turn dark, like black clouds gathering in a storm, and suddenly she's pulling my face down to hers, pressing her lush lips to mine.

I groan like a man who's just come in from a bone-chilling ride out on the range to a blazing fire.

Fuck me… This is my heaven.

I pull her body even tighter against mine, and when our tongues meet, she whimpers, my cock aching between us. She tastes sweet and spicy and I can't get enough of her as she grinds against me, exploring my mouth, driving me to desperation.

I take her hands and wrap them around my waist, kissing her neck. "Shit, darlin', I wanna taste every inch of you."

"Yes…please," she moans, clinging to me.

Arghh… We need to talk first. Before she regrets anything, and before we destroy this entire wonderful thing.

I pull back and take her face in my hands. "Paige… We can't do this. Not until we talk."

"Talk?" Her brow furrows, her eyes still clouded with desire.

"Yes, talk." I tuck a couple of stray hairs that have come loose from her braid behind her ear. "There's something you should know before the animal sanctuary comes to life."

She blinks a couple times, as if coming out of a trance, and I reluctantly leave her for a moment.

I step over to Ollie and remove the blanket I tied to the saddle earlier. I flap it open and lay it on the grass. "Get comfortable. I brought lemonade."

She takes a seat on the blanket, and I grab the bottles and hand one to her.

"What's going on, Reece?" Her face is lined with concern.

I sit next to her and down half my lemonade at once.

"Well…" I rub the back of my neck. "Do you remember that first day we met?"

CHAPTER 5
PAIGE

What the hell.

First, Reece and I are kissing, and it's better than I ever could've imagined. Better than any of my fantasies all these years. My body is hot, achy, and hungry for more...and the next thing you know he's pushing me away and asking about the day we met?

Is this some sort of sick joke?

Oh god—maybe Eden found out what I'm up to and put him up to it.

At least that enormous bulge in the front of his jeans is no joke.

I take a long, shaky breath, my heart beating so hard I'm afraid it will explode.

"Well, yes," I say. "But what does that—"

"Let me explain." He takes my hand, stroking the back of it with his thumb.

I nod, my nerves raw and fragile.

"About four years ago, I met the most beautiful woman I'd ever laid eyes on. I was ridin' down Main Street on Ollie. She was about to get in her truck, and I struck up a conversation with this angel. And all I could think about was that this was the woman I was gonna marry."

My breath catches. *What did he just say?*

"I wanted to tell you right then and there. But I found every excuse in the book not to. Every single one rooted in fear. Fear I'd make a fool of myself, but more to the point, fear of the completely different version of myself I'd become in a flash when I met you."

He chuckles and squeezes my hand fondly. "I mean, this cowboy had never said the word love or marriage to anyone, let alone himself. I'd never wanted those things before. I had a mind to see a doctor, thinkin' I might be touched in the head."

My stomach drops, like I'm on one of those rides at a theme park.

"*That's* why I broke up with Eden a few days later. Not because I thought anything would come of you and me. But because I realized she deserved a man who felt about her the way I feel about you."

I'm dizzy. I can't shake the fog of disbelief from my mind. Reece had the same moment I did all those years ago? The one that changed me forever?

"Say somethin', darlin', please," he begs, searching my eyes.

There's too much to say. But the first thing that springs to mind and bubbles up out of me is, "Then why did you tell my sister she wasn't good enough for you? That she wasn't good enough for anyone?" I clear my throat. "Reece, you told her she was a disgrace to the town."

He rears back as if I had punched him. "Paige, I said no such things. I swear on Buck's grave."

"Why would she make that up?"

He pulls my hand closer. "I don't know. But I wouldn't

ever say something like that, especially not to a sweet girl like Eden."

I put my face in my hands. Did Eden lie? To me, to mama, to everyone? She couldn't have. But why would Reece lie? After all this?

When I finally drag my gaze back up to him, Reece is looking at me with the saddest eyes I've ever seen.

"You have to believe me, Paige. About everything."

God, I want to. So, so much.

I cup my hand against his stubbled jaw, and he leans into my touch. "I do believe you. Because I remember that day, Reece. It changed me, too. I fell hard for you. So hard I thought I was insane. I'd never felt that way about a man before. And since then, no man has come close to making me feel like you did that day."

The widening smile on his face quickly turns feral, and he tosses aside his lemonade bottle. "Thank fuck," he growls. "I hereby vow to do everything in my power to keep it that way, always." He pushes my empty lemonade bottle off the blanket and crawls over me. "You're mine, darlin'. Please let me show you what that means."

There's no thinking straight when he looks at me that way. "Yes," I whisper, before his mouth meets mine in one swift rush.

His tongue sweeps into my mouth as he presses me into the blanket in the tall grass.

His.

The word echoes in my head as he rolls his hips against me. I cry out into his mouth, my body aching everywhere.

I thrust my hands into his soft hair, pulling him closer.

He snarls, his kisses moving to my ear. "My sweet Paige…" he whispers, his breath hot on my skin. "I need you naked. Now."

He pulls at the buttons on my shirt and shifts so I can get up and slide it off. While I'm there, I untuck his shirt and undo the buttons. He rips it off along with his undershirt, and I'm left staring at his hard pecs and mouthwatering six-pack abs.

My hands roam over his skin as he unhooks my bra. The cool air hits my bare breasts, and I lie back. "So goddamn beautiful," he groans, then goes straight to removing my boots and jeans.

Through my panties, he rubs small circles with his thumb. I moan. "Reece…"

"Fuck, darlin', you're soaked."

I arch back, his thumb sending bolts of pleasure through my core. My legs involuntarily spread. "Don't stop."

"Ah, baby, is just this tiny motion driving you crazy? Making that pussy throb and ache?"

"Oh…" I raise my hips to him, craving his touch.

As I close my eyes, he slides both hands up my sides and lowers down. "Not yet, my sweet. I have plans for this needy body." He cups and massages one of my breasts, teasing my nipple between his fingers. He presses kisses onto my other breast, licking and sucking, laving the peak until I'm buzzing underneath his mouth.

His fingers graze my ribs. "Paige…" he gasps in alarm. "Are these bruises from yesterday?"

My eyes fly open and I hesitantly nod.

He curses. "I'm so sorry, hon. Every single one will get kissed better, I promise."

I smile as he softly kisses my ribs, my arm, my knee and my shin, leaving me breathless. He peels down my panties and kisses low on my hip. "But I don't have a bruise there…" I venture playfully.

"I know," he replies. "But I also know how much this is aching right here." He drops a kiss right on my pussy, his tongue sliding into my folds. I moan, nearly bucking my hips at the shock of pleasure.

"See, you need my tongue and mouth to heal you up good." He pushes my thighs apart and dances his tongue over my tender, wet flesh until my hips tremble and my very toes curl.

"Your taste is addictive," he whispers against my pussy, coaxing more gasps and moans from me. He sucks and licks at my skin, moving toward my clit. My core clenches in anticipation.

He feathers a hand over my belly. "I love how your body reacts to me. I can't wait for you to come all over my face."

I reach down, grasping at his hair as he rasps over my clit, teasing and licking. I pull at his hair. "Yes, Reece. God, *yes*."

He squeezes my thighs, moaning into my pussy, sending delicious vibrations all over my skin.

My legs shake and I suddenly explode, my hips rocking up. Reece doesn't let up, drinking in my orgasm, playing with my hyper-sensitive skin. "Yes, my girl. That's it. More. Come for me."

"Yes, Reece. Yes!"

My body jerks under his tongue and still he holds on, wrenching every ounce of pleasure from me until I've come down. My breathing is heavy as he kisses the insides of my thighs, my hips, my belly, then teases my nipples before snaking his way back to my mouth. He kisses me deeply and I savor the taste of myself on him.

"You are the most gorgeous creature when you come, Paige," he says, his voice hoarse and deep. He gets up onto his knees, straddling me. "Ready to do it all again?"

I'm hypnotized as he unbuckles his belt and opens his fly. His big cock springs out of his boxers. I gasp.

"I hope you like it, darlin'," he says, rolling off to the side to remove his boots, jeans, and boxers. "Because every inch is for you and only you."

I reach down to touch his thick cock. "I do like this, Reece. A lot." I wrap my hand around the tip and spread the slickness that is seeping out the tip.

His eyes close, and he purrs. "*That* is nice…"

He's big, and rock-hard. As I rub over him, his skin glossy and velvety smooth under my fingers, he gasps and jerks. I'm dying to know how it would feel sliding against the inner walls of my core, how the thick veins would throb inside me.

As I roll to face him, he groans. "I don't have a condom."

"I'm on the pill. Have you been…tested recently?"

His eyes focus on mine. "I was, a while back. But I haven't needed to be since. I haven't been with a woman since the day we met."

"What?"

He nods. "Swear on a stack of bibles."

"I want you inside me, Reece. So much. But I'm…"

"Nervous?"

I duck my head. "A little. I've never, um, had sex before."

"Darlin'…" He groans and strokes my cheek. "If this is too much too soon—"

I squeeze his cock, and he inhales sharply. "No. I want to do this. With you," I say. "Now."

"Yes, ma'am." He grins and pushes me onto my back. He positions himself on top of me, kissing my face, my neck. "You're an angel…" he growls, and I feel his hard length pressing against my opening.

His green eyes never leave mine as he slowly pushes into me. I bite my lip at the stretch, the burning pinch.

"Breathe, hon. The pain will pass."

I take a few deep breaths and try to focus my spinning

mind. *Reece Callahan is making love to me.* How the heck did this happen?

Reece rocks his hips, and the motion does indeed begin to feel better with each movement.

His face is still, almost pained.

"Am I doing something wrong?" I ask, worried.

He laughs. "No. *God*, no. Everything's so right. I'm just tryin' not to come so soon. It's been a long time, Paige."

I smile as his thrusts get deeper and harder. My head falls back. "Oh, Reece… That feels incredible."

He moans, grabbing at the nape of my neck, kissing me. "Fuck, yes. I wish it could last forever."

"We can always do it again," I say, feeling the tremble in my legs.

"Always," he replies. "I'll always be ready for you." His words come out choppy and stunted.

"I'm going to come."

"Goddammit," he says. "Me too."

I wrap my arms around him as he thrusts into me, his rhythm erratic, his breathing turning ragged, and his moans becoming raw and desperate.

"I love you, Paige," he rasps in my ear.

And I'm coming in an instant, back arched as my body convulses yet again.

He roars as he comes apart in my arms, holding onto me for dear life. "Fuckkk," he cries, and I feel a blast of wet heat shoot deep inside me.

"Damn, baby…you…" He trails off, heaving over me, muscles spasming.

I close my eyes against the afternoon sun, spent and satisfied. Reece finally slides out and rolls off me, pulling me close against him. My leg rests over his, our bodies sweaty, muscles like jelly.

"I love you, Reece," I say on a happy sigh.

He kisses the top of my head. "You made my day, darlin'."

I smile into his shoulder, inhaling his delicious musk. "We should probably get dressed. Any of your guys could see us if they rode out this way. And poor Ollie and Mabel have already seen more than any horse should."

He chuckles. "The guys have no reason to come out here." He pats my ass. "But I'm definitely getting hungry. What say we go back to the house and get some lunch?"

My stomach rumbles and I roll my eyes. "I guess that's your answer."

He grins, sweeping me into another deep kiss that I feel all the way down to my toes. A girl could get used to this.

"Shit, any more of that and we'll never get home," he says, giving me one more peck before rolling away.

We get dressed, and I try not to get caught admiring his body—all muscled and tan. I shake my head in disbelief. How could I ever have thought this man would turn *grizzled*? He's only getting better with age.

As he's tying the blanket on Ollie's pack, I see his phone in the grass. I bend down to get it and a text briefly pops up on the screen.

Okay. See you then.

It's from Eden.

Why would Reece need to see her? And why wouldn't he tell me about it?

Something doesn't feel right.

I grab the phone as I get up. "Reece—your phone."

He pats his jeans, turning to look at me. "Shit, thanks, hon. Must've fallen out of my pocket in the rush to take off my pants." He grins, his tongue poking out playfully as he takes it from me, jamming it in his back pocket. "What would I do without you?"

I chuckle faintly as he gives me a boost up onto Mabel. "No idea."

"I'd be lost, darlin'. Lost." He swings up onto Ollie.

I *know* I should give him the benefit of the doubt. I mean, he just told me he loves me.

But what could he possibly want with Eden? Especially now?

I'm still sore as we head out, and feverishly hoping the pain won't be spreading to my heart anytime soon.

CHAPTER 6
REECE

Mama Alvarez opens the door in answer to my quiet knock.

"Reece," she says, her eyes shooting daggers.

I fiddle nervously with my hat as I hold it in my hands. "Afternoon, ma'am. May I please talk to Eden? She's expecting me."

"If you must," she sniffs. She moves back and gestures for me to enter. "She's out in the side yard, helping me with the laundry."

I step in and the heady smell of savory spices mixed with flowers hits me. Mama Alvarez is known for her green thumb, and the array of indoor plants makes her quaint home look more like furniture sprang up in the middle of a garden than anything. And I can tell she's making something delicious for dinner.

"Through that door," she says, pointing to a simple door with a homemade curtain over the window.

I nod and head out, closing the door behind me.

Sheets on a clothesline are gently flapping in the afternoon breeze. A clean freshness is in the air.

Eden is at the far end of the yard in a bright housedress and light sweater, taking down a pillowcase and folding it into a wicker basket. Her dark hair is pinned back, her lips the same cherry red that I remember.

She's pretty. And I see a lot of her mama…and Paige…in her dark eyes and figure.

"Why are you here, Reece?" she asks flatly, not taking her eyes off the laundry she's folding. "Your text was cryptic, to say the least. Did you change your mind about me? Because that ship has sailed, mister."

I fight the urge to roll my eyes. Before I met with Paige, I'd set this meeting up so I could make amends for what happened between Eden and me all those years ago. But that was before Paige dropped that bomb about what Eden had told her. "I need to know why you told Paige, your mama, and god knows who else that I said all those cruel things to you when we broke up."

She stops but doesn't look at me. "I…how did you—"

"Paige told me."

Her brow furrows and she puts her hands on her hips. "Paige?" She exhales and swivels her head toward me. "You're keeping company with my *sister* now?"

I nod. "For what it's worth, Paige came to me. We're going in together on her animal sanctuary. We'll be using my property."

"What? That little sneak—"

"Now hold up. Don't you dare. You know full well I only had good things to say about you, Eden. And yet, Paige and the rest of the town all seem to think I'm some monster, thanks to you. Why is that?"

Her knuckles turn white as she grips the laundry basket. "I was hurt, okay?! I thought we were at the start of something amazing and you just ended it! Men never want a relationship with me, they just want a few dates and a roll or two in the hay. When you showed interest beyond that, I thought I'd hit the jackpot. The wild and free cowboy wanted to be with *me?* And *only* me?"

She drops the basket onto the grass. It tips over, spilling the clean sheets. "But no. Eden strikes out yet again." She perches on a small wooden table under the clothesline. "So I made something up. Something that made you sound like a jackass. People finally felt I'd been wronged for once, rather than shaming me for what they call *promiscuous behavior*."

I take a deep breath. No wonder the townspeople were suddenly less friendly to me. Especially Mama Alvarez. She makes it very clear she hates my guts.

"I'm sorry, Reece. It's just every time someone mentions your name, I get upset all over again. It's hard to forget those feelings of rejection."

I scratch my jaw. "While I'm not at all happy you spread lies about me, Eden, you should know that one reason I initially asked you out was because you aren't like other women. You don't play games, you go after what you want, and you make no apologies for who you are. I like that about you, and many other men—good men that will stick around—will too."

She huffs out a breath and smiles weakly.

"Why do you have to be so darn nice, Reece?"

I chuckle. "Am I really that nice?"

"Unfortunately...yes." She slides off her perch. "I guess I have to tell everyone the truth now."

I cock my head. "It would be the right thing to do. But if that's too much, I'd be happy if you just told the important people."

"Like Paige."

I nod. "And your mama."

She cringes. "Oh god. She's going to kill me."

Yeah, I got nothin' there. I know if Buck was still alive and I'd pulled a stunt like this, Buck would've made me pay, too.

"So… Paige convinced you to lease her the land on Callahan Ranch?"

"Something like that." I grin. "I'll let her tell you all about it." I walk closer and open my arms. "Friends?"

She nods. "Friends."

And I pull her into a hug.

"Thanks for being so good about this, Reece," she says. "Honestly, you have no reason to be."

I pull back with a warm smile. "It's nothin'."

Hopefully, we can laugh about this once I'm her brother-in-law.

CHAPTER 7
PAIGE

As I pull up to my mama's house, I see Eden's car and Reece's truck both parked out front.

I should've guessed.

I headed home after Reece and I had lunch to help mama with family dinner for the weekend. Reece had said he was off to the feed store.

Liar.

As I get out of my truck, I hear the low murmur of voices. I walk over to the fence and peek through the wooden slats.

Reece and Eden are locked in an embrace.

I think I'm going to be sick.

Tears spill down my cheeks and I run inside, slamming the door behind me.

Mama comes out from the kitchen, a furious look on her face. "Paige! The door!"

I just mumble an incoherent sorry through my tears and head to my room, bawling my eyes out.

So much for my strength, independence, and carefully guarded emotions.

One stupid man has turned me into a blubbering mess.

Now I know how Eden felt. Well, she can have him back if that's what she wants. But why would she want a cheating cowboy?

Oh god, and now he's my business partner.

"Paige!" Mama yells through the door, knocking. "What's wrong?"

She rattles the knob, but it's locked.

"Tell me," she says, softer.

"Men! I hate them! They're a bunch of lying jerks!"

She huffs out a laugh. "Well, no argument from me there."

I can hear more voices behind her now.

"What did you do this time, Reece?" I hear mama say angrily.

"I—"

"He didn't do anything, mama," Eden interrupts. *Eden, you traitor*! "Just hold on. Let me talk to her."

"No!" I yell through the door. "I don't want to talk to you or anybody. Go away and leave me alone!"

"Paige, please… Let me explain." It's Reece, and his voice still makes my heart and body sing. But who cares, he doesn't want me. He wants *Eden*. My stomach roils.

"Haven't you done enough to my girls already?" Mama says. "You should leave right now."

"Mama, stop!"

"How about I wait outside," Reece says quietly, before I hear the front door open and shut.

"I have the key, Paige. I'm coming in." The doorknob jiggles, and Eden opens the door.

"Go away," I say again dully, before turning and shoving my face down into my pillow.

"Stop it." The bed moves as she sits on it next to me. "You're acting like a child."

I push myself up and glare at her. "Don't you start with me, Eden. I saw you and Reece out back, all chummy. Getting back together with the man who tossed you out like so much trash when he was done with you? I mean, how desperate for a man *are* you?"

As soon as the words fly out of my mouth, I regret them.

She crosses her arms. "Wow. Seriously low blow, Paige. Are you done slinging insults so I can clue you in?"

I groan and roll up to a sitting position. "Sorry, I just—like —*how could you*?"

She shakes her head, looking at me strangely, confused. "I'm not back with Reece. We're just friends again. He came here and confronted me about…"

She trails off, as if searching for the right words. "About…?" I prod.

"I lied about how it went down when Reece broke up with me. He never said all those horrible things that I said he did. I was…just trying to get a little sympathy, I guess."

So she *did* lie! Reece was telling the truth!

"Eden… That's really shitty. How could you?"

She takes a deep breath. "Like I said, I wanted pity rather than shame. I *know* what people say about me, Paige. It… hurts."

I glance down at my hands.

"Reece didn't ask me to make a public apology, but I'm going to. I don't know how, but I will. He deserves that. I wanted to tell you and mama first, though."

"So you're *not* getting back together," I say, wiping the tears from my face.

"No, not even close." She gives my shoulder a little shove. "But why would you be so upset about that, anyway? Even if you are going into business with him?" She grins. "He might have told me about the animal sanctuary. But why would you care if I was involved with him?"

As soon as the words leave her mouth, I can see realization dawning on her face. Her eyes go wide. "You're in love with him."

"N-no…" I say, avoiding her eyes, my cheeks heating.

"That's it, isn't it? It's the only thing that makes sense. You're not just business partners. You're in love with him." She shakes her head. "That was fast. It's been like, what, a couple of days?"

"Well…"

And then I tell her all about that day four years ago, and the reason Reece told me he broke it off with her. That he thought she deserved better, someone who felt about her the way he felt about me.

She leans back on the bed, taking a deep breath. "My god, I messed up even more than I thought, didn't I? He's actually a really decent guy."

I nod. "He is."

"Well then, what are you waiting for, girl? Go to him!"

I wipe my face with my sleeve. "You're really okay with it?"

She grabs my hand as I get up and grins. "Oddly… Yeah, I am. I want you to be happy. If he makes you happy, I'll support that. I love you, Paige."

I feel a happy tear fall down my cheek, and I tackle her. "I love you, too, Eden!" I say into her hair as I hug her tight.

She laughs, I laugh, then she rolls me up. "Now *go*. I'll tell Mama everything so she doesn't worry—or chase after Reece with her biggest, scariest spatula."

I take one last long look at Eden smiling at me on the bed, then run out the door.

Reece is out front, leaning against his truck. He looks up

and tears off his hat, tossing it in the open window of the cab. "Darlin'…?" he whispers.

And I'm off running toward him.

He steps forward and I hurl myself into his arms, kissing him all over his face, then on his sexy mouth, as he grips my ass and pulls me close against him.

I don't want to stop, I'm so completely consumed by him, but I finally come up for air.

"I guess Eden explained everything, then?" he asks, his voice hoarse.

I nod. "Yes. And I'm so sorry for what she did to you."

"It's in the past. All I care about is what you think of me now. Everyone else can go to hell." He kisses me quickly, then pulls back. "Well, and I'd prefer it if your mama didn't hate me."

I smile. "Eden's talking to her now."

"Good. Then there's only one thing left to do to make this right." He sets me down on the ground, then takes my hand and drops to one knee, pulling a small box from his jacket pocket.

"Paige Alvarez, I've waited way too long to do this. You're the woman of my dreams, and I'm happy beyond belief you came back into my life. I don't want to spend one more moment apart from you, so I hope you'll marry me and let me make you the happiest woman in the world."

I blink back happy tears as he opens the box. The ring is beautiful—antique, for sure. Two diamonds set in silver with a simple, timeless design.

"This was Buck's wife's ring. He left it to me to give to the woman I marry. I honestly never thought I'd use it. But here we are."

I chuckle. "I never thought I'd get married either. But—yes."

His smile widens, and my cowboy's green eyes glisten with what might be tears.

He eagerly slides the ring on my finger, and miraculously, it fits.

And then he wraps me in his arms and kisses me like I know he will for years to come.

EPILOGUE - REECE

ONE YEAR LATER

I tiptoe into the single stall as quietly as I can after checking on the rest of the animals for the night.

The light is dim, but I can see Paige seated in the soft hay, back against the far wall, eyes closed, precious lips parted in sleep. In her lap, I can just see the little fuzzy head of our newest resident, Timmy the donkey, sleeping peacefully. Timmy's previous owner's property went into foreclosure and we were notified of a neglected young donkey that needed a special home.

Timmy, sadly, proved to be one of the worst cases of animal abuse we'd ever seen, having known nothing but cruelty from humans for his entire short, sad life. Everyone on our team has tried working with him, but he responds best to Paige, so she's made it her mission to earn his trust.

It's clearly working.

I approach them from the other side and slide down to sit next to her. Timmy opens his eyes sleepily, but when he sees me settle down next to Paige, they close again.

It's great to see him curled up with her like he feels

completely safe, and I'm thrilled he's starting to feel comfortable with us.

It's been a year since C & A Animal Sanctuary opened—we decided that our full last names made it a bit of a mouthful, so it usually gets shortened like that—and it's been a huge success. We currently house about sixty animals: chickens, goats, pigs, sheep, horses, cows, even a llama or two. It's hard work, both physically and emotionally, but at the end of the day, I'm proud of what we do. The community has embraced our program as well, and they've donated time and money to us in many thoughtful ways.

And Paige herself never ceases to amaze me with her energy, commitment, and passion for these animals. I love her more and more each day.

I turn and nuzzle her neck, pulling the collar of her shirt back to kiss her skin, loving her scent, her taste, and every sweet sound she makes.

She stirs and moans. "Hi, Reece," she whispers, glancing down. "Timmy went out like a light." She strokes his head.

"Hey, darlin'. Yes, he even saw me sit down, but didn't budge."

"Excellent," she says, turning her head to kiss me. Her tongue slips into my mouth, and I growl.

I can't resist. I undo a couple of buttons of her top with one hand and slide it inside. A gasp escapes her lips as I tease the stiff peak of her tit.

"No fair," she sighs, as I play with her nipples. "You know I can't reciprocate right now."

"I know," I say. We've been exploring her body and all the ways I can please her since the day I proposed. I've discovered I can bring her to orgasm simply by teasing her sensitive places and talking dirty to her. I can't wait to continue experimenting.

I truly have the best life a man could ever ask for. A sexy, loving wife, a fulfilling business, good friends... I'm as content as little Timmy snoozing in my beautiful wife's lap.

"You gonna stay out here all night?" I ask.

She yawns. "Maybe just a little longer. Unless I can bring him into the house with me?"

I level my gaze at her. "I draw the line at livestock in the house." Although really, I'd probably let her do whatever she wants. She knows it, too.

She smiles. "You go in. Maybe you'll wake up later with my mouth on your cock."

I groan. "How am I supposed to get to sleep now?" She chuckles as I get up and open the stall door quietly. "Love you."

"Love you too," she replies, as I head out.

Walking back to the house, my phone buzzes and a text comes through from Gavin. Cool. I haven't heard from him in a while.

> Remember when I caught the garter at your wedding?

> > You didn't exactly catch it. It landed in the champagne glass you were holding when your back was turned. It's the one time I might've believed in magic.

> Caught, landed, whatever. I have some news.

This should be good.

HIS BIG SPARK

CHAPTER 1
GAVIN

"Until next time, Mr. Layne. Always a pleasure."

The young pilot presses his back against the cabin wall to allow me through the exit of the small plane, flashing an impeccable, pearly-white smile.

He's at least fifteen years younger than me. The flight attendant looked like she was right out of high school.

I slide into my car in the private lot adjacent to the tarmac, idly wondering if I'm getting too old for this.

These international consulting jobs seem to take more and more out of me every year. I enjoy myself while I'm there, of course—make some good money, see the sights, sample the local food (and sometimes the women). But these days I miss my daughter Willa, my friends, and my newly remodeled home in Deepwood Mountain…not to mention the absolutely *magical* massaging recliner in the den.

Yep, I'm officially old.

I loosen my tie and undo the top couple of buttons of my shirt, sinking into the buttery soft driver's seat that fits me like a glove. I'm so beat I could take a nap. But last time I checked this Bentley convertible was made for driving, not sleeping in.

Typically, I sleep on the plane home, dreaming about my next adventure. It's a habit. But this time, something was off. Probably my aging body telling me to slow the hell down.

Wonderful.

I crank up the music for the ride home and pop the top down, letting the sunshine warm my skin and the mountain air fill my lungs.

Halfway through the three-hour drive, which is how long it takes on the scenic route, the car drops suddenly. There's a horrible scraping noise as I pull off to the side of the highway.

What kind of pothole from hell was *that*? Jesus.

When I get out, I notice the lean at the front of the car immediately. That doesn't look right. I shrug off my suit jacket and roll up my sleeves before squatting down to take a closer look. I'm an electrician, not a mechanic—that's my best friend and now son-in-law, Dash, who builds motorcycles for a living —but even I know the bent metal I'm looking at is not ideal.

I huff and give the tire a swift kick for good measure.

"Call Sam's Towing," I say into my phone.

A rough, familiar voice answers after two rings.

"Sam!" I cry. "Gavin Layne here."

"Gavin, my friend. Long time no see." The sounds of a drill and clanking metal are blasting in the background. "What can I do ya for?"

"I'm stuck out here on Highway One just past Porter's Corner. I think I hit a pothole pretty hard. I'm no expert, but it doesn't look good."

He makes a pained whistling sound through his teeth. "Oh boy. You in that new Bentley I heard about?"

"Yeah." I lean back against the door glumly, pinching the bridge of my nose.

The hiss of compressed air gets louder over the phone. "Hang tight, brother. I'll get someone out there in a tow truck."

"Thanks, Sam." I hang up and settle into the driver's seat to wait.

It really *is* comfortable. I tilt the seat back a little and let my eyes drift closed under my sunglasses. With the music playing and the warmth of the sun, it's not long before I drift off.

CHAPTER 2
KAT

D*amn, she is one sweeeet ride.*

    I wolf-whistle as I pull up behind the shiny new Bentley GT Convertible in midnight blue.

I'd only ever seen older model Bentleys in L.A.—and *those* were drop-dead gorgeous. But this one had to be brand spanking new! And a convertible, to boot! Always a playful choice on a luxury car.

Sam knows I have experience with cars like these. He just doesn't know exactly how I *got* that experience.

And…well… If he's not asking, I'm not telling.

He'd mentioned in passing that the owner of this beauty, Mr. Layne, was a good guy. Hmm. In my experience, people who own this kind of car rarely are. More like, snobby and rude.

No big deal. I have no problem putting an arrogant prick in his place. I just have to remember to watch my damned mouth around customers. I need to keep this job.

I slide out of the tow truck and see Mr. Layne reclined in the driver's seat. Even after I shut my door, he doesn't move. Probably on his phone, oblivious to the world around him.

Figures.

His loud snoring makes me pull up short as I walk up to the side of the car. The guy sounds like an injured moose.

I snort. Mr. Luxury-Car-Designer-Sunglasses-and-High-End-Suit is gonna scare off potential gold-diggers with that racket if he's not careful.

Getting closer, I study him. *Wow...dude's a looker.* Mouth hanging open and everything, I can still see his clean-shaven jaw is chiseled to perfection. He's got thick sandy blond hair and there's a powerful chest hiding under that crisp white dress shirt, muscles straining at the fabric.

Mr. Layne's got it going *on.*

Okay, enough checking out the sexy sleeping moose.

"Sir..." I murmur.

He doesn't budge.

"Sir," I say again, louder.

Nothing.

I reach out and tentatively poke his bicep. Fuck, it's rock hard. I'm tempted to run my fingers over it, but manage to stop myself, thank god.

"Mr. *Layne.*" I jostle his arm.

"Nothing to drink, thank you," he mumbles, then opens his eyes and starts.

"Oh, shit...sorry." He yawns and wipes a bit of drool from the corner of his mouth. "I must've drifted off." He pushes his sunglasses up onto his head, and I'm struck by his dreamy eyes, the same deep blue as his car.

They give me the once over. "You sure I'm awake? I'm only used to seeing women as stunning as you in my dreams."

A sweet talker too? He smiles, and I admit... He is *fine.*

"Oh, you're awake all right. The god-awful snoring has stopped." I put a hand on my hip.

He presses the button to return the seat to upright, letting his sunglasses fall back into place. "You heard that, huh," he says, wincing.

"I don't think anyone could *not* hear it, Mr. Layne."

He licks his lips, and my gaze zones right in on them. *Dammit, Kat.*

"Well now you know my only flaw," he says, staring up at me with a playful smile. "And, please—call me Gavin."

I step back so he can get out of the car. And again…wow. He's tall, broad, and bulky in *allll* the right places. I rarely look twice at clean cut guys. But this one oozes something raw and heady and undeniably masculine.

I zero in on his tan forearms, where he's rolled up his sleeves. When he catches me, he flexes, shoving his big hands into his pockets. *Busted.*

I clear my throat, "I'm Kat. Sam sent me."

The corner of his mouth quirks up. "For the tow? Really?" It's clear he wasn't expecting a woman to come out to help him.

I square my shoulders. "Is that a problem?"

"Not in the least…Kat," he replies, his voice low and gravelly and doing weird things between my legs.

"I haven't seen you around Deepwood before," he adds.

"I've been gone for a while. I'm staying with Gran for now."

He cocks his head to the side as his eyes narrow. His brow pops up. "You wouldn't be Mrs. Holloway's granddaughter, would you?"

I cross my arms over my chest, and his eyes flick to my cleavage for a moment. I'm sure he's heard a ton of things about me from the town gossips. Unfortunately, most of it was probably true, but despite that, I hold my head high. "That's me."

"Well, welcome back then," he says, and pauses before turning back to the car. "Apparently, unbeknownst to me, there are gaping caverns on this highway, and I went right over one without a care in the world." He pouts. "The poor car didn't stand a chance."

I chuckle. "Let's take a look, then." I admire the car's sensual lines and whistle. "She's a real beauty, you know."

He moves aside. "Indeed," he replies. When I glance back, he's still looking at me. A shiver runs up my spine. *Stop. No. Do not let yourself get carried away by these feelings.* Men like Gavin don't go for women like me. Maybe as a dirty little secret for a quick fling. But I'm too thick, rough, and tattooed to be anything more. Besides, I'm in my coveralls and combat boots. There's nothing alluring about this get-up.

"You have experience with cars like these?" he asks anxiously, as I lean down to inspect the wheels and under-carriage.

"I did work in L.A. that exposed me to all kinds of luxury cars." I don't mention that it was less-than-legal work.

I see the bent metal. A shame, for such a sweet ride. "You do have some damage. It's not a difficult fix, but I'll have to tow it back to Sam's. You shouldn't drive it like this."

"I'll trust your expertise," he says, sighing. "I'm pretty useless with cars, which annoys my best friend Dash to no end. He's tried over the years to teach me, but I think my brain's too full of electrical knowledge for there to be room for anything else."

"Oh! So you're part of the Blue-Collar Millionaire Club?" I ask, as I get his car ready for the flatbed.

The Blue-Collar Millionaire Club is the nickname the town gave the six best friends who started blue-collar businesses that eventually made them all millionaires. It makes the town of Deepwood Mountain unique out here in the middle of rural Montana. Those guys and their businesses have helped the town immensely. They've brought in new people, new business, and new development, without the big city problems that usually come with all that.

It's something I hadn't really noticed before, growing up. Or maybe I'd been too young to appreciate it and instead just desperately searched for a way out of what I thought was a sleepy, dead-end town with nothing to offer. Bottom line, I took it for granted...and ended up paying the price.

Gavin nods. "BCMC for life." He flashes a ridiculous attempt at a gang sign, and I can't hold back.

"Please never do that in public again," I say in between giggles.

"But...why not?" he asks, with a not-so-innocent grin that makes my pussy tingle.

Kat, you need help.

"Oh, and I've noticed two more flaws," I say.

"What? *Two*?" He scuffs the dirt.

"Useless with cars and...kinda dorky." I shrug.

"Come on!" he groans. "I'll give you the car thing, but dorky? You don't think I'm cute? In a silly, adorable way?"

"I'll think about it," I say, and he nearly pouts.

After I finish hooking up the Bentley, we get into the truck. His expensive cologne mixed with his natural musk fills the cab. It's very distracting, as is the way his eyes follow my every move.

I start the engine.

"Hey, Kat," he says, voice low.

"Yeah?" I turn to him.

"Thanks for coming out to save me." He leans closer. "Don't tell Sam, but you're my favorite tow truck driver now."

I grin. "I won't tell him. I wouldn't want to hurt his feelings."

He chuckles. "Aww. And you're a kind soul, on top of being a knockout."

I turn back to the road. He needs to quit with that, right now.

Or else... I'm going to start believing him.

CHAPTER 3
GAVIN

W ho *is* this gorgeous creature?

Mrs. Holloway's granddaughter, that's who. The one who upped and left five years ago, just like that. Mrs. Holloway never talks about it, but from what I heard, she ran off with the leader of a motorcycle gang from Los Angeles.

It broke Mrs. Holloway's heart. She'd taken Kat in after her parents died in a car crash when Kat was a teenager. But Kat was a handful, always getting into trouble and finally getting kicked out of school. She loved cars but learned about them from some of the scummiest dudes around.

But my god, Kat is beautiful. That curvy, sultry body under those coveralls, which is unzipped far enough for me to salivate over those big, luscious tits. Long, glossy red hair cascading from her black bandana tied around her head Rosie the Riveter style. Hazel eyes enhanced by winged eyeliner and dark lashes. And sweet red lips, as plump and dewy as I can imagine her decadent pussy—

Settle down, Gavin.

She's young. Probably younger than my daughter, who's twenty-five. I'm over forty now. I shouldn't be obsessing over a woman half my age. Besides, why would she want to waste her time with an old fart well past his prime?

"What brings you back to Deepwood?" I finally ask, resigned to being friendly. Not flirty. Just friendly. *Sigh.*

She's quiet for a while as we drive past the tall trees and grass, mountains in the distance. I wonder if she's going to answer.

"Peace and quiet."

Interesting. I heard she was looking for the exact opposite when she left.

"I'll bet your grandmother is thrilled to have you back."

She huffs. "Can we please not talk about me right now?" She shakes her head, her hands gripping the steering wheel tight.

"Oh. Sure. You want to talk about me instead?" I suggest, leaning back in the seat.

She chuckles, and there's a dimple in her cheek. It's adorable.

"I guess." She glances over at me. "Were you coming back from a trip? I saw a suitcase in your trunk."

"I just got back from a consulting job in Koh Samui, Thailand. Decided to take the scenic route home from the airport."

"You do that a lot?"

"Travel for work, or take the scenic route?"

She shrugs. "Both."

"Well, I do keep busy taking jobs that require me to travel throughout the year. But when I come home, I like taking it easy. It gives me a chance to drive the Bentley." I pause. "Time to think, too. Been doing more of that lately."

"Sounds like you lead a pretty adventurous life."

"I've seen the world and taken the time to enjoy it, yes. But peace and quiet sounds better and better after each trip." I wink at her.

"Feeling your age, then?"

I huff, my ego deflating a bit.

"I'm *kidding*, Gavin," she says.

But there's some truth to it. Obviously.

"I *am* old."

"Please. Old men don't look this hot in a tailored suit."

What now? I look over at her and she's hiding a smile, her cheeks an adorable shade of pink. "I mean—"

I put my hand up. "No. Don't explain. Let me just live in that fantasy for a little while longer."

"What fantasy?"

"The one where the sexy young woman with her name embroidered on her coveralls thinks I'm hot."

She snorts and gives me some serious side eye. "Don't do that."

"Do what?"

"Patronize me."

"Ah, feels different when the shoe is on the other foot, doesn't it?" I tease. "Hon, I swear to you, I would never patronize you. How many times do I have to tell you you're beautiful before you believe me?"

She sighs and shrugs. "I dunno. Maybe ten?"

I laugh. "You got it."

We go quiet, and my stomach rumbles in the silence. "You mind if we stop for some snacks? I didn't eat much on the plane."

"We can do that."

At the next off-ramp, she exits and parks at a truck stop on the corner.

We get out and head into the store. I open the door for her and try not to stare at her spectacular ass as she walks past.

"Thanks," she says, brushing by me, igniting all my senses.

"My pleasure." *Seriously*.

I grab a bag of chips and she goes for a bottle of iced tea.

"A drink?" she asks me, pausing at the cooler.

"You asking if I want to go out for a drink with you sometime?"

I'm hopeless.

She levels an unimpressed gaze at me. "That was a reach...and pretty lame."

I make a face. "But did it work?" I get up close, breathing in her spicy scent. A tattoo peeks out from her coveralls near her neckline, and I stifle a groan, imagining tracing over it with my tongue, exploring her sweet skin.

I reach past her to grab a bottle of water. She doesn't move back, but I swear she trembles. There's no way this goddess is afraid of me, so I take that as a good sign.

"No," she finally whispers. The word doesn't match the smile on her lush mouth, but I won't cross that line. Even if my heart sinks a bit.

I head over to the cash and put my items on the counter, plucking the iced tea from Kat's hand. "This too," I say to the guy behind the register.

She opens her mouth to protest, but I cut her off. "Please. I insist."

She sighs and finally nods. "Fine."

The teenage clerk is staring directly at Kat's chest as he rings up the items.

"Eyes up here, bud." I tap my card on the terminal and slip it back into my pocket. "She's not a piece of meat."

He scoffs. "The fat cow should be so lucky," he grumbles under his breath.

"Say that again, asshole." Kat pushes past me, glaring.

I level my gaze at him. "Apologize to the lady. Now."

"Or what? She'll sit on me?"

I reach over and grab his collar. "Really, kid? You're going

285

to insult a woman you're attracted to because you're too chick-enshit to give her a compliment?"

The guy yells for me to let go, as he struggles in my grip, his shirt about to tear.

"I'm not opposed to putting you in a headlock, little boy."

"Okay! *Okay*! I'm sorry. S-sorry!" he sputters.

"Yeah, whatever, dickhead." Kat grabs our things and heads out, flipping him off.

I shake my head and push him back as I let go. "Learn to treat people with respect, okay? Especially women. Grow up."

CHAPTER 4
KAT

I'm used to men staring at me.

Either they're attracted to my body or not. But that's their problem, not mine. I've learned that how people feel about me is none of my business, just as long as they keep their opinions to themselves and stay respectful.

My shitty ex didn't care why a man talked to me or looked at me. He'd punch him out for it every time, but not because he gave a shit about my feelings. He'd punch him out because in his mind the guy was messing with his things. That's what I was. A thing. An object he could control.

And he definitely never stood up for me. I had to do that for myself.

So it feels kinda good to have someone looking out for you just because it's the right thing to do.

Gavin and I get into the truck in silence.

"Sorry you had to hear that," he finally says, taking the bag from me.

"He's just a punk kid."

He cracks the bottle and takes a sip of water. "I know, but you still don't deserve to be treated like that. By anyone."

I reach over and pull him closer by the loose tie around his neck. His brows lift in surprise when I kiss his cheek.

He smells good. Like fresh linen and rich soap. A five o'clock shadow has left his skin rough, and I get wet thinking about how it would feel against my inner thighs.

"What was that for?" he asks, his voice hoarse, eyes hooded.

"For being a gentleman." I pull back and smile, letting go of his tie.

He sits back in his seat, looking dazed, and I kinda like that I had something to do with that.

He shifts in his seat. "I'd really love to know more about you, Kat. You fascinate me."

I let out a long breath and turn onto the road. "Maybe I'm willing to talk now." I glance over at him. "Since I know you better and all."

He grins. "Okay. Why'd you leave Deepwood back then?"

He offers me the open bag of chips and I shake my head.

"A lot of reasons. I wanted to see what I was missing. I thought Deepwood was holding me back from being the strong, independent woman I wanted to be. When Bones came along, I was ripe for the picking."

"Wait, dude's name was *Bones*? And you willingly left with him?"

"Yes." I stick my tongue out at him. "I was naïve, okay? And stubborn."

"You, stubborn? Surely you jest."

I chuckle. "Fuck, the way I felt about Deepwood back then, any man could've gotten me to follow him. Just as long as it was away from here."

"What did you do out in L.A.?"

I pause. Did I want to tell him? I haven't even told Gran

everything yet. Just getting her to look at me has been hard enough.

"You don't have to tell me if you don't want to." He pops a few chips into his mouth. "I'm not one to judge." He winks. "Well, not much."

"I was…stupid," I confess.

"We've all been that."

I do trust Gavin. He genuinely seems to be a good guy. And it's like he gets me on a different level, which is something I've not had much luck with when it comes to men.

"So being stupid that one time is your only flaw?" he asks with a smile.

I chuckle. "You could say that."

"Then I'm all ears."

"I should start from the beginning," I say.

He nods and scarfs another handful of chips. "That's usually the best place."

"Basically, Bones was passing through Deepwood one day with his crew, saw me working on a car, and swept me off my feet. Like, literally. Hauled me up and onto the back of his bike. In the beginning, he was really charming." I shrug, remembering how sweet he was with me at the beginning. "I ran away to L.A. with him, filled with hope and his promises. Gran tried to reason with me, but there was no stopping me once my mind was made up. Stubborn, right?" I glance out the window. "I might have said some nasty things to her when I left. I regret them all."

My throat gets tight, but I continue.

"L.A. turned out to be a nightmare. We lived in a house with a bunch of other gang members and their women. The place was gross—filthy and falling apart—in a shit part of town. Everyone was always drunk and angry. The gang would steal cars, targeting the rich and their fancy rides. My job was to help remove parts for us to sell. We made good money, but these guys were always fighting and spending the money on booze, drugs, and other stupid shit."

I bite my lip and look over at Gavin.

"You're doing great," he says, and gives me a reassuring smile. He opens my iced tea and hands it over.

I take a sip, the cold liquid refreshing. "If ever I spoke up, or stood up to Bones, he'd hit me. He wanted me to 'know my place'. He wanted complete control." I shake my head. "Soon, I was always drunk and angry, too. Then one day Bones cut me during a fight, so deep I had to get stitches. After that, I was done. I planned my escape and pocketed enough money to take the bus back here."

Holy shit. I can't believe I just told him all that crap. It feels good to get it out, but saying it out loud somehow makes it more real, as real as one of those true crime documentaries I used to watch on TV.

Gavin's quiet next to me. I wouldn't blame him if he decided to jump out of the truck and book it down the road in the opposite direction.

"Pull over," Gavin finally says. It's an order.

I move the truck over to the shoulder and come to a stop, waiting for him to get out.

"Where did he cut you?" he asks, staring straight ahead, his jaw set. The words come out sharp.

I hold out my arm and to show the inside of my forearm. "There. Near the elbow. I was pushing him away, and he lashed out with his knife. See the scar?"

He takes a deep breath and holds my arm in one hand, running his finger over the welt. Tingles shoot through me from his soft touch.

Gavin's jaw grinds. He looks like he's about to explode.

"Are you mad?" I ask.

"Furious," he grits out. "At the pathetic excuse for a man who did this to you. He deserves to be locked up."

"Does he ever," I reply. He's still stroking the underside of my arm and it's making my belly flutter.

He looks up into my eyes, and I wish I could see his behind his shades. He cracks a smile. "You know you're completely amazing, right?"

"What?"

"You're the strongest person I know, Kat. And I know some pretty tough people."

Suddenly, my heart is fluttering, too.

"Yeah, well, apparently not strong enough to stay out of this fucking mess in the first place," I say, shifting in my seat.

"Hey—life doesn't always work out the way we'd like. I struggle with anger issues. But I got help and now I'm working on it." He lets go of my arm and I already miss his touch.

"That's what a grownup does," I say. "We all need help sometimes."

He smiles. "Well, anytime you want to talk, I'm here." He pauses and takes out his wallet. "I also know a therapist—my buddy Logan's daughter. She's friends with my daughter. You're all about the same age, actually."

He hands me a business card, and I nearly drop it. *Gavin has a kid my age?*

"I was married a long time ago," he says, noticing the look on my face. "My daughter Willa works with your grand-mother, as a librarian."

"No shit."

Fuck me. What am I doing flirting with this guy who's old enough to be my dad? A guy with a daughter my age, that for bonus points works with my Gran!

And why does my heart suddenly hurt over it?

CHAPTER 5
GAVIN

Kat's gone silent ever since I told her about my daughter.

Shit. Maybe I shouldn't have put that information out there so soon.

But if she can't handle the existence of Willa, then whatever we have going on here is moot.

If we have anything going on here.

If it were up to me, I'd make her mine right here and right now. The woman is incredible—beautiful, and sexy, and tough as nails. I just hope she'll give me a chance to show her how a real man treats his woman. Who the fuck cares if I'm...*shit*... twice her age.

By the time we make it to Sam's, he's already closed. Small town living means it's hard to find a shop open after five on the weekend.

She lets me out to wait while she gets the Bentley down and eases it into the garage to secure it for the night.

"Not going to lie, she sounds like crap," she admits as she gets out. She slides her fingers along the front fender, almost caressing it, and a shock of pleasure travels up my spine. Who knew a woman touching my car would make me so hard? But then again, there isn't much Kat could do that wouldn't turn me on.

Suddenly, the lights in the shop go out.

She gasps, and I instinctively reach for her, wrapping my hand around her waist.

"You okay there?" I ask.

"Yeah," she breathes. "Just caught me off guard." She doesn't pull away.

"You know where the electrical panel is? I can take a look if you like."

"Oh, right. You're the electrician. How convenient."

"Who better to be stuck with in the dark?" I whisper.

She scoffs, but when I let go of her to grab my phone from my pocket, she moves closer and holds onto my arm. My bicep flexes under her grip, and I feel goosebumps on her skin.

"The panel's in a closet just off the office," she says, as I boot up the flashlight. She tugs at me. "This way."

She guides us into the office and to a small closet in the back. She opens the door, revealing the panel. "Hold this for me?" I ask, giving her the phone.

Our hands brush as she takes it, and I feel electricity pulsing through my body like a conduit.

I quickly find the switch after I open the panel and flip it. The lights pop back on.

"That was fast," she says.

I take the phone back from her. "You'd rather stay in the dark with me?" I tease, and her cheeks go that shade of pink again.

She smirks, playfully punching my shoulder. "Get out so I can change. Then I'll take you home."

I should've just said I'd call a friend, or Willa, to come pick me up. But I selfishly want to spend as much time as possible with Kat.

I walk out and busy myself checking my email when I hear a commotion from the office. Then she curses. Repeatedly.

I knock on the door.

More cursing.

"Kat? I'm coming in," I say, before stepping inside.

Kat is sitting on the edge of the desk, a few strands of her red hair exploded out of her scarf, her coveralls zipper down near her belly button. She's wearing a sports bra, but it's not leaving much to my imagination. I gulp loudly.

"The goddamned zipper is stuck!" she yells, blowing her bangs up with a quick breath. "And I can't get these coveralls over my gigantic ass."

Oh, baby… "Can I help?"

"I hope so," she replies. "Or else I'm stuck in these fucking things forever. What happens when I need to pee?"

I laugh as I go over to her. I try not to look at the creamy skin of her belly, and the colorful butterfly tattoo on the left side of it. God, I want to touch her bare body everywhere. My mind spins, but I realize that we have to get the zipper up first, before it will come down.

"I'm going to pull it up, then add some graphite," I explain, grabbing a pencil off the desk. "To get it slick."

"Okay, MacGyver," she says with a smirk, her sweet face mere inches from mine.

I steady myself with a hand on her hip as I pull the zipper up. Then I draw the pencil over the zipper teeth in the area giving her trouble. It's difficult to concentrate on the job at hand, rather than her luscious tits at my chest and all that delectable skin in front of me, but I manage. When I get the zipper down near her belly button it sticks a little, but when she sucks in a bit, it cooperates and continues on down until I see her sexy red panties. The zipper is really slick now.

This woman is killing me.

I clear my throat. "Sorry, I didn't mean to go down that far."

Her cheeks redden. "S'okay. I'm just glad I'm finally free. You're my hero."

"I was hoping I could impress you *somehow*."

Her hazel eyes go wide. "Gavin... You've defended my honor against Cash Register Jerk, gotten the lights back on, and now saved me from the polyester queen's evil grip. How much more could you possibly do?"

"As much as it takes to get you to go out with me," I say with a wink, before turning to go. "I'll let you finish getting changed."

"Wait."

I turn back.

She bites her lip.

"I think I need more help getting out of these coveralls," she says huskily, arching her back slightly, pushing out her tits.

My cock thickens in my pants and I walk back to her, staring down into her pretty eyes, stroking her cheek.

Her eyes fall closed, and she shivers under my touch.

"Does that mean what I think it means? You said you didn't want to go out with me before."

Her eyes fly open. "I'm allowed to change my mind, right? Woman's prerogative and all that good shit?"

My heart thumps. "You can do anything you want, Kat." I run my thumb over her cheek. "I just want to make sure I'm reading your signals right. Tell me what you want."

Her eyes flash, and she grabs my tie, pulling me down to her lips.

I let out a groan as she kisses me, my hands sliding into her hair.

When her tongue touches mine, I shudder. She tastes like honey and sweet tea, and I'm instantly hooked.

She shrugs off the coveralls, and I'm helpless to stop myself from exploring her soft skin. I kiss, lick, and bite my way down the column of her throat to her shoulder. I slip my fingers into the straps of her sports bra and slide them off, lapping at the angry red marks underneath, soothing them with my tongue.

Kat moans as I pull the sports bra down, releasing her big, beautiful breasts. More colorful butterflies ink her skin and I lap at each one. I bury my face between her flesh, massaging them in my hands. I'm in heaven.

Her hands lock my head to her chest, but I manage to find a dusky pink nipple and suck and nibble until she's trembling beneath my lips.

"Touch my pussy, Gavin," she moans, and I slide my hand into her coveralls, feeling her wetness through those hot red panties.

"God, you're wet. Get up for a second, baby. I need to get these things off you." She stands and wriggles as I pull the material down. She steps out and, at the same time, pulls the sports bra straight over her head.

I attack her mouth, reaching around to get my hands inside her panties.

"I'm obsessed with this gorgeous ass," I growl against her lips, as I grab two massive handfuls. I could get off just grinding against her like this, but hell, I want more.

"I can tell," she whispers. "That hard cock of yours is going to make me come if you keep doing that."

"Mmm...tempting. But I want to see if your pussy tastes as

sweet as the rest of you. I want you screaming from my tongue." I pull her panties down as I say it, and she gasps.

"Lie back." I press her against the desk and pull over a chair. "I didn't get any dinner."

"You had a snack!" she exclaims, her laughter making her bare tits jiggle. I'm overwhelmed by everything I want from her body. This woman is a feast.

I start high, my hands on her belly, then move them down to caress her hips and inner thighs. I trace the tattoos on her pelvis with my fingertips as I gaze at her core. Her pussy is bare, and so wet and plump and pink I could get lost pleasuring it.

Pulling her hips to the edge of the desk, I place her feet on my knees.

I tease her from the bottom up, licking at her wet folds. She moans and writhes under my tongue, her sweet noises making my cock even harder.

"You smell like a summer meadow," I whisper, as I spiral my tongue around her clit.

She pulls at my hair, breath coming fast, hips rocking.

"I'd love to tease you all night," I rasp.

"Fucking hell, you're driving me batshit crazy," she whines, her body shaking.

I hum as I delve deeper into her body, licking and kissing, sucking on her wet flesh. Closing in on her clit again, she's a sputtering, shuddering mess. I flick and roll my tongue over her most sensitive spots, and she moans, clawing at me. "Oh god oh god oh god. Please, Gavin. Don't stop. Don't ever fucking stop!"

"Never," I say with a snarl, like a dog worrying its favorite bone.

Her hips grind against me, and I feel the trembling of her legs until finally she snaps.

"Fuck!" she screams. "Gavin, I'm coming!" Her pussy pulses under my mouth as I lick her through her orgasm.

"Kat, my sweet baby," I say, my voice hoarse and raw. "You're mine now."

And I've never meant anything more.

CHAPTER 6
KAT

My body quakes as Gavin wreaks absolute fucking havoc on my pussy.

Best. Orgasm. Ever.

And just from a man eating me out? That's never happened before.

I never came with Bones. He was too rough and full of himself to care what felt good for me. It was always about him.

But Gavin just read every single cue my body gave him perfectly. Maybe it's his experience talking. Age. Or maybe he just actually listened.

And goddammit, *I want him*.

I don't care if he's older or has a daughter who's my age.

I've never felt like this.

Hell, even before we got here, I wanted him. I just didn't want to admit it.

He *did* say I'm his just now. Did he mean that?

I lean up on my elbows and pull his head out from between my legs. He looks so hot there, his tanned skin a stark contrast to my white, inked thighs.

"Fuck me, Gavin. You're a keeper."

He grins, running his hands over my hips. "Your body drives me out of my mind. I could worship it forever."

And looking at the hungry way his eyes rove over me, I believe him.

"It's my turn to touch you. I want to see your sexy cock."

His brow arches. "Careful, baby. Hearing you talk like that will set it off."

I chuckle as he pushes the chair back to stand.

"That's the point." I wink. "Now, you work on your shirt, and I'll get you out of these annoying pants."

He growls and it sends a thrill straight through me.

As he unbuttons his shirt, I unfasten his belt and zipper, and reach in to feel silk boxers. "Ooh, fancy," I whisper, as he inhales sharply. "Almost too fancy for this old beat-up office of a mechanic's shop."

"You want to stop and go somewhere else?" he asks.

I squeeze his cock through his boxers, and he groans. "Shit, no."

"Thank fuck," he says, voice rough.

I finally free his cock from the boxers and stroke him slowly. He's big and thick and breathtaking. His head tips back. "Shit... No, no more of that, hon. I want to come inside your heavenly pussy."

I smile. "I can't even get a li'l taste of you?"

His eyes look pained. "If I see those gorgeous red lips around my cock, I'm done for. And I'm not afraid to admit it." He reaches down to fish something out of his pocket, and I watch as his naked body flexes and curls. The man has abs like a washboard. Yeah, I'll be licking those later.

He brings out a condom in a wrapper, then rips it open with his teeth.

I snatch it from him and roll it over the slick head of his

hard, raging cock. His belly contracts as I give him a few more strokes for good measure.

"You're a fucking dream," he chokes out. He takes my face in his hands and kisses me deeply, his tongue stroking mine with such passion and tenderness, tears prick the corners of my eyes.

What is the matter with me?

His hands rove over my body, palming my tits, before leaning over to line up his cock and my opening. He guides the tip slowly up and down my folds before pressing inside.

"How's that, beautiful?" he groans, filling me up to the brim.

I'm struck by the sincerity in his question. "Amazing."

He grins and begins to thrust into me.

"Holy fuck, that feels good," I moan. "You're so huge."

"Yeah? Glad you like it. I'm in another world here, baby." He grunts. "I'll warn you, I'm trying not to blow too soon."

I clench.

"Oh god…" He pumps into me faster, and I splay my knees outward, knocking over some folders on the desk. Oops.

"Yes, Gavin…*yes*." He's so big he's finding the deepest spots. Places I've never been touched before.

Leaning forward, his breath comes hard and fast, his big, heavy balls smacking my ass with each thrust.

"I'm so close," he whispers.

I clamp my hand down on his arm. "Me too…"

"That's my girl," he says, and that simple phrase zaps my core and sends me over the edge.

"I'm coming. *I'm coming*!" My pussy throbs and contracts, and I let myself soar, my head falling back, as I explode into a million pieces.

"God, Kat. This is… You're…" His words come out

between curses as he jerks and moans, his body hot and sweaty, his muscles taut. It's a magnificent sight.

He keeps pumping into me with slow, languid strokes. Finally, he grasps the edge of the desk for support and slides out. He tosses the condom in the garbage and falls into the chair. "My legs are shot."

I laugh. "Same."

He massages my thighs. "Shot, but stunning." He trails kisses all over my damp skin and I sigh contentedly.

"Hand me those clothes over there on the cabinet, please?" I ask.

"If I must," he grumbles. He gives me my clothes and we both get dressed.

"You're coming over to my place to spend the night, right?" he asks, then adds, "And the rest of your nights?"

My heart leaps into my throat. "Gavin! Surely you can't be serious."

"Dead serious. And don't call me Shirley," he smirks. "Sorry. My *age* is showing."

I shake my head, though I can't stop smiling. "You're a dork. But you're a cute dork. And for the record, I *don't* think you're old."

He grabs my hand. "Kat, I want to cut way back on the jobs I take. Hell, maybe even retire, I'm not sure. All I know is whatever I do, I want you at my side when I do it. You're the only woman I've ever felt this way about."

"We've only known each other for a few hours—"

"Which is how I know you're the one." He chuckles. "I've been around the world so many times. I've never met anyone like you."

He squeezes my hand, and I'm overwhelmed with a ton of conflicting emotions. Excitement. Fear. Doubt. Longing. All of it.

I do want him. But will he be able to handle *me*...forever?

"I'm not saying no," I say carefully. "But I can't go tonight. I need some time to think, and Gran will be worried. She's still not really talking to me, and I need to win back her trust."

"Of course," Gavin says, kissing me softly. "I understand."

Suddenly, my phone buzzes with a text, and I grab it from the desk.

It's from Gran.

> Stay away from the house. Bones is creeping around the property. The Sheriff has been called. I'm hiding.

"What's wrong?" Gavin asks, noticing the way I've paled.

"I'm sorry, I can't give you a ride. I have to get home right away."

He grabs hold of my shoulders. "Kat, what is it?"

"Bones," I say, trying not to tremble. "Gran says he's at the house, sneaking around. She's called the Sheriff and everything."

"I'm coming with you. You're not going alone."

I shake my head and look into his eyes. "No. It's too much, Gavin. You don't want to get mixed up with me and my mess. I'll just drag you down, because frankly my life is shit right now. Honestly, you should just leave me alone."

His gorgeous blue eyes bore into mine. "Listen. When I said I wanted you, I meant all of you. Not just the good stuff. Every secret, every heartache, every messy bit. When I'm in, I'm in. For better or for worse, like the saying goes. Got it?"

I've never had a man talk to me like this. And I can't believe how much my heart swells with hope to hear it, jaded as I am. My stomach legit flip-flops, and I feel faint.

Crap. Is this what swooning feels like?

"We'd better go," he says, running a hand down my cheek.

I nod with renewed determination. "Yes. Let's."

CHAPTER 7
GAVIN

"That's his car," Kat says, pointing to the beaten-up Mustang as we pull up to the Holloway house. I'm behind the wheel of one of Sam's loaners, since I didn't want Kat to drive in her current state of mind.

The Mustang is parked off to the side, near some trees.

Kat squints at the car. "I don't see him."

I ease in closer. "The police aren't here yet, either."

"I can't let that asshole hurt Gran," Kat says. Before I can even come to a stop, she jumps out and starts racing toward the front door.

"Kat!" I call, getting out to go after her.

A man dressed in black appears from behind a column on the front porch and grabs her.

No!

He forces a knife to her throat as she struggles and screams.

Blazing hot anger courses right through me and my heart slams against my ribcage.

This douchebag is asking for it. I'll kill him, for real.

No, Gav. Play it cool, for Kat's sake.

I mentally count to ten and take some deep, steadying breaths before I walk up.

"You come any closer, Daddy Megabucks, I'll slice her throat open," Bones snarls.

I put my hands up. "Take it easy, man. I'm not trying to—"

"Shut the fuck up, Pops. This doesn't concern you. This here is *my* bitch." He presses a sloppy kiss to her cheek, and I seethe.

"Ugh! Fuck off, Bones," Kat spits out. "You treated me like trash. I was stupid to trust you at all. You're nothing to me."

He yanks her back, pressing the knife into her neck. "Ungrateful skank." He laughs. "You think this rich old man is gonna make you into somethin' better? You'll always be trash, Kitty Kat."

She yelps, and the front door bursts open. Mrs. Holloway appears on the porch with a shotgun levelled straight at him.

"The only trash around here is your pathetic sack of bones in a soiled leather jacket."

Kat's blocking her grandmother's shot. But when Bones hears Mrs. Holloway rack her gun, his gaze drops.

I seize my moment and charge as Kat pulls down on Bones' hand, twisting his arm behind his back.

The knife clatters to the ground and away.

I tackle him, pinning him to the porch with all my weight.

"I'm not afraid to shoot if Gavin moves," Mrs. Holloway says calmly.

"I've seen her at the range, Bones. She's a good shot," I add, as Bones yells, cussing us all out from under me.

"Like, where do you think I get my spiciness from?" Kat taunts, ready with the knife.

Sirens get closer and closer as the police converge on the house, their red and blue lights flashing in the darkness.

Deputy Barlow runs up, hand on his holster. "Hey Gavin,"

he says, readying the handcuffs and kneeling down next to me. "This our trespasser?"

"He also attacked Kat here with a knife. Threatened to cut her throat."

"Bullshit! All bullshit!" Bones screams, but I push his cheek down to the wood of the porch, muffling his words.

"It's all true," Mrs. Holloway says, the gun now lowered and at her side.

"I'll take it from here, then," Deputy Barlow says.

"Be my guest." I get up and let him take over, cuffing Bones.

The piece of shit won't stop yelling and cussing, even as he's hauled up and away. "You're going down, Kat! I'm taking you with me, you fucking bitch," he snarls and spits, as he's put in the car.

Sheriff Quinn arrives just as I put an arm around Kat, squeezing her tight.

Later, after we've given our statements to the Sheriff, he says he'll have to follow up on Kat's involvement with the stolen cars in Los Angeles and advises her not to leave town.

"I'm not going anywhere," she says, her smiling eyes darting from Mrs. Holloway to me. "I'll do whatever it takes to make things right."

Sheriff Quinn leaves, promising to be in touch, and we all head into the house.

Mrs. Holloway walks to the dining room table and hunches over it, her withered hands shaking.

"Gran…?" Kat says, rushing over.

"I can't lose you again, Kat," Mrs. Holloway sobs, turning

to face her. "First I lose your father, then you run off… My heart can't take any more, sweetie. It hurts too much."

Kat throws her arms around her, her face stricken. "You won't lose me again, Gran, I promise. I'm sorry. I'm so sorry."

They both begin to cry, holding onto one another, apologizing over and over and making new promises. My eyes well up despite my best attempts to keep it together.

Mrs. Holloway dabs at her eyes with a tissue. "And how did *this* come about, Kat?" she asks, looking suspiciously in my direction.

"I'm sure you know Gavin Layne, Gran."

"Of course I do. He grew up here. But he always seems to be around when trouble is afoot. That's why I'm asking."

I cringe and bite my lip. I mean, she's not totally wrong.

Kat grins. "He had some car trouble and needed a tow. I'm not sure how or when it all happened, but I guess he just got under my skin. And I'm real glad he was there when I needed him." She gives me a wink.

I lean back on my heels. "I'm not sure either of you ladies needed me, anyway. You and Mrs. Holloway could've handled this on your own quite well."

"Yup, Holloway women are tough," Kat says, looping her arm through her grandmother's.

Mrs. Holloway pats Kat's hand. "That we are, dearie, but it's still nice to have a doting man around." She gestures to the table. "How about you stay for a piece of cake, Gavin?"

Kat comes over to give me a hug.

"Sounds perfect, Mrs. Holloway, thank you."

"Yes, this is a much better match, in my opinion," Mrs. Holloway says, watching us together. Then she side-eyes me. "As long as you plan on spending more time here in Deepwood, Gavin."

"There's nowhere else I'd rather be," I say, kissing Kat's temple.

EPILOGUE - KAT
ONE YEAR LATER

I t's been a long day, and it's late when I pull into the garage
of our house. *Our house.*

Well, it was Gavin's first. But he's let me do whatever I
want with the gigantic mansion. I haven't done much with it,
to be honest, because it's a beautiful home. All I really need is
for Gavin to be in it.

It's amazing how much of a homebody I've become since I
moved in with Gavin. And I don't mind one bit.

I testified against Bones and his gang in exchange for
immunity, and they were put away for a long time. Since then,
I haven't looked back.

Gran and I are closer than ever. We're constantly together
over the course of the week, either running errands or having
meals, or sometimes I come to visit her at the library.

Gavin and I got married after six months, but I moved in
with him after only a couple of weeks. We just couldn't wait.
Gran has supported us from the start and even gave me away
at the wedding. I couldn't ask for a better grandmother.

Willa and I became fast friends, which I was happy about.
She's kind and smart, just like her dad. But really, all of the

women in this town have welcomed me back with open arms. Willa invited me to join the rest of the girls one night at the Rustic Ridge Bar and the rest is history. When Willa, Maddie, Violet, Paige, Zoe, Eden, and I all get together it gets pretty wild. Not L.A. wild, but enough for me.

I enter the house after punching in the alarm code and smell Gavin's cologne hanging in the air.

Delicious.

He had his buddy Sully over tonight. Talk about a home-body. *That* man is a borderline recluse. But he's got his hands full with his new neighbor, from the sounds of it. She just bought the Deepwood Inn and is fixing it up. Sully is beside himself with all the construction noise.

I head up the stairs. It's quiet and dark, and Gavin's clearly gone to bed, but he's left a few lights on for me because he's considerate like that.

Entering the bedroom, I hear him snoring before I even see him. He's lying on his back, mouth wide open, in all his moose wailing glory. The guy's lucky he's so hot, I tell ya.

I slip out of my clothes and join him, naked, underneath the satin sheets. He likes the feel of the satin sheets on his skin. We both do.

Pulling down the sheet, I find his cock hard and ready. The man is *always* hard. Not that I'm complaining.

Moving lower, I stroke my hand over his hip, and he jerks awake.

"Mmmm…I'm glad you're home, baby," he rasps.

I lick up the length of his warm shaft and take him in my mouth.

"Fuck, now I'm *really* glad you're home."

He tastes salty-sweet as I tease his tip, swirling my tongue around him, then softly delving into his slit.

"Oh…god…that's—" He chokes on his words as I take him

311

as deeply as I can, until he's touching the back of my throat, then I pull off, letting my teeth graze him in that way I know drives him crazy.

"Shit, hon…"

I caress his balls as I lick and suck, chasing those desperate sounds of his that make me so wet. Soon he's writhing underneath me.

"Please, Kat. Please…"

I've never had a man beg as much as he does in bed, but it makes me feel like the most powerful goddess in the universe.

I moan and hollow out my cheeks, and he curses again.

When I slide down and bury his cock between my tits as I suck the tip, he finally roars.

"Fuck, I'm coming…so hard!"

I swallow his seed as he convulses, pumping between my breasts.

"Kat…my Kat," he whispers, as he comes down from his orgasm.

I move to his side, my head on the pillow next to him.

"I love you," I say, feeling his heart beating wildly in his chest.

"Oh hon, I love you more than I can say." He turns and strokes my cheek fondly.

"How was your night with Sully?"

"Lonely without you. He's turning into a complete sourpuss. All he did was complain about his new neighbor."

"I'm sorry." I play with his chest hair.

"*And* he didn't bring dessert like he said he would."

"That sucks. I would've brought you something if you'd asked me."

His eyebrows waggle. "Oh, but you just did."

His hands are already roaming down my body.

"You're insatiable."

"Not bad for an old man," he says, going in for a kiss.

And once again, I thank my lucky stars that I found my way back to Deepwood Mountain.

∾

HIS BIG PIPE

CHAPTER 1
SULLY

S ix letter word for *collide with*.

The sun bounces diamonds of light off the gentle waves of Deepwood Lake as I squint down at my phone. I don't *need* my glasses to see the crossword puzzle. It's just really bright out here, that's all.

Yeah, let's go with that.

Impact!

I type the answer into the boxes, much too slowly. Fine. I'll go and get my glasses.

When I come back out, I settle into the comfy new Adirondack chair my buddy Logan made for me and grab a slice of my lunch. Frozen pizza again. Terrific.

Yuck. How can something be both mushy and stale at the same time? Not to mention bland.

I toss it back on the plate. Maybe I should learn how to cook…

Oh. Right. Because I burn toast.

Birds chirp as they flit through the trees and a family of ducks swims across the water. It's the kind of day I built this house for. Sunny…peaceful…the only sounds from the animals, the water, and the wind.

I lean back in the chair and close my eyes—

THUMP! THUMP! THUMP!

The birds take flight in a flurry of chaos.

"Goddammit!" I bark, jumping up.

The noise is coming…*of course*…from the property next to mine. Ever since that woman bought the Deepwood Inn and moved to town two weeks ago, she's been renovating at all hours of the day.

I've already left two strongly worded notes on her door to keep it down.

BANG! BANG! BANG!

Jeesus.

I tug on my baseball cap and trudge through the forest toward the Inn.

With each step, as the noise gets louder, I get angrier.

By the time I reach the front door, I'm fuming, ready to give her a piece of my mind. Not to mention a few more choice words.

Just as I raise my fist to knock, the tell-tale sound of rushing water comes from inside.

"Nooooooo! Stop! Shit!!" a woman yells, and then there's more banging.

Pipes.

I pound on the door. "Hello? Are you okay in there?"

"Help!" she cries. Screw it. I barge into the front room. I can hear her and the water in a room on the left. Probably the kitchen.

I burst through the doorway.

The woman is drenched from head to toe and desperately holding onto the faucet as it sprays water in all directions. Everything's wet - the floor, the counter, the windows. Her.

But even half-drowned, this woman is stunning. She's the most beautiful woman I've ever seen.

Long black hair, petite frame, sweet little tits, and a mere handful of ass.

I'm frozen in place.

"Little help here?!" she yells over the sound of the water when she sees me.

"Where's the main water shut-off?" I holler back, shaking off my surprise.

"Basement! Ack!" She gets another spray in the face. "Straight back, to the right."

I fly down the stairs to the basement to shut off the water. I bound back up, taking the steps three at a time, and find her leaning over the sink. Her body is heaving with her ragged breath as she pushes her wet hair out of her face.

"Thank you," she says, turning to face me. She blinks rapidly, droplets of water on her eyelashes, lips parted. I can only gaze back at her, rendered speechless.

When she finally tears her eyes away from me, she scans the kitchen. It might as well be a swimming pool. It's a complete mess.

"Oh god," she groans.

Then her pretty face crumples and she bursts out sobbing.

CHAPTER 2
TALIA

"What am I going to do?" I wail, ugly crying in the kitchen of my newly acquired bed and breakfast that was already painfully unfit for guests even *before* the kitchen got flooded with water.

It all bubbles up and tumbles out. "The windows need replacing, the roof needs fixing, the electrical is fucked…" I point to a switch near the pantry despairingly. "That switch turns on the light in the front hall closet!! Why?" I hiccup. "I've done all I can cosmetically, but I'm in way over my head. I thought I could fix the faucet myself—like, how hard could it be— but now I've just made it worse! What was I thinking?"

I bury my face in my hands. Suddenly I feel the big sexy stranger that barged into this fiasco put a gentle hand on my shoulder. I'd almost forgotten he was here, he's been so quiet. Poor guy. What a shit show to walk in on.

This is *not* me. I don't cry. I'm the eternal optimist. Miss Sunshine and Rainbows! I should just tell him I'm fine and pull myself together.

Except…I've officially hit rock bottom. I'm broke. I've sunk everything into this place. I wanted it to work so badly. I wanted to show my grandmother, God rest her soul, that I could make something happen for once. Prove that I'm not a failure.

But there's only so much I can take.

Instead of collecting myself and wiping away my tears, I grab onto the stranger's flannel shirt, bury my face into his strong chest, and let the tears flow. My face is as wet and sloppy as the rest of me, but I'm beyond caring at this point. This man smells like lemons and the forest and you know what, it's good for my nerves.

I let it all out. I tell him everything. All the things that are wrong with the property. My growing suspicion that I should just give up.

The stranger pats my back awkwardly. Crap, I've made this weird. But it's fucking amazing to feel something so solid, warm, and real against me. It's been a long time. And his chest is firm and muscled. I wish it was bare so I could feel every swell and ripple.

Talia! Down girl!

"It's okay," he rasps. My god, his voice is deep. I feel it down to my—

Talia, you're being ridiculous. Just cut it out.

"Don't cry. Please," he says. It's obvious he's uncomfortable.

I finally push myself out of his arms and wipe my face, gulping down the sobs. "Okay. I'm good. Sorry."

He stands there and shoves his hands in his pockets after tugging his cap down nervously. His pale green eyes can barely look at me. Poor guy must be shy.

And damn, really big. Tall, sexy…

"Let's start over," I say, collecting myself as best I can. I put out my hand. "I'm Talia Yang."

He shakes my hand. "Sully O'Neill. I live next door." I'm

trying to ignore the electricity shooting up my arm as his big hand envelops mine.

I pull out of his grasp hastily.

"Wait, you're the jerk who's been leaving the nasty notes on my door about the noise?" My heart sinks a bit. Just my luck. My hot savior is also a bona fide douche canoe.

He glances down at his feet. "It's pretty loud and disruptive. Kinda makes it hard to enjoy the peace and quiet the lake is known for."

I put my hands on my hips. "I'm sorry, but how am I supposed to do construction quietly?"

His eyes flick away again. I can tell he doesn't like confrontation. "You could keep it to specific hours, maybe? Especially nothing after dark?"

I shake my head, painfully aware of how uncomfortable my wet clothes are. "I need to work every second I can. Every day this place isn't ready to open, I'm losing more and more money."

"You're doing everything yourself?" He's looking around and I know he's thinking I'm out of my mind.

I mean, he's right. But still.

"Mostly." I stick my chin out.

"Do you have any experience with renovation?"

Now it's my turn to avert my eyes. "I've been watching YouTube videos and tutorials."

He whistles. "That's commendably brave." He takes his cap off to scratch his head, and I notice how thick his dark hair is. "But unrealistic. You really need professionals for a big project like this."

I remember with a jolt that I'm not supposed to like him.

"Thank you for the vote of confidence," I say, sarcasm dripping off my tongue. "But as I'm sure you heard when I was blubbering before...I'm broke."

He sniffs the air, ignoring my comment. "What smells so good in here? You order in?"

The change in subject practically gives me whiplash. "Oh, um, I made pork siu mai. You know, dumplings. I cook when I'm stressed."

His brow raises.

"I made a lot of them." I give him a sheepish smile.

He licks his lips. Damn him for having such a sexy mouth.

"You're a good cook, then?" he asks.

"My dad was a chef. He taught me everything he knew." I pause. "I might not cook in Michelin starred kitchens like he did, but I've never had anyone complain."

He cocks his head to the side, rubbing his jaw. "Maybe I can help you with the plumbing."

"What are you, some kind of contractor or something?" He does look the part—all rugged and in flannel. Yummy.

"Not exactly. I'm a plumber." He digs in his pockets, searching, until he pulls out a dog-eared card and hands it to me.

O'Neill Plumbing. Where have I seen that before? Probably one of my many internet searches in the area.

"I own the company but haven't actually done any jobs in a while." He glances out in the direction of the lake. "I've been trying to, ah, enjoy the fruits of my labor."

"I get it, I get it. I'm noisy!" I roll my eyes, then try to hand the card back to him. "Thanks, but I couldn't afford you anyway."

He doesn't move to take the card from me. "How about we make a deal?"

"What kind of deal?" I'm skeptical, but he's got me intrigued.

"You cook your best dishes for dinner for me this week, and I'll get your plumbing in order."

Dinners? That's it? A plumbing job like this might cost thousands!

Tempting. But I don't even have money for groceries.

I'm shaking my head to decline when he adds, "I'll give you money for the ingredients, too," as if reading my mind.

Getting the plumbing done *would* allow me to get some guests in and generate some cash to pay for the remainder of the projects this place needs.

This is starting to sound too good to be true. "What's the catch?" I narrow my eyes suspiciously. "You're not expecting sexual favors or anything, are you? Or to watch me cook naked? I'm not—"

"No, no!" He waves his hands in front of him frantically. "Nothing like that. I'm just sick of frozen pizza. And...not to stereotype or anything...I do love Chinese food."

He's gone beet red, and I try to hide a smile as his pale eyes dart away.

He really is cute. I'd be a fool to pass this up.

"Deal," I say, with newfound hope.

CHAPTER 3
SULLY

Homemade Chinese food for a whole freaking week?
Score!

Sure, I didn't give her the piece of my mind I meant to... but she was crying, dammit. She's clearly down on her luck. And I'm not heartless.

Not to mention, she's fucking beautiful. A sexy, pint-sized dream.

Suddenly, I'm nervous as hell.

Plumbing I can do with my eyes closed.

But women? I'm not good with them. They scare the crap out of me. Especially raven-haired little spitfires who make my jeans tight.

"I'll go get my shop-vac and fans to clean and dry this place out," I say, getting back to business. "But we won't be able to turn the water back on until I can do some diagnostics."

"So... I won't have water tonight?"

I shake my head. "You can stay at my place if you want." Sully! what the hell are you doing?

"I can?"

"Sure. I've got guest rooms."

"You could be a murderer."

"Think about it. I wouldn't get a week's worth of dinners if I murdered you."

She wrinkles her nose. "True."

"Besides, equal opportunity. You could be a murderer. Who's to say I'm not the one putting my life in danger?"

She rolls her eyes and I fight back a chuckle.

"It's not like I have a choice. I can't afford a cabin rental."

I pause and take a breath. "I can pay for a cabin, if you're really concerned."

She smiles at me. My jeans get even tighter. "That's really nice of you, Sully. But you're already getting the raw end of this deal. I'm sure one night at your home would be just fine."

I like hearing her say my name. I have visions of her whispering it in my ear. Or screaming it as I'm buried deep inside her.

Damn. I'd better leave before I do something inappropriate and ruin everything.

When I return with the shop-vac and some fans less than an hour later, Talia's already dried almost everything except the floor with towels. She's opened all the windows and I get to work vacuuming out the water and setting up the fans.

As the sun begins to set, she packs up some food from her refrigerator.

She pats an insulated bag. "This is most of our dinner. I still need to prepare some rice and vegetables to go with the dumplings."

"Sounds delicious," I reply. I decide to leave the vacuum, in case I need it again. "You have an overnight bag packed and ready?"

She hands me the food. "Yep. You carry this, and I'll get it."

We get into my truck and head to my place. When we pull up, she gasps.

"When you said 'lake house' I pictured a little cabin on the water, not this. This is gorgeous."

I open the door for her as we walk in. "Thanks. My friends and I built it together."

She puts her bag down, then tries to take some of the food from me.

"'S'okay, I got it," I say, blocking her playfully. She grins and follows me into the kitchen.

"Wow. Beautiful." She gazes out at the lake, then looks longingly at my chef's kitchen that's barely been touched. "This kitchen is begging to be used, Sully. Why don't you cook in it?"

I set the food down on the counter and shrug. "Never got into it, I guess. But I do miss home-cooked meals."

She begins to unpack the bags, taking out containers and produce. "Who cooked for you when you were growing up?"

My thoughts turn to the old table at my parents' house laden with lamb stew, colcannon soup, and soda bread. "My mum mainly. Her sisters, when they came to visit."

"Are they nearby?"

I shake my head. "Ireland. I was raised here in Deepwood by my mum and dad, but when they retired, they moved back to be with family."

"That must be tough." She puts on an apron she pulls from her bag.

"It is, but they're happy. That's the main thing."

"You know, my mom's Irish," she says. "Her maiden name was Doyle."

"No kidding! And your dad's Chinese? And a chef?"

"Yep, they met when my mom was in China teaching."

"Where are they now?" I ask, getting a couple of beers out of the refrigerator and opening them.

"Mom's still in China. She's a professor. And my dad…"

She taps her fingers on the counter. "He passed away a while ago."

"I'm sorry."

"Thanks." She starts grabbing pots, pans, and utensils from drawers like she's done this hundreds of times before. Even in a kitchen that's unfamiliar.

She gets to work rapidly chopping an assortment of vegetables.

"So why are you here in Deepwood?" I ask, setting the beer bottle next to her.

"My grandmother on my mom's side just died. We didn't see each other very often, but I often felt she understood me the best. Like kindred spirits or something. She left me a nice chunk of money with instructions to follow my dreams."

I nod.

"My dream is to have a nice bed and breakfast. I hope that will make her proud." She smiles wistfully, then downs a huge swig of beer.

My kinda girl.

She looks perfectly at home as she moves around the kitchen, setting the dumplings in a bamboo steamer basket, starting the other dishes. She talks as she fills a couple of different pots with water to boil. I admit, I like seeing her here. She seems comfortable, happy. Like she belongs. Not for my benefit, of course. But because cooking is what gives her the most joy.

I'm already lost in her smile and the delicious aromas beginning to swirl around us.

"Why don't you set the table?" she asks, and I nod before I take off my cap, wash my hands, and get to work.

My mouth is watering like crazy by the time we finally sit at the dining table where I've only ever played board games and done jigsaw puzzles.

She points to a dark sauce in a small dish. "This is for the dumplings - it's black vinegar with ginger, plus a hint of chili oil. I hope you're okay with a little spice?"

"I love spice."

"Duly noted," she says with a wink.

My face heats when she hands me some chopsticks. "Oh. Uh. I'm not good with these."

I start to put them down but she stops me with a smile. "I'll teach you. It's easy once you get used to it. And it's part of the experience. I'm not going to let you eat my dumplings with a knife and fork."

After I pile some food onto my plate, she pulls up a chair next to me and demonstrates her own chopstick technique.

"Put the first one in the crease between your thumb and palm, resting against the inside of your ring finger." She shows me, and I follow. "Then put the other in between your thumb and index finger, with a little help from your middle finger." I copy her once again.

She delicately picks up a bok choy leaf and pops it in her mouth. I watch, mesmerized, as she chews.

She gestures toward me. "Your turn, big guy."

I grab a piece of bok choy and try to lift it to my mouth but drop it halfway.

"Yeah, it's a little slippery," she giggles. "But here." She leans over to put her hand on mine, and I try not to tremble. Damn, I must be hungry.

"Keep this thumb straight." She strokes her thumb over mine, and the tiny motion has my cock stiffening. "It'll give you more control over this stick."

Speaking of sticks…

When she turns to look at me, our faces are inches apart. I can feel her soft breath on my cheek.

Fuck, I could kiss her right now.

What am I thinking? I just want to help someone out of a dire situation and get some home-cooked meals into the bargain. There's no need to be acting like a horny teenager.

But I'm staring at her mouth like I could devour her faster than the meal on the table.

She clears her throat and moves away, saving me from myself, thank god.

"*Qing man yong*," she says cheerfully. "Or *bon appetit*."

Miracle of miracles, I manage to snag a dumpling with my chopsticks, dip it in the sauce, and get it to my mouth without bobbling it.

Flavors of juicy pork, earthy mushroom, chili, sesame, and ginger explode across my taste buds, setting fire to them in the best way.

"My god, I could eat a bucket of these." I grab another. "They're spectacular."

She laughs, the sound melodic and bright. "I didn't make a bucketful. But I have plenty of dough to make more for later in the week."

"Perfect," I mumble, my mouth full. Forget manners, this is the best thing I've eaten in a long time.

She grins and takes another swig of her beer. "I saw a cross-word puzzle on the counter. Maybe we could give that a whirl after dinner?" she asks.

Jesus. If I'm not careful, I'll be under her spell by the end of the week.

Or sooner.

CHAPTER 4
TALIA

I throw a wrap over my pajamas and tiptoe down the hall to the kitchen.

I can't sleep. My mind is on overload…and so is my body.

Sully and his big, rugged self keeps barging into my thoughts, demanding food and other more carnal things. And I would thoroughly enjoy giving him what he wants. Not just dumplings, either.

I must be losing it.

This Inn is driving me crazy. Even if Sully fixes the plumbing, I worry I won't be able to keep it for long.

Why do I have to be impulsive like this? Jumping into things without looking?

I rifle through Sully's pantry for herbal tea, but all I can find is coffee and liquor. Warm milk it is.

As it heats on the stove, I think back to how much Sully loved my food. He was completely absorbed in it. It filled my heart with pride and maybe a little longing. It's been a while since a man has made me feel needed and wanted like this. Even if only for my cooking.

And then after dinner, when we sat outside and did the

crossword puzzle together, I felt completely at home. To be honest, I feel like that in this kitchen, too. I's silly, but there's just something about this place—and Sully—that makes my heart happy.

I clean up and am walking down the hall with my milk when I hear my name.

"Talia…"

I freeze, stunned at how desperate he sounds.

Sully moans my name again and I creep over to his half-open bedroom door, holding my breath as I peek in.

Holy shit.

There, in a perfect shaft of moonlight, is Sully's muscled, naked body, writhing on top of the sheets. And in his meaty palm is his thick, hard cock.

If I wasn't so frightened of being found out, I'd come right there and then.

Instead, I try not to breathe too loudly.

Watching him pleasure himself is the sexiest thing I've ever witnessed, especially when I know he's thinking of me.

Damn, I want to touch myself.

He's pumping his cock so achingly, maddeningly slowly, his eyes shut in ecstasy.

"God…" he whispers, and I can't help it. I press my back against the wall and slide down to the floor. Setting my cup of milk to the side, I dive my hand into my flooded panties.

I rub my wet and swollen pussy, watching him, listening to his ragged breathing and soft whispers.

I press my head back and bite my lip as Sully moans like no one's listening. When his sounds and movements speed up, I match his rhythm.

He groans as he comes, and I'm right there with him.

Then he grunts, and the bed creaks as his body jerks and convulses as he shoots his load.

I turn my head to watch the last splashes of his seed fly from his massive cock. Oh my…

My orgasm rips through me and I clamp a hand down over my mouth to keep from screaming. Pleasure ignites all over my body and I ride the waves, my eyes screwed tightly shut, my pussy throbbing with the aftermath, drunk with pleasure.

I roll away from the door, catching my breath.

Creaking, a grunt, and the sound of footsteps sober me up quick.

He's walking toward the door!

I flatten myself as close to the wall as possible, barely breathing.

Then the door closes with a soft click.

My body still shaky, I grab my milk and get up to walk back to my room.

After all that, I probably won't need the milk after all.

CHAPTER 5
SULLY

Before I even set foot into my kitchen I can smell breakfast.

The tantalizing aroma of bacon beckons me and I follow it like a swirling tendril of scent you see in those old cartoons.

Just like yesterday, Talia's moving about the kitchen as if she's been here for years.

It's adorable—and she's so fucking sexy it hurts.

"What's this?" I ask.

"Breakfast," she deadpans.

"That's not part of our deal."

"I know. I just felt like making breakfast for you, is all."

"Why?" I ask.

"To be nice. Is that okay, Grumpy? Here. Get some caffeine into you. I get the sense mornings are not your strong suit." She pours me a cup of coffee as I sit at the counter bar.

I take a sip. *Fuck.* Even her coffee tastes better. "Just don't want you to feel obligated," I say, after another sip.

"I don't," she chirps, then beams at me. "By the way, I used the eggs in your refrigerator. I hope that's okay. They smelled super fresh."

I nod. "Reece's wife brings those over from the ranch sometimes. Glad you could use them."

I can feel her eyes on me. "You really don't cook... anything?"

I shake my head.

"Not even eggs?" She sounds scandalized, and maybe a little sad.

"Nope."

"Do you go out?"

"Not if I can help it."

She chuckles. "What about on dates?"

"*Especially* not on dates."

She eyes me and quickly looks away, cheeks pink. She hums to herself as she plates the food and I can't help but think how nice it is waking up to a woman in my house. Although it would be even better if she'd just come from my bed.

Last night I had the hardest time getting to sleep. Emphasis on *hard*. I couldn't stop thinking about Talia riding my cock, her head thrown back until we both came loud and fast.

Pipe dreams. Pun intended.

I should forget those dreams asap. Why would an outgoing, fun-loving woman like Talia want a shy grump like me? Never brave enough to make a move. It's why I'm still a virgin.

Talia is a bright, shining light. Sunshine in a bottle. She needs a man with experience who could make her feel like a queen and bring her to climax every night. There's no way I could ever do that...though if given the chance, I'd gladly spend the rest of my life trying.

We eat breakfast together and everything about it is delicious. I savor every moment because I don't know if it will ever happen again and I want to remember it all—the taste of the food, the smile on Talia's face when she set the plate in front of me at my table. I keep telling her how great everything tastes until she blushes and playfully smacks me with the dish towel.

Later, I hand her a wad of cash to buy food in Missoula for the rest of the week plus some gas money to get there and back. Nolan's General store here in town doesn't carry all the specialty spices and produce she'll need.

"Is that enough?" I ask doubtfully.

Her dark eyes go wide. "Plenty."

"Better to have too much than not enough."

"Are you sure?"

I nod. "I'll start on the plumbing."

"Well, okay. Thank you again." She hesitantly puts the money in her bag and pats my shoulder, and her hand lingers there, searing through my flannel shirt.

I tip my ball cap and move away, desperately wanting to gather her in my arms instead and take her straight to my bed.

She leaves to walk over to her place to get her car and drive into town, and I finally let go of the breath I'm holding.

I spend half an hour packing up my tools before driving over to the Inn myself, ready to get to work.

Hopefully getting knee deep in stinking pipes corroded with mildew and muck will take my mind off this woman.

CHAPTER 6
TALIA

I pull up my shopping list on my phone as I maneuver through the aisles of the grocery store. I run through the various dishes I plan to make for Sully this week—dumplings, cashew chicken, maybe sweet and sour pork if they have decent pork shoulder butt today.

As I reach for a bottle of soy sauce, I hear a cheerful voice behind me.

"Hey—aren't you Talia, the one who bought the Deepwood Inn?"

I turn to see a smiling woman with long, sleek dark hair pulled back in a chic ponytail, pushing a shopping cart over-flowing with items. Beside her a tall, rugged guy with piercing green-blue eyes plays with the chubby-cheeked toddler sitting in the front of the cart.

"That's me," I say, and she extends a hand.

"Violet," she replies, and we shake. "This is my husband, Nick, and our little munchkin, Ethan. Welcome to Deepwood Mountain."

Nick waves in greeting, and Ethan gives me a shy grin.

"I'm glad to finally meet the one driving Sully crazy with all the renovation noise," she winks.

I roll my eyes. "Sheesh. For someone so quiet, he sure has no problem complaining to everyone about that."

Nick chuckles. "Honestly, I think it gives him something to do."

Violet levels her gaze at him. "Hey, don't be mean. He's one of your best friends."

"Which is why I give him such a hard time," he replies, grinning.

"He's actually been helping me with the plumbing at the Inn. It…needs some work."

"Uh, Sully?" Violet's eyebrows fly up. "Sully *O'Neill*?"

I nod. "We have a deal—he's helping me with the plumbing, and I'm cooking him dinner for the week. Chinese food, to be specific."

Nick and Violet exchange surprised looks.

"Sully's not usually one to sacrifice his alone time," Nick says cautiously. "You must be one hell of a cook."

I smile, feeling more than a little proud. "He seems to enjoy my food." Suddenly, an idea strikes. "You guys should come over tonight! I'd be grateful for the company, and I'm sure Sully would love to see his friends."

Violet's eyes light up. "That would be great! It's been ages since we've been out. And trying to find decent Chinese food around here is pretty difficult." She chews her lip and glances at Nick. "I bet the rest of the gang would love to join, too."

"There's an official gang?" I ask, laughing.

"Yeah, there are five couples in our little group," Nick explains. "We used to hang out more often, but life gets in the way, you know? Timing's great, actually. I think we're all in town."

"But that's a lot of people, Talia," Violet says. "If it's too much—"

"Nonsense! I love cooking for big groups. Invite them all," I say enthusiastically. "It'll be a blast. And don't worry about Sully—I'll handle him. I mean, I'm inviting you to my place, not his."

Nick chuckles. "All right, we'll see you tonight. But Sully might give you a hard time—don't say we didn't warn you."

"Nothing I haven't dealt with already," I reply with a grin. "See you at seven?"

"Can't wait," Violet confirms, grinning at Nick. "Text the sitter, babe. We're going out!"

"Whatever," Sully grumbles, going back to work under the kitchen sink.

Wow, Nick wasn't kidding. I told Sully I'd run into Nick and Violet at the grocery store and that his whole crew was coming over for dinner, and the man got even grumpier, if that's possible.

I guess he really is a homebody at heart.

But watching him under the sink, his thick, muscled body flexing as he tightens something here, loosens something else there, adds plumber's tape, a clamp... I realize I don't mind that he's a homebody. And to think that he's doing all this to make my place run smoothly is...hot.

Okay, remembering last night and picturing him stroking his cock, imagining I was there with him, is damn hot too.

Who cares if he's not a social butterfly like me?

"Done," he says, wiping his hands and turning to face me. His shirt is damp from a mix of stray water and sweat. Ugh, so sexy.

I reach over to the sink. "Really? I can turn it on and won't get attacked?"

His mouth turns up at the corners. "Try it."

I hesitantly lift the handle and water pours out from the faucet straight into the sink, just like it's supposed to. My mouth makes a pleased little O shape.

Turning, I throw my arms around his neck. "Thank you, thank you, thank you!"

Oh god. *Big* mistake. That smell. All man and musk—it's overwhelming.

"You're...welcome." He awkwardly pats my back. Great— once again, I've managed to make this weird.

I back away.

He takes off his cap and runs a hand through his damp hair.

"I gotta go home and get changed," he says, grabbing his tools. "To look presentable for your big dinner party and all."

"Okay. Thanks again. And don't be too long, it would be great to have some help as I make dinner."

He grunts, which I assume is a yes, steps onto the porch, and heads for his truck.

By the time he returns, I've changed clothes as well. The kitchen is dialed up to eleven—all burners going, every available surface covered in ingredients, containers, and utensils.

"Grab an apron," I say, glancing up as he steps in. He looks delicious yet again, in dark jeans and a green Henley that brings out his eyes.

"Smells amazing," he says, putting on the apron that I toss him, and I grin.

"Welcome to Dumplings 101," I announce, rolling out the dough on the floured countertop, my hands moving quickly to keep it from drying out. Sully watches me with a mix of curiosity and intent concentration, his large frame looking almost out of place in the crowded kitchen.

"All right, big guy: time to get your hands dirty." I hand him a small ball of dough. "I'll show you how to fill them."

He nods, taking the dough from me. His hands dwarf mine, and I suddenly worry that pinching the dough might be challenging with his big fingers. Ech, we'll manage.

"First, you roll it out like this," I demonstrate, pressing and rolling until the dough is a thin, even circle. Sully mimics my actions carefully.

"Not bad at all," I say, inspecting his work. "Now, we take a spoonful of this filling and place it in the center. Not too much, not too little. Then fold the dough over and pinch the edges to seal it."

I show him how to do it, my fingers working quickly. He copies me, a little clumsily at first, but soon he's getting the hang of it.

"Your dad taught you this?" he asks, his voice deep and soft.

I smile. "Yep. He used to say that making dumplings is like creating happiness, one little pocket at a time."

Sully glances at me, his eyes warm, and the familiar ache forms in my chest. "I miss him a lot. But cooking always makes me feel closer to him. Almost like he's here with me, watching over my shoulder."

Sully nods, a small smile on his face.

Suddenly, I feel the need to apologize. "I hope it's okay that I went ahead and invited all your friends to join us for dinner. I'm sorry about that."

He shrugs. "It's fine. I don't mind them and their families. But sometimes I can't help but feel a little jealous spending time with them these days."

I look up at him, surprised by his honesty. "Jealous? I wouldn't have guessed that. You always just seem…grumpy."

He chuckles, a deep rumble that makes my heart skip a beat. "Yeah, I guess I do. It's easier to be grumpy than to admit you're lonely."

"I get that."

We work in silence for a moment.

"We're not a bad team," I say, admiring the neat row of dumplings we've made.

He scratches his jaw. "Kinda fun working together, too. You're a good teacher."

"Oh, stop." I feel a blush creeping over my cheeks as I drop the first batch of dumplings in the water to cook.

Sully's eyes darken as he continues to watch me. "I like it when your cheeks turn pink," he says, reaching over to stroke my face with the backs of his fingers.

My heart pounds in my chest as I look up at him. The kitchen suddenly feels even smaller, the air thicker. Sully might be too shy to make any move, if he even wants to, but me, I want to try.

I tilt forward, pressing up on my tiptoes, and kiss his parted lips. They're warm and firm against mine, and for a moment, I revel in the way my body thrums.

He doesn't move, and I open my eyes again to see his are still closed.

Oh boy. Did I break him? Is he okay? Did he enjoy the kiss?

Then he comes to life, wrapping his arms around me.

"Talia…" he whispers. Well, maybe more of a half-groan, half-growl. It takes me right back to last night, listening to him pleasure himself.

Then his mouth is on mine, his tongue sliding against my tongue. His hands roam over me and I shudder against his big, hard body. One specific area is particularly hard.

He lifts me onto the edge of the counter, and I know I'm getting flour all over my ass. I don't care.

I wrap my legs around his waist and he presses even tighter against me, his length a steel rod between us.

He groans deeply as we explore each other's mouths with frantic need, then he breaks the kiss to tongue down my neck. Sucking on the column of my throat, his growls vibrate straight through to my soaked pussy.

A loud knocking on the door has us breaking apart quickly.

Sully pulls me off the counter. "Shit."

He looks frazzled, and I start patting the flour off my pants.

Glancing at the front of his jeans, it's obvious that his cock is still raging.

"I'll go answer the door. You get that bad boy under control," I joke. But his grumpy expression has returned, and he doesn't even crack a smile.

CHAPTER 7
SULLY

"Thanks again for having us, Talia," Nick says, lifting his glass in a toast at my dining table. "We've missed everyone getting together."

"Yeah, it's been too long," Willa adds from a few seats away, grinning. "This food looks amazing."

Talia blushes at the compliments, waving them off with a modest smile. "I'm just glad you're all here. It's nice to cook for a full house. Eat up while it's hot!"

I watch from my seat at the end of the table as Talia flits around, making sure everyone's got what they need. She's a born hostess, her smile bright and infectious. I can't take my eyes off her.

I can still taste her on my lips, that kiss lingering in my mind like a sweet, forbidden memory. She surprised me, kissing me like that. But I shouldn't have given in. Now it'll be even harder for me to resist her, knowing how she feels against my body.

But resisting is exactly what I need to do. Talia doesn't want me. She might think she does, but I know who I am. I'm a hermit. A grump who likes his peace and quiet and who wouldn't even know how to please her. I'd just dim her light.

As everyone digs in, the conversation turns to the Inn. Gavin's wife Kat feeds him a dumpling, then turns to Talia. "So, how's the renovation going?"

Talia takes a deep breath, her expression suddenly turning serious. "Honestly, it's been a lot tougher than I expected. There's just so much to fix—leaky roof, faulty wiring, not to mention the plumbing. Sully's been a lifesaver with that."

All eyes turn to me for a moment, but I just keep my focus on my plate.

Talia continues, "There's a lot of projects I can't handle on my own so it's going to take time for me to be able to get the place completely as I'd like it. But at least now I can start booking guests, thanks to Sully."

Eyes are back on me. The attention is killing me. "She's one hell of a cook," I finally say, my voice gruff. "You're lucky to have her feeding you tonight."

"Seriously. This food is incredible," Paige says, her eyes wide. "I can't remember the last time I had Chinese food this good. And I appreciate you making some vegetarian dishes for me and Maddie."

"Of course, I love finding ways to adapt a recipe for those with special dietary preferences."

"Well, you knocked it out of the park," Logan says, resting a palm on his gut happily.

"Sully helped," Talia offers. "He's actually pretty good at making dumplings."

Dash chuckles and slaps me on the shoulder. "And I've never known him to use chopsticks with such skill. Who knew you had so many hidden talents, Sully?"

I roll my eyes at him and he flashes me a wink.

As my friends chat around me, I keep stealing glances at

Talia, marveling at how effortlessly she fits in with this group. It's as if she's always been a part of it, and the thought fills me with a strange sense of contentment.

But she's still so different from me. I could never be enough for her.

"How about a game?" Willa suggests after we've finished dinner and are seated around the main living room. "Trivial Pursuit, anyone? I think I see the box over there." She nods her chin at the bookshelves.

I raise an eyebrow, feeling a flicker of interest. "You know I can't ever say no to that, Willa. It's my favorite." I throw a look to her husband, Dash, who I can one hundred percent guarantee put her up to it.

Talia's eyes light up. "That's a wonderful idea!"

There's more enthusiastic agreement, and soon enough, we're all gathered around the coffee table with the game board spread out. Talia sits next to me, our shoulders brushing. I try to ignore the heat that spreads through me at the simple contact.

"All right, teams?" Gavin asks, waggling his eyebrows at his wife.

"How about couples," Talia says with a grin. "And since Sully and I are the odd ones out, we'll pair up."

There are playful groans and teasing comments, but everyone agrees. Talia and I exchange a competitive look, and I feel a surge of excited determination.

The game starts off with a question for us about ancient history. I'm impressed when Talia answers it with ease.

As the game progresses, we fall into an easy rhythm. Talia's extroverted energy balances out my more reserved nature, and we complement each other perfectly.

"Stop showing off, you two. You're making the rest of us

look bad," Nick teases, when we get another colored pie piece for our wheel.

"Talia's got to be a ringer, some secret professional Trivial Pursuit player," Reece says with a smirk. "This is all one big ruse that Sully orchestrated to get us back for all the poker nights where we cleaned him out."

I chuckle and stroke my jaw deviously. "Damn. Busted."

Talia laughs, a sound that's quickly becoming one of my favorites. Our eyes meet and this time I'm able to hold her gaze, captivated by her sweet smile.

By the time we reach the final round, it's clear that Talia and I are the team to beat. Our last question to complete our pie is a toughie about classic literature. I rack my brains, but it's Talia who comes through for us, her eyes lighting up with recognition.

"It's Jane Austen," she says confidently. I nod, trusting her judgment.

"Final answer?" Gavin asks, grinning.

"Final answer," we say in unison.

There's a dramatic pause before Gavin announces, "Jane Austen is correct! Talia and Sully win!"

There's a round of applause and playful groans of defeat from the others. Talia and I share a triumphant look and bump fists.

"Good game, everyone," Maddie says, beaming. "And congratulations to the winners."

Talia nudges me with her elbow, her eyes sparkling. "See? Told you we make a great team."

"Yeah," I say, my voice softening. "We really do."

Later, I step out onto the back porch, wanting a moment to clear my head. The cool night air feels good in contrast to the warmth inside.

I hear the door creak open behind me and turn to see Nick and Gavin stepping out. They exchange a look, and I know immediately that something's up.

"What?" I ask, leaning against the porch railing.

Nick smirks. "We were just wondering about you and Talia."

Gavin nods, a grin spreading across his face. "You like her, don't you?"

"What is this, high school?" I feel my cheeks heat up, but I try to play it cool. "Sure, she's…nice enough."

Nick rolls his eyes. "*Nice enough*? Come on, man. We can see it a mile away. You've got it bad."

I sigh, running a hand through my hair. "But what am I supposed to do about it?"

Gavin steps closer, clapping a hand on my shoulder. "Just tell her. She's really great and honestly kinda perfect for you, Sully. We all see it."

I shake my head, feeling a knot of anxiety forming in my chest. "You guys know I've never… What if I screw it up?"

Nick's expression softens, and he squeezes my shoulder. "You've got to trust that she'll understand. If she's the right woman, she will. She'll get it."

Gavin nods in agreement. "Just be honest with her. You're a good man, Sully. She'd be lucky to have you. And vice versa."

Slowly, I let their words sink in. They're right—I can't let my insecurities hold me back. Talia's worth the risk.

"I guess I just need to find the right moment," I say, more to myself than to them.

Nick grins. "That's the spirit. If you need any advice, you know where to find us."

Gavin chuckles. "Just don't wait too long. Women like Talia don't stay single forever."

I nod, feeling a mix of determination and nervousness. "Thanks, guys. I appreciate it."

They both clap me on the back, and we stand there for a moment, the silence filled with unspoken support. It's moments like these that remind me why I value these friendships so much—

"Dead arm!" Gavin yells, breaking the mood and punching me in the arm as he and Gavin head back inside.

"Damn it!" I grab my arm, pain throbbing in my bicep. "Asshole," I mutter under my breath as they leave chuckling.

Why am I friends with them again?

The house is quiet now with everyone else gone, the lively energy from earlier fading into a peaceful hum. Talia and I clean up the happy mess that is the mark of a successful dinner party against the background noise of clinking dishes and running water.

"That was fun," Talia says, her voice soft and content. She hands me a towel to dry the dishes.

"Yeah," I agree, taking the plate from her and wiping it dry. "You really know how to bring people together. And they were complete strangers to you!"

She smiles, clearly a little tired but happy. "It's nice to have a full house. It reminds me of when my family would gather for holidays. Lots of noise, lots of food, lots of love."

I nod, feeling a pang as I remember gatherings with my own family. "Everyone had a good time. And they all really like you."

She blushes, looking down at the dish she's been washing over and over. "I couldn't have done it without you. The plumbing, the company...you've been great, Sully."

I'm not quite sure what to say to that, so I just keep drying the dishes, my mind spinning. I know I need to say *something*, but the words stick in my throat.

We finish the last of the dishes, and I set the towel aside, feeling a sad sense of finality. I'm terrible at this stuff. "Well, I should go."

Talia turns to me, her eyes searching mine. "Do you really have to?"

My stomach churns as the question hangs in the air. I feel my heart skip a beat, the weight of the moment pressing down on me. This is it, the chance to make my move.

"I don't *have* to, no..." I admit, my voice barely above a whisper.

She steps closer and grabs my shirt. "Good. Because I want you, Sully O'Neill."

I open my mouth to say something, but I'm speechless. My cock has decided to speak for me, rising high and hard in my jeans.

She notices and slides her hand over my bulge.

"*Fuck*," I groan.

Her eyes widen. "That's some piece you're packing."

She squeezes me again, watching me moan, and I reach for her.

She gasps as I pull her into a kiss, tangling my tongue with hers. She tastes like sugar and spices, and I can't get enough.

"Bedroom?" I ask, breaking the kiss just long enough to gather her into my arms.

"Upstairs...directly to the...left." She's breathless, and any nervousness I might be feeling dissipates.

I throw her over my shoulder and bound up to her room. She's laughing as I toss her onto the bed.

"Impressive speed and strength," she says, sprawled on the comforter.

I take a deep breath, gathering my courage. "There's something I need to tell you."

She looks up at me, her eyes hooded and full of lust. "What is it?"

I crawl over her and drag my thumb over her lower lip. "It's a little embarrassing for a man my age. I'm…a virgin."

Her brow furrows. "Really? But grabbing me just now…the way you kiss—"

"Oh god, was it bad?" The world spins for a moment as I second guess myself. "I just did what felt right."

She grabs my shirt. "Not bad at all. Hot! Very, very hot!"

I let out a breath. "Oh." I smile. "Thank fuck."

Her eyes soften, and she strokes my cheek. "Thank you for telling me. But for the record, it's no big deal."

"No?"

"Not in the least. You're clearly a natural," she purrs. "You just tell me what you need from me."

I thrust a hand through her silky hair. "What makes you come?"

She giggles. "Oh, lots of things, hot stuff." She kicks off her shoes. "Do whatever feels right, like you've been doing already, and we won't have any problems. As long as you don't mind a teensy bit of direction every once in a while."

"Yes please…" I say, leaning forward to kiss her again. She runs her hands up my back, pulling up my shirt. I sit back and pull it the rest of the way off.

Her mouth falls open. "Sully. These abs…" Her fingers drag over them and I can't help myself, I flex for her. She latches onto the waistband of my jeans and unfastens them. I kick off my shoes and pull down my jeans, leaving me in just my boxer briefs. The fabric is barely able to contain my eager cock.

She pushes me back onto the bed, then removes her jeans.

She crawls over me and my breath catches as her top goes flying, followed by her bra. Her sweet little tits have me reaching for them, and she shivers as I stroke her dusky pink nipples.

Fuck, those are pretty.

She moves to kiss my neck, my chest, flicking her tongue over my nipples, and it's wonderful. Then she drags her tongue down my stomach, and her hands massage my cock through my underwear.

"Oh, damn…"

She pulls my boxer briefs down and I lift my hips to help her. She slides them all the way off and returns to my dick. I'm so hard it hurts, the skin stretched tighter than it's ever been before.

"You're huge," she whispers, as her fingers stroke up my length. My muscles are tense, and I'm almost frozen in place, but when her small hand curls around the tip, using my pre-come to slip and slide all around my sensitive head, I buck.

"Talia!" I'm trembling, already on the edge. "I can't… You're going to make me come too soon."

She continues her maddening motions. "I want you to come fast. Means you'll last longer later." She grins and lowers her mouth to me.

Shit. Is she going to—?

She takes me in her mouth, and my hips jerk. "Oh hell…" Her mouth is so hot and wet, and that tongue is like magic.

I glance down when she cups my balls.

And that's it. I'm done. My climax hits me *hard*.

Before I can warn her, I'm pumping into her mouth.

"Baby…" I try to push her away, but she grabs onto my hips and just sucks harder, taking my come willingly into her mouth.

I writhe and jerk. *"Fuck me.* Shit, my god, Talia."

When I'm just a sweaty pile of flesh, my heart racing as if I'd just run a marathon, she slides off my cock. She kisses up my body, until she's nibbling on my ear.

"How was that?" she purrs.

My voice comes out like gravel. "I can barely move."

She chuckles and I pull her against me. "But I'm not sure that's going to hold me as long as you hoped. Not when I'm starving for your pussy."

CHAPTER 8
TALIA

I gasp as Sully rolls me underneath him.

He moves his mouth down my body, sucking at my nipples. I mewl, grasping his head to me, my fingers spearing through his hair.

I love how responsive he is to everything. Hearing him moan and whisper my name turns me on more than anything.

He kisses over my belly, licking at my navel. His fingers brush over my pussy through my soaked panties.

He groans. "These panties are drenched."

"All your fault," I breathe.

He leans down and inhales. A snarl bursts from his throat, and he rips off the thin fabric.

He exhales over my now bare pussy, and it's excruciating. "Please, taste me, Sully," I beg, spreading my legs.

"Fucking hell," he says, before he lowers his head. "I'm afraid I'll devour you whole." Then he licks me like I'm his favorite ice cream cone, his tongue swirling over every inch of me. It feels incredible.

I grind and writhe against his face, but he holds my thighs

down and apart. "Good?" he asks between licks. "Am I doing it right?"

"Soooo right," I manage, as he finds all my secret, sensitive spots and works them over with his lips and tongue. "Ohhh… ohh…*shit*, Sully…"

I'm shaking, my body on fire.

When his tongue sweeps around my clit, my voice cracks. "Yes, right there. That's…perfect…"

"You're so sexy," he says, his voice muffled, his mouth buried in my folds.

My orgasm detonates, and I reach down to grab his hair. "I'm coming. Fuck, I'm coming."

"Goddamn, Talia, yes," he snarls, continuing to work me over.

I moan like a madwoman under him, my toes curling and my voice rising to a shriek. "Oh god. Oh gaw*wwd*."

He doesn't stop until my breathing slows way down, and little gasping cries escape me when he hits a particularly tender area.

Finally, he lets go of my thighs and sits up, his hand stroking his cock. It's already as hard as it was before.

I lift myself up on my elbows. "Wow. I'm having trouble believing you've never done that before."

"Yeah?" he grins, his cheeks flushing red.

"Yeah," I reply. "And what are you planning to do with that?" I ask coyly, gesturing to his cock.

"I was thinking about burying it inside you and making you come again."

I bite my lip. *Virgins. So eager.*

I roll over to check my nightstand drawer. "I'm on the pill. But even if you wanted to use a condom, I don't think I have one big enough for the likes of you."

He smiles and palms my ass. "I'm fine with the pill." He

looks down at my pussy when I roll back toward him. "Do I need to...prep you, or something?"

"I don't think there's much more you can do to prep me for that monster." I trail a finger down his chest, tracing his thick muscles. "I'm already relaxed from the orgasm. And soaking wet. Just fuck me already."

He crawls over me and I let one leg fall to the side. He runs his tip over my opening and slowly presses in.

"Oh...my..." I choke out. Sully looks pained.

"About...that," he replies, his words choppy. "You... okay?"

"Mmm...yes." There's a slight burning sensation, but I focus instead on how he's stretching me and filling me up in the best way.

"God, this is—"

"Yeah," I manage, as he finally bottoms out.

When he starts to move his hips, it's tight. But it feels amazing, too.

"Oh damn, Talia. I didn't...expect it to feel this good."

I grip the sheets under me and clench them.

"Fuck!" he growls. "That's..." He pulls me closer as he thrusts into me.

And even though I've just come from him going down on me, I'm right on the edge for a second time.

I cry out. "Sully, I'm going to come again."

"God, yes," he rasps against my cheek. I feel him shudder as he kisses me. It sets me off, my climax tearing through me.

He's coming too, his noises like a man possessed. He jerks and I grab his ass tight, pulling him toward me.

We ride out our orgasms, clinging to one another, kissing and whispering expletives, until I'm spent and gasping on the bed from one of the most satisfying experiences I've ever had.

"Best. First time. Ever," rasps the grumpy plumber who stole my heart.

~

I wake up to an empty bed in the cold stillness of the morning light. For a moment, I lie there, hoping he's just in the bathroom or the kitchen. The utter silence of the house tells me otherwise.

A hollow ache throbs in my chest. We had such a great time last night, both at the party and…afterward. I thought it meant something to him, too.

Clearly, I was wrong.

I sit up, wrapping the duvet around me, and let out a deep sigh. I'm determined not to let this ruin my day. There's too much to do at the Inn, too many things to fix. But as I shower and get dressed, the sense of loss lingers.

A knock at the door startles me out of my gloomy thoughts. I open it to find Nick standing there with his construction crew out front. Beside him are Logan and Vi, all smiles and ready for action as well.

"Good morning!" Nick says brightly. "We're here to help with the renovations."

I blink in surprise. "What? How? Why?"

"Because Sully asked us to," Vi explains, stepping forward. "Although honestly, we were eager to help anyway. We all want to see the Deepwood Inn flourish, and we think you're the perfect person to make that happen."

"Especially if you make your amazing cooking part of the Inn experience," Logan adds with a grin.

"Really?"

"Really. You're a fantastic hostess, Talia," Vi says. "You deserve a place to let that talent shine."

Her words fill me with joy, and a feeling I'm not familiar with—satisfaction. Contentment. Maybe this really is what I'm meant to do: provide an experience for guests that's unique to Montana. Bring part of my heritage, my culture, here.

"Thank you for saying that," I say, a little choked up.

Vi rubs my arm. "I'm glad you're here, Talia. It seems like just yesterday I was the new girl in town. But this community welcomed me with open arms. Now it's our turn to welcome you."

Nick flashes her a smile and I can see the love in his eyes.

My thoughts turn back to Sully. "Where is the big guy, anyway?" I ask, trying to sound casual and keep my voice steady.

Logan grunts as the rest of them begin pulling out equipment and measuring tapes. "He's gone back into hiding."

Nick gives me a pointed look. "He's afraid of his feelings… for you."

I swallow hard, the ache in my chest deepening. "I see." So he does have feelings for me. Then I clear my throat brusquely. "Well, enough about me. Thank you all so much for coming. I'm grateful for your help. Where, in your professional opinion, should we start?"

We get to work quickly as I tell them my plans. Their energy and enthusiasm fills me with excitement and it leaves me all abuzz thinking how this place will turn out. But my mind keeps drifting back to Sully.

As soon as I can, I slip away and make my way to Sully's cabin. I find him on the back porch doing a crossword. A duck out on the lake quacks and he looks up, surprised to see me.

"Talia," he rasps, his voice sending shivers through me. "Aren't you busy at the Inn?"

"It seems I have a full crew handling things back there. Thank you for asking them to help. That was really sweet."

"I could barely finish asking them before they said yes. They were more than ready and willing to help after they met you last night."

I smile. "Yeah...speaking of last night. I thought we had something special."

He averts his eyes, his face taut. "We did—we do. I'm sorry. I just...I don't know how to do this."

"What do you mean? You've done almost everything right so far." I lower myself onto his lap. "Sully...I've fallen for you."

He looks up at me, his pale eyes filled with doubt and worry. "I'm not like you, Talia. I'm shy. Grumpy. Boring. You'll get tired of me."

I run a hand down his rough cheek and shake my head. "There's nothing boring about you at all. You're smart. Engaging, when you want to be. We make a great team at trivia. And honestly? Your grumpiness has kinda grown on me." I grin. "Besides, you're invaluable in the kitchen. Who will help me with my dumplings?"

He smiles a little at that, a flicker of hope in his eyes.

"And what you did to me last night. What we did..." I touch his sexy mouth, my panties getting damp just from the memory. "A girl could get used to that."

His eyes darken and I feel the bulge of his hard length underneath my hip.

He clears his throat. "Well, *technically*, you still owe me five more dinners."

I laugh. "And you know, I think I could be convinced to sign on for more, as long as you were there to help me."

He squeezes my hip, his grip possessive. "You really mean that?"

"I do," I say, my voice steady. "You still owe me more plumbing, right?"

His brow furrows. "I thought I finished everything yesterday."

I smirk. "Oh, trust me. You have a *lot* more pipe to lay."

He groans at my terrible joke, then kisses me. I feel it all the way down to my toes.

The gentle lapping of the water, the birds, the rustling of the trees—it's so serene.

Then a buzzsaw screams to life out in the distance, shattering the moment and causing a flurry of birds to squawk and take flight.

We break our kiss and I gaze out toward my property, stricken.

"Okay, point taken about the noise," I acknowledge.

And Sully tickles my sides, my laughter echoing out into the sky.

EPILOGUE - SULLY

THREE MONTHS LATER

The sun sets over the lake, casting a brilliant orange and yellow glow over the water. Sounds of laughter and conversation fill the air. We're gathered on the back patio of the Deepwood Inn, celebrating the end of a successful summer season. The wrap-around deck, built by Nick, is filled with happy people. Logan's handcrafted wood furniture adds a rustic charm to the space. And Gavin's lights strung up all around the roof, pergola, and umbrellas create a magical atmosphere.

I lean against the railing, a cold beer in my hand, and watch my friends and neighbors enjoying themselves. I over-hear Maddie, Logan's wife, chatting with Willa about the new website she set up for the Inn, complete with a page high-lighting Talia's amazing Chinese cuisine. Reece and Paige are discussing their latest addition to the C & A Animal Sanctuary, a Berkshire pig named Norman Rockwell. Willa talks to Talia about flyers she's promised to put up around town and in the library promoting the Inn to locals now that the summer tourists are leaving.

My life has been turned completely upside-down since Talia came into it, but she's brought me more joy than I ever thought possible. My friends helped make Deepwood Inn what it is, and I'm grateful for every one of them for bringing her dream to life.

But it's Talia who's truly transformed *my* world.

I watch her moving among our guests with ease, her smile lighting up the evening. She's in her element, and I feel a swell of pride in my chest. And love. So much love.

She catches me eyeing her and makes her way over, her dark eyes sparkling.

"Hey, you." She wraps her arms around my waist. "Enjoying the party?"

"Yeah," I say, my voice thick with emotion. "Amazing job, Talia. This place, these people…you did it. I know your grandmother would be so proud."

"I think she would be, too. "She smiles, stretching up to give me a kiss. "But you know I couldn't have done any of this without you, Sully. You're my rock."

I look into her eyes, mesmerized by her, and the words tumble out before I can stop them. "Marry me."

She blinks, stunned, and I realize I've done this all wrong—not at all how I had planned it in my head. I scramble to drop to one knee, pulling out the ring I asked my mom to send to me after just two weeks with Talia, a family heirloom from my grandmother.

"Let me start over," I say, clearing my throat officially. "Talia, I love you more than anything—"

"Stop. The first way you asked was perfect." Tears well up in her eyes, a smile breaking across her face. "I want nothing more than to marry you, Sully."

I slip the ring onto her finger and stand, pulling her into my arms.

"She said yes!" I yell to the assembled crowd, my heart swelling ten times bigger.

Cheers and applause erupt around us, and I look around at my best friends and their growing families. It just doesn't get any better than this.

And I plan to yell it to the world from the very top of Deepwood Mountain.

~

Now that we've come to the end of the Deepwood Mountain series…what's next?

Husky Valley
A Deepwood Mountain spin-off series featuring some of your favorite characters from Deepwood Mountain and a whole bunch of new ones!

Prefer your men with a little more meat on their bones? Then Husky Valley's got just what you need. These men are large and in charge, and looking for that one special woman who can handle all they have to offer. So head over to Husky Valley, where big-hearted boys get the love they deserve…and more.

Check out the Husky Valley series page here:
www.lexihayes.com/series/husky-valley

You can sign up for my newsletter via my website:
www.lexihayes.com
It's the best way to hear about new and upcoming releases, plus get access to subscriber exclusives and bonus content.

And as always, if you liked this story, please post a review on any of your preferred platforms. Reviews are the lifeblood of independent authors like me, and I welcome your opinions and feedback.

Thanks for reading!

ABOUT THE AUTHOR

Lexi writes short, steamy, over-the-top romance with a heaping dose of humor. She is a long-time superhero lover, book sniffer, and Mr. Darcy fanatic. Raised in the same SoCal city as Will Ferrell, she now resides in sweltering Las Vegas with her husband and two spoiled cats. She dreams of lush green foliage, ocean waves, and Henry Cavill. Or Tom Hiddleston. It's a toss-up really. ;)

Join Lexi's mailing list for new and upcoming releases (and exclusive content!) here: www.lexihayes.com

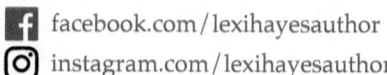

       facebook.com/lexihayesauthor
       instagram.com/lexihayesauthor

www.ingramcontent.com/pod-product-compliance
Lightning Source LLC
Chambersburg PA
CBHW020517260626
47156CB00006B/2034